About the author

Campbell Armstrong was born in Glasgow and educated at Sussex University. After living in the USA for twenty years, he and his family now live in Ireland. He has been in the front rank of modern thriller writers for many years, and his bestselling novels include the highly acclaimed *Jig* series. His heartbreaking memoir, *All That Really Matters*, was also a remarkable success around the world. Detective Lou Perlman also appears in his two previous novels, *The Bad Fire* and *The Last Darkness*, both available from HarperCollins.

WHITE RAGE

CAMPBELL ARMSTRONG

HarperCollins*Publishers*

This novel is entirely a work of fiction.
The names, characters and incidents portrayed in it are
the work of the author's imagination. Any resemblance to
actual persons, living or dead, events or localities is
entirely coincidental.

HarperCollins*Publishers*
77-85 Fulham Palace Road,
Hammersmith, London W6 8JB

www.harpercollins.co.uk

Published by HarperCollins*Publishers* 2004
1 3 5 7 9 8 6 4 2

A catalogue record for this book
is available from the British Library

ISBN 0 00 714963 8
ISBN 0 00 714962 X (trade pbk)

Typeset in Palatino by Palimpsest Book Production Limited,
Polmont, Stirlingshire

Printed and bound in Great Britain by
Clays Limited, St Ives plc

*This book is for Joy,
for her unstinting support
of my books down the years.*

1

She hadn't planned on letting things go this far. She'd been ambushed by a variety of influences, the effect of wine and grass, the slow-burning jazz. His persistence was also a factor, probably the major one.

He wanted her with a passion that was an anger.

Fine. It suited her to have him off-balance. She lay beneath him on the rug and looked at the ceiling and listened to him whimper. He uttered words that made no sense, long vowels, sawn-off consonants punctuated by tiny grunts and plosives. The weird language of a man about to explode. Brutespeak.

He groaned, then roared, and she thought of a zoo creature filling the night with anguished noise. She saw his mouth open, and the shadow at the back of his throat. His roar died suddenly. He let his face drop into her shoulder and whimpered. Then he sighed as if he'd run a marathon and was approaching meltdown, a coroner's slab.

She made a tiny sound that was intended to be one of appreciation or gratitude, designed to reaffirm his 'manhood', or whatever he called that quality he needed to prove. He was of slight build, thin-shouldered. He slid out of her and rolled away, reached for his cigarettes, lay on his back and flicked his lighter. It was a smoothly cinematic motion. She saw it as if she were a camera. She often looked at the world like this, tight shots, close-ups: it gave her a sense of control over her perceptions.

'Are you satisfied?' she asked.

'Spent,' he said. He laid a hand on the back of her neck. 'I hope I didn't hurt you. I get carried away –'

'If there was any pain, it was sweet,' she said. Mr Bigcock, she thought. Major Dick. And I'm just cunt, poontang, beaver. I'm just something to poke on the floor of his flash flat among the empty wine bottles. A pick-up in a club, a shag. The things you have to do.

'You want a drink?' he asked.

'I'd prefer some air,' she said.

'You mean you want to go *out* somewhere?'

'Just the balcony,' she said.

She got up, found her panties, pulled them on. She stepped into her jeans. She put on her white silk blouse.

He reached for her ankle and held it. 'Don't leave me,' he said. 'You'll break my heart.'

'Then join me.'

'In a minute. I'm a bit stoned.'

'Bring some wine. We'll drink it outside.'

'Anything for you.'

She slipped her feet into her shoes. Jeans, blouse, shoes: what else had she brought with her? An overcoat. A bag. That was all. She didn't want to leave anything behind.

Come and go, no trace.

She slid the balcony door open. The night was dense with the aroma of wet trees and rain on stone. Sparse traffic moved along Great Western Road towards Anniesland Cross. Up here, on the sixth floor of Kelvin Court, she had a good view of the northern reaches of the city: the high-rises of Drumchapel, the dense tenements and streetlamps of Maryhill. Further north, Glasgow gave way to the mysterious dark of the Campsie Fells. She'd camped up there once as a little kid in the days before her father had walked out and she remembered the smells of canvas and Calor gas and baked beans burning in a saucepan. The memory caused her a flicker of sadness. Baggage she didn't need.

He came out onto the balcony in a thick black robe. Looking pleased with himself, she thought. Freshly laid. Ashes newly hauled. He carried two glasses of red wine. He swayed, almost slipped.

'Just set it down for me,' she said.

He put the glass on the balcony ledge. 'You're a skinny little thing,' he said.

'With tiny tits,' she said.

'I'm not a breast man, personally.'

'I eat like a horse, and I can't gain a pound.'

'You work out, I bet,' he said. 'You're hard. Muscular.'

'I do some press-ups. I jog.'

'You dance nice,' he said.

'I'm flattered.' They'd met in the Corinthian, once a bank, now a club and bar refurbished like a vast flamboyant wedding cake. After some desultory conversation, they'd danced. She remembered the music, the thunder of the bass, the staccato drumming.

'You really move. Eye-catching.' He smiled, opened his mouth as if he meant to say something, but a drugged synapse must have collapsed. He drank his wine in silence. She didn't touch hers. She felt a pain between her legs. She was tender inside. She despised him for the hurtful way he'd used her body. She hated his skin and the idea of allowing him to fuck her.

He said, 'Christ, it's chilly. You had enough air now?'

'I like night. I like the air.'

'I just realized I don't know your name.'

'I thought it was uncool to exchange names on one-nighters.'

'Who said it was a one-nighter?' He touched her shoulder. 'I'd like to see you again.'

'You never know,' she said.

'Tell me your name. Come on.'

3

'Pass me my wine and I might.'

He laughed. He was giddy, but full of himself and his prowess. He'd fucked her into ecstasy. She'd come back for more. Bound to. He stooped with mock courtesy. 'At your service,' he said.

He reached for her wine.

She pushed hard against his back, forcing all her considerable strength into her hands and arms. His glass went spinning from his fingertips and out into space and he said, 'Hey, what's this game?' And she pushed again even before he had time to turn his face round, bringing her hands up from a lower angle than before, shoving him just under the hips and causing him to tilt forward.

It was easy. He was wasted. He wasn't expecting it. He weighed as much as a shadow. He went over the edge and fell into the same downward path as the wine glass. She heard him shout. He struck the ground, the hard crack of his body smacking stone. Then immediate silence.

She didn't wait. She didn't look down to see how he'd landed. She emptied her wine glass, hurried inside the flat, put on her coat and stuck the glass into a pocket. She picked up her bag from the coffee table. She looked round a couple of times, then she let herself out.

She walked quickly from Fifth Avenue to Great Western Road, where she found a black taxi trawling for custom. She climbed inside and told the driver to drop her at an address in Govan, south side of the city.

'Nippy for the time of year,' the driver said.

She hated idle talk. She settled back and watched the city go past in a series of streetlamps and shuttered shopfronts, gaunt tenements and closed pubs.

A dead city, heart of night.

4

2

Lou Perlman struggled with his broken umbrella as he walked westward along Bath Street. The mid-morning wind blew rain under the black canopy, which had begun to collapse around a crown of bent metal spokes. Buy cheap, he thought, you get what you pay for. He tried to readjust the bloody thing. Rain smeared his glasses.

He gave up on the brolly, dumped it in a litter bin. He wasn't far from Force HQ in Pitt Street – so what was a little rain, a trifle of discomfort, when you were about to sit down in the same room as the man who'd killed your brother?

He was uneasy. He needed a dispassionate distance between himself and Leo Kilroy, the killer. Sorry: *alleged* killer. Kilroy's lawyer, Nat Blum, believed all his clients were innocent. On Planet Blum, where the air was so thin only lawyers could breathe it, Leo Kilroy was innocent of any crime.

Perlman started to cross the street. Ahead, he saw the unappealing red-brick edifice of HQ. He paused to adjust his collar against the rain. He didn't notice the big Dalmatian on the pavement slip its leash and bound with mighty steps and spring at him like a ball of iron shot from a cannon. He was blasted flat on his back, winded. The dog, whose breath smelled of rancid corned beef, licked his face with a hot tongue.

'Get this beast away from me,' Perlman said, and pushed at the dog with no result.

An elderly man in a green rainproof jacket appeared. 'Clem, Clem, come on now, get back, get back,' and he clipped the end of a leash into a hook on the dog's collar. 'I'm awfy sorry, he's hyper, but he usually doesn't run away from me like this. Let me help you up –'

'Just get the dog out my face,' Perlman said.

'Clem's a good boy. Aren't you, Clem? He wouldn't do any harm. It's just –'

'Boisterous good fun, eh?' Perlman got to his feet.

The owner's face was red from the effort of curbing his panting animal. 'Are you injured?' he asked.

'I'll survive.'

'I wanted to audition Clem for that film, you know.'

The elderly often made comments out of the blue. Perlman wondered if the same fate awaited him when he retired; days spent practising conversations in the hope that you might be lucky enough to engage a total stranger in one of them. *Here's a non sequitur I prepared earlier.*

Perlman asked, 'What film was that?'

'*One Hundred and One Dalmatians.* But it meant travel.'

'I get the impression he wouldn't make a good traveller.'

'Aye. But he's got star quality.' The dog was all rippling muscle and power, trying to burst free of his restraint.

Star quality. Perlman brushed his damp coat with sweeping gestures, and felt a rush of sympathy for the elderly man. Lonely, a widower, say, probably lived in a little flat overlooking the fumes of the nearby motorway, loved his dog, dreamed his dreams, dragged out old photographs and studied them. People who harboured outrageous ambitions for their pets were a little odd, but usually harmless.

He entered Force HQ. The air smelled of damp coats and wet shoes. A tiny ache played in the small of his back from the encounter with the dog. Just what he needed, something *noodged* out of alignment. He headed to the stairs, nodding at the uniformed constable behind the reception desk.

'Wet one,' the constable said. His name was Jackie Wren and he had a walrus moustache. 'Where's spring, eh?'

'Round the corner, I hear,' Lou Perlman said. He glanced at his watch. The encounter with the dog had made him late.

'Whatever happened to all yon global warming stuff, eh?'

'I look like a meteorologist?' Perlman, surprised by the snap in his reply to Wren's light-hearted question, climbed the stairs.

Tense is all. It was the prospect of seeing Leo Kilroy.

Come to think of it, where the fuck *was* spring anyway? Christ, how he longed for it, the earth warm, winter no more than a memory. He thought of his brother Colin gunned down last December on a cold black street. The recollection was hard as crystal. Icicles hanging from eaves and sills, the big blue car slowing almost to a halt, the gunman's hand in the window, the gaseous white flash as a shot was fired.

Lou had held his dying brother in his arms. He still saw Colin's face in his dreams. Eyelids fluttering, mouth slack, neck bent to one side. He thrust the images away. They angered and saddened him. If he was going to maintain his cool in Kilroy's presence, he didn't need rollercoaster rides of the heart. Calm down.

Easier said.

He reached the landing, paused. Sometimes he tried to absolve his brother from his sins, but absolution wasn't his to bestow. He wasn't God. Even if he could grant forgiveness, would he? Colin had committed various crimes, the least of which was his embezzlement of a large amount of money from a group of idealistic Israelis and Palestinians working to structure an improbable peace in the Middle East. And if Colin had left it there, okay, that would have been bad enough, but still tolerable up to a point. After all, what was embezzlement except robbery wrapped in layers of paper?

But no, no, Colin had gone far beyond fiscal chicanery. He'd crossed the border where paper malfeasance became bloody, and greed led to murder. He'd killed to cover his crimes. Three men had died.

Shovel that one aside too, Perlman thought. My *bruder*, the murderer. It was a tough one to budge. The tide of publicity that had roiled in the wake of Colin's death brought Lou into the public eye in a way he'd never sought. *Glasgow Cop's Brother A Killer* – Colin's world was aired in black type, scams exposed, the convoluted web of violence unravelled. Hacks wanted to interview Lou: tell us, did you ever think your brother capable of these things?

What did he have to say about Colin that the hounds hadn't already sniffed out? Old girlfriends popped up like goggle-eyed glove puppets to testify to Colin's sexual appetites. *He was a tireless lover for his age*, a woman in Edinburgh told the *Sunday Mail*. *He definitely liked younger girls:* this allegation came from a female blackjack dealer in London.

Perlman wondered how these public revelations had affected Colin's widow, Miriam. He didn't want to think about her right now. When his head was less cluttered, when he had time to ponder how she was handling her life, maybe then –

The babble of HQ assaulted him suddenly. Phones ringing, a toilet flushing, a young man speaking from behind a half-shut door: 'I'm telling you. Celtic have too many diddies in the squad. Exact same thing with Rangers.' The cantankerous fluctuations of weather and football: Glasgow preoccupations.

He disliked the confines of this building. One reason he was happier in the streets: Force HQ was a cig-free zone. Death by clean air.

'I was about to give up on you, Lou.' Detective-Inspector Sandy Scullion stood at the end of a hallway, tapping the face of his wristwatch.

'You don't enjoy a cliffhanger?' Perlman asked.

'No head for heights.' In dark suit and red tie, thin ginger

8

hair combed back, Scullion had one of those sympathetic faces that lighten bleak days. He was an optimist by nature; he had a tendency to look for anything that glinted in the malodorous shite of the world.

'Ready to face the demons?' Scullion asked.

Perlman said, 'Call me fearless.'

'Kilroy's lawyer is building up a head of steam strong enough to foam milk for a cappuccino.'

'Fuck him. What I have got to lose?'

'I hope nothing,' Scullion said.

Perlman didn't hear a ring of confidence in the Inspector's voice. Sandy's doubts were usually grounded in caution. He liked ideas to mature slowly. 'If you prefer to postpone, Sandy –'

'It's your call,' Scullion said.

'You're not happy with it.'

Scullion shrugged. 'I didn't say that.'

'You're about as subtle as a tabloid, Sandy. You could always pull rank.'

'Aye, right, I could. Except I'm taking the easy way out. I'm leaving this one entirely to you.' Scullion was Perlman's superior officer, but always treated him as an equal. Certain Very Big Shots who occupied the upper slopes of Force HQ, the men who sent out reams of brain-numbing bumf weighted with stats and regs to the foot soldiers, thought Scullion gave Perlman a wee bit too much freedom. Lou, twenty years older than Scullion, reckoned that his long experience in the Force compensated for the difference in rank.

He'd never aspired to a level beyond Detective-Sergeant; the higher you rose, the more tangled the thickets of politics, the more demanding the bureaucracy. You had to play too many daft games. He'd seen good men bleached of vitality by promotion. He'd seen them vanish for ever inside the wormholes of the system or mutate from humans into rubber stamps. Not for him, thanks.

'I'd like to make Kilroy sweat, Sandy.'

'And Blum? What about Blum?'

9

'I doubt if he has the glands for it. Maybe it'll give him something to think about.'

'Like what? His conscience?'

'A lawyer with a conscience? That must be a rare beast.'

Both men paused outside the door of Scullion's office, and Perlman sighed and looked suddenly serious. 'Sometimes I wish I'd led a life of the mind. A cloistered wee world among the spires of Glasgow University. Harris tweed jacket, leather elbow patches. Prof Perlman, surrounded by nubile undergrads. I'd sit on committees and eat decrusted sandwiches. I'd have no seedy villains and their sordid lawyers to deal with.'

'Bullshit, Lou. You love your work.'

'One of love's flaws is the fact it grows cold,' Perlman said. 'Faulty heat-retention system.'

'You signed on for life,' Scullion said. 'Divorce isn't an option.'

'Feh,' Perlman said. He suddenly remembered the dead gull he'd found in his driveway yesterday morning. It had dropped mysteriously from the sky. No evidence of a wound, no broken wing or leg. It occurred to him that the bird had fallen about twenty yards from the place where Colin had died. Practically on my own doorstep, he thought.

And hadn't he heard on the car radio only this morning of somebody falling from the balcony of a flat in Great Western Road? A suicide? He couldn't remember what the newsreader had said.

The leaping dog, the stiff gull, the balcony jumper – were these all signs of some kind? Did we live in an age of portents? Maybe. But who was wise enough to interpret them?

He had an image of the gull. Eyes void, claws paralysed.

I'd fly away if I had wings, he thought. Who are you kidding? Without your job, life would be one long *kvetch*. Unemployed, you'd go down Domino Drive and shuffle the ivory tablets with the other old Jewish geezers in a senior citizens' centre, and bitch in the bittersweet language of mightabeens. *If I'd gone to Israel when my son asked me, I'd be sucking fresh oranges in Tel Aviv instead of. I shoulda saved harder for my old age, here I am counting pennies and.* He thought: I need the city, the streets, a sense of purpose. Sandy was right: you signed on for life.

I belong to Glasgow. Dear old Glasgow.

Where else would I go?

3

Bobby Descartes wrote in his journal with a ballpoint: *I hate Pakis and Indians, and jews and Nijerians and niggers in jeneral.*

He was a man with pale lifeless grey eyes. He had a tiny mouth he often forgot to close – a trap for flies, his father used to say. He breathed through his open mouth a lot. He had nasal problems and often *thunked* at the back of his throat. He wore purple and green tracksuit trousers of a shiny synthetic material, and a green fleecy top with a hood. He also wore a pair of chunky black running shoes. He liked the mazy footprints made by the contoured rubber soles.

He closed his journal, which had a hundred and twenty pages. So far he'd covered eighty-seven of them with his tiny handwriting. One day he'd have to start a new journal, all blank crisp pages. *Volume Two of Bobby's World View.* He had a lot to get off his chest. Two times one hundred and twenty pages was two hundred and forty. He liked numbers, the act of counting. Arithmetic was an orderly world all to itself.

A TV jabbered in the next room, where his mother lay on her decrepit velvet sofa. She was addicted to self-humiliation shows imported from America. Mountainous men and women, ranting blubbery persons who came screaming and strutting out of the wings. *Check my fucking attitude.* There were Brit clones of these shows on telly. What was wrong with the UK mentality that it had to mimic the American? Turn your head one way, wham, another big fucking yellow McDonald's M in the sky. Swivel it the other, you get an eyeful of long-necked Budweiser bottles lying broken in the gutters and discarded packets of Camel Lights. Newsagents were filled with glossy magazines devoted to the troubled histories of Hollywood film stars. Sluts, shoplifters, cokeheads.

I give a fuck, he thought.

Credit where it was due all the same: the Yanks understood love of country. Yessiree, they did. *My Country, Love It Or Leave It.* Bobby had that bumper sticker tacked to the plywood-panelled walls of his room. He wondered how come national pride had been trashed. Who stood up these days when the band played 'God Save The Queen', eh? Patriotism was just a bad word. The nation was under an evil spell. An air of despair hung over the land. Try to find a decent hospital. Trains a joke. Buses always overcrowded. Post Office workers downright fucking rude. Factories shutting down. Ordinary people couldn't pay rent.

The country reeked of decay.

He teased back a strip of plywood from the wall and concealed his journal behind it, then he looked from the window down into the street. He saw a burnt-out old Vauxhall and a bunch of shaven-headed locals – he counted six – smoking skunk under a twisted lamp-post that hadn't had a bulb replacement in eight years. A teenage Temazepam addict Bobby knew as Annie swerved along the pavement in the manner of a twig shuttled this way and that by a wind.

Pretty wee thing, Bobby thought. Always dazed and bone-white and nothing in her eyes.

Drug dealers were royalty around here. The police did bugger all. They drove past in their cars like slumming tourists. Look,

13

there's a druggie, just drive on. Upholders of the law, o aye, sure.

He stared at the crummy flats across the way. Some windows had been blocked with sheets of steel. A spray-painted message splattered on one sheet read: *Welcome to Hell*. When he considered how dopers and hoors and an influx of immigrant scum had wrecked this corner of Glasgow, and by extension the whole United Kingdom, he heard a blood-red hum in his brain and his vision went dark at the edges. His rage, which he struggled to maintain on a low-altitude frequency for the purposes of making it through the day, rose to radioactive levels.

In a dark room, by Christ he'd *glow* with fury.

He sat down in front of his computer and checked his email. He had one message. The one he'd been expecting. Even so, it caused a rush of blood to his head.

Go, the message read.

He sent a reply to Magistr32@clydevalley.net. He tapped the keys in picky little strokes. The note he transmitted read: *Beezer will do his duty.*

Beezer, his war name. Magistr32 had given him that one. He didn't know why. He didn't want to think about Magistr32 right now because it was a line of thought that always disturbed him, and he gave in to feelings he didn't need. He had to be absolutely fucking *focused*.

He deleted all his messages in and out, shut the machine down and slid open the drawer of the woodwormed table on which the computer sat. The Seecamp was wrapped in a dirty linen handkerchief.

He removed the gun. He admired its compact design. Amazing how this wee thing, less than five inches long and weighing about ten ounces, could kill. He balanced it in the palm of his hand, and thought *lovely*. He stuck the gun in the right pocket of his tracksuit trousers.

When the time comes. Reach, find, remove, fire.

Today's the day, he thought. No turning back. Enough's enough.

14

He walked inside the room where his mother, Her Highness, lay. Sandrine Descartes, sixty-six and leathery from half a century of smoking, adjusted her shawl. She looked as if some high-tech latex special effects had been used on her face; her eyes were bright but her skin was pure crone.

Ugly old cow, Bobby thought. Day after day she lay in this dim room and smoked cigarettes with the blinds drawn. She lived in a state of perpetual shade. One day he expected he'd come into the room in time to see her fade into infinity.

On the telly a white-faced woman with long greasy hair was weeping. '*I never told her I loved her,*' she said, tears rolling down her cheeks.

The show's hostess squeezed the moment. '*It can't be easy to admit you have lesbian feelings for your own sister –*'

Bobby picked up the remote and zapped the TV.

'I was watching that, Robert.'

'It's shite,' Bobby said.

'It interests me. The whole human drama.' She smoked a Kensitas.

'You see more human drama from your own window.'

'It depresses me to look out, Robert.'

He had the feeling his mother was about to launch into her usual mumbo about her late father, an important Frog lawyer with a big house in the Loire Valley. Fine wines, crystal, silver candlesticks, the works. Bobby sometimes wondered how much of this story was true.

The plotline was total suds: young French woman of a certain class marries beneath herself, falling for a charming adventurer called Jacques Descartes, who drags her halfway round the world in doomed pursuit of lost gold mines and oil deposits, riches based on wild rumours eavesdropped in the taverns of shabby port cities where travellers traded dodgy map fragments or dog-eared geological reports for a few drams of booze or some cash. The lovers marry in Mozambique and, having survived various disasters – a shipwreck, an earthquake, according to Sandrine – they wash up in Glasgow many years later because

15

Monsieur Le Loverboy has learned of a forgotten silver mine in the hills of Lanarkshire.

Of all places. Lanarkshire. The sticks.

The story culminated in sickness and poverty, Jacques dying from TB, and Sandrine living out a miserable widowhood in this unpleasant corner of a cold Scottish city, her only legacy Bobby, who remembered his dad, his *papa*, as an embittered man with a frighteningly big head and thick white hair, who sometimes sang 'La Marseillaise' if he was pished. Which was often.

It was all rubbish, Bobby sometimes thought. Pure *keich*. Or maybe there was some nub of truth, enough to keep Sandrine warm on cold nights. Fuck did it matter?

'I'm going out,' he said.

'Where?'

'Don't interrogate me, Ma. I'm thirty-seven years old.'

'In your head, ah, you are an adolescent.' She made a Gallic gesture, shrugging then throwing her hands up in the fashion of a juggler. 'No job. No prospects. No girl, Robert. No love. Where is love? Life needs love.'

Her accent turned Robert into Robair. She pronounced their last name Daycart instead of Deskarts. He hated that. Daycart. It was like something with wheels.

'You do not make anything of yourself.'

'At least I don't lie around on a clapped-out old sofa watching crap TV.'

'Ah, no. You are so busy acquiring a university degree, of course. Forgive me, I forget.'

Her sarcasm. Her love story. Her broken heart. Her maroon sofa and that bloody shawl. What else didn't he like about his mother? He headed towards the door. 'One day you'll be proud of me.'

'I hold my breath.'

He paused on the way out. Just for a second his nerve wilted, but he pushed his uncertainty aside and shut the door before hitting the stairs. Beezer – one of whose ancestors was a famous French philosopher, a fact Sandrine had fruitlessly tried to impress on her son years ago – was on the go.

With murder in his heart.

4

Leo Kilroy weighed twenty-five stone, give or take. He dominated the space of Scullion's small office. His great jellied jowls
wattled his neck; his eyes were lost in mounds of flab the shape
of gnocchi. Perlman never knew which was more overwhelming:
the man's sheer presence or the garish nature of his clothing. He
wore a long red leather coat, a suit of brushed blue suede, an
antique brocade waistcoat, and a broad-brimmed beige hat with
a wide band of neo-Aztec design. It was difficult not to think of
an overstuffed trotter got up for a fancy-dress ball.

'You look pale, Lou,' Kilroy said. 'Peely-wally.'

'It's the effect you have, Leo. You drain the blood from
my face.'

Kilroy smiled. 'Have you changed your hairstyle or did you
just get your finger stuck in a light socket?'

'Tell me where I can catch your stand-up act.' Perlman went
to the window of Scullion's office, which overlooked Pitt Street.
He needed light, even if it was only this insipid grey muslin that
enclosed Glasgow like yesterday's ectoplasm. Kilroy's presence
was oppressive, an eclipse.

Kilroy said, 'A sea cruise in sunny climes might be just the thing to get some colour into your cheeks. I can recommend a first-rate vessel sailing the Caribbean. I know el capitano.'

'I don't have holiday time coming up.'

'Too bad.'

'Mibbe this has escaped your notice, Leo, but the majority of people work for a living. Most of us are on schedules and incomes that don't allow much time for globe-trotting. Most of us aren't on first-name terms with the el capitanos of seagoing vessels.'

'My, don't tell me we're going down the slope to snide, Lou. My ears are pricked. Will you be calling me Fatso next?'

Perlman stuck a hand in his coat pocket and fingered his cigarettes. He regretted his brief foray into cheap sarcasm. There was no dignity in it. Kilroy would see it as a victory: I got under the Sergeant's skin easy as breaking wind, heh heh.

A smoke, a smoke, Lou thought. His need for a stick of tobacco was profound. In the street below he saw the Dalmatian still hauling its owner along the pavement. What did a little old man want with such a big dog? Protection against the terror of the city, of course. Tenements were fitted with security doors and alarm systems. Fear of violence was a condition of the world. Old people were lost in a savage jungle they didn't understand.

Leo Kilroy's lawyer, Nat Blum, stood directly behind his client. Blum was as slim as Kilroy obese, a spindle of a man with a narrow face and dark eyebrows. He was handsome the way the head of an axe might be handsome. His black hair was glossy. Perlman wondered if it was dyed.

'Let's try and keep this cordial, Lou,' Blum said.

'Working at it, Nat. Sweating over it.'

'After all, we're here in the service of the due process of law. The least you can do is show appreciation.'

Appreciation. Perlman choked back a number of responses, none witty. He glanced at Scullion, who was rearranging the framed pictures on the desk. Sandy's private icons – his pretty wife, Madeleine, his two sweet kids. The Inspector had an existence beyond Pitt Street, a home to go to. Perlman's life was laundry he never got round to doing, a ton of old newspapers he'd never managed to discard – some of them dating back to a misty age when tramcars swayed on electric wires through cobbled city streets, and the coins in your pockets were big hefty pennies or chunky florins.

Blum looked at his watch and said, 'Let's get to the point. You have some quote unquote fresh evidence, so I'm told.'

Perlman propped himself against the window ledge. He remembered the blue classic car pass under the streetlamps, and heard the blast of the weapon rolling through his head like a memory of thunder. He said, 'Kilroy's car, the Bentley –'

Blum interrupted. '*Again* with the car? We dealt with the bloody car months ago.'

Kilroy said, 'The night your brother died my Bentley was stolen. It's a matter of record. A felonious person, or persons, made off with my pride and joy.'

'The car was subsequently torched,' Blum added. 'The charred ruin was found a couple of months ago in a godforsaken part of Ayrshire. This is ancient history –'

Perlman said, 'I know that –'

'In any case, haven't we already proved that my client had nothing to do with the slaying of your brother?'

'Not to my satisfaction,' Perlman said.

'I'm heartbroken to learn that you aren't happy, Lou, but the Procurator-Fiscal threw your case out, or have you forgotten?'

'I'd forget a thing like that?'

'I'm sorry Colin's dead, but you can't keep trying to dump the blame on my client.' A greased lank of black hair had fallen over Blum's forehead, and he swept it back. 'You saw a gun in the window of a classic Bentley one night last December. Somebody, whose *face* you didn't see, fired a shot that killed your brother. My client doesn't even know how to *use* a gun, for God's sake. You don't have *anything* that links the killer to Mr Kilroy. What's so interesting about the car all of a sudden?'

Blum's confidence riled Perlman. Nat was infatuated with

himself, the slickly dressed man about Glasgow familiar to maître d's and chefs alike, one who drew waiters to him as a magnet attracts metal shavings. Nat's world was champagne cocktails in the Rogano and a penthouse flat in some flash new development on the river. He was the boy who'd risen from a mean background – Dad an impoverished tailor – to become the high-paid legal representative of assorted gangsters and criminals. He'd bought himself expensive implanted teeth, and buffed the rough edges from his Glasgow accent. He never swore. As he'd risen in the world, he'd elevated his language.

Perlman said, 'If you'll just listen without getting your silk boxers in a fankle, Nat, I might get a word in . . . An eyewitness says he saw Kilroy driving the Bentley *after* the time of my brother's murder. If that's true, it hammers a stake through the heart of your client's alibi. Correct me if I'm wrong.'

'An eyewitness, Lou? Four months later and suddenly an *eyewitness*?' Blum looked at Scullion. 'Is the Sergeant in his right mind, Sandy?'

Scullion said, 'A person made contact.'

'A person made contact? How exactly? Letter? Email? Did he tell you my client was driving the car after it was reported *stolen*?'

Scullion blew his nose, then glanced at Perlman. 'Lou, why don't you tell Blum your story?'

Perlman was quiet for a moment. Okay, this was a shot in the dark with a crooked crossbow, but the important thing was to appear confident, a man privy to great secrets. 'The contact was made by telephone last night.'

'And the caller left a name and address?' Blum asked.

Perlman smiled at the lawyer. Hold the smile, sustain the confidence, the ease. 'As a matter of fact, no.'

'I'm hitting rewind. A total stranger phoned, spun you a story, then – what? He gave you *nothing* by way of ID?'

'He said he'd call back.'

'And he hasn't?'

Perlman nodded. 'No, but it's only a matter of time.'

21

Blum said, 'And you recorded the message, I assume.'

'I don't tape my calls. He said he'd call with more details –'

'And that's *it*? Some schmuck phones you with a message he doesn't substantiate, he gives you no indication of its provenance, he doesn't even *identify* himself, and you have me drag Mr Kilroy down here on *this* basis? It's a nonsense. I know what you're doing, Lou. You're harassing my client. This is part of a pattern you've established over the years.'

Perlman waved a hand dismissively. 'Fuck's sake, Nat. I'm not harassing anyone. I'm presenting you with a simple statement of fact that contradicts your client's story.'

'An anonymous phone call doesn't constitute a statement of fact, Lou. Is this all you've got?'

Perlman shrugged. 'Somebody out there knows something, Nat. I just thought you should be aware.'

'And I'm supposed to take your word that this phone call actually happened?'

'Are you saying I'm a liar, Nat?'

'I've had consommé that was thicker than what you're trying to serve up,' Blum said. 'Just because some murderous bastard with a pistol stole Leo's car, you jump – no, you *leap* – to the conclusion that it was Leo who killed Colin. Now you're reduced to anonymous eyewitnesses. You're a sad old bastard, Lou –'

Perlman said, 'My phone'll ring again. Today. Tomorrow, Whenever. And when I pick it up, wham!'

Blum looked at Scullion. 'Do I have to listen to any more of this, Sandy? Perlman's been harassing my client for years. Every petty little thing he can dream up. If it's not contraband cigarettes, it's some kind of protection racket for the better boutiques and clubs of our dear city. Or it's alleged bribery of some city official. One fake accusation follows another.'

'My brother and Kilroy were involved in serious fraud, Nat,' Perlman said.

'So you claim,' Blum said.

'All right, I don't have documentary evidence, and I don't

have corroborating statements because the people who might have been in a position to make them are all fucking boxed and dead.'

'Anything you've got is either fabricated or circumstantial.'

Perlman ignored the lawyer: let a lawyer rabbit on and you're shafted. 'Your client killed my brother because Colin knew the scam in and out and up and down, how it worked, who profited and who was cheated. And because Kilroy feared exposure, he killed Colin. Just the way Colin killed the men he thought might expose *him*.' Perlman felt an ache in the lower area of his spine. That damn dog. That big spotted hellhound. 'One day, Nat, I'll nail your fucking client to the wall. I promise you.'

'You're going too far,' Blum said. 'You're really pushing your luck.'

Kilroy said, 'Boys, boys, boys, this talk of nails is *troubling* me. It's upsetting my ulcer. There's been a misunderstanding here. These things happen.'

Perlman noticed a sharp little light of something – malice? manipulation? – beneath the flaps of Kilroy's eyelids. You saw Kilroy in the pantomime clothes, and it was easy to forget that his heart was black. Now he began to rise, a monstrous undertaking, a complicated process of flab displacing flab, a series of soft rings of flesh yielding so that muscle and bone might be liberated long enough to allow him leverage to a standing position.

He made it. Kilroy Erectus, a mighty sight.

'Lou, a word in your ear,' he said. 'I bear you absolutely no hard feelings. I swear. Justice hasn't been served. The killer's still out there. But I'm not the answer, Lou. I was awfully fond of Colin. And I miss him sorely. I do.'

'You expect some thanks for this speech?' Perlman asked. *I want to murder you*, he thought. He had the wild urge to gather the ends of Kilroy's long silk scarf and choke him slowly. But you can't do stuff like that, you're a policeman, you obey the book of rules, and so you live your professional life in a series of small acts of restraint.

Blum laid a hand on the fat man's sleeve. 'He's not listening, Leo. Let's get away from this . . . pesterment.'

'Pesterment? Nice word that,' Perlman said.

Blum escorted his client to the door, where he turned round. 'Any more stupid stunts, Lou, I'm going all the way up to Chief Superintendent Tay, and even higher if I need to. At which point you go in the grinder and you come out sausage. Loud and clear?'

'Loud anyway,' Perlman said. He listened to lawyer and client go along the hallway. He imagined Blum reporting him to the straight-faced William Tay, Presbyterian Church elder, a man suffering a terminal humour deficit. *Perlman's waging a private war on my client. Perlman's acting beyond his authority.* Tay would hear him out unblinkingly, all the time storing away the lawyer's complaints. It was no secret William Tay disliked Perlman, whom he considered a dinosaur living on borrowed time. Tay wanted Perlman to retire; it was even rumoured that the Chief Superintendent had composed a farewell speech for the occasion of the Last Supper. *We come to say goodbye to a valuable comrade . . .*

Scullion asked, 'What do you think?'

Perlman watched ragged clouds blown west across the city. 'I'm deeply impressed by that look of wounded innocence Blum's cultivated. Then the way he switches in a flash to outrage. He'd get my BAFTA vote. As for the fat man, who knows? I enjoyed the quiet word of confidentiality, and the woeful expression he tries on. *Sorry about your brother, Lou.* I felt like asking him for the loan of a hankie so I could dry my fucking eyes.'

'I'm a wee bit troubled I didn't see Kilroy *squirm*, Lou,' Scullion said. 'Nor did I see Blum miss a beat. He didn't go all pale and trembly. Quite the opposite. He went on the offensive.'

'I'm hearing a tiny off-note in your voice, Sandy. You think I jumped the gun? I should've waited for the caller to get back to me? I should've put some meat on the bones before we brought the *khazer* and his lawyer here?'

'Maybe.'

'I just thought I'd plant a tiny seed, see what grows. You said to go for it. You had the chance to stop me.'

'You were hot. I didn't want to burn my fingers holding you back.'

'I wanted to niggle them, ventilate some of that bloody *smugness* out of them –'

'I know what you wanted, Lou. But you didn't think this little confrontation *through*. I understand you're in a hurry. I know what you feel. You want Kilroy in jail where he belongs, and you want it yesterday. But now that you're asking me, okay, with the benefit of hindsight I have to say we should've waited for a second phone call from the mystery man, more info, some kind of verification, before we pulled Kilroy down here, I was wrong to let you rush –'

'I've lost my objectivity, Sandy?'

'In this matter, aye. How could it be any other way? Your own brother. You're haunted.'

'I need an exorcist. Where's the Yellow Pages?'

'You need a diversion, Lou. You're too close to the situation.'

Perlman was quiet for a time. The sky was surly. Glasgow had a veneer of gloom. He thought: I saw the slaying, I recognized the car. And I don't believe for a moment Kilroy's claim that he doesn't know how to handle a gun, even if the Procurator-Fiscal had bought into it.

He laid the palm of a hand on a window pane. He noticed liver spots on his skin. Decay and deterioration. How soon they set in. He thought of Colin decomposing in the soil. Four months in damp earth, what was left?

He said, 'I loved my brother.'

'I know you did.'

'He was a bad bastard. I loved him anyway.'

'You love who you love, it's all a bloody mystery.' Scullion drummed his fingertips on his desk. 'Change of topic. Madeleine's expecting you for dinner tonight. Remember?'

25

'How could I forget?'

'I don't know why, but she's got a soft spot for you.'

'I'm blessed with a certain charm. Only people of discretion see it.'

'Let's get some perspective here. Madeleine's also very much taken with lost dogs and stray cats as well.'

'So she has a soul,' Perlman said.

Scullion propped himself on the edge of his desk. 'No matter what she serves up, Lou, say you like it. I know she's not exactly Nigella in the kitchen –'

'Maddy does fine,' Perlman said.

'Your idea of fine is a bag of greasy chips drowned in malt vinegar.'

'The fuck you say. I like a greasy sausage to go with the chips.'

Scullion made a face. 'Do you want to know what she's preparing?'

'So long as it's not fish pie.'

'Fish pie? Did you say fish pie?'

'Break it to me gently, Sandy.'

'I wish I knew a way of breaking anything gently to you.'

Fish pie, Perlman thought. His mother Etta used to make it every Tuesday. In her limited repertoire of dishes, fish pie was far and away the most scary. It transgressed all the rules of inedibility. Lou and Colin used to deconstruct the pie and shove soggy pastry round their plates, trying to create an illusion of having eaten at least something. Etta was never fooled. She served the same dish the next Tuesday, and all the Tuesdays after that: Tuesdays were an infinity of uneaten scraps of haddock, cod and other slimy marine matter afloat in a lumpy white sauce.

'You'll eat it,' Scullion said.

'Is that an order, Inspector?'

'Take it any way you like.'

Before Perlman had a chance to reply, his mobile phone rang; it played the first few notes of 'Take Five'. He spoke his name into the mouthpiece. He was surprised – *astonished* – to hear her voice. His heart felt like the tight-stretched skin of a drum.

'Can I see you, Lou?' she asked.

5

Bobby Descartes pulled the hood of his jacket over his skull and knotted the drawstring, which gave his head a cylindrical look. Wind whined through the thin stand of trees and whipped slanty rain at him.

He stared at the building beyond the trees. One storey, squat, functional. He'd come here many times before. He knew this place. He knew the specs: diesel-fired central heating fuelled from a six-hundred-gallon tank, twelve rooms, three toilets, a kitchen. The number of windows. Twelve in front, twelve at the back. One at each end. Twenty-six in all. There was one front door and one back, where four big green wheelie-bins sat.

He gathered these details as a miser might hoard coins. A good plan was an accretion of small facts and you memorized them all. The number of people inside the building – that was important. On an average day, with no absences, there were about fifty, which included staff. The part-time kitchen staff, two plump women of about sixty who were almost twinlike in hairstyle and bearing, a couple of bollards, usually left around 2 p.m. Bobby had followed them once or twice. They lived nearby in an estate of two-storey houses where, years before, there had been the tenements that had housed generations of immigrants, Jews, Irish, Poles, Latvians, all the dross of Europe that had washed up in central Scotland.

He felt a rant begin to rip through his head. Don't go there. You don't have time to waste. Rain dripped from leaves and slicked over his hood. He heard the rush of traffic on the nearby M8, where the motorway cut through Kinning Park and Kingston, and then crossed Paisley Road. It traversed the Clyde at the Kingston Bridge and headed, in the manner of a surgical scar that would never heal cleanly, through the west of the city centre.

He checked his watch. The face was blurry. Two thirty. The hour approacheth. No nerves, Beezer. This is your destiny.

He left the trees and crossed the yard quickly. Ten seconds, maybe fifteen, he reached the side of the building. He ducked his head under the window and slipped round the back.

He opened the rear door quietly and stepped inside a storage room adjoining the kitchen. He was surrounded by big bottles of ketchup and industrial-sized tubs of bright yellow mustard. Monster cans of baked beans formed a huge stack on a shelf. He thought: I'm breathing a little too quickly. Pulse up, heartbeat raised a notch.

Cool it, Beezer. Keep your mouth closed. Breathe through your nose.

He gazed across the empty kitchen: steel surfaces, pots and pans hanging from hooks. It was the cleanest room he'd ever seen. Scrubbed, sanitized, polished; the air smelled of strong disinfectant. It was almost a shame to step into the kitchen with your muddy running shoes. Besides, they made a distinctive pattern, and he wasn't happy about leaving a trace behind; you might as well lay your business card on the counter-top. He took off his shoes and hooked them over the fingers of his left hand and only then did he enter the kitchen.

He heard a woman's voice in a room down the corridor. 'This little piggy went to market.'

Bobby felt suddenly very calm, like he wasn't attached to

himself any more, he was weightless in space. It was similar to the feeling he got when he'd been in pain with a broken leg one time and the doc had shot him with morphine, max strength, deep into the vein, a lovely wee ship sailing on a tranquil blue surface straight to his brain.

He moved across the kitchen, opened a door, stepped into a corridor. The woman's voice was louder. 'And what did the next little piggy do? Justin, can you tell me?'

'Don't know.' A wee boy's voice. Presumably Justin.

'Come on, Justin. You do know.'

'Don't know.'

'Yes, you do,' the woman said.

Bobby thought: Leave Justin alone, you bullying cunt. The next little piggy shit his pants. Tell her that, Justin, wee man. Or tell her the next little piggy had a fucking good wank.

'Can *you* tell me, Alexandra?'

'Went to market,' a girl said.

'No, Alex, pet, that was the first little piggy.'

Bobby thought: Who gives a shit where any of the piggies went? Why drum this crap into the heads of kindergarten kids?

No time to waste, he knew which door to enter, which room he wanted. Room 2. The doors were all bright red. Each had a small pane of reinforced glass set at eye level.

Bobby stopped outside 2. He pressed his face to the glass.

There she was. That bitch. She didn't see him. She was busy yacking about the comings and goings of pigs. You cunt, leave the kids alone, they don't need this.

'Which little piggy ran all the way home?'

Bobby opened the door and said, 'I am that fucking piggy.'

The woman stared at him. She was brown-skinned, good-looking if you liked that dark-eyed, brown-skinned, long-lashed type. The pale green sari, the headscarf, where did she think she was, bloody Bombay?

Leave your mark, Bobby. Leave your sign. Go on.

'You know this is private property?' she asked. 'What business do you have here?'

30

'Private business,' Bobby said. The air smelled of sour milk, chalk: did every school and every kindergarten in the world smell the same damn way?

'I must ask you to leave.'

'Ask me. See what happens.'

'Go, please, you're scaring the children,' she said. She had a Glasgow accent. Her type always thought that if they pronounced their words like locals, if they dropped their 't's' in 'bottle' or 'spittle', that was enough to fool everybody into believing they belonged.

It ain't fooling me, Bobby thought. He said, 'I know you.'

'I don't think so. Please. Just go.'

The kids were in motion now, shrinking away from him, moving towards the woman. She gathered some of them around her. A few weans, four years old or so, had begun to snivel. You hadn't foreseen that, Beezer. Crying kids hadn't been part of the plan. What did you think? She'd be alone in the classroom and you'd just do your stuff and walk away? What does it matter, you don't have to harm the kids. You just do the thing and go.

Yeh. Now.

He took a couple of quick strides forward. 'Indra,' he said. 'I fucking know you, you bitch.'

'We've never met,' she said.

'I know your name, I watched you, I saw you coming and going, all airs and graces and floating along the street like your shite didn't stink, what do you think you are, eh? Some fucking rajah's bint? Eh? Look at the clothes. You don't belong here.'

'Go, please please go –'

'Scared, right? I've got you scared. Scared and running, pishing your knickers. You pishing, Indra? Hiss hiss.'

Reach, find, remove, fire. He realized he had the tiny gun in his hand. He didn't remember taking it out.

Kids were screaming.

'Put that gun away,' she said.

'Aw, fuck you.'

He fired at a range of four feet directly into her forehead.

31

She made a weird sound, as if her breath had all been sucked back into her throat, then she slipped to the floor and lay on her side. Little kids were sprayed with her blood and brain-soup and bone fragments. He wanted to linger, say something to calm them down, explain why he'd had to shoot the woman, and how he was sorry they witnessed it, but some things had to be done, he had a duty.

They'd thank him one day. Some of them anyway.

He rushed from the room. A man appeared at the end of the corridor. He was big and bearded, and wore a white turban.

A raghead, Bobby thought. This school was crawling with these fuckers.

The man shouted. 'What the devil do you think you're doing?'

Bobby fired a shot that hit the man in his chest.

The man slumped against the wall and said, 'Oh no, oh no.'

Bobby raced down the corridor, crossed the kitchen, left the building the way he'd entered it, and skidded across the yard to the trees. Then he was moving quickly beneath a sky the colour of cold volcanic ash. He was running, and the motorway roared and spat damp spray nearby.

When he'd run as far as Scotland Street he remembered he was still carrying his shoes. He sat on the pavement and put them on and he thought: You're a prince, Beezer. A national hero. He didn't feel the rain now. He didn't feel his sodden feet inside the chunky shoes. He was running a Union Jack up the flagpole of his imagination, then saluting it with great dignity; and the brass bands in his head played patriotic marches.

6

Perlman drove his battered Mondeo east along Edinburgh Road, past housing estates that had been built in the mid-1950s and early '60s to accommodate the mass exodus of people from the doomed slums of the old city. These communities, Cranhill, Easterhouse, Barlanark, were once considered part of a great utopian experiment in living. But entire blocks of flats had decayed, some in the space of less than twenty years, while others lay gutted and abandoned. So much for the dark, wacky craft of social engineering, Perlman thought.

He smoked one blue Silk Cut after another.

The idea of seeing Miriam after four months brought him pleasure, but also tension. He pictured her as he'd last seen her: black-veiled and sad-eyed at Colin's funeral, and yet in some way *above* her grief, as if an inner grace prevented her from a public display of loss. She'd floated over her sorrow – assuming sorrow was what she felt. Who could say?

She'd told Perlman last December she'd known for years of her husband's philandering; so maybe her love for him had died long before his death. The revelations that came later, the murderous secrets of Colin's life, would surely have harmed her more than any exposé of his infidelities. Marriage to a serial philanderer was heartbreak, but a less brutalizing shock to the system than marriage to a killer.

Miriam, *hartzenui*.

Perlman lingered over her name. He loved the way it began and ended with the same letter, self-contained and private, as if the M's were two strong doors. He loved how the name included 'i am', like a concealed statement of pride. I Am. This is me. How I am. The sound of the name pleasured him –

Christ, this is a daft road for you to take, Lou, he thought. This is some retarded adolescent *mustang* rearing in your head. The lover denied his true passion. The bandage you've kept wrapped round your heart for more years than you can remember. He believed Miriam knew what he felt. How could she not read it in his face or his eyes, or in the clumsiness he showed in her company?

This line of thinking derailed him; what were the rules when it came to loving the wife of your dead brother? Was a matter of taste involved, an etiquette unknown to him? He concentrated on the rattle of his Mondeo. The car was dented side and front where it had been struck twice in separate minor accidents.

Music. He needed music. He stuck a CD in the deck he'd had installed recently. An old Paul Butterfield album, *Buried Alive in the Blues*. The sound zipped him back to the early '70s, when he'd been a constable pounding a beat in Partick. Colin had already graduated and worked five years in a local brokerage firm, before leaving, as so many Scots did, for London and fortune.

Lou remembered seeing him off at Central Station in the dreamy haze of a midsummer night. Colin, drunk on ale and giddy with notions of prosperity, had climbed clumsily inside a carriage, suitcase in one hand, crumpled coat slung over his arm, a burnt-down cigar between his lips. He'd worn his best suit, a blue single-breasted worsted he'd bought at Burton's. It was probably the last time he'd ever shopped at a chain of off-the-peg tailors.

Details came back sparsely. The unexpected press of Colin's lips on Lou's forehead – *ae fond kiss*, Colin had said, *and then we sever*; the only time Lou had ever been kissed by his brother. The splatter of cigar ash on Colin's dark blue lapel. He looked, Lou remembered, so damn *confident*. He knew he was going to make it in the big city, in the toughest playground of them all.

London changed him. Money changed him. And what a fatal talent he had for making it.

Perlman turned off Edinburgh Road and into Barlanark. He drove slowly down Hallhill Road. The rain had stopped at last. In the eastern sky a weak sun carved a thin rainbow beyond a water tower. A tiny miracle. Another sign, Perlman thought. Maybe it's spring. Finally.

Got caught up in a landslide, Bad luck pressing in from all sides . . . Perlman pressed the stop button of his CD deck as he entered the cemetery. He hadn't been here for months. The dead didn't care if you neglected them, so why did he feel guilty? He parked, got out. His legs were stiff and he felt the dull ache the hellhound had caused. Did you reach a time when you were nothing but the sum of all your petty pains? Take me away, stick me on a codeine drip.

He turned from the ranks of headstones and looked across the street beyond the cemetery wall. He saw a row of shops: a Chinese restaurant, Haddow's off-licence, and – ah yes – the inevitable tanning parlour. These establishments were the rage in Glasgow. People who'd never been further than the Gallowgate strolled the streets looking as if they'd just come back from Jamaica.

He walked between the headstones. He was the only visitor in the cemetery; there was no sign of Miriam. He wondered at the existence of a Jewish burial ground in this part of Glasgow, where there was no Jewish community. It was probably safe to assume that Barlanark's Jewish population was close to zero. The Jews generally hadn't settled in the east of the city – although Perlman chose to do so, in a small area known as Egypt located in a network of streets behind Parkhead Cross. His *klatsch* of aunts berated him whenever he saw them. Why choose Egypt? Always you have to be the contrary one, Louie? What is it, this need to live in the east end? The Aunts – he thought of them as a chorus from a Greek tragedy – managed to make 'east end' sound like Hong Kong, exotic and just a little dubious.

He liked Egypt. He found it a friendly place. He was reasonably popular, perhaps on account of being a cop, an accessible one: he'd responded a few times to a local burglary or a streetfight. He induced a sense, however small, of security – although there were a few in the community, ex-cons and small-time neds, who regarded him with sullen suspicion. He was known to the local kids as The Detective. Sometimes they clustered round him on the street and questioned him about baddies and guns and what it was like being a polisman.

He read headstones. *Deeply mourned by. Sadly missed by.* He came across the grave of Nancy Meizenburg, buried in 1975 alongside her husband Joe. Nancy, a small bright-eyed sparrow of a person, had given Lou piano lessons when he was twelve, thirteen. He could still hear the incessant tick of her metronome, and see the yellowing keys of the piano. She coerced him into playing 'The Merry Peasant' until he had it down note-perfect.

Memories of the dead, the lost music of boyhood.

He kept moving. Damp earth sucked at his shoes. He glanced at other stones. Krasewitz. Matafsky. Guberman. Old European Jews, survivors of pogroms, camps, who knows what they had to live through and how far they had to travel to reach Glasgow?

The sun was milky. The air still smelled of rain. Overhead, a coven of crows, sinister in their concentration, flew quickly. He walked the lettered rows where more recent graves had been dug. No headstones here. It was the custom that a year pass between the funeral and the raising of the stone. The new graves were marked with simple plaques of wood. In Row S, he found Colin's name, and he stood before it, lowering his head a little.

A little leap of association made him think about the voice on the telephone: *I think you should know, Sergeant, I saw Kilroy drive his Bentley the morning after your brother was killed . . .*

Lou had asked, 'Who is this?'

The man said: *I'll be in touch . . .*

Or maybe he'd said: *I'll get back to you with details . . .* Whatever, the sense was the same. Who was the caller?

He stared at his brother's name hard, as if he might somehow conjure an answer from the grave. A stranger's voice. *I'll be in touch . . .* Maybe it was only some *nishtikeit* bent on causing mischief, but he'd sounded authoritative, knowing. So who was he and what did he want and why hadn't he called back?

Perlman bent to pick up a stone. It was wet in his fingers. He placed it on the grave to mark the fact that the site had been visited. He became aware of a figure moving in his direction between the graves.

She wore a long black coat and boots. Her head was uncovered. Her hair, shoulder-length the last time he'd seen her, had been cut short. It gave her face a stark kind of beauty. She moved across wet earth with glorious balance. Perlman's heart was a leaf in the wind. *I should learn to unfeel*, he thought. What would the Aunts say if they knew his secret? Your dead brother's wife, you crazy? It's incest practically.

He walked a few paces to meet her. He felt coy, unsure of how he was expected to behave. Four months without seeing her; he was out of practice. He wanted to hug her, touch her face, kiss her forehead. And more, God help him: his urges were carnal and deep. When she was close enough, he opened his arms instinctively. She stepped at once inside his embrace, and pressed her face against his chest. He held her this way for a time and thought it strange to feel so alive in this place of the dead, and stranger still to be holding his brother's wife a few feet from the place where Colin lay.

'I missed you,' he said. Christ, he longed to let his language soar. *I missed you*. A weary wee platitude. He wanted to speak of love and commitment, and open all the doors of his heart for her to see how he'd furnished the rooms. Come live with me in these chambers.

'I went to Florence,' she said.

'I heard.'

'I had to get away.'

'Did you paint in Florence?' Why couldn't he think of a scintillating comment, an insightful response?

She stared across the cemetery. He detected a slight flicker of hurt in her eyes. It must cause her pain to come back to this place; a dead husband, after all – there was surely some sense of loss, a quiet grief. There had to be a few memories of good times. It couldn't all be anger and regret and the bitter taste of betrayal in her mouth. She took a couple of steps away from him and studied Colin's grave. Then she set a pebble alongside the one Lou had left.

'I didn't feel much like painting. I bought canvas and some paints. But . . .' She shrugged indecisively.

'When did you come back?' he asked.

'Nobody told you? Last week.'

'How was Florence?'

'Quiet,' she said. 'I like Florence. Off-season anyway.' She gazed at him and smiled. He thought that smile would melt the polar ice-cap and swell oceans. Her voice, low-pitched, almost husky, belonged in an old-style Left Bank café where candles burned and the chanteuse sang with painful intimacy of broken hearts, and the zinc counter was dented.

She said, 'Poor Lou, you don't know what to do with your hands, do you? You never did.'

He was unaware that he'd been tapping the pockets of his coat in a pointless way. Big hands. Hard to hide. Thick fingers. 'I find them useless except for brushing my teeth and buttoning my coat, just about.'

'You obviously don't use them to run a comb through your hair.'

He raised a hand to the spiky disarray of his hair, suddenly self-conscious. Leo Kilroy had made some comment about his hair earlier, which had irked him. But he'd gladly let Miriam say anything she liked about his appearance. She could reconstruct

38

him if she wanted. Build me up into a new man, love. Consider it a challenge.

'My hair has a mind of its own.'

'It's so *you*. That just-out-of-bed look.'

'Is that compliment or critique?'

'You work it out.' And again she looked across the cemetery, as if something in the distance had demanded her attention. He followed her line of sight. The arc of the rainbow still hung beyond the water tower, colours fuzzy.

'How did two brothers turn out so differently?' she asked.

'Who knows? I like your hair, speaking of hair.'

'I needed a change,' she said. She reached out and took one of his hands. 'There. I'll keep it still.' She held it pressed between her own. Her skin was cold. She no longer wore a wedding ring, he noticed.

'Do you know a cop called Latta?' she asked.

'Not very well. Why?'

'He's one of the reasons I came back.'

'I see him around from time to time. Fraud Squad. Black hair, bad teeth.'

'Very scary teeth,' she said. 'He's been asking me questions.'

'About Colin?'

'Right. Latta makes me feel as if I was some kind of willing accomplice in Colin's financial schemes. As if I know where there's a vast cache of money and bonds or something.'

'Is he pressuring you?'

Miriam shrugged. 'I suppose he's just doing his job. In the charm stakes, he's a total *golem*. I don't have a clue about Colin's transactions. I never did. He had his world, I had mine. He had his spreadsheets, I had my paintings.'

'Did Latta say it might be useful if you came back to Glasgow?'

'He came all the way to Florence to tell me so.'

'Nice junket,' Perlman said. 'I'll speak to him if you like. See what he's up to.'

'No, you don't have to do that. One day he'll find out for himself that I know nothing about Colin's business.'

39

Perlman shrugged. 'There's no harm if I talk to him.'

'Let me deal with it, Lou. I have to cope with all kinds of things now. Fend is the word.'

He felt a vague disappointment: he wanted to help. He wanted to check this thing out with Latta. But no, she didn't need him for that. He saw a quiet determination in her face. She was going to be her own person. And he let this realization disappoint him also. What had he expected? A useless sorry widow, dazed by misery, looking for support and guidance, and turning to him? *Oh, Lou, you're the only one I can count on.* The selfish heart projects its own needs. She was free. Allow her that.

'You said Latta was one of the reasons you came back. What were the others?'

'I don't know yet.' She drew away from him. His hand, released suddenly, slumped back against his side. 'To visit this grave, maybe. To see if I could pick up my life again in Glasgow. I have spells when everything just *shines* with the possibility of a new life. I'm restless, energetic, I want to paint. Then the next day I'm tumbling down this spiral of gloom and I hit bottom and nothing has any electricity.'

'You don't put your world back together overnight. Why the rush?' He wanted to add: I'm here for you all the hours God sends.

She said, 'Tell me about the investigation.'

'Don't ask. One of the nightmares of a cop's work is knowing the identity of a criminal and not being able to do anything about it. Something might break, I might get a nibble of luck. Some days the wind blows your way.'

She raised a hand to her neck where the skin was smooth and firm. He'd thought a thousand times of kissing her throat, unshackling himself in the intimacy of the gesture. She had tiny lines at the corners of her lips, and a darkness under her eyes, but otherwise the years had been charitable to her. She was slender. She had the body of a retired ballerina, and the kind of elegance of movement nobody can teach.

40

'You want justice for Colin,' she said, and her voice was thin and strained.

'Of course. Don't you?'

'What do you think?'

'He was murdered. Murderers go to jail. That's a simple equation. It doesn't matter what Colin did.'

'In your world,' she said. 'It matters in mine.'

'I understand –'

'I'm not sure you do, Lou.'

'You're angry. You're hurt. This I understand.'

'I'm neither angry nor hurt. Maybe I just don't want to talk about Colin. I've almost managed to leave him behind. I've been training myself not to feel his absence. After a while, it gets easier. So let's drop him.' She pressed a finger to his lip as if to silence him. He smelled her skin, a trace of whatever perfumed emollient she used to rub into her hands.

They walked a little way between graves. 'Tell me what's new in your life. Is there a woman? Have you met somebody?'

'Have I *met* somebody?' He studied her face. Was this mischief? Was she *serious*? 'What makes you think I'm even *looking* for somebody?'

'I bet women find you attractive. You've got that wee boy thing. Women want to brush your hair and make sure your socks match. You look like a kid who's become separated from his mum in a big department store.'

'Miriam, I'm a fifty-something cop, and I'm staring down the barrel of retirement.'

'Quit making yourself sound like an old man, Lou.'

'You know what lies in wait for me? A pension. Walks in the park, probably in the company of some loyal wee schmuck of a dog. I'll spend some of my endless spare time wondering what my life really amounted to, did I achieve anything, did it go the way I thought it might, all the big searching questions, et cetera. Who knows? Maybe I'll gorge myself on Viagra and trawl senior citizens' bingo clubs in search of casual sex.'

'Funny man. I don't see you doing any such thing.'

41

'So help me out. What will I be doing? Look into your crystal ball.'

'I see clouds,' she said.

'Heavy or passing?'

'Hard to say.'

He moved his weight, shifted his feet. He was uncomfortable whenever he talked about himself. He gazed past her, unable to hold her eye for long, as if he might give too much of himself away. The headstones reminded him that life was a mercilessly brief business altogether, and if you didn't reach for the prize when you had the chance, you woke up one day and you were out of time. He heard sands whispering through the glass, demented clocks ticking. *I left it too long, but how could I have done it any other way?* Cowardly of you, Lou. You've faced down some vile criminals in your time, but you can't confront the notion of saying aloud what's inside you.

Then it occurred to him that maybe Miriam *didn't* know what he felt, that he'd been mistaken in assuming she did. Perhaps he fell into that sad category of a man who wants to be the lover, but is destined for ever to be the best friend.

There's an epitaph: *His love was never noticed.*

Should he have made a pass at her, chanced his arm? A different kind of man might have done that. Not you, Lou. You're too courteous for your own good, old-fashioned in matters of the heart. Was it out of a weird respect for your dead brother that you didn't tell this woman, once and for all and beyond any doubt, what you felt for her, what you've felt for many long dry years?

Miriam folded her arms against her breasts, and moved slowly away. He followed her. A slight glumness had descended on him. He was delighted to be with her, but what had possessed him to rabbit on in such an inane way about life and retirement – and Viagra, of all things? If you were trying to make yourself seem an attractive proposition, or even a promising one, you really fucked up the sales job, *shlub*.

Try another tack. 'Have you got time for afternoon tea?'

'I'd like that.'

'The Willow is nice.'

'I love the Willow. I haven't been there in ages.'

Uplifted suddenly, he was suffused with warmth; tea with Miriam, cakes on doilies, genteel sandwiches, cream and scones. Miriam facing him across the table, those chocolate-dark eyes of hers suggesting wild encounters where you adventured beyond the boundaries of your shy staid self.

His mobile phone rang. The sound startled him. He took the device from his coat pocket with a gesture of irritation.

It was Sandy Scullion. 'We've got a situation, Lou.'

'Don't tell me. The fish pie is off the menu.'

'There's no menu. You better come in. Fast.'

Perlman shut his mobile off and looked at Miriam with an expression of annoyance. 'Shite. I'm sorry . . .'

'A policeman's lot,' she said. 'Call me. By the way, that cloud in the crystal ball?'

'Aye?'

'It may pass.'

7

In the back of his plum-coloured chauffeur-driven Mercedes, Nat Blum sat with his briefcase on his lap. He was conscious of Kilroy's cologne, which was a little on the effete side.

Kilroy said, 'Perlman made it all up. Plain and fucking simple.'

'I have any number of reasons for disliking Perlman, Leo. One thing I can tell you, he's no liar.'

Kilroy issued a derogatory *pah* sound. 'Everybody lies, Blumsky.'

'Lou Perlman doesn't. Fact of life.'

'Then he's a bloody rare bird.'

'He's got some notion of honour, granted.'

'Unlike his brother, who'd have shagged his grannie if it meant extra points on a deal. Hungry man, Colin.'

Blum gazed at the back of his driver's bald head. 'Colin was greedy to the marrow. Lou, on the other hand, thinks he has a shot at sainthood.'

'Do you Jews have saints?' Kilroy asked.

'We canonize all our best accountants.'

Blum drummed his briefcase and considered this fat beast who was his client. He'd heard the usual stories, which he found prudent to ignore, about the series of boys who shared Kilroy's bed. Other reports suggested Leo was rampantly bi, and had access to a harem of pubescent girls. Blum had no idea if the rumours had a basis in fact, nor inclination to ask: if Kilroy was the most flamboyant queen in the city, or if he was AC/DC to the point where he drained megawatts from the National Grid, he was still good for a retainer of £200K+ per annum.

Besides, it was potentially dangerous to ask too many questions about Kilroy's private life, or cause him offence; he was said to have an army of thugs at his disposal. They were allegedly fond of the occasional after-hours bone-breaking in alleys, just for the sport of it. Kilroy had lethal clout. You gave him counsel, but crossed him at your peril.

Kilroy, a devotee of musicals, briefly sang a phrase from *South Pacific*. He had a voice that would chill a hangman. 'Bali Ha'i' was quickly choked. He fell silent, and looked out at the stout respectable houses along Crow Road, which led eventually to suburban Bearsden and home, a big tree-shielded, electric-gated mansion, ersatz Spanish-style, in Ledcameroch Road, where his flamboyant presence annoyed his neighbours.

Kilroy's love of his native city was selective. On warm sunny days, ah good God, he *adored* Glasgow. There was no place on earth like it, you could take your New York and your Paris and stuff them right up your crack. Okay, Glasgow had rough areas, no-go neighbourhoods – what city didn't? But it had hundreds of acres of parks, and more wondrous Victorian architecture than you could find anywhere else on earth.

He also loved being a man of influence in this city. He was close to cardinals and bishops, contributed generously to a number of Catholic charities, dined with MPs and city councillors, and he was on first-name terms with the Lord Provost.

But come long dreich winter, or cold damp spring, he preferred escape. He cruised the warm blue waters of another

45

hemisphere, exposing his pendulous dugs to the sun, sipping drinks festooned with parasols and cubes of pineapple.

'Just for a minute, assume Perlman is telling the truth,' Blum said. 'Who do you think could have phoned him?'

'The fucking truth, Blumsky, is that any number of neds would like to see my empire collapse. I live in a state of siege. There are all kinds of fucking villains trying to climb my walls. Sometimes I can't sleep at night thinking about all this *hostility* out there. So some envious wee nob picks up a phone, calls Perlman, and lies in his teeth. Ach, let's not waste time on it. Perlman's trying to con us. I always trust my gut. It's an inbuilt shite detector.'

Blum listened to the smooth motor of his car. People like Kilroy helped keep this Merc on the road. They were scum, these high-flying crooks of Glasgow, men who ran the scams that ticked and hummed unseen beneath the surface of everyday life. Blum had chosen to blind himself to the fact that these characters lacked, for want of a better phrase, a moral sense. They were his clients, and any client was entitled to confidentiality and your best work. So you went bare-knuckle for them. And you accepted their lies as truths.

Leo's car, for instance. Blum had serious doubts that it had been stolen in the manner Kilroy claimed. *Parked it outside my house around 10.30 on the night Colin was shot, fucking hell, some naughty bugger had magicked it away by morning.* It was within the realms of possibility that Kilroy had paid somebody to steal the car. Money stuffed into a lackey's hand, a quick handover of keys. Or, if the message Perlman had received was true, it was also possible that Leo *had* been seen driving the car after Colin's death.

But who was this anonymous individual and why would he report it? Where was the gain? It was a tangled business. Lies and half-lies; the truth, never unvarnished, always seemed to be concealed at the bottom of some murky river – which was probably also the fate of the murder weapon too, covered by silt on the bed of the Clyde.

46

Whether you believed your clients was of no consequence. Once upon a time he'd been an idealistic student; he'd considered the law beyond corruption. Hey, look at me now. He wondered if he should laugh or cry at the loss of his youthful naivety.

'Here's the thing. Perlman's not going to go away, Leo, no matter how many Hail Marys you say.'

Kilroy settled back in his seat and smiled. He had peculiarly small teeth, almost baby. 'Speak to me straight. You admire Perlman?'

'How do you mean, admire?'

'Say you're playing the black pieces against his white.'

'As an adversary? Admire? More like . . . respect. I can't say I could ever befriend him. He's too dogged. Also, and I know this is a petty thing, Leo, but he hasn't a clue how to dress. Did you see those flannels? They looked like windsocks at some abandoned airfield. And when did you last see anyone wearing specs like his? They must be National Health issue, circa 1960.'

'Never mind all that. Does he worry you?'

'Up to a point.'

'He's going to get up my nose a lot, right?'

'All the way up.'

'He thinks I'm just some fat dimfuck in poncey feathers.'

'I doubt that.'

'I don't think he gives me respect. He doesn't see there's a lean shark hidden deep down inside me, Nat. This big body, these clothes – okay, I happen to like eating, *gluttonous* eating, and I enjoy a certain mode of dress that some might find a touch extrovert in our dull-arsed society. But sometimes people make the mistake of thinking they're dealing with Coco the fucking clown. Big blunder, believe me.'

'I don't think Perlman would make that mistake, Leo.' A lean shark, Blum thought. Extraordinary how people perceived themselves. He had an image of a huge killer fish with Kilroy's face gliding through an aquarium tank.

Kilroy sat back. He gazed out at Bearsden Road. He felt

a twinge of weariness, a tweak of discontent. A shadow of unhappiness fell across him. For years he'd been juggling this business, that business, and it was hard work to stay ahead of the pack. He tried to keep his affairs cloaked in a fog. He was the exclusive supplier of bootleg Aberdeen Angus beef, Thai prawns and certain popular brands of alcohol to many of the city's elegant restaurants. He had a majority holding in a chain of motorway cafés – cheap eats for the masses on the move – and a huge investment in a no-frills airline. There were rumours of more nefarious activities involving contraband single malt whiskies and, as the Jew Perlman had intimated in the past, a high-dollar protection racket involving boutiques and hotels.

True or false, no matter, he'd been the subject of scrutiny and envy for years. The Strathclyde Police, in the form of Perlman, harassed him without mercy. And his business associates were jealous of his successes. Why the hell didn't he give this place a wide fucking berth altogether? Why not lie on a teak deck in sunlight all the days of his life? Simple answer: he didn't want anyone to think he'd run. He didn't want anyone to believe his nerve had failed. And he still had precious fragments of Glasgow in his heart.

He said, 'I hope Perlman doesn't fuck with me, Nat. I wouldn't like that. It wouldn't sit very well with me.'

Blum said, 'I understand.'

Kilroy closed his eyes, cleared his throat and in his rasping voice ruined the first lines of 'Some Enchanted Evening'.

The fat man sings, Blum thought. Alas.

8

The kindergarten was surrounded by police vehicles, TV vans, cameramen, and a swarm of reporters whose duty it was to scurry here and there with microphones, searching for likely heads to interview. Perlman, who disliked the ostentatious light-show of roof strobes on cop cars, blinked behind his wet glasses.

He parked his Mondeo and skipped around the assembled news-gatherers, then walked past two uniformed constables, neither of whom he knew. They were standing, arms folded, outside the front door of the school, and they stepped aside to let him pass. They recognized him, didn't ask for ID. They nodded, looked grim, two young men solemnized by the proximity to a killing.

He entered a corridor, where Sandy Scullion stood in conversation with Detective Superintendent Mary Gibson, a middle-aged woman in a beige trouser suit and a floral scarf. She reminded Perlman of the models you saw in clothing catalogues aimed at the forty-five plus market. The Mature Woman. She was handsome and tall, and she always dressed as if she expected a last-minute invitation to afternoon tea with the Queen. She was completing a PhD at Glasgow University in Sociology, for reasons best known to herself.

Doors lay open on either side of the corridor. In one room clusters of small whimpering children and their shocked parents talked quietly to three uniformed cops. Two of the cops were women. Perlman heard sniffling and the occasional sound of a nose blown and the hesitant voices of tiny kids trying to answer questions. There was quite an ethnic mix in the room – Indians, Pakistanis, a few Africans and Orientals, a clutch of whites: Glasgow was a cauldron of colours.

Scullion said, 'One teacher dead, another wounded. A single gunman.'

Mary Gibson glanced inside the room where parents hugged their kids. 'They saw their teacher killed. They say the killer wore a hooded jacket. Green, maybe blue. Navy. Nobody's sure. The guy's trousers had stripes in them. Sound like tracksuit bottoms. Some kids say green and red, others green and blue, others purple and blue. Take your pick. They all agree the man was carrying his shoes.'

Scullion said, 'A gunman who doesn't want to get the floors dirty.'

'Who were the victims?' Perlman asked.

'The dead woman was Indra Gupta. The wounded man is Ajit Singh,' Scullion answered.

'How is he?'

Mary Gibson said, 'He's not expected to survive, Lou. They'll operate, of course . . .' She looked at Perlman a little sadly. 'Call me a brontosaurus, but I remember a time when guns were truly rare in this city. If you killed somebody, you used a knife or a razor.'

'Or a hatchet. Those were good old days.'

'You could say,' Mary Gibson remarked.

At the end of the corridor a police snapper was photographing a pool of drying blood. Bulbs popped. A young constable called Dennis Murdoch scribbled something in a notebook: scene-of-the-crime notations, position in which the wounded man had been found, manner of wound, the stuff you were taught to write down for the record.

Perlman scanned the room where the kids were gathered. He knew very little about children. Their sensitivities, perceptions of reality. He'd never been exposed to them for any length of time. His one shot at marriage, a doomed nonsense, had been mercifully barren. He gazed at the small faces and heard quiet anxious voices tremble as narratives were stitched together out of confusion. He admired the tenderness and patience the uniforms showed.

'What kind of sorry bastard walks into a kindergarten and shoots teachers?' he asked.

'The same kind who did it in Dunblane,' Mary Gibson said.

Perlman, like so many people, had shoved the events of Dunblane inside the pit at the back of the head where you stored the kind of unbearable human slurry you didn't have the heart to re-examine. In March, 1996, a certain Thomas Hamilton had walked into a primary school in the quiet Perthshire town of Dunblane where, armed with an assortment of handguns, he'd killed sixteen children and their teacher; an atrocity unprecedented in Scotland. Even now, seven years on, Perlman found it difficult to picture this massacre. The country had haemorrhaged that day; and nothing had ever been quite the same since.

Scullion said, 'Hamilton killed kids, though. This one didn't.'

'So his only targets here were teachers?' Perlman asked.

'Teacher singular,' Mary Gibson said. 'From what I've been able to gather, Ajit Singh came out of his classroom only because he heard the gunfire.' She looked in the direction of PC Murdoch and the photographer. 'That's where he was shot.'

Perlman said, 'Okay, the hooded man is only out to get Indra – why can't he wait for a less public moment?'

Scullion said, 'He's crazed. A lover's thing? A falling-out? A heartbreak? He's off his rocker.'

Perlman sighed. 'Or she dumped him. She was unfaithful to

him. She was just sick of him and wanted to move on. He was blinded by rage. Any of the above.'

Mary Gibson said, 'Check Indra Gupta's background. Family life. Boyfriends. The usual.'

Perlman nodded. 'Will do. Who's in charge of this school?'

Scullion said, 'A woman called Amy Blyth. Her office is at the end of the corridor.'

'I'll have a wee word with her,' Perlman said.

'This school is her baby, and she's shaken,' Mary Gibson said. 'Go easy, Sergeant.'

'I'm a sweetheart.' Perlman was about to move when one of the uniformed cops, a WPC he knew as Meg Gayle, came out of the classroom. She was a very tall young woman who slouched in a self-conscious way. She wore her black hair cut short and fringed at the front. A pretty girl, Perlman thought, a good-hearted face.

'I need a wee break,' she said. She looked at Mary Gibson for approval.

'It's tough in there,' Perlman said.

'Children shouldn't see anything like that,' Meg Gayle said. 'This man comes in and starts calling the teacher names and then he whips out a gun and shoots her in the face from a couple of feet away. And these kids see it all. It's sickening.'

'What kind of names?' Perlman asked.

'Bitch. Bint. I don't know what else. Words like that.'

'Did any of the kids say he gave the impression that he knew Indra?'

WPC Gayle had shadows under her eyes. 'It's a difficult situation to piece together, Sergeant. The kids tell you different things. Apparently he said he knew her name. I don't know how much stock to put in that, to be honest. The children are all . . . they just want to go home. They're tired and upset and horrified.'

Mary Gibson said, 'Fine, if you think you're finished, send them all home. We can contact them later if we need to.'

WPC Gayle went back inside the room and Perlman continued

52

along the corridor. He stopped briefly outside the door of the room where Indra Gupta had been shot. A couple of crime-scene technicians were dusting in silence. Perlman noticed lower-case words written on a blackboard in coloured chalk: *tree sun dad mum*. Blood dotted the chalk and darkened the white wood frame of the blackboard. Paperchains hung from the walls. There were shelves of kiddy stuff, plastic figures, plasticine models, puppets.

He shivered unexpectedly, although the cold he felt had no external source. You're four years old and you see somebody gunned down from a distance of a few feet, does the memory stay deep inside you and fester like a wound? How does it change you – bad dreams, anxieties? And then later in life, recurring flashes of memory?

He kept moving down the corridor. He paused beside PC Dennis Murdoch, whose expression was sombre. 'Singh didn't look good when they took him into the ambulance, Sergeant. The wound was chest, dead centre. I'm no doctor, but –'

'So you can't make guesses.'

'No, Sergeant, I can't.'

'Speculation's for the stock market, Dennis.' Perlman liked Murdoch, which was probably why he felt the need to temper the young man's enthusiasm every now and then with caution; it was a tricky craft, the practice of giving advice without coming off like a stuffy old fart, and Perlman was never sure he accomplished it. He wondered if he saw a slightly deflated look in Murdoch's eyes.

The police photographer snapping the spot where Singh had fallen was a dark-bearded man called Cameron 'Tizer' Dunlop, nicknamed after the soft drink to which he was addicted. Tizer was bent forward, knees locked, as if he was shooting a model from an oblique angle.

Perlman said, 'It's not a fucking fashion shoot. It's bloodstains. It's not going on the cover of *Vogue*.'

Tizer made a faux gay gesture, limping a wrist. 'I am *constantly* berated by philistines.'

'I'd watch out. You do that a little too convincingly.'

'Bitch,' Tizer remarked.

Perlman stopped outside a door with a small wooden plaque that read: *Amy Blyth*. He knocked, heard a voice from inside, then he entered. Amy Blyth, a fair-haired woman in a pink shirt and black trousers, sat behind her desk with her hands clenched in front of her; an attitude of prayer, Perlman thought. She wore a tiny silver crucifix and gold-rimmed half-moon glasses.

He introduced himself. Amy Blyth acknowledged him with a slight gesture of her hand. She had a big lipsticked mouth and the foundations of a double chin. She didn't rise.

'It's a total disaster,' she said. She was about to weep, but managed to contain herself. 'The parents will blame me for not providing proper security. This is the last thing you expect. You read about . . . you never think. A gun. A man with a gun.'

Perlman observed a moment of quiet sympathy. 'We don't live in a safe world, Miss Blyth. Even security guards can't keep everyone out. Somebody wants inside a place badly enough, they find a way. What are you supposed to do? Electric fences, watchdogs, a platoon of armed men? Don't blame yourself.'

Amy Blyth remarked, 'Easy to say.'

Perlman glanced round the room. Amy had scores of diplomas in frames. Certificates from colleges, teaching associations, civic groups. She had a document naming her as the registered owner of this kindergarten, which was called the Sunshine Day School.

'I'm going to phone my lawyer,' she said. 'I was just about to when you came in. If the parents think about damages for, I don't know . . . mental and physical distress, I have to know where I stand. I worked so bloody hard for this place.' Amy Blyth whipped her glasses off and pressed the tips of her fingers into her eyelids. 'Really I did. Built it up from . . . Worked hours, long hours. It isn't easy. Handling parents and children. Finding staff.'

'Tell me about Indra,' he said.

'Indra? Oh, the kids adored her. She was gentle. She enjoyed her work.'

'What about her personal life?'

Amy Blyth replaced her glasses. The lenses made her brown eyes look very big. 'I make it a rule not to intrude in the private lives of my staff, unless there are exceptional circumstances.'

'I'll need her address.'

'I have her file here.' Amy Blyth opened a drawer of her desk and took out a manila folder, which she slid towards Perlman.

He picked it up. 'I have to borrow this,' he said. 'Has anyone contacted Indra's family?'

'I think one of the teachers did.' Amy fingered her crucifix, a small gesture of uncertainty.

Perlman tucked the folder under his arm. 'I'll get this back to you.' He stepped from the room, shut the door, walked into the corridor. A small boy emerged from a toilet and almost collided with him.

'You in a big hurry, wee man?' Perlman asked.

'Going home,' the boy said. *Gaun hame.* He had untidy red hair and freckles and green eyes, and he wore a blue pullover and flannel shorts. A Glasgow face, Perlman thought. He'd seen this boy thousands of times in different incarnations, in buses, on street corners, a face in a crowd on the way to a football match.

'Somebody kilt Mizz Gupta,' the boy said.

'Did you see it happen?'

'Aye. Man had a gun. Know what he said?'

Perlman leaned down, bringing his face level with that of the child. 'Tell me.'

The kid whispered. 'Are you pishing your knickers.'

Absent-mindedly, Perlman removed a length of white thread attached to the boy's sweater. 'He said this to Miss Gupta?'

'Aye.' The kid ran off down the corridor.

Perlman watched him go. *Are you pishing your knickers.* Was that some nasty jibe before the trigger was pulled and the gun exploded? A moment of verbal brutality imposed upon Indra Gupta before she died? Think about that. A young woman is staring into a gun and her killer is goading her. What does that tell you about your man, Lou? Cruel. Granted. But what else?

55

Something more. He *enjoyed* killing Indra Gupta. He made sport of it. He prolonged it. A fucking sadist.

He found Sandy Scullion inside the murder room. The technical people had gone. There was no sign of Mary Gibson. Sandy sat squeezed behind one of the small wooden desks. He looked grotesquely huge.

'The Inspector relives his childhood,' Perlman said.

'I was trying to imagine everything that happened here through a kid's eyes. But I've forgotten how a child sees the world.'

'It's called growing old. It's the deal you get the day you're born. The nappy, then the shroud.'

'It's happening faster than I like,' Scullion said.

'You know what it does to *me* when a thirty-six-year-old man such as yourself tells me *he's* getting up in years? I feel like I'm a Polygrip junkie in Weetabix City.'

Scullion got up from the desk, stretched his legs. 'When I was four or five I wanted to be a bus conductor. Instead, here I am at a murder scene in a kindergarten. At some point I'll go back to Pitt Street and stick coloured pins into wall maps and talk to forensic guys and collate facts – which is a far cry from how I saw my life.'

Perlman surveyed the classroom, his eyes drawn to the blood on the blackboard. A gunshot. A young woman falls dead. Little kids scream and cry. He imagined echoes. He didn't like the sounds they made in his head. He remembered something, a flicker out of childhood. 'My earliest ambition was to be a rabbi.'

'What stopped you?'

'An awful weakness for ham,' Perlman said.

Both men walked outside where Mary Gibson was surrounded by a thicket of reporters. She handled them as she always did: good manners and careful words. The assembly never interrupted her. Mary Gibson had that quality people called 'presence'. She had an educated Glasgow accent, unlike Perlman's; hers was authoritative, with crisp diction, while his was rough and unschooled, forged in his boyhood in the old south side.

'Your car or mine?' Scullion asked.

'Mine's shite on wheels,' Perlman said.

They went towards Scullion's car, a Citroën. Scullion unlocked it, and sat behind the wheel. Perlman climbed into the passenger seat. He looked up at the sky. The early evening sun, free of cloud and rain, glowed orange over the city. When it lay under sunlight, Glasgow always reminded him of a patient liberated from a long recuperation. Sandstone tenements cast off their austerity, like creatures shedding a wintry skin. Belated spring, blue skies, maybe even people strolling in the great parks of the city: Glasgow stirred, but warily, because those skies now clear might chuck down rain again in the morning.

Scullion drove out of the car park, and Perlman felt a familiar old electricity zap him. The first foot over the threshold of an investigation: you don't know what lies in the room beyond the door. Corridors, other rooms, staircases, whispers, whatever. You followed, you listened. You waited. Sometimes you obsessed.

'Where are we heading?' Scullion asked.

Perlman opened Indra Gupta's file. 'Pollokshields,' he said.

9

She sat on a bench in Elder Park, a couple of hundred yards from Govan public library. There was a dead air about Govan, she thought, an aura of unemployment, lives scratched out of nothing. She imagined a camera shot from high overhead, depicting the tenements along Govan Road, and the cranes perched at the river's edge, where only a couple of small shipyards now operated.

Her grandfather had worked in the shipyards in the days when glorious ocean-going liners were built on the Clyde. Her father might have done the same if the industry hadn't collapsed. He'd gone to Canada in search of work. He said he'd find a job in Toronto, he'd write, send money, and one day she and her mother would join him. Big shot, big promise.

Nobody ever heard from him again.

Sometimes she wondered if he'd started a new life in a Toronto suburb or wherever, and just erased the old entirely. New wife, kids, house. He disappeared inside a mist of memory, and even when she tried to bring his face to mind she wasn't sure if the image bore any resemblance to the man. Ten years after he'd vanished, her mother – who'd indiscriminately taken a series of casual lovers, sailors, salesmen, drifters – died of diabetic complications.

The past is over, she thought. You don't need to go there. But she could smell her father sometimes, stale tobacco hanging in his clothes, the damp stink when he took his shoes off and stuck his feet in front of the coal fire. And she could hear her mother have sex in the recess bed in the kitchen with strangers, the racketing of mattress springs, her mother *hushing* her partners into quiet, the eventual gasps and cries of release and intoxicated laughter. Some of these men were black. She remembered them leaving in the middle of the night, or at daybreak, faces glistening with sweat, steps stealthy. Once, late at night, she'd bumped into one of them in the narrow hallway that led to the toilet, and he'd reached out to stroke her face or pat her head, and she'd recoiled from the strangeness of his skin, and the strong odour of his sweat: from his naked *blackness*.

Little girl, he'd said, and laughed in a deep way. *I'm just being friendly*.

She'd run to her room, which was a closet containing a tiny mattress, and she'd pulled her face under the sheets and lain there trembling. A black man, black as that oily tar spread in summers by road crews, and he'd haunted her dreams for a long time after.

The sun was slipping beyond trees now. Two adolescent boys with long shadows threw a lime-green tennis ball back and forth. She thought of the man going over the balcony. Dropped into the night like a stone.

Yes. It was the right thing. The only thing.

She thought of him inside her. Fucking her. She felt unclean.

She gazed at the lights in the windows of the library. Some of her time she lived in a third-floor flat in Langlands Road, a few blocks from the park. The nameplate nailed to her door read *RJ McKay*, probably the previous tenant. She kept the name because it afforded her anonymity. Uncarpeted, sparsely furnished, the flat wasn't a home. She stored a few suitcases of clothing there, but not all. Her possessions were scattered in other rooms and bedsits about the city. She liked this dispersal of her belongings; anyone trying to track her movements would find a series of false trails and tantalizing clues.

She rose, walked round the bench, felt darkness gather in the greenery. She checked her watch: 7.30. She wasn't sure what time the park closed. She shoved her hands deep into the pockets of her blue jeans. A chill was forming in the night air. She zipped her brown leather jacket shut and kicked damp grass with her burgundy Docs. She was impatient.

7.42.

She saw him come from the direction of the library. He was looking down at his feet like a child counting his steps. You can't always get the people you need, she thought. You take what's available. The gullible, the lonely who wanted to belong to something, anything. Only a few had potential.

She sat on the bench, crossed her legs. She raised her face just as he reached her: it was always a rush to see the effect she had on him. He was severely smitten. His lunar white face flushed. She knew how to turn his head the full three-sixty.

'I heard on the radio,' she said.

'Went like a dream.'

He sat beside her. She smelled booze on his breath. She said, 'I told you no drinking. Emphatically. What did I tell you?'

'One pint zall I had. Cross my heart.'

'Alone or what?'

'On my tod,' he said.

'Where?'

'Does that matter?' A small rebellion in his voice.

'This is serious. The whole structure's serious. We're not playing some fucking game, Beezer. If I ask a question, you answer. You don't like the rules, get on your bike.'

'Awright. Brechin's Bar.'

'You talk to anybody there?'

'Not a soul.'

'You think I'm a bossy bitch.'

'No, no, I don't –'

'I have people I answer to. The people I answer to have people they answer to. It goes on. I don't know where it finishes. We keep secrets. You think I'm a bitch, that doesn't matter a fuck to me. The world's going down the kludgie and I don't have time for your petty-arsed concerns.'

'I don't need lectures. Jeez-*us*.' He looked offended. He stared in the direction of the boys throwing the ball. The dog was running this way and that, confused and frothing.

'We all need reminders,' she said. She pushed a hand through her black hair, which she wore back in a ponytail held in place by an elastic band. She snapped off the band and let her hair go loose over her shoulders. She could almost feel Beezer shiver as strands drifted close to his face. Gossamer, spiderwebs – he caught the slight updraught and liked it. She looked at his hands on the knees of his gaudy trousers. His nails were bitten down and ragged. And those shoes, those weird boats on his feet. What were they for?

'You got the item?' she said.

He reached into his pocket and slipped a folded hankie towards her. She peeled back the dirty linen an inch and glanced at the gun, then tucked it in the breast pocket of her leather jacket.

'It's the same bloody weapon,' he said.

'I have to check.'

'You don't trust me, eh?'

'Trust isn't the point. I have to return the gun. So it has to be the same gun.'

'You think I did a swap or something? Where would I find a gun anyway even if I *wanted* to swap?'

'Sometimes I think you don't get the whole picture.'

'I get it all right. I know what the fight's about. Don't you worry about me.' He looked tense. He pouted, then exhaled, relaxed his shoulders. She'd detected a slight madness about him in the past; he carried a worrisome buzz around in his head. It made him useful, but also unpredictable.

61

'I did the job. I carried it off.'

'Your assignment was one target. Only one.'

'The fuck was I supposed to know a guy was gonny come into that corridor? He was a raghead anyway. What does it matter?'

'If he recovers and gives a description, it matters.'

'My hood was on tight. He couldn't see my face. I got the one that counted. I got that bitch. Clean and fast and I was out of there in a minute. Oh I was great. I was great.'

His voice rose in a disturbing way. His pendulum was out of kilter. She had to play him. She had to keep him sweet. Under control. 'I'll send you a new email address.'

'You keep changing it.'

'I keep changing a lot of things. Only a fool stays in one place, Beezer.'

'Just don't forget me, eh? I mean, I'm ready. Any time. Say the word. You know that.'

She let her hand fall to his shoulder. A small squeeze, an inconsequential intimacy. Give him a wee thrill. What was his life like anyway? Bare bones bleak, she thought. Look at him, the tracksuit trousers, the hooded top, the noise he made at the back of his throat as if he was trying to regurgitate something. He had hands like putty. She couldn't imagine those hands touching the flesh of another person. Without the battle, what would he do with his time? He had the forlorn look of a man who realizes he has no great talents to sell.

She had a thought. Why not. Okay. It would either be the making of him, or the end. Take a chance. 'You free later tonight?'

'I've got nothing planned.'

'You know the Victoria Bar in Dumbarton Road. Be outside at nine fifteen.'

'What are we going to do?' he asked.

'Tell you then. Don't disappoint me.'

She turned, broke into a run, jogged quickly out of the park, disappeared in the direction of Langlands Road. Streetlamps had come on and burned in the twilight. In the distance an ice-cream van chimed for custom; an ambitious Glasgow entrepreneur trying to squeeze a few quid out of the summery illusion created by the change in weather.

Bobby Descartes, concrete hard-on poking a puncture in his pants, watched the woman run out of his world. Face like Mona fucking Lisa, he thought: aye, Mona Lisa with a ponytail and a gun.

It took a great effort not to follow her. One day he might, oh he just might. One day he'd like to give her a good fuck. She'd do whatever he demanded. She'd suck him and he'd come in her mouth and ooh –

Magistr32. A wee bit on the thin side, not much meat to pick at, but gorgeous, and he wasn't getting a lot of nooky these days anyway. He'd never had a lot of it, come to think of it. Some guys got all they wanted. But not Bobby. Never Bobby.

In fact, okay, he wasn't getting any.

Magistr32 and her long black hair; he'd take strands of it and weave it round his dick –

Aye, right. He didn't even know her name, only the one she used on her emails. And that wasn't a real name. Nobody was called Magistr32, for Christ's sake. How did you even pronounce it? Majister? Did you drop the numbers?

He'd met her in Maryhill on a wet night last January. He'd been drinking alone, and she was standing beside him at the bar, and they just sort of drifted into conversation; she *listened* more than she spoke – at first anyway. She listened to his views on the state of the nation. She was sympathetic, even when he launched into a long beer-fuelled rant, the memory of which embarrassed him.

The more she listened, the more attractive he found her. She was quietly lovely. No flash, no eyeshadow and warpaint, but definitely a face you'd look at a long time because the features –

green eyes and thick black hair and an expressive mouth – were a delight to him.

Despite the slender body and the sweet face, she was as gentle as a howitzer. She had firm views about the world, and a way of expressing them that silenced Beezer, and made him feel inadequate. He was transported by her passion and the funny manner she had of chopping the bar with her small clenched hand when she had a point to make.

There were solutions to the sickness in Britain, she told him, but they'd take time and courage. Did he have that courage?

And he'd said, Fucking right.

She'd asked if he wanted to meet a few people who felt the same way. Kindred spirits, a kind of loose group.

I'm in, he said.

A few nights later, in a ground-floor flat in Garnethill, she introduced him as Beezer – a name she bestowed on him for no apparent reason – to a long-haired cadaver of a man she called Swank, who wore a beaded choker. By candlelight, Swank spoke of revolution and blood in a serious monotone. Bobby Descartes thought he looked completely wasted, a doper. Swank created a dire picture of the future: the United Kingdom would be plummeted into third-world chaos. Total breakdown. Nightmare. Bloated corpses floating in rivers. War in the streets. The last great battle, Swank said. Do you want to be a soldier, Beezer?

Bobby was overwhelmed by Swank's gloomy vision. He said he'd gladly be a soldier. Just point the way. Swank told him it wasn't that easy, the movement needed to evaluate potential recruits, he'd be observed and assessed, and when the time was right – maybe, maybe – he'd be given an important task. Swank stared at him red-eyed for such a long time Beezer felt uneasy, sort of spellbound.

A week later, Magistr32 took him to a pub near Bridgeton Cross. At a corner table in the lounge bar, she introduced him to a man by the name of Pegg, who wore an eyepatch and talked in a buzz-saw rasp about how the heavy guns were going into action. People would die. But somebody had to take a stand. Pegg raved about the number of illegals now in the country, and how they were draining the system dry; decent people were being taxed all the way up the anus so that black and yellow and brown immigrant scum and an assortment of unwanted unwashed foul-smelling asylum seekers could ride the Great British Gravy Train. Hello, newsflash. This train was out of freebies. This train wasn't running any more.

We must fight the good fight, Pegg said.

Beezer said Jesus, he'd fight. He'd be at the barricades. By Christ, he wouldn't let anybody down. Suddenly he belonged to something, a *cause*, he was meeting like-minded people – even if he'd never seen the men called Swank and Pegg again.

But that was how it worked: the less you knew the better. The fewer faces you remembered, the better chance the organization had. Magistr32 said the organization was big, even she didn't know many members; he accepted that.

An organization. I belong to an organization, he thought. He cherished the notion.

A tennis ball came bouncing towards him. He caught and squeezed it. He enjoyed the feel of crushing it in his hand; it was like demolishing the swollen testicle of somebody he hated.

A kid shouted to him. 'Can you toss the ball back, mister?'

'Fuck off,' Bobby Descartes said. 'Fuck you and your fucking ball.'

He turned away, swung his arm, launched the ball in the other direction. It rose into the last light of day and vanished as it fell against the backdrop of darkening trees. It must have gone up a hundred, a hundred and twenty feet, he thought.

'Yer a shite,' the boy shouted. 'A total shite.'

'That's me,' Bobby Descartes said. 'That's what I am. A total shite.'

He flashed a vigorous V-sign at the boy. You don't know the

half of it, sonny. I have killed. I have killed another human being, and I'm ready to do it again.

Any old time.

10

Perlman felt edgy whenever he travelled deep into the southern part of the city; Pollokshields was too close to the neighbourhoods where the Aunts lived. Hilda and Marlene and Susan had small tidy bungalows in Giffnock and Newton Mearns, and led comfy lives behind lacy curtains. They baked a lot. They forced hefty scones and slabs of fruitcake on him whenever he visited, which wasn't often. They slaughtered him with kindness and well-intended counsel. *There's a lovely woman you should meet, Lou, Sadie Plotkin, recently a widow, such a shame . . .*

Scullion parked his Citroën outside a red sandstone Victorian villa sheltered from the street by trees. Perlman was first out of the car. He walked to an iron gate that led to the driveway and paused. Gupta. Why did that name suddenly ring a tinny little bell in his private steeple? He rummaged his memory; nothing came up. Store it away. Once upon a time, his memory would have pounced on any loose fragment like a piranha in a feeding frenzy. Not now: synaptic difficulties. Sometimes they self-repaired, sometimes not.

He pushed the gate and walked up the path. Scullion followed. The house was imposing and self-assured in the Victorian way;

the future will always be British, old boy, the colonies eternally grateful. Confident nineteenth-century dreams of infinite commerce and infinite profit, Perlman thought; the city of Glasgow had been one of those dreams, where tobacco barons grew rich and built grand houses like the mansion that faced him now.

He rang the doorbell. The sky was almost entirely dark. A breeze blustered through the trees. A young man appeared in the doorway. He was Indian, wore a stylish grey suit and a grey shirt and a brown tie. Perlman and Scullion showed ID and the young man introduced himself, in a Glasgow accent, as Dev Gupta, Indra's brother. He invited them inside a foyer that was a deep burgundy colour; a mellow spice perfumed the air. Cinnamon, Perlman thought, but he wasn't sure. Candles burned on a sideboard.

The house was crowded. He listened to noises from rooms whose doorways lay open: a woman crying, other voices offering comfort, and from elsewhere a man speaking firmly and with obvious anger in what Perlman assumed was Hindi.

Dev Gupta led them into an empty room at the rear of the entranceway. 'It's quieter in here,' he said.

'We can come at another time,' Scullion suggested.

Kind-hearted Sandy, Perlman thought, showing respect in this house of death. But the process of law doesn't stop. We can go away, but we always come back later.

'This time is as good as any,' the young man said.

Perlman glanced round the room. The furniture was old-fashioned; there were a few tapestries of stylized dancing girls, which he imagined had some religious significance.

'Krishna dancing with the *gopis*,' Dev Gupta said. 'My father's fond of these old things. If this was my house, I'd change a few items around. But it's not.'

An old family resentment, Perlman thought. It was in the voice.

Scullion said, 'Let's talk about Indra.'

'What do you want to know?'

'Anything at all. Her personal life?'

68

'She didn't have one. She lived for that school. Bloody awful place. Nobody in the family wanted her to work there.'

'Why?'

'She spurned the chance of a good marriage because she wanted a career. Great career, eh? Look how it ends.'

'Who did she turn down?' Perlman asked.

'The man she rejected lives in Calcutta. The marriage was one my father had arranged.'

The arranged marriage. The amalgamation of families and business interests, Perlman thought. 'So she went to work, came home, never went out? How did she fill her spare time?'

'She read. Watched a little TV. Mostly documentaries. She was into ecological issues. Most nights she planned her classes. She was conscientious, despite the fact she earned a pittance at that Sunshine school or whatever it's called. And now she's dead.'

'And we have to find her killer,' Scullion said quietly.

Perlman noticed a bowl of fruit. He realized he was hungry. With a younger man's sense of acute anticipation, he'd been looking forward to afternoon tea with Miriam, but that prospect had been set aside for another time. Now he longed to reach for a pear, an apple; his belly had begun to grumble quietly.

He gazed at Dev Gupta, who gave more an impression of anger than grief. He thought of the arranged marriage Indra had refused and imagined the arguments that must have rolled around this house. The daughter defies the father's will. The daughter remains firm. The brother sides with whom? Father? Sister? They all fall out. The atmosphere is tense, one of uneasy truces shattered by outbursts of belligerent reproach.

Gupta said, 'She once thought somebody was following her.'

'Did she know who?' Scullion asked.

'Just some man. She didn't know him, and she wasn't absolutely sure he was a genuine stalker anyway. Then she stopped mentioning him, and we assumed he wasn't hanging around any more. My sister, you have to understand, hated making a fuss. All she wanted was to contribute – her word, not mine – to the lives of the kids in her school. That was her choice. She could've chosen a different path, and she'd still be alive.'

'And married,' Perlman said. A stalker who might not have been, he thought. A young woman who didn't want to make a fuss. He glanced at Scullion. Over the years they'd developed a kind of silent communication; Perlman's present expression, and the accompanying tiny shrug of the shoulder, was a way of saying that there had to be more than this to Indra Gupta's life. Otherwise, why was she killed? Did somebody just drift in off the street and shoot her randomly?

Scullion paced the room as if measuring it for a new carpet. 'She didn't have a boyfriend?'

'Right,' Gupta said.

'You're absolutely sure?'

'I knew my sister, Inspector.'

Perlman eyeballed the fruit longingly, and imagined the flesh of a pear dissolving in his mouth. 'So she never kept any secrets from you?'

'She wasn't the furtive type.'

'With all due respect,' Scullion said, 'sometimes we think we know people better than we really do. Sometimes they surprise us.'

'Not my sister.'

Perlman picked up an apple. He remembered how WPC Meg Gayle had suggested that the killer might have known Indra's name. Might have. A child's impression. 'Did she ever say anything *specific* about this possible stalker? A description? What he wore?'

Gupta shrugged. 'Nothing I remember. She'd seen a man a couple of times at the end of the street when she walked to the bus stop in the morning. She also thought she saw the same man in the vicinity of the kindergarten once or twice.'

'She never talked to this guy?'

'I seriously doubt it.'

A tall white-haired man came into the room. He wore a black three-piece suit and a white shirt unbuttoned at the collar. He had an air of proprietorial authority; this, Perlman thought, was Gupta Senior. Dev Gupta faded immediately into the margins of the room, diminished by his father's presence. It was obvious where the control of this household lay.

'These men are from the police, Father,' Dev Gupta said.

The older man scanned Scullion and Perlman. A sharp eye, Perlman thought. The flick of a shutter, snap, picture taken and filed in the memory. 'I am Bharat Gupta, gentlemen. People call me Barry. Why this need for abbreviation, who can say? The Glasgow way, I suppose. Here, everything is shortened. Robert to Bob. Names are shortened. Lives too, it seems.'

Scullion was quiet a moment, then he introduced himself and Perlman.

'There is enormous sorrow in my house today,' Barry Gupta said.

Scullion said, 'You have our sincere condolences.'

Bharat Gupta, who spoke English in the slightly formal way of a man who has learned it as a second language, made a gesture with his hand, palm overturned, as if to suggest grief and emptiness. 'Sometimes language is deficient for the expression of the heart.'

Barry Gupta talked to his son in Hindi, then turned back to look at the two policemen. 'Dev says he has told you all he knows. For myself, I can add very little. Indra was a private person, perhaps a little too self-willed for her own good. Of course, she was born in Glasgow, and went to school here, and possibly she learned certain ways of behaviour of which I didn't approve. But times change, the old customs are abandoned . . .' He paused and plucked a handkerchief from the pocket of his jacket. He buried his face in it for a while.

Perlman wanted to say something, a phrase of comfort, but all you could ever offer were crumbs that made no difference. Scullion stood very still, head stooped. Dev Gupta touched his father's elbow and led him to a chair, but the older man refused to sit. He dropped the handkerchief from his face; a glassy track of tears slipped from his eyes to his lips.

71

'You will forgive me, gentlemen.'

'Of course,' Scullion said.

'Find this man who killed Indra. That's all I ask. Find him. My son will show you out.'

Bharat Gupta walked from the room, leaving the door open. Perlman saw him move to the stairs, his hand pressed flat to the wooden rail as he climbed. His step was slow and heavy.

Dev Gupta asked, 'Anything else I can do for you?'

'Not at the moment,' Scullion said. 'We'll be in touch.'

Gupta led them to the front door. Perlman could hear only the sound of the woman still weeping in another room. He followed Scullion down the path to the street. When they reached the gate Perlman paused. Gupta, Gupta: why did the name come back to prick him like this? He reached into his coat pocket, pulled out an apple, crunched into it.

'I didn't see you pilfer that,' Scullion said.

'Sleight of hand,' Perlman answered. 'I was dying of hunger.'

Scullion gazed back at the house. 'What do you think?'

'Indra was all work and no play.'

'Is anybody that cut and dried?'

'Look at me,' Perlman said. 'Ever see me having fun?'

Scullion smiled and walked to his car. Perlman devoured the apple and tossed the core into a clump of shrubbery. He sat in the passenger seat and shut his eyes and listened to the faint hum of the Citroën.

He opened his eyes. 'Gupta,' he said.

'Do you know the name?' Scullion asked.

Perlman said, 'I might be having one of those rare moments of insight. I think I'll call Terry Bogan in Partick.'

'Why?'

Perlman fished his mobile out of his pocket. 'Check on something.'

'Check on what? You know, you can be bloody irritating at times, Perlman. You're secretive, furtive, unforthcoming.'

'Now tell me my bad points.'

Perlman punched in the number of the Strathclyde Police

Office in Partick and picked a sliver of apple from his teeth while he waited for a reply.

Detective-Sergeant Terry Bogan, who'd joined the Force the same year as Perlman, came on the line.

'It's your favourite Jew here,' Perlman said.

'And how can humble Terry Bogan be of any help to the great Perlman?'

'This jumper you had? What's the story?'

'An odd one,' Bogan said. He had a growl of a voice, like pebbles rattling inside a pewter jar.

'Can you meet me at your usual place? Fifteen minutes?'

'Can do.'

Perlman cut the connection and watched the dark expanse of Queen's Park slip past. He lit a cigarette and Scullion, devout non-smoker, rolled down his window. The night air was cold.

'Explain,' Scullion said.

'It might be nothing.'

'Explain it anyway.'

11

At 9.20 p.m. a man called Jachay Ochoba stepped from Hillhead Underground station. In Byres Road he buttoned his overcoat to the neck. Even on the *hottest* day in this city, he was cold: a man couldn't get warm in this place. Then you weighed such discomfort against the uncertain political and economic situation of your homeland, and you decided that cold and wet were preferable, ice and snow and blizzards all godsends.

Byres Road was crowded as always. The people who drifted past bright restaurants and shops were mainly young. Many were students, like himself. He thought of the 5000-word essay he had to turn in to Professor Bain. He'd only completed half of it. It was called *British Imperialism: why did it fail?* In brutal language the answer was simple: the Brits fucked the natives over every chance they got. They still did. Of course, one couldn't render an essay that way and ever expect to graduate, but that was the gist of Ochoba's approach.

He was going to meet Helen; his second date with her. He'd encountered her at a Getting to Know You party in the Student Union. She was studying economics. Nice girl, pretty, a little on the shy side. She had a sly sense of humour. She wore her thick black hair centre-parted; she had two clasps in the shapes of butterflies on either side of the parting. He fantasized that they'd fall in love and she'd become his wife one day. They'd emigrate. Australia. New Zealand. They'd have kids. Dreams sustained him.

He took a right turn into Ashton Lane. He had an impulse to check the Grosvenor, see what movie was playing. He might ask Helen to a film. He enjoyed films, especially American ones, where the love interest always ended well. If you believed such movies, couples in America lived happily ever after.

Ashton Lane was crowded with boisterous young people. He reached the entrance to the cinema and studied the poster: a revival, a James Mason and Judy Garland movie, *A Star is Born*. He'd seen it years ago. Helen might like it. He was jostled by two or three people whose faces he didn't see. He knew it was best to keep your head down and carry on walking, because sometimes if you caught the eye of people looking for trouble it only made things worse.

Somebody tugged sharply on his sleeve. He was spun halfway round. He felt a terrible stinging sensation in his ribs, and he wondered if he'd been punched, but it wasn't like that. He boxed a little as a middleweight, he knew what a punch felt like. He gasped, and slammed the palm of his hand to the area of pain. His fingers were wet. He heard a woman scream. He didn't see her face. He didn't have the strength to stay upright. He went down on his knees. The woman screamed again. Somebody said *you okay there you okay jim, haud on we'll get an ambulance.* The words came from a far place.

He lay flat on his back and looked at the sky and thought of Helen waiting for him and checking her watch and wondering where he was. Maybe in a few minutes, if he could get some treatment, he'd be okay, he'd meet Helen, and he'd say, you will not believe what happened to me on my way here. Somebody gripped his hand and said *just wait just hang in there big fella we're getting an ambulance* and he imagined speeding through the streets of the city listening to sirens.

I'll be okay.

Hang in there, big fella.

Helen sat in the Tinderbox and drank cappuccino. Maybe Jachay – or Jay as she called him – had been delayed. Maybe he'd decided not to come. He wants nothing to do with me, she thought, only he is too nice to say it to my face. Or too cowardly. Or just a man, crude and cruel and selfish. The fact was, he hadn't turned up. Forty minutes late.

He'd seemed so kind, so genuine, at the Student Union. You cannot tell the inside from the outside, she thought. Men were like cards; they were usually played face down.

She turned to smile at the young woman at the next table. They'd been conversing idly for the last twenty minutes. The girl was friendly in the way Glaswegians often were. Sympathetic, a ready ear.

'I think I've been stood up,' Helen said.

'Some fellas are just congenitally late,' the girl said. 'I'm Sally, by the way. Kincaid.'

'Helen Mboto.'

'Care to spell that?'

Helen smiled. She had a smile that dazzled. 'Spell it just the way you say it.'

'You want another coffee?'

Helen shook her head. She'd already had two cups and she felt jumpy. 'A glass of water might be pleasant,' she said.

'Plain or sparkling?'

'Sparkling, please. But you –'

'I'll get it. No problem. I've been stood up myself by some numpties in my time.'

Numpties. Helen didn't know this word. She deduced its meaning from the context. It certainly wasn't a compliment.

Sally Kincaid, slim-hipped in blue jeans, went to the counter, and returned with fizzy water and a small shot of espresso. She sat down facing Helen Mboto.

'Where you from, Helen?'

'Zambia.'

'You like it here?'

'I get homesick sometimes. But, yes, I like this city. After I graduate, I hope to stay here and work. If I can.'

Sally Kincaid stirred sugar in her coffee. 'Those butterfly things in your hair. What are they made of?'

'Coral.'

'They're very pretty.'

'My grandfather gave them to me when I left home. To remember him.'

'You live nearby?'

'In Kinning Park.'

'You have a flat over there?'

'I rent a room in somebody else's flat.'

'I live round the corner,' Sally Kincaid said. 'It's convenient for the city centre. And for work.'

'What kind of work do you do?'

'I write for one of the local papers,' Sally said.

'You're a journalist?'

'Way down low on the ladder. I get the obits to write.'

'Obits?'

'Obituaries? When somebody dies.'

Helen Mboto felt relaxed in this woman's company. She'd already begun to shed her irritation about Jay. There was a good expression she'd learned in Glasgow: *he could go take a running jump at himself.*

'Is it interesting work?'

'It gets gloomy. Dead people all the time.' Sally Kincaid had a big brown leather bag she placed on the table. She plunged a hand into it. Helen heard the sound of keys, coins, matches rattling in a box.

Sally brought out a packet of cigarettes. 'Want one?'

'I don't smoke,' Helen said.

Sally stuck a cigarette in her mouth and struck a match, but she didn't light up. 'I don't like smoking in cafés and restaurants any more. You always get dirty looks from non-smokers. They make you feel like a leper. Listen, you fancy a cup of tea somewhere I can smoke?'

'I should wait for Jay,' Helen said.

'Forget Jay. Look, if he turns up and you're not here, he'll be on the phone to you before the night's out. Men are all the same. Whip the rug out from under their feet, suddenly they're all attention. Like puppydogs. Come on. I know a place round the corner.'

Helen Mboto hesitated. 'It's kind of you, but . . .'

'Wait, wait, you don't think, oh no . . .' Sally Kincaid laughed. 'This is some kind of pick-up?'

'No, but –'

'You'll realize how ridiculous that is when you know me a wee bit better. Men are my weakness. I don't need extra vices.'

Helen got up from the table. She was embarrassed. Sally was only offering friendship. Sometimes city life made you suspicious. You wanted to feel free and open-minded, but it wasn't always possible.

Sally was already moving towards the door. She took a black raincoat from a hook in the wall. She said, 'Never trust the weather here. You've learned that already, I suppose.'

'It was the first thing I learned,' Helen said. They went out into the street. She found herself staring into the headlights of traffic coming down Byres Road, and hoped she might see Jay running towards her, apologizing for being late. But there was no sign of him.

'This way,' Sally said. She took a few steps along the pavement, away from the main thoroughfare. 'It's only a few blocks. I live in Havelock Street. Tell me what kind of tea you like.'

'We're going to your house?'

'Flat. Two rooms and a bathroom. I call it home.'

'I thought we were going to another café. Are you sure this is no problem –'

'Problem? No way. I've got green tea, Typhoo, Darjeeling,

some herbal stuff, nettle. You know what they call people in Glasgow who love tea? Tea-jennies. That's me. C'mon. Let's get a move on. I think it's going to rain again.'

Helen hurried after her. They entered a street where the lamps were less bright. Sally took a big bunch of keys from her bag. She unlocked the security door of a tenement and stepped inside a long tiled close leading to a flight of stairs. Helen followed. On the first landing Sally stuck a key in another door and turned it.

'Home sweet home. It's not a palace. Be my guest.'

Helen stepped into the flat. The living room was barely furnished. A sofa, a coffee table, no decorations on the walls. A fireplace with imitation coals. The air smelled damp. The wallpaper depicted seashells and sea horses.

'I know, I know, it's pretty basic.'

Helen said, 'My grandfather always says we allow possessions to own us.'

'Wise man. I'll put the kettle on.' Sally Kincaid opened a door that led to the kitchen. 'You fancy Darjeeling?'

'It's fine,' Helen said.

'Sit down. Get comfy. Meet my flatmate.'

'You have a flatmate? I didn't know. Will she mind you bringing a visitor?'

Sally Kincaid didn't answer. She went inside the kitchen.

Helen sat on the edge of the sofa. Webs hung in high corners of the room, and dead flies lay inside the overhead lightbowl.

A man stepped from the kitchen. 'Hello. I'm the roomie.'

'Oh. I think I expected a woman,' Helen said.

'See what expectations can do?'

His face was ordinary, neither benign nor cruel, but for some reason she didn't like it. Instinct. She couldn't say why she felt uncomfortable. She looked at her watch. How long was she expected to stay? She had no grasp of the local etiquette.

He stood over her, leaning slightly towards her. 'Our Scottish hospitality is famous all over the world.'

'Tea'll soon be ready.' Sally Kincaid appeared in the kitchen doorway.

'I have to prepare for a class tomorrow,' Helen said. 'I can't stay long.'

The man said, 'You'll stay for tea, surely.'

'Mandatory,' Sally said.

Helen Mboto stared at the cheap synthetic material of the man's trousers. She could smell him. The sweat, the material, perspiration and chemicals. The smell was offensive. She got up from the sofa and the man placed his hands on her shoulders and shoved her down again.

She was baffled by his aggression. A joke, maybe some playful gesture? A local custom? But he wasn't smiling.

'You'll fucking stay,' he said.

'What's going on, Sally?' Helen asked. 'Does your friend have a problem?'

Sally said, 'You don't leave until you've had your tea. Rule of the house.'

'This is some kind of, what, joke?'

The man said, 'No joke. You don't leave until we tell you.'

Helen Mboto remembered something she'd read, an old newspaper story about how foreign girls were press-ganged into lives of vice, bought and sold and shipped off to the Middle East or Japan. Is this why she'd been brought here? No, her imagination was flying away with her. She was panicking.

'Sally, explain this, please, I don't understand,' Helen said. 'Your friend's behaviour –'

Sally said, 'We're only trying to be hospitable.'

The man said, 'The very words I used.'

'I'd really like to leave,' Helen said.

'No chance,' the man said.

Helen Mboto was too proud to make an imploring gesture; she'd never begged for anything even though she wanted to beg now: *please let me leave*. She felt endangered, cornered by an incomprehensible hostility. She made to rise, but the man stopped her again. She reacted the only way she knew how. She lowered her face and sunk her strong teeth into the man's thigh and he howled even as he tried to step away from the clamp she had on his skin. She released him and he backed off a few feet, eyes filling up with tears.

She got up from the sofa and thought she'd rush for the door, she had time, maybe a few seconds, she was strong, athletic, quick. Before she'd gone a few steps she felt pressure against the back of her neck.

Sally Kincaid said, 'I'm holding a gun. Stand very still.'

'That black cunt bit a hole out of my leg,' the man said. 'That fucking nigger cunt.'

'Sit down, Helen. Sit down and drink your tea. You, Beezer, quit moaning.'

'You'd moan if you'd had her fucking fangs sunk into your leg.'

Helen sat. 'I want to go home.'

Sally said, 'Be a good girl. Do as you're told.'

The man limped inside the kitchen. Still complaining about his wound, he came back with a cup of tea. The string of the tea-bag dangled over the rim. He thrust the cup at Helen.

'Drink, Helen.'

'I don't bloody want to drink.'

Sally Kincaid pressed the gun into Helen's ear. 'Do it.'

Helen took the cup. 'Please don't shoot.'

'Then drink.'

Helen didn't trust the tea. Why should she? It was probably drugged. Or poisoned.

She dropped the cup to the floor.

'Oh my,' Sally said. 'Clumsy. What are you going to do about her attitude, Beezer?'

The man punched Helen hard in the mouth and said, 'Black fucking cunt.'

Helen felt a shellburst of pain. Blood flowed from her lips. 'Let me go home. Please. I'll say nothing about this.'

The man had something in his hand. 'Looks like silver, swings like lead.'

Helen stared at Sally and said, 'Tell him not to harm me, Sally. Please.'

Sally Kincaid said, 'He's a very bad boy, Helen. I can't tell him anything.'

12

Perlman and Scullion met Detective-Sergeant Terry Bogan at Cottiers pub, formerly a Presbyterian church. It was a big untidy room, usually noisy, clientele young. This was why Bogan favoured the place: he could check out young women to his heart's desire. An unlikely gigolo, Perlman thought. He looked more farmer than cop – beery red face, frizzled side-whiskers, brown tweed suit.

Perlman said to Scullion, 'Take a gander at this man, Inspector. He's a Highlander. A *teuchter*. Even does farmyard impersonations. Cows. Ducks.'

'Only when I'm smashed,' Bogan said. 'Anybody want a wee drink?'

'A lemonade,' Sandy said.

'Half a pint of lager for me,' Perlman said.

'Still the hard-living Jewish playboy, eh?'

'I boogie from dusk to dawn,' Perlman said.

Bogan went to the bar and ordered drinks. Perlman checked out the room. Dear Christ, did he need to be confronted with so much ripe youth? So many fecund girls, with rich lustrous hair and slender bodies? A couple danced in a corner, although

83

there was no audible music: Perlman wasn't altogether sure it was dancing as he remembered it, more a voracious form of sexual prelude.

'Bogan comes here because he considers himself a ladies' man,' he said.

'Is he successful?' Scullion asked.

Perlman shrugged. 'Lives with his mother. What does that tell you?'

'He's saving on rent?'

Bogan came back with drinks, which he set down on a table. The three men sat, tapped glasses together.

'Life treating you kindly?' Lou asked.

'Smashing. See that redhead near the door? Don't all look. She'd raise anybody's spirits more than a notch.'

'You know her?' Perlman asked. He squinted at the woman through his murky glasses; a tall beauty, legs to the moon.

'Advances have been made.'

'And rebuffed?'

'Rebuffed, my arse. See these whiskers? Like Velcro to women.' Bogan stroked his steely fuzz. 'She's called Cynthia, she's a nurse, and nurses don't play tiddlywinks.'

'I'm impressed,' Perlman said.

Scullion looked at his watch. 'This is all very jolly, but let's get to the point . . . About your jumper, Terry.'

'The jumper, right, okay. That boy had everything to live for, according to what we've learned. Wealthy. Export business flying full speed. Top-of-the-line BMW. Expensive flat in Kelvin Court. Why end it all?' Bogan sipped his dark stout.

'You have any reason to think he didn't jump of his own free will?' Scullion asked.

Bogan shrugged. 'My best guess is he had a bit of a daft moment and climbed on the ledge and slipped. He had a high alcohol level in his blood. Plus he'd been smoking reefer. Maybe he thought he could fly. One other thing. He'd had sex shortly before his death. But there was no woman at the scene and nobody saw one coming or going.'

Perlman said, 'Maybe she saw him fall, didn't want to get her name involved, so she shot the craw.'

'Could be.'

'Or she shoved him.'

'Your imagination's dark as ever, Lou.'

'But a push is possible,' Perlman said.

'Aye. It's also possible I could get my leg over Nicole Kidman.'

'You're talking in the realm of a miracle now, Terry. You need to find this woman who was with young Gupta.'

A white froth of stout adhered to Bogan's upper lip. He wiped it away with the back of his hand and gazed in the direction of the redhead. He winked at her. He managed to make it suggestive, Perlman noticed. How had Bogan cultivated that trick? I wink, it looks like an eye infection.

'Why does this kid interest you anyway, Lou?'

'You're not listening to the tom-toms of the city, Terry. He's the second dead Gupta today.'

'Oh Christ, *right*,' Bogan said, and slapped his hand against his forehead. 'That kindergarten teacher was called Gupta. I just didn't make the connection between her and Tilak.'

Perlman said, 'I remembered the guy's name from the radio, which gobsmacked me because my memory's usually like a fishnet stocking. Then I wondered, this Gupta – could he be related to the slain teacher?'

'Neither Dev nor Barry Gupta mentioned anything about the dead man,' Scullion said. 'Wouldn't they have said something?'

'Perhaps the young guy who fell off the balcony isn't related. Or perhaps they didn't *want* to mention it. Bad timing.' Perlman drank some lager. He'd never really enjoyed the taste of alcohol. 'If there's a family relationship between Indra Gupta and the jumper, we've got a coincidence. And I don't always trust those bastard things.'

'So we find out,' Scullion said.

'You mean *I* find out,' Perlman said.

Scullion said, 'If you feel you're overworked, Lou –'

'Overworked nothing. I can cope.'

'He always liked it coming thick and fast,' Bogan said. He clapped a hand on Perlman's shoulder and looked at Scullion. 'He's a good soul, Inspector. Really. We go back more than twenty years, mibbe longer. Under that gnarly exterior beats a heart of total melancholy.'

Bogan drained his stout just as a uniformed constable, a young Sikh, appeared at the table, and whispered in his ear.

Bogan set down his empty glass. 'It seems we have another casualty of the city, gentlemen.'

13

Leo Kilroy played bagpipe CDs on his ultra high-tech sound system, custom-designed to blast music from speakers strategically placed in the back garden of his house for the express purpose of annoying his snooty neighbours. The night positively *whined*. Dressed in kilt and tartan socks, he sat in his conservatory and watched water spout from jets hidden artfully under terraces of rock in the back garden. Spotlights of silver and gold illuminated the waterfalls. The Black Watch Pipe Band played 'Farewell to Gibraltar', 'The Black Bear', and other military favourites.

It was all deeply stirring, if you were Scottish.

He pressed a bell set into the wall.

Frankie Chasm appeared from the shadows, dressed in black jacket and pinstripe trousers and shiny black shoes. He carried a tray: one bottle of Gordon's, a litre of tonic, a bucket of ice, and a frosted glass. He fixed a drink. Kilroy sipped.

Chasm said, 'That old rat's arse Mrs Gradley phoned to complain about the pipes.'

'Tell her to shove a yam up her fanny.'

'She's called the gendarmes,' Chasm said.

'Oh she's such a predictable *tweedy* wee bitch. All right, turn off the music. When the officer shows up on the doorstep, as he will, give him a generous contribution to the charity of his choice – his own bank account, I don't doubt. Then deliver a bottle of something from the cellar to Mrs Gradley. She's an old port-hog.'

'Port's her tipple all right,' Chasm said.

'Make sure she gets a bottle covered in dust. Old fart won't drink anything younger than herself.'

Alone, Kilroy listened to 'The Skye Boat Song'. He became grudgingly sentimental when he heard Jacobite tunes, and all that romantic guff about Bonnie Prince Charlie leaving Scotland for ever. Chasm cut off the music from the central control unit in the sitting room, and the night collapsed in silence.

Annoying the neighbours was a mischief of diminishing returns, Kilroy thought; the solicitors, the petitions gathered by irritated householders, the court cases and the fines, it had become all too tiresome. He sipped his G&T and watched the lights play on the waterfalls and he pondered Lou Perlman. He'd been pondering Lou Perlman too much lately. It wasn't healthy. That Yid tec. What was he *really* up to with the alleged anonymous caller?

Blum hadn't been especially comforting, hadn't said the soothing words lawyers were paid to say, such as: forget about it, Perlman's a scam artist, he's talking out his spout, I'll deal with it. Instead, Blum had rabbited on about Perlman's honesty. If you listened to Blum you'd think Perlman was George Washington. Daddy, I cannot tell a lie. I whacked the cherry tree. This fucking axe is mine.

The kilt felt heavy against Kilroy's thighs, like some pleated beast dying in his lap. He adjusted his sweaty legs under the stifling burden of the garment. He toyed with the notion of taking his business away from Blum. That would shake Blumsky up, because he lived in massive fear of poverty.

Chasm returned. 'I paid the cop. I also delivered a bottle of port.'

'Pull up a pew.'

Chasm did so. He sat down facing Kilroy. Frankie Chasm, born Chasmofsky of Polish parents, was a pale, muscular man. He had eyes the colour of cigarette ash. His nose was just slightly bent. His face was a map of a life led violently for almost fifty years. A streetfight or two, casual battery, a bad attitude to authority in general. Years ago, he'd been arrested for chainsawing fir trees on the Queen's estate at Balmoral while under the influence of rough cider; it was an anti-monarchist act of eco-terrorism, he'd told the police after a lengthy stand-off between big Highland cops armed only with batons, and Chasm, who menaced them with his chainsaw until it ran out of fuel and he was rushed off to the slammer.

He had an IQ of one hundred and thirty-one. When he'd been released from Peterhead after thirteen years, he'd come to work for Kilroy, who liked to describe him as a 'factotum' or 'butler'. But Chasm had gradually become more than a mere dark-suited appendage to Kilroy's world. Confidant, companion, and perhaps most importantly *minder*, he was Nat Blum's equal in Leo's hierarchy of support. Chasm had a special quality Blum couldn't bring to the party: he wasn't afraid of physical violence. He didn't go looking for trouble, but it frequently found him. He was a hard bastard with a deceptively quiet voice and manner.

'Anything special you want to do tonight, Leo?' When the social calendar was zero, Chasm dragged out a chessboard or a pack of playing cards or Monopoly to keep Leo amused.

Kilroy said, 'Fucksake. I can never relax, Frankie. Why can I never relax?'

'Too much on your mind?'

'What's on my mind is that Perlman.'

Chasm said, 'Every problem has a solution, Leo.'

Kilroy looked thoughtful. 'I don't believe he received that phone call. Not for a minute.'

'Then fucking let it go,' Frankie Chasm said.

Kilroy said, 'I simply have to get out of this bloody *skirt*. Can you believe people went to *war* wearing these hefty big things? How did they manage? Did they just *drag* themselves across the ground to fight the enemy? Here we come, you Jerry swine. Sporrans at dawn.' He stood up, undid straps, let both kilt and sporran fall to his ankles. He wore cavernous purple boxers. 'Ah, now that's better, that's a load off me.'

'Fancy three-card brag? Texas cut-throat?'

Kilroy sipped his G&T and dismissed Chasm's suggestions with a gesture of his hand. 'Frankie, Frankie. I sit in this bloody mansion in my underwear, I've got wads of cash stashed in such a bewildering variety of bank accounts I can barely remember them all, I can have the city's finest young sexual playthings here at a moment's notice to keep me amused, I can eat at any fine restaurant I choose . . . so what's my problem? Is my Catholic upbringing giving me the willies finally? Are all those fucked-up nuns and jerk-off priests of my boyhood catching up with me and telling me I'm going to hell, as they predicted lo these many years? Am I afraid of failing to pass through the eye of the needle?'

'Would you be happy if you were poor?' Chasm asked.

'Don't talk shite.'

'Then rejoice. You want to go out somewhere?'

Kilroy considered this, and yawned. 'I don't think so. I may watch some TV before I call it a day. Is it time for the news?'

Chasm got up, and obligingly wheeled a TV out of the corner of the room. Kilroy liked it right in his face, the full glare. Chasm flipped the channels with the remote control. 'Tell me when you want me to stop, Leo.'

An array of images flashed past: a whale giving birth, a football match from South America, a masked man shackled and sealed inside a block of ice, and some character with a pimp's blow-dried hairstyle reading the news. 'Stop,' Kilroy said. He looked at the screen.

The newsreader said, *'The victim was in his late twenties . . .'*

The image changed. OB camera. Kilroy recognized Ashton Lane, just off Byres Road. Café Brel and the Ubi Chip and the cobbled street. A group of policemen wandered in front of crime-tape. They were blocking something from view. A small crowd stood idly around: ghouls from the local chapter of freaks. Somebody waved at the camera. *Hello, Ma and Da, this is your grinning turnip of a son.*

Kilroy leaned forward, drawn into the picture. He pointed a finger in excitement. 'Good fucking Christ, *look*, there's Perlman. See him, Chasm! On the edge of the picture. Perlman, for Christ's sake. Look! Ah, shite, he's gone.'

Cut to studio. The newsreader said, '. . . Mr Ochoba, from Lagos, was a student at Strathclyde University, and planned to graduate this year. It is the second murder in the city today. Earlier, a kindergarten teacher was shot in the city's south –'

'Off off off,' Kilroy said. 'I've seen this kindergarten story more times than I need to.'

Chasm flicked the remote. The picture vanished.

'Perlman on TV.' Kilroy gazed at the blank screen. 'On my TV, in *my* fucking conservatory, in *my* house. One day he'll be the face I see when I shave in the morning.'

Frankie Chasm said, 'Relax. Just relax, Leo. Here, you think that Nigerian's dead because he hadn't paid his witch doctor's bill?'

Kilroy smiled, perhaps for the first time all day. 'I don't doubt it. Witch doctors are said to have seriously strict collection policies.' He rose, grunted. 'You better phone our friends, Frankie.'

'On my agenda.'

Kilroy climbed the stairs to his bedroom. He sat on the big green velvet quilt of his California kingsize, and stretched his legs. He thought of the encounter that morning with Perlman. He lay back and absent-mindedly fingered his pudgy dick and, since he had a hand in the general vicinity, scratched his balls for good measure.

He frowned, remembering Perlman at the scene in Ashton Lane. Was there no end to the man? The cop who goes wherever the crime takes him. He was like a fucking one-man posse.

Kilroy waddled into his pink-tiled bathroom. Lifelike mermaids had been painted on the ceiling, swimming in an array of stucco bubbles. He opened his medicine cabinet and swallowed two Zantac and pondered the dead Indian girl in the kindergarten.

Frankie Chasm took a shotgun from a rack on the wall and moved quietly through the house. This was his job at night. He patrolled. He jiggled locks and made sure the electronic security system was set. He wondered at his life: you grow up to become Big Billy Bunter's minder. It was never my ambition, he thought.

Outside, beyond the metal gates at the front of the house, lay an incalculable number of threats and menaces, according to Leo, who claimed he had enemies everywhere – people jealous of him, those who plotted to seize his power, and others, callous brutes, who simply wanted to burn his huge fat arse.

Chasm was under orders to shoot intruders on sight. He knew Kilroy had enemies. A man so involved in criminal society as Leo had a whole bloody mob of people who wouldn't exactly be *well-wishers*. Chasm had seen all sorts of gangsters come to this house to talk business in hushed voices with Leo. Jimmy 'Bram' Stoker, an ostentatiously rich bookmaker who took bets lesser bookies offset; Gordy Curdy, nominally a restaurant supplier, but also the city's major hoormeister, running high-class girls in and out of the better hotels; Errol 'Bungalow' Wilkes, whose fleet of taxicabs was used more for the carriage of stolen pharmaceuticals than ferrying human beings. There were others, men who had small standing armies and who ploughed their illegal earnings into financing hotels and underground car parks and shopping malls.

If you lived in this milieu, you lived on an edge: Kilroy knew it, and had always enjoyed the risk factor, just as he'd enjoyed lording it over lesser crooks. He was, after all, the crime de la crime in this society . . . But lately he'd lost a bit of his energy, Chasm thought, and the long afternoon meetings with his fellow crooks didn't happen with their previous regularity. And why was he allowing Perlman to bother him, when normally he'd have brushed the cop's attentions aside like a man flicking a spider from the back of his hand?

Tired of the stress and hassle of protecting his empire from predators and pirates? Could the Fat Man be pondering retirement? It was hard for a career crim like Kilroy to retire; it would be seen as something of a weakness in the criminal fraternity – and that was when the vultures began to gather, drawn by the whiff of an edible corpse.

Kilroy's best option, if he really wanted out, was to empty his bank accounts and bugger off to a distant trop island with de luxe lodgings. But somebody would eventually remember an old grudge or offence, because in Kilroy's environment grievances were neither forgiven nor forgotten. And this somebody would find out where Kilroy was living, and an emissary sent from Glasgow with a machete in his golf bag, and on a balmy tropical night Leo would be chopped for sharkfood, blood and fat and intestinal matter floating on the tide.

Not nice, Chasm thought.

He checked the deck of monitors that received pictures from security cameras scanning the front driveway, the gardens, the sides of the house. Sensor lights had been installed all over the place. They were so sensitive a passing snail could set them off. Nothing out there. But he felt jumpy anyway. He was letting Kilroy's edgy mood get to him.

Walk the hallways, hug the shotgun, check the monitors. Oyez, eleven o'clock and all is well.

How soothing this house became after the Fat Man had gone to bed. How pleasant without Leo's whims and crybaby demands for amusement and reassurance. It was a wonderful house; great ceilings, cornices restored by artisans shipped in from Turin, a private thirty-seater screening room.

He paused at the foot of the stairs. He heard Kilroy snore. Did the Fat Man dream? Did his dormant mind throw up paranoid images of enemies, gangsters who plotted his downfall – or maybe even Lou Perlman, his private gargoyle, popped up in the midst of his dreams and turned them all into nightmares?

Chasm remembered the phone call Kilroy had told him to make. He went inside Leo's office, where the walls were decorated with photographs of Fatso in the company of dignitaries. Here he was shaking hands with Glasgow's Lord Provost. Here he was with some bishop or cardinal. And here he stood with a famous Glasgow comedian, arms linked, the best of buddies. Kilroy enjoyed the company of the rich and famous. He liked having their private phone numbers in his book.

There were also pictures from long ago: Kilroy as an obese young child astride a skinny donkey on the sands at Rothesay, circa 1950. Kilroy at five or six, cherubic curls and velvet suit, clutching the hand of his mother, a very tall veiled woman in a black coat. A shot of a gravestone: *Effie Kilroy, 1927-1962, Much Loved Mother of Leo.* Creepy, Chasm thought.

You better phone our friends, Frankie.

Right, boss. Right away, sir. Even as you sleep, massa.

14

Perlman felt like a weary animal burrowing into the darkness of the city in search of a place to hibernate. It was raining again, albeit finely, and the lamplit streets were enveloped in the strands of a damp web. It wasn't the rain that afflicted his mood, nor the prospect of going back to his house in Egypt, and the silences of rooms which often struck him as curiously unfamiliar – it was murder that had brought him down into an emotional slump. This city had shed too much blood in one day.

He drove the streets of Merchant City, an area of converted warehouses adjacent to George Square. Miriam had a loft in this neighbourhood and he played with the notion of ringing her doorbell, regardless of the hour. Maybe she'd still be awake and offer him a cup of hot chocolate, or a coffee. A smile would do. A brush of her hand against his would be enough, more than enough. It would lift his heart.

He parked his Mondeo in Virginia Street and sat smoking for a time. He stuck a tape in the deck and listened to Gram Parsons' 'In My Hour of Darkness'. What was this '70s kick that had possessed him lately? Usually he listened to jazz from the

'50s and '60s, but recently it had been Paul Butterfield, Gram Parsons, The Band – was it some kind of compensatory visit to his history? A way of reassuring himself that once he'd been young and life unlimited?

Good morning, mortality, what's new?

He gazed the length of Virginia Street. A few black cabs drifted along Argyle Street at the bottom. I'm sick of the dead, he thought. I need life around me. A kindergarten teacher is gunned down, and her colleague Ajit Singh lies comatose in an IC unit. A Nigerian student is knifed in a busy street, a sneaky job, a stiletto blade slipped through the material of his coat and between his ribs and into his heart, and he perishes on cobblestones. He thought of the quiet black face of the young man, the eyes open wide, the lower lip distended as if in some last sulk at the abysmal cruelty of the world.

And a young man falls from a balcony, maybe pushed.

Quite a fucking casualty list.

The things I see in Glasgow. The places I go on this job.

His mobile rang in his pocket. He answered.

'I got your message, Sergeant.' It was Dev Gupta.

'Thanks for getting back to me. Talk to me about Tilak Gupta.'

'What do you want to know?'

'He's family?'

'A cousin,' Dev Gupta said.

'You think he was suicide material?'

'How would I know something like that?'

The connection became crotchety; the hiss in Perlman's ear was like a snake in his brain. He shouted to be heard. 'An informed guess would be useful, Dev.'

'He drank and he drugged. It might have been an accident. He might have been wasted. Or depressed.'

The hiss quit. 'Did he have a girlfriend? A regular partner?'

Dev Gupta said, 'He knew a lot of women. I can't imagine him restricted to just one.'

Now this is all very helpful, Perlman thought. Dev Gupta's a quarry of info. Nothing useful to say about his sister, even less about his late cousin.

'You never mentioned Tilak earlier,' Perlman said.

'I was preoccupied, Sergeant. You might have noticed.'

Fair enough. Perlman stared into the rain. 'Where was he likely to hang out?'

'The Corinthian was one of his haunts. Sometimes he went to the Tunnel. What has this got to do with my sister's murder anyway?'

'Maybe nothing,' Perlman said. 'If you think of anything useful, get back to me. Any time of day. Obviously I keep long hours.' The line was off its rocker again, sizzling and roaring like all manner of echoes picked up in deep space. These mobile monsters. He disliked them. Everybody had one attached to his or her ear. Schoolkids yakked on pavements. Fragments of weird ringing tones irked you in cafés and pubs. Maybe in the future somebody would dream up a way of implanting Nokias into the brains of babies. Wired at birth. Born with the gift of sending text messages. *Hello world, my name is Karen and I am two minutes old :)*

Perlman shoved the Thing into his pocket, then turned off the tape just as Gram Parsons was singing 'O Lord, *grant me vision'*. Grant it indeed. Tell me the secret purpose of the universe. Or if that's too much of an ask, reveal to me the deeper strata of Glasgow.

He got out of the car and sighed, crossing the street to the door of Miriam's building. He lit a fresh cigarette and when rain soaked into the paper he tossed it aside. His throat was raw from tobacco anyway. Ring the bell, don't ring. What are you, Lou, standing here in the rainy dark like a *yold*?

He looked at the nameplates that studded the frame of the door: *Miriam Perlman*. He raised his finger and moved it towards the brass button at the centre of the nameplate. Just as he did so, the door opened and a man emerged; Perlman, surprised by recognition, stepped to one side.

Detective-Inspector Latta, tall, hunched shoulders, thick black hair, uneven teeth – some white, others brown, some pointed, others blunt: like a mouthful of chuckie-stones – gazed at him. *Midnight, Latta is coming out of the building, he's been to see Miriam – who else?* Perlman wondered if these facts made a sound case for the sudden pang of envy and suspicion he felt.

Lunacy lay along the faultline of this thought. *Latta and Miriam, lovers.* He cursed the sorry streak of adolescence that burned inside him; at this stage of his life all such fires should have died out. He was being an arsehole, succumbing to this silliness. Stop and think about it. What would Miriam see in this grotesque man anyway?

Latta smiled in a squeezed-out way; he was clearly conscious of his awful choppers. 'Small world. I've just been talking to your sister-in-law.'

'You always work this late?'

'Tell me when crime stops, Perlman. Show me a criminal and I'll show you an insomniac.'

'And which one is Miriam?'

Latta shrugged, and tapped Perlman's sleeve. 'Fraud's a tough nut to crack, Perlman. You need an eye for the seemingly insignificant detail that turns out to be the smoking gun. Reams of paperwork get sifted. If I got paid by the tonnage, I could retire.'

'What's she supposed to have done, anyway?'

'I'm not sure she's done *anything* yet. Might turn out to be very simple. Bad choice of a husband, say. No crime in that. End of story, and I go home happy. Might turn out to be something else.'

'You think she knows where Colin stashed illegal loot?'

Latta said, 'Anything's possible, Perlman. I've given up being surprised.'

'She didn't have a clue about her husband's line of work.'

'I'd expect you to say that. She's family, right?' Latta grinned briefly. 'For all I know, she might be even more than that.'

'Don't talk crap.'

'She's a damn fine-looking woman, Perlman. Don't get so bloody shirty.'

'You should start investigating me, Inspector. I might be her accomplice. Maybe we divvied up spare cash Colin left lying around. You thought about that?'

'Everything crosses my mind sooner or later, Perlman. I pick and I pick, and I examine every wee thread.'

'All my adult life I've been on the force, Latta, and I never took a penny illegally.'

'Aren't you the paragon?'

Patronizing fucker. Perlman felt his initial daft response of jealousy turn to anger. He had the scary urge to smack this creep between the eyes, which would have led directly to a committee of inquiry, then suspension. Maybe even a goodbye boot up the arse on the steps of Force HQ, and all his figurative medals ripped from his chest.

'I'll say goodnight, Perlman.'

'I'd say the same if I thought I fucking meant it,' Perlman remarked.

'You want to watch your tongue,' Latta said. 'We're not all like your friend Scullion, *Sergeant*. We're not all so bloody tolerant as good old Sandy, *Sergeant*. Bear that in mind.'

Latta walked away. He had a shuffling step, like a man whose shoes fit badly. He got inside a car and slammed the door. Perlman heard him rap the horn, then the vehicle headed towards Argyle Street.

He felt suddenly weighted, lead in his bones. Everything's a trial, he thought. You hunt criminals and killers. You bruise yourself against the brick and iron of this complicated city and sometimes that hurts. You don't sleep well. Or you encounter a colleague, a superior officer, a real *farshtinkener*, who tries to drag you inside a nasty little web he's weaving because he suspects you of knowing where stolen treasure lies buried. Think: Latta gossips in the lavatories of Pitt Street. Cops in cubicles, trousers round their knees, listen. Men standing with damp hands under the hot air of dryers tilt their heads attentively. Before long, Lou Perlman is tainted, a fucking *gonif*, a bad cop. This I need, he thought. A rotten rep at my time of life. Fuck Latta. He's not getting to me.

He pressed Miriam's doorbell.

From the intercom: 'Yes?'

'It's Lou. Can I come up?'

He heard a buzz. He entered the building. The lift was out of order. He'd been here a couple of times in the past, and it had never been working. He breathed deeply and badly as he climbed the stairs. He coughed when he reached the third floor. One more floor to climb. He wanted a smoke, regardless of his whining lungs. Once upon a time I could've had these stairs for breakfast . . .

Miriam was waiting for him in the doorway of her loft. She wore blue jeans and a black denim shirt that hung outside the jeans. 'The midnight caller, what a pleasant surprise,' she said. She led him inside a large high-ceilinged space where a long skylight enclosed the night. Canvases were stacked against walls. An easel stood in a corner.

Miriam asked, 'Coffee? Or something with a bit more bite?'

'I'll risk a very small Scotch,' he said. 'A nip.'

'I can count on one hand the number of times I've seen you drink booze. Let me guess. You've had a shitty day, and to top it off you just ran into Latta as he was leaving.'

'We had an encounter.'

'And?'

'You and me, we might be partners in some kind of financial scam,' Perlman said.

'Dragged you in, has he?' She smiled and Perlman's mood brightened at once. What a tiny movement of lips can do.

'He'd love to.'

'He's the kind of man who suspects the whole world of wrongdoing,' she said. 'Every face he looks at, he clocks it as dishonest. Every statement he hears, it's a lie. I wonder how he got like that.'

'Burn-out,' Perlman said. 'Been doing the same job for too long.'

'And *you* haven't?'

'I'm different.'

'Are you? Tell me how.'

'I'm immune to cynicism.'

She opened a cabinet, filled a tumbler with Scotch, and handed it to him. She poured a shot of vodka for herself. 'Here's to immunity,' she said.

There was a period of silence, exaggerated by the way the space in the loft seemed to stretch into an infinity of shadow.

'I think Latta would like to believe we're lovers into the bargain,' he said.

'That bothers you?'

'I give a damn what he believes?'

'I can't imagine you would.' Caught in a wedge of light created by an overhead lamp, she looked suddenly impish, an elf of mischief. 'He's probably thinking right now that we're copulating with abandon.'

'Probably,' Perlman said.

'Heavy breathing and passion,' she said.

Was she teasing him? he wondered. Playing him like an old penny whistle? Whatever, he felt a pleasing flutter, a shiver of desire. An image passed through his head, him and her, lovers in a bedroom, curtains drawn and a candle burning down in a slow-dying flame reflected in a wall mirror where, if he raised his head a little, he could see himself and Miriam naked in the glass, oy –

'He probably gets his thrills that way. Mental voyeurism. A man with a grubby wee mind,' he said.

Miriam sat on the arm of a chair and sipped her drink. The mischief had gone from her face. 'Forget Latta. He can't prove Colin hid any money away. No money, no case for complicity. He can excavate and interrogate all he wants, he's wasting his time. He even hinted he works hand in hand with the Nazis at the Inland Revenue, but that prospect doesn't worry me either. What have I got to hide?'

Perlman experienced decompression; the few seconds of elation and arousal had withered away. She hadn't been teasing *him*; instead, she'd been ridiculing *Latta*. That talk about copulating, heavy breathing and passion, it had been directed at the folly of Latta's imagination. She didn't know she was having any effect on *you*, Lou. What are you to her, anyway? Brother-in-law, that's all, that's how she perceives you. It's never going to change, forget it, let it go, toss out the obsession –

'I saw that kindergarten murder on TV,' she said. 'Are you involved?'

Perlman nodded. 'It came my way,' he said. He wanted to lock Indra Gupta inside a secure room at the back of his head. Why not? Other people switched off, they didn't drag their work home with them, they didn't brood and sit up until dawn smoking and doodling and drinking rank black coffee and jangling. Take a break. Indra Gupta will still be dead in the morning.

'There was another killing later,' he said.

'I didn't know.'

'A Nigerian student. Off Byres Road. Stabbed. I'm only flitting round the periphery of that one. I happened to be in the vicinity.' Even as he said this, he wasn't sure it was true: he'd get sucked in if he was asked to help. Suddenly he felt like a man trapped under an avalanche: the investigation of Leo Kilroy and his role in Colin's death, Indra Gupta's slaying, the suicide/jump of her cousin in Kelvin Court, and now this bastard Latta – all these were beads on an abacus, and he was sliding them this way and that along the wires, looking for a design.

'You're exhausted,' she said.

'This city roughs you up sometimes. You get punchy.'

'Sleep here tonight. The sofa folds out. It would spare you the drive home.'

Three miles, Perlman thought. If that. 'I've got some things to do,' he said.

'Cleaning house? Silverware to polish?'

'Paper stuff, office stuff . . . thanks anyway.'

She moved towards him and stood up on her tiptoes and

kissed him on his cheek. He realized he hadn't shaved. He must feel like a bear's arse against her soft mouth.

'What's that for?' he asked.

'Fondness. Gratitude. I don't know. Does it matter? Does there have to be a *reason* for everything, Sergeant?'

'Force of habit,' he said. 'I'm glad I dropped in. I needed to see a friendly face.' He could still feel her kiss on his cheek.

'When are we going to have tea at the Willow?'

'Call you tomorrow,' he said.

She opened the front door for him. She kissed him again, same spot. 'Drive safely.'

He went down the stairs and out into the street. Rain fell softly. He sat inside the Mondeo and looked up at the pale light glowing from her loft. Then darkness, almost shockingly sudden, as she switched the light off. He thought of her undressing for bed.

Your age, horny as a boy.

He drove into Glassford Street and then south to the Trongate, which was dead save for a drunk man lurching between lamp-posts like a figure trapped in a pinball machine. Trongate to Glasgow Cross, and along London Road; the city was bolted down for the night. Dead pubs. Dark cafés. He passed one bright blast of light, an Indian takeaway. It was empty except for an Asian man reading a newspaper behind the counter. Perlman caught the beguiling whiff of tandoori and for a moment was tempted to pause and grab a fierce vindaloo to take home.

Carrying curry to Egypt.

He didn't stop. If he went inside the Indian takeaway, he'd invariably start thinking about Indra Gupta, and tonight he wanted the full six hours of doss sweet doss, no interruptions. He was almost asleep at the wheel.

London Road was a gulch of darkness. He passed St Peter's Cemetery. His eyelids felt heavy; he turned on his radio for some quick wake-up noise and found a station playing 'Itchycoo Park'. The Small Faces, he remembered. Another passageway into the past – but he was too tired for time-travel.

He turned left into Braidfauld Street. Home territory now.

The last few blocks. He parked outside his house, a black brick two-storey affair that looked as if it had been dipped many years ago in soot. He locked the Mondeo, went up the driveway and let himself into the hallway. He stroked the mezuzah as he habitually did. It was concealed under a skein of old blue paint. When had he last painted this house? Ten years ago, fifteen? He couldn't remember.

Inside the living room he slumped into a decrepit armchair. A pile of newspapers lay on the floor, also a couple of CD boxes whose discs he'd misplaced. Monk's *Paris Concert*. Brian Kellock Trio's *Live at Henry's*. They'd turn up. Everything rose to the surface eventually.

He entered the kitchen, examined the contents of the refrigerator, grabbed some raspberry jam and cottage cheese, and slathered both between two slices of white bread so old that even the massive infusion of preservatives was beginning to lose its protective power. He bit into the sandwich; the best he could say about it was that it killed the taste of whisky in his mouth.

He yawned, imagined Miriam in her bed – did she sleep on her side? Or on her back with her legs parted a little? Pyjamas or in the buff? Such images, ah.

He checked his answering machine.

The message indicator read: 1. He pressed the playback button and listened. Familiar voice.

He listened to it twice. Then, intrigued, agitated, he listened a third time before he went upstairs to his bedroom. He couldn't sleep for the sound of rain running down the window, and a cat howling a randy song in a nearby alley, and the prospect of all the things he had to do in the morning.

15

2.30 a.m. Sandrine Descartes always stayed awake until her son came home. She loved Robert – mothers loved their sons, flawed or otherwise – but something about him scared her. A terrible admission to make where your own child was concerned, certainly, but true. She saw absolutely nothing of Jacques in him, and even less of herself. When she looked at him she sometimes wondered if there had been a switch at the maternity hospital, one of those mistakes one sometimes heard about. *He is someone else's child.*

He was a blob of a man, a thirty-seven-year-old stranger who tapped constantly on his computer keyboard and made quiet phone calls in the dead of night. He received letters and circulars from all over Britain. She never pried into his life. His room was out of bounds. He hadn't imposed this rule himself; rather, she'd come to realize that she preferred to keep herself separate from her son's world.

His only source of income was from the Department of Social Security. He was 'disabled' and claimed benefits. The disability was a fiction stemming from an 'accident' that had occurred three years ago when he injured himself on a building site. He'd tripped and broken his left leg and alleged that it had never healed properly, so he'd developed a limp for the purposes of fooling the DSS.

She heard drunks in the street scream sectarian songs: *we are ra people, we are ra people, the Pope's a fuckin tampax.* Bottles shattered on the pavement, and somebody shouted from a window: *Shut yer fuckin gobs we're tryin to sleep.* The drunks roared with laughter. *Away tay fuck, ya wanker.*

Sooner or later the drunks would move on and an uneasy silence come back. She thought of Jacques, as she did most of her waking hours, and wished he hadn't died and left her in this damnable place. Poor Jacques, he'd simply wasted away, assassinated by the climate. He'd grown small, shrunken, gasping as he died. Jacques, love of her life . . .

She heard Robert's key in the front-door lock. She knew from the clumsy scratching sound he made that he was drunk and incapable of letting himself in. She got out of bed and walked through the sitting room to the door. She turned the handle. Robert staggered into the room, lurched against the sofa and toppled clownlike over the arm. He fell on the floor.

Sandrine tutted, and kneeled beside him. 'Let me help you up.'

'Don't move me, Ma, want to lie here, need to.'

'Please, Robert, you can't sleep on the floor.'

'Sleep where I fucking please. *Robair*, sweet Jesus Christ. *I'll sail my ship alone, with all the dreams I own* . . . Oldie but a goodie, sonny boy.'

He was always objectionable and utterly incoherent when he was drunk. Half-done sentences, snatches of song, outbursts of remorse mixed with expressions of anger. He opened one eye, a tiny scarlet parting, and glared at her. How ugly he looked, she thought. How sad and stupid and, yes, common. Oh God, it was so hard to love him. He reeked of booze and sick. There were red marks on his cheek. What had happened to him? A girl, perhaps. Somebody he'd made unwanted advances to.

He managed to sit upright. He leaned against the side of the sofa, head drooped. She wondered how life might have been different if she'd taken her son and gone back to France after Jacques' death, but by then her father had passed away, and the estate had been divided between her brothers, and she'd been cut out of any inheritance. Her brothers never answered her letters. France had become an unattainable place of half-remembered scenery.

Forget the château. She lived in Possil, Glasgow, and there was no escape.

'Robert, please, I will help you to get up. You need a bath.'

His limp head rolled. Blood had congealed in his hair. He'd been struck on the skull.

'What happened? Did somebody hurt you?'

He leaned towards her. He toppled forward, his face in her lap.

Like a small boy again, she thought. Like a little child. She stroked the side of his head gently. Unexpectedly, tears filled her eyes. This pathetic drunken manchild. She was consumed by a huge sadness. Her life had gone nowhere. It was all cul-de-sacs and deprivation. She heard herself sing to her son as she'd done when he was very small. *Mon ami Pierrot*. He'd never been able to learn French. At school he was always close to the bottom of the class. He wasn't stupid, he just hadn't applied himself.

'Ma,' he said. 'I feel like shite. Like total *shite*. The fucking room's spinning. Jesus Christ.'

He vomited riotously into her lap, then rolled away from her and lay on his back and stared at the ceiling.

'Oh God,' she said. 'What a mess, what an awful mess.'

'There's wee cracks and lines in the ceiling Ma didya know that. Mibbe one day it'll all fall down. I am totally pished Ma. Blootered.'

She got up, went inside the kitchen, soaked a sponge and started to clean her robe. The smell was rancid. Undigested foods, stale beer. She took the robe off and held it under the hot water tap. Dressed only in a slip, she shivered.

She heard her son crawl across the sitting-room floor. He made it into the kitchen. He got to his feet somehow and stood directly behind her, placing his hands on her shoulders.

'Ma I'm sorry sorry really sofucking sorry.'

'It cleans, Robert. Look. I'm cleaning it now.'

'No Ma you don't you don't follow my drift I am sorry I am fucking *sorry* and I am not talkin about that old robe.'

'I understand,' she said.

'But you don't know Ma why I'm sorry you don't know you just think I'm talkin total shite coz I'm pished out my skull right eh right eh?'

'Sleep it off, Robert,' she said.

Balance gone, moaning quietly to himself, he slid to the floor and lay on his side, eyes shut and mouth open. He made that terrible *noise* at the back of his throat. She got a blanket from a cupboard and draped it over him. She gazed at him a moment, then turned out the kitchen light.

She sat on the sitting-room sofa. She thought, thirty-seven years ago I gave birth to a beautiful boy who turned into this – this drunken lump asleep in his own vomit on the kitchen floor.

She heard him shout in his sleep. *Ten times eleven is a hundred and ten.* She wondered what he was dreaming about. Sometimes at night she heard him roar incomprehensibly while he slept, as if he was in unbearable pain.

She moved in the direction of her bedroom, and stumbled over something on the floor. She bent down. Something of Robert's. What was he doing with this? It was moist and unpleasant to the touch.

She dropped it almost as soon as she'd picked it up.

16

Perlman found a parking space in Cadogan Street, west of Central Station, and walked a couple of blocks north to Waterloo Street. The morning was dry. A frisky wind tossed used tissues and discarded plastic and all manner of paper material into the air.

He paused outside an office building in Waterloo Street. He caught his reflection in the smoked-glass door. Dark coat, flannels, brown shoes, glasses that indented the sides of his nose. Get a new lightweight pair, he thought: these heavy specs add years to your appearance. His hair, which he'd soaked and flattened before leaving home, was all over the place now, wind-tormented. He saw his face in the dark glass, hollow-cheeked, aye, but the mouth was a good firm line that suggested purpose. There was some wear in the skin of the neck, a sagging.

Not handsome, not like Colin had been. What had Miriam said? *You've got that wee boy thing.* Which was fine, he supposed, if you were seven – but for a grown man?

He pushed the door open and entered a marbled reception area. He checked the list of companies on a wall chart, found what he was looking for, then rode a lift to the fifth floor. He exited into a carpeted corridor and encountered a big oval sign that read: *Nathan Blum & Co, Solicitors*, in fancy script. A pretty receptionist, a good-looking fair-haired *shikse*, sat behind a desk. Perlman could have guessed that Nat would have a blonde for front office purposes; image was the key, from the big car to the riverfront penthouse.

'Help you?' she asked.

'Here to see Nat Blum,' he said.

'Got an appointment?'

He showed his ID, which didn't generate great enthusiasm. The girl barely glanced at it. 'You need an appointment, Detective-Sergeant.'

'Aye, right. Watch me.' Perlman walked past the reception desk and along the corridor.

The girl called after him. 'Here. You can't just go in like that.'

He didn't look back. The receptionist picked up a phone, probably to forewarn Blum, but Perlman had gone out of earshot and didn't hear what she was saying. He approached a door with a plaque that had Nat's name on it and he pushed it open. He relished this action, walking directly into Blum's lair without going through any basic civilities.

Blum was sitting behind his desk in shirtsleeves. He wore bright red braces. His keen-eyed hatchet face registered only a slight expression of surprise, which passed away quickly. You had to admire Blum's facial control.

'They outlawed knocking when I wasn't looking?' Blum asked.

'Nice room, Nat.' And so it was, book-lined, rich in blond wood and bright with chrome. Daylight came through the white slats of venetian blinds.

Blum pushed aside a folder he'd been examining. He looked at his watch. 'Nine sharp. My my. I didn't think your generation of policemen got up so early.'

'I'm with the crack-of-dawn brigade, Nat.'

'You're glowing, Perlman. I don't like it when you glow.'

'Are these chairs for sitting in or just for show?'

'Test-drive one and see.'

Perlman sat in a steel-framed leather chair. 'Not comfy, Nat. Reminds me of the seats in the old La Scala picture-house in Sauchiehall Street. Before your time.'

'Give me notice if you intend to drop in again, I'll get you a recliner.'

Perlman patted his coat pockets, located his cigarettes, took the packet out. He lit one. 'Have you got a tape-deck handy?'

Blum smiled. 'Let me guess. The phantom caller struck again. Only this time you captured the voice.'

Perlman took an audio-cassette from his pocket. He flashed it in the air. 'You'll like this, Nat.'

'Over there.' Blum nodded across the room where a sleek metal-grey sound system sat on a shelf between neatly stacked law books. 'I assume you know how to operate it?'

Perlman walked to the cassette-player. 'Highly futuristic, Nat. I'm impressed.'

'Cutting edge,' Blum said. 'Beyond cutting, for all I know.'

Perlman surveyed the smooth lines of the equipment, the recessed buttons. He searched for the tape slot. Christ, this was a complex set-up. He didn't want to be seen fumbling. He shoved the cassette into the first appropriate opening he could find and mercifully the tape vanished into the heart of the system. He looked for the power button, but Blum was a step ahead: the system lit up suddenly, glowing a discreet orange.

'Remote.' Blum held a tiny black rectangle the size of a credit card. 'Now I just hit the tape symbol on this wee gadget and we can relax and listen.' He sat down and folded his hands behind his neck and looked very calm.

The cassette played. The man's voice was deep, Glaswegian accent. *'Perlman? You there? Come on, man. Pick up if you are. I don't have all night and I badly need to piss . . . Waiting waiting . . . Awright, I presume you're not at home. Here's the crux of the matter. I saw Leo Kilroy drive his Bentley on the night of December 15 at approximately eleven. He was heading along Dalness Street, driving at about twenty-five mph . . . You sure you're not listening to this,*

Perlman? You'll want some evidence that I'm telling the truth, I suppose . . . Fine. I'll get back to you.'

The tape ended.

Perlman asked, 'Will I run it again?'

'I don't see the point,' Blum remarked. 'It's nothing.'

'Nat, Nat. Don't be a schmuck. It's a long way from nothing. I *live* in Dalness Street. Somebody saw your client in his *car* in fucking Dalness Street.'

'How do I know you didn't get some dodgy friend of yours to make that phone call?'

'Below the belt, Nat.'

'How do we know anything about this caller? How do we know he's not some joker stringing *you* along?'

'For what purpose?' Perlman pushed a button; the tape slipped from the machine into his hand.

'Malice. Money.'

'He says he has evidence.'

'Evidence I'll believe when I see it.'

'The law's made you a cynic.'

'Show me a gullible lawyer, I'll show you a tosser in a dosshouse.' Blum stood up. 'I've got an appointment.'

'So have I,' Perlman said. He moved towards the door, paused. 'It's up to you, naturally, but you might want to inform your client about this tape.'

'And tell him what? I've just heard the latest fairytale from the wizard of Pitt Street? I don't think so.'

Perlman laughed. 'The wizard of Pitt Street. I like that. Big pointy hat. Secret lining in the cloak. Abracadabra. That's me.'

Blum said, 'Before you go. One thing puzzles me. Why do you suppose this killer didn't shoot you as well? After all, you're an eyewitness. You saw the car.'

'My guess is he didn't have time. You fire from a moving car, hitting your target isn't easy. He wanted Colin more than he wanted me. By the time he shot my brother, he's already forty, fifty yards down the road. He doesn't want to wheel round and try his luck again. Gunfire at night in a quiet street? Nope. So he decides against the risk of drawing attention. He drives the hell away.'

Blum took his jacket from the back of his chair, and put it on. 'It's a plausible theory. Problem is, as I keep telling you, you've got the wrong suspect. My client wouldn't know a firearm from a walking stick.'

'And you think I'm convinced of that?'

Blum smiled. 'The burden of proof isn't mine, Lou.'

Perlman paused in the doorway of Blum's office. He knew that as soon as he left this place, Blum would be on the blower to the fat man.

'See you around, Nat.'

'Not too soon, I hope. Don't you have that serious kindergarten killing to keep you occupied? Why are you flogging this dead pony? Give it a break.'

'There's life in it yet, Nat.' Perlman hesitated before tossing the cassette through the air. 'That's for you. I've got another copy.'

Blum snatched at it and caught it.

Perlman stepped out of the office, walked past the reception desk where the *shikse* glowered at him. He winked at her and moved towards the lift, feeling jaunty.

17

Every morning of their lives Billy Parsonage and his wife Matty played nine holes of golf at Knightswood Park Golf Course on the west side of the city. Billy had retired fifteen years ago from his position as assistant manager at a city branch of the Clydesdale Bank, and Matty had given up her career as personnel supervisor at the House of Fraser department store in Buchanan Street the same year.

Like some long-married people, they'd come to resemble each other; each had a small round rosy face set in a permanent frown, as if they mutually disapproved of the world. Golf was their passion. Matty was the better player. Billy was a stranger to coordination. He studied golf improvement books, and watched instructive videos, but nothing helped. He was cack-handed, doomed to mediocrity.

On the fourth tee he sliced his drive and the ball went wide of the fairway. He lost sight of it.

Matty said, 'Not so hot, Billy. Not so hot.'

'It's the wind,' Billy said.

'Knocked you off balance, did it?' Matty played a lovely shot. The ball rose straight and true in the direction of the green.

Billy Parsonage fumed quietly. He dragged his bag and followed his wife along the fairway. The wind puffed up the sleeves of his rainproof jacket.

'It's coming out of the east,' he said.

'What is?'

'The wind, woman. The wind is.'

'And how is this significant?'

'It interferes with the flight path of the ball, *obviously*.'

Matty Parsonage thought her husband sometimes talked utter ballocks. He was a bore of the first order, a self-proclaimed expert on meteorology, the global economy, the Kennedy assassination, and the ventilation of buildings. He just blethered on. She didn't listen much. It would be more fun to read a book about embalming than listen to Billy.

She located her ball in line for the green. 'You'll have to look over there,' she said, and she pointed firmly with her club towards a scrubby clump of bushes. 'That's where your ball came to rest, Billy.'

'Are you sure?'

'I saw it fall.'

Billy stalked off in the direction of the bushes. He muttered to himself furiously about the horrible gloating *pleasure* Matty took in his misdirected shots. He contemplated the possibility of getting up very early one morning and catching a plane to a faraway place. Alone. Rio came to mind. So did Kuala Lumpur. Matty would never find him. She might not even look for him.

That thought worried him.

He rummaged in the bushes. He snagged his skin on a thorn and said, 'Dammit.' He sucked the back of his finger, where blood had broken his skin.

He'd never leave Matty, he thought. It was just something to dream about. She still had shapely legs despite the fact she stuffed them into asexual opaque stockings and wore two-tone brogues and tweed skirts and looked for all the world like the retired headmistress of a certain kind of private academy that no longer existed.

He wished they'd had children. He missed his job at the bank.

He spotted the ball and reached for it.

His eye fell on something else. He failed to recognize it at first – some kind of dark organic matter, he wasn't sure. He peered closer, parting the thorn bush very carefully. An eye looked back at him, red and swollen and human and dead.

His mouth filled with tepid saliva. He dropped his ball and went running towards his wife, calling her name. Matty would know what to do in a situation like this.

Whatever this situation was.

18

In St Vincent Street Perlman drove past the mighty edifice of the church designed by Alexander 'Greek' Thomson. Dark, uninvitingly dour, its size and austerity always had a spooky effect on him. Massive pillars created impenetrable shadows in the early morning light. If God lived in Glasgow, this would be his HQ.

Perlman drove over the motorway, past the high-rise towers of new hotels and office blocks. Old Glasgow, dead or dying, was buried under motorways and skyscrapers. Shame. Something irreplaceable was lost in the ruthless process of renewal. So much of Perlman's Glasgow had already disappeared. Trams, the Treron et Cie department store in Sauchiehall Street, J D Cuthbertson's music shop where they sold pianos upstairs and records in the basement, the Empire Theatre. St Enoch Station was now a big glass shopping structure.

A litany of the extinct.

He remembered a call he wanted to make. He drove one-handed and punched digits on his mobile with the other. Terry Bogan answered.

Perlman said, 'Tilak turns out to be Dev Gupta's cousin. I don't know how helpful this is, but Tilak frequented the Corinthian and sometimes the Tunnel. There's always a possibility he was in one or other of those places the night of his suicide, if that's what you're still calling it.'

'What are you calling it, Lou?' Bogan asked.

'I'm not calling it anything yet,' Perlman answered.

'You're thinking – cherchez la femme, right?'

'Aye, and if you cherchez deep enough, who knows?'

Bogan said, 'I like the Corinthian. I'll check it out first.'

'Scruff like you get past the doorman? That place has gone downhill fast. What's the story on the Nigerian?'

'Newby took that on himself. He's a glory-seeker.' DI Paul Newby was Bogan's immediate superior. Perlman knew him only vaguely. Newby chaired TV discussions about law enforcement matters on BBC Scotland; he was telegenic and enjoyed his modest local fame.

'I hope you find your mysterious lady, Terry.'

'So do I.'

Perlman hung up. He was driving along the extreme western section of Argyle Street, past the Kelvin Hall and the red sandstone extravaganza of the Art Galleries. The wind roared round the car, hammering the chassis.

He parked close to a fish and chip shop called Cremoni's in a side street off Dumbarton Road, a couple of blocks from Partick Underground station. The restaurant had been founded by a family of Italian immigrants, but now it belonged to a man called Perseus McKinnon, the black offspring of a one-night stand between a sailor of Senegalese origin and a red-haired stripper from Leith. Perlman always had the sneaky feeling that a limerick lurked somewhere in McKinnon's history. *There was a young stripper from Leith, Whose method of giving relief* . . . He couldn't come up with the next line.

He knocked on the door and Perseus McKinnon, who habitually wore shades, appeared behind the glass pane.

'I gave at the office,' McKinnon said.

'Fuck off and let me in.'

McKinnon opened the door. Perlman stepped into the empty

118

restaurant. He clapped McKinnon's arm in a gesture of greeting, then made an exaggerated sniffing motion. The air reeked of last night's frying; battered haddock, chips, black pudding, the whole high-cholesterol diet on which generations of Glaswegians, dicing with premature cardiac death, had been reared.

'Air fresheners, Perse. Perfumed sprays. I keep telling you.'

'My customers would stay away in droves. They expect the fragrance of lard.'

Perlman followed McKinnon into an ill-lit back room, which served as an office. There was an array of computer equipment and a number of metal filing cabinets. The fish and chip shop was a front for McKinnon's real interest.

Perseus sat behind his cluttered desk. 'Here's your trivia question for the day, Lou.'

Always with the trivia question for openers, Perlman thought. It was like being asked for a password. 'Who played alto sax on *Monk's Mood*, November 21, 1947?'

'Sahib Shabib. Try stretching me next time.'

'You just got lucky,' McKinnon said. 'Your turn. But don't ask me about any of that cowboy shite or that rock'n'roll you listen to. That's not real music.'

Perlman thought quickly. 'Name the drummer on Sonny Rollins's recording of "Long Ago and Far Away".'

'1991?'

'Right,' Perlman said.

'Easy. That was Steve Jordan . . . You still trying to wrestle Kilroy to the mat?'

'I'm giving it some attention.'

'I haven't been able to turn up a damn thing to suggest he ever handled guns. I've looked, Lou, and I found sweet eff-all. His live-in stormtrooper Frankie Chasm would've been the perfect candidate for the shooting, but Frankie didn't enter Leo's employ until early January, as far as I can make out. Pity. It might have been nice and tidy. Fat Leo driving the car, Chasm doing the shooting.'

'I didn't get the impression of a second man in the car,' Perlman said. He remembered Chasm from past encounters;

a man cursed with a misguided intelligence and a heart like a
Brillo pad. Perlman had once arrested him on a charge of GBH;
the victim of Chasm's violence had been a twenty-two-year-old
man who'd stubbornly refused to yield his place at a video
game in a public house. Frankie had swiped the unfortunate
from ear to ear with the jagged lip of a broken bottle, disfig-
uring him for the rest of his life. Chasm could be smooth, and
convincingly civilized at times, but he wasn't a man you'd keep
company with.

McKinnon stared at him for a moment with a sympathetic
expression. 'A warning, Lou. Just beware a fucking obsession,'
and he gestured around his office, the computer, the disks,
the filing cabinets. 'All this began with a simple interest in
the criminal mind imparted to me by my late mother, who
dragged me off day after day to every bloody cinema in this city
that was showing a gangster flick. Peter Lorre freak? Big-time,
man. She also had a serious thing for John Garfield. She loved
Robert Taylor in *Rogue Cop*. Now take a good long look at me.
I'm devoured by baddies. I dream criminals. I don't have time for
the fish shop. I couldn't tell you the wholesale price of haddock if
you asked me. I don't know the kind of potatoes we use for making chips either. Pentland Dells? Kerr's? Buggered if I know.'

'Point taken,' Perlman said. An obsession. How easy it was to
develop one. Your brain, devoid of will-power, goes over the
same terrain time and again, like one of those remote buggies
they use to explore the surfaces of distant planets. 'Can we get
down to the reason I phoned you? What do you know about
the Gupta family?'

'The Guptas, eh? I've stored a few snippets.'

McKinnon turned his computer on. There was a slight wheeze
and a couple of clicks, then light from the console illuminated
McKinnon's dark glasses and turned his skin more blue than
black. His passion was Glasgow crime, and the people who
committed it. He had a small legion of informants throughout
the city who sold him scraps of info. Who was doing what.
Who was getting out of prison. Who'd been seen loitering in

whose company. Who was planning what job. As some men spent their spare time haunting auction rooms in obscure Border towns in a demented search for first editions of Walter Scott, and others trawled derelict railway stations for precious scraps of old timetables or anything connected to the golden age of the steam engine – a fragment of sleeper, a button from a signalman's sleeve – Perseus McKinnon gathered crime data and fed them into his computer, a task that had been occupying him for more than ten years. It didn't matter the nature or gravity of the crime – a bad cheque, a random act of violence, murder – it was all porridge for McKinnon's unappeasable appetite.

Perlman treasured the man's usefulness. When you needed information, and it wasn't available on the National Criminal Intelligence Service computer, and you didn't have time for the basic slog of acquiring it the old-fashioned way, you came here and you sat in the back room of Cremoni's with Perseus, whose accuracy rate, when it came to arcane information about Glasgow's criminal fraternity, was high.

McKinnon tapped a password into his keyboard. 'Which Gupta intrigues you, Lou?'

'All of them. I'm wondering why the hell Indra was killed. She seems to have been a harmless wee soul, so why does she get shot? If it isn't some loony with a demented reason of his own, maybe it's connected to something inside the family. I don't know. I'm beating the heather, Perse. See what flies. Anything on Dev?'

McKinnon typed, looked at the screen. 'Not much. Possession of cocaine, 1997. The NCIS computer could've told you that.'

'I want something beyond dry kindling,' Perlman said. 'What else have you got?'

'Only this. Dev associated with the late Ben Fogarty.'

'The greyhound trainer?'

McKinnon nodded. 'Dev somehow connected with Fogarty, and they hatched a race-fixing scheme. It wasn't big-time. Three or four dogs doped. Fogarty had his licence cancelled, and Dev walked away free as a sparrow.'

'I remember Fogarty had his throat slashed in Carntyne walking his hounds one night. Bled to death on the pavement. The local cops found the dogs slurping up his blood.' Borscht came to Perlman's mind. 'The crime was never solved.'

'He'd ripped off a lot of people,' McKinnon said. 'He was a star when it came to making unkept promises.'

'Anything else on Dev?'

'That's it, Lou.'

'Try Tilak Gupta.'

'The boy who fell to earth?' McKinnon adjusted his shades and stared at the screen. 'Man about town, ladykiller. The reason he's in my machine is because he was an associate of a certain Morton "Eggs" Benedict, whose name will be familiar to you.'

'Eggs I remember,' Perlman said. 'He had premises in the basement of a Chinese restaurant called – gimme a minute while the connections get made – the Won Ton Palace in Bellahouston where he operated an illicit gambling den. High-stakes roulette, poker, et cetera. Unfortunately, Eggs forgot to apply for a gaming licence.'

'Right,' McKinnon said. 'Busted three years ago. He got out of jail and vanished. South Africa is the general assumption.'

'Eggs ran, so to speak,' Perlman said. 'So Tilak and Dev were both connected with gamblers and gambling. You think that means anything? Was Tilak still involved in that racket?'

'I don't have any more information,' McKinnon said.

'Pity. If you hear, let me know.'

'Moving up the Gupta family tree, we now come to the patriarch.'

'Barry I met already.'

'Sharp as a new razor. Came to Glasgow from Calcutta in the early 1960s and set up a dry-cleaning business in Dennistoun. He moved up in the world with considerable velocity. Money-lending was his first rung on the ladder. His clientele came from the dispossessed, those poor fuckers banks toss out into the street with a snort of derision.'

As McKinnon scrolled screens, Perlman gazed through the half-open office door and across the dining area. He could see traffic pass along Dumbarton Road. The wind puffed hard. It shuddered the awning of a flower shop across the street. Several bunches of daffs rolled down the pavement, pursued by an anxious florist whose hat blew off.

McKinnon beat the surface of his desk vigorously with the palms of his hands. A jazzer at heart, a drummer *manqué*. 'Okay. Here we are, Lou. The patriarch makes a killing money-lending. His enforcement methods for delinquents seem to have been discreet. He's got a growing family and he's ambitious, so he uproots and moves to desirable Pollokshields. Big house.'

'I've been there.'

'And young Dev gets sent to Fettes College, no less. Expelled a year later for selling porno tapes to classmates. The daughter, well, we know her sad destiny. Meanwhile, Barry is financing schemes all over the place. Apartment blocks. Private housing estates in all four corners of our dear green city. He owns or co-owns a couple of Indian restaurants on the upscale side of the tandoori trade. He's rolling.'

'And all you've got on him is the illegal money-lending stuff? Nothing else?'

McKinnon pushed himself back from the desk. His chair had tiny wheels that squeaked. 'One other thing. Gupta Senior has a majority stake in a trucking company.'

'And?'

'The word is contraband cargo.' McKinnon's shades had slipped, and he pushed them back up his nose.

'What kind?'

'My source didn't know.'

'Can your source find out?'

'These characters come and go. You know how it is. If I don't buy their information, their next port of call is the blood bank to flog a litre of their own claret.'

'You know the name of the freight company?'

'Bargeddie Haulage.'

Perlman said nothing for a time. Crossword puzzles. What could link Indra Gupta, mild-mannered kindergarten teacher, to the dubious activities of her father, brother, or even her cousin? And how had Tilak Gupta really died? And who was the chickadee inside whom he'd blasted off his last fireworks?

'Thanks for your help, Perse.'

'If anything new turns up, I'll be in touch.'

Perlman walked into the restaurant. McKinnon followed him. Outside, the wind was awesome, whacking the plate-glass window as if it meant to break through. Something flapped under the restaurant door.

Perseus McKinnon bent to pick it up; a leaflet. He barely glanced at it. 'Second one this week.'

'What is it?' Perlman asked.

'You haven't seen one of these already?'

Perlman shook his head, studied the leaflet. He rubbed its surface between index finger and thumb. Good quality yellow paper, big bold black font:

WHITE RAGE

Do you realize how many immigrant families and so-called 'asylum seekers' are sponging off social security?

Do you know why there is such a long wait for hospital beds in this country and our people are dying?

Do you know why schools are overcrowded and our kids exposed to diseases?

Do you know where our kids are getting their drugs?

BLACKS, INDIANS, PAKISTANIS, ARABS, ILLEGAL IMMIGRANTS, ASYLUM SEEKERS ARE RUINING OUR COUNTRY!!! IT'S TIME FOR BLOOD & ACTION . . .

WHITE RAGE IS COMMITTED

'White Rage. New to me,' Perlman said. 'Sounds like a heavy metal band.'

McKinnon dismissed White Rage with a gesture of his hand. 'Every now and then you get these total arseholes who crank themselves up about blacks or Pakis, so they print a few leaflets. If they're really tanked up, they'll burn some old warehouse down. Then they get bored and vanish again. You know the score.'

Perlman folded the leaflet, tucked it inside his pocket. He couldn't dismiss racist tracts and movements as lightly as Perseus McKinnon. They invariably disturbed him.

'They don't mention Jews,' McKinnon said.

'Give them time.'

Perlman opened the door. The wind gusted. It was magnificent and fierce. Facing into it, he couldn't catch his breath. It was a day for chimneypots to be blown off roofs, slates skirled across the sky, satellite dishes frisbeeing through the air.

'Take care,' McKinnon said.

'You too.' Lou walked into the blast, which hauled at his coat and threatened to rip his hair from his skull. Jesus Christ. He staggered to where he'd parked his car.

He yanked the door open and got in. White Rage, he thought. He wanted to imagine a group of the demented and the bitter cranking out messages of hatred on mimeograph machines in abandoned rodent-infested slum shops. But he knew that this perception of greasy-haired loners with a deranged mission, marginal Glasgow figures churning out smudged sheets on a dilapidated machine, was outmoded. The yellow paper wasn't cheap tissue, but a high-quality bond. The printing had been done by a laser device because no ink rubbed off when you touched the letters. Spacing and alignment were immaculate, the fonts varied and well defined, even artful.

White Rage obviously had access to some funds, enough at least to buy computer equipment, and decent paper, and a good printer. Funds meant contributions, membership dues, supporters of racist dementia. Friends of White Rage. He wondered how many, and where and when they met? Were they strong and crazy enough to carry out threats? *It's time for blood and action* . . .

Blood. He'd had enough blood.

He took his mobile from his pocket and dialled Force HQ and asked for Constable Dennis Murdoch. Young Murdoch came on the line, his voice filled with a breezy enthusiasm.

'Do me a favour,' Perlman said.

'Will do, Sergeant.'

'Check on a company called Bargeddie Haulage.'

'Anything specific in mind?'

'Nothing in particular. Run the company through the computer. Also, take a trip out to their depot, which I assume is in the wilds of Bargeddie. Have a quiet wee look round. Can you be inconspicuous, Dennis?'

'I can try.'

'It helps if you leave your uniform behind.'

Perlman hung up. He drove towards the city centre through a storm of windblown matter, much of it paper; it was as if layers of skin were peeling off the city in flakes.

19

She waited in the doorway of the Ramshorn Church in Ingram Street. The old church, now a theatre, belonged to Strathclyde University. Students carrying big musical instruments jostled her as they entered the building. She stuffed her hands into the pockets of her jeans and wondered what her life would have been like if she hadn't dropped out of university. Speculation, pointless. All those dreary lectures she'd attended with naive enthusiasm in the beginning; what did she remember of them? Practically nothing. You learned on the streets all you needed to know.

Pegg came along the pavement in her direction. The wind flapped his coat so that it trailed behind him like a cape. He walked with purposeful little steps. She moved forward to meet him, and they turned the corner into Albion Street to get out of the blast. They passed the glossy black building that had once been the offices of the *Evening Times*.

Pegg said he was hungry. She knew a cheap quiet café in Wilson Street. They picked up cheese and tomato rolls and coffee at the counter, and carried them to a table in the corner. She observed Pegg's clenched little face for a time. His black eyebrows made him fierce. The fawn eyepatch that covered the left socket seemed to conceal an even deeper intensity about him. How he'd lost the eye was unclear. She'd heard stories – an explosive had gone off unexpectedly, a firearm mishap. She didn't know the truth, and Pegg, who reinvented his history on a constant basis, wasn't about to tell her. He hinted he'd been a member of the old British National Party, and then later the National Front, that he'd lived in America for some years and joined the American Nazi Party. Too dull, he'd said once, of Lincoln Rockwell's organization; drenched in mediocrity. Americans trivialized every political instinct. American politics were as interesting as sugar-free muesli.

He finished his roll and picked at crumbs on his plate. 'So tell me about your flawed recruit.'

'He did what I asked.'

'But you said on the phone he's a liability.'

'I didn't take his boozing into account.'

'Serious oversight.'

She sipped her coffee. 'We all make them.'

'And we all regret them. You know how fucking careful we have to be. We're walking on eggshells.'

'I don't need you to tell me that.' She realized that although she called him Pegg, she had no idea what his real name was. Same with Swank. Same with the man called Oyster she sometimes met in Kennyhill Square who gave her money. They were all strangers, shadows. They lived furtive lives, like her own – except maybe for Oyster. He was different. He didn't have the haggard look of the fugitive, that projection of dread and the signs of an unhealthy life, dry lips, dandruff, discoloured teeth: he suggested quiet prosperity and a certain toughness. She didn't have him sussed out yet, and maybe she never would. She thought about him sexually quite often, attracted by his projection of mystery.

Pegg said, 'Infantry is always expendable. Christ, we're *all* expendable. You. Me. Swank. Anybody on the inside.'

'I can get one last gig out of him,' she said.

'Like what?'

'Trust me.'

'In other words, don't ask.'

She watched a recently arrived diner munch into his mutton pie, and she remembered how quickly Beezer had become drunk in the pub in Maryhill Road late last night, how he'd declined into talking brain-fried nonsense about his French parents, buried treasure, bullshite, his red-hot disgust at the way Great Britain had become diminished, how it was Not-so-fucking-Great Britain, a country destroyed by fucking immigrant scum – his voice rising all the time until it reached the level of a roar, his face growing as purple as a bruise, people in the bar turning to stare. Then he'd climbed onto a table like a soapbox orator. In full-rant mode he'd started in on a scheme to create camps, bloody *concentration camps*, hundreds of them.

Somebody called him a Nazi cunt and smacked him on the skull with a beer bottle, and then he'd been dragged out into the street and a couple of hard characters had laughingly kicked him as he lay on the pavement, still speechifying. She'd slipped away then. She didn't want to be seen in his company.

'You need help to deal with him?' Pegg asked.

'I can do this on my own.'

He rose. 'If you say so.'

She watched him step out into the street. He didn't look back. He didn't wave. There were no little social courtesies in Pegg's life. He drifted out of sight, an inconspicuous figure in a raincoat, the beige eyepatch his only distinction. You'd never imagine him capable of stabbing a man in a public street. If he'd done it. Maybe Swank had been the killer. It was also possible they'd acted together. She had no idea why they'd chosen Ochoba as a target. Colour was enough. No reasons beyond pigmentation were ever necessary. And Helen Mboto. Maybe Pegg had seen Helen and Ochoba together in a café and the sight of two black people being openly affectionate had revolted him and he'd decided something had to be done about it. Maybe he and Swank wanted the effect of a double slaying. Big press.

They'd plotted it together. They'd learned that Helen would be waiting in the Tinderbox, and so they'd asked her to deal with the woman. They'd followed Ochoba into Ashton Lane and murdered him even as Helen Mboto, anxiously clock-watching in the coffee shop, was about to be led to her own execution.

Something like that.

She watched the street. A woman the colour of milky coffee went past; a child of mixed race clutched her hand. The child wore a hood against the strong wind. The woman bent down to pick the child up; she tucked the kid inside her coat. It was touching in its way, a mother protecting her daughter from the elements.

Motherhood. A universal. Black, white, yellow, it didn't matter.

Except I never felt that need to reproduce, she thought.

What was the point of bringing a kid into this overpopulated shithole of a world? this place of sorrow and strife and famine? She felt a slight edge of loneliness, which she pushed aside: unworthy.

Helen Mboto's face flashed across her brain. She saw the woman's pink palm rise to fend off the first fierce hammer blow.

Detach yourself.

She got up from the table and went outside. The city huffed and creaked all around her. Wind-ruffled pigeons huddled in front of the Cenotaph outside the City Chambers. She walked across George Square to Queen Street Station, where she'd call Beezer from a public phone.

20

Perlman entered Force HQ and passed the reception desk where Jackie Wren was fidgeting with his walrus moustache; a furry upper lip, Perlman thought, was a silly vanity, like having a miniature stole attached to your face.

'Windy enough out there for you?' Wren asked.

'Blows the cobwebs away,' Perlman said. He'd been short with Wren the day before, he remembered. He smiled in a conciliatory manner. 'I'm sorry I snapped at you the other day, Jackie.'

'With all the tensions in this place, Lou, it's no surprise. Apology accepted. By the way, DI Scullion's been trying to contact you. You're to report to him right away. I get the impression he's not a happy chappy.'

Perlman climbed the stairs. If Scullion wanted him so badly, why hadn't he called? He stuck a hand in his coat pocket and took out the phone and looked at its small dead screen. Shite. He'd switched it off after he'd called Murdoch. He was technologically challenged, that was the crux of it. He belonged in an age where PCs and bytes and phone text and the whole intergalactic freeway of electronic data hadn't been invented.

He was a neanderthal. Granted, he'd tried to get the hang of all this technology when he'd signed up for a computer course two years ago, but after three sessions he'd fallen out of the loop and returned to his cave, defeated.

Scullion appeared at the top of the stairs.

'Before you jump all over me, Sandy –'

'Your phone's been off.' Scullion wore a dark suit, a white shirt that had clearly been ironed – by Madeleine's hand, of course – and a rust-coloured tie that almost matched his hair. 'We should find some bloody way to hard-wire you, so that you're always available when you're needed.'

'What's the big commotion anyway?'

Scullion said, 'You'll see. Satisfy my curiosity, first. Where have you been?'

Perlman thought that if a hard-boiled egg could speak it would sound exactly like Sandy Scullion right now. 'I got a message from my anonymous caller. On tape already. I took it to Blum.'

'Caller leave a name?'

Perlman shook his head.

'You recognize the voice?'

'No.'

'Then you've still got nothing.'

'I don't consider a tape nothing, Sandy. Listen to it.'

'I will, Lou, but right now there's this meeting –'

'What meeting?'

'The one you'd know about if you kept your phone on,' Scullion said.

'You don't even want to *hear* the tape, Sandy?'

'Later, I'll sit down, I'll play it. Not now.'

Both men moved along a corridor. Perlman was disappointed and a little angry. He'd expected Scullion's understanding, the way he'd always expected it in the past. 'Tell me, Sandy. Did you roll out of bed on the wrong side, or did an alien pod take you over in your sleep?'

Scullion turned to look at Perlman. 'I'm just a little pissed off,

Lou. First thing this morning, even as I'm drinking my coffee, I'm practically *third-degreed* by George Latta, who's not my favourite human being to begin with. If I see Latta on the street, I cross to the other side and toll my rosary beads. He tells me a story. You're screwing your late brother's wife.'

'Screwing Miriam? Hold on, Sandy. Just hold on –'

'He further tells me you and Miriam might be accessing funds your brother stowed away illicitly.'

'He's talking utter shite,' Perlman said angrily.

'I *know* he's talking utter shite, Lou. I told him so. I've known you long enough to know you're not crooked. And even if you and Miriam *were* in a romantic relationship, it's personal, it's got nothing to do with me so long as it doesn't interfere with what we do around here –'

'If I was having an affair with Miriam, you'd be able to read it from my face because I'd be beaming like the fucking Bell lighthouse. I can't believe you'd let a toerag like Latta get to you. Why give him the time of day? He's a lying bastard. The only tool in his box is innuendo. I think it's more than George Latta that's getting to you.'

'You don't miss much for an old fart, do you? Twenty minutes after I ease Latta out of my office, who calls me? Chief Superintendent Tay. His majesty. Wants me upstairs on the double. He's had reports, he says. Some senior cops don't like the freedom Perlman gets, he says.'

'Feh. For years they've been saying that.'

'They've been making noises, agreed. But now he thinks it's time you were . . .' Scullion paused, lost for a word.

'Restrained? Downsized? Decommissioned?'

'More *focused*.'

Perlman thought of Tay, a man with a head as square as a concrete block. He rarely encountered the Superintendent, who lived in a place where no ordinary policemen could go. He sat in a grey suit in a grey room located in the upper corridors of the building where all the grey spirits congregated and conspired.

'So twenty minutes after you have a contretemps with Latta, you get a call from Tay? A man with no nose could sniff collusion.'

'Sure. Latta goes running to his pal the Super. The Super carpets me. Tells me to carpet you.'

'And how am I to be more "focused", Sandy?'

'Tay says your logs on your brother's case are vague. You have whole passages of time unaccounted for. Your reports are skimpy and careless.'

'I'm a slow typist.'

'That's not the point, Lou. He thinks you're not making progress. He wants this case solved and closed.'

'How can I close it, Sandy? And how am I to spend more time writing detailed reports? Suddenly I'm a journalist?'

'Lou, he wants to see specific. To the minute. Where you go. What you do. Who you see. He's suddenly got this bee up his arse about Colin.'

'Why now? He never seemed interested before.'

'I don't know why.' Scullion adjusted the knot of his tie. 'Play his game a little more.'

'What game?'

'The procedural game,' Scullion said.

Perlman thought of Latta stepping out of Miriam's building after midnight, the encounter in the street, the misaligned teeth of the man. So Latta casts a shadow over my life, he thought. More than a shadow; aspersions as well. Fuck Latta. Fuck the 'detailed' reports. You reached an age when you couldn't make the changes people demanded of you. You couldn't adapt to a new set of regulations because you only knew how to work the old ones. You were who you were; you'd put years of labour into yourself. Okay, so you weren't the finished article. You weren't a fucking gemstone, all nicely polished. You had flaws and warts and idiosyncratic manners, but that was how you'd turned out. Too bloody bad.

Scullion looked at Perlman with unusual seriousness. 'Do it for me, Lou. You don't know how many times I've gone out on a limb for you. You have no idea how often I've covered for you.'

'I'm grateful.'

'So do what Tay asks.'

'I'll try, Sandy.' Perlman didn't like the uncharacteristic gravity in Scullion's voice.

'Lou, listen, I'm sorry. It's been a shit morning and I'm stressed to hell, and the day's hardly started.'

'Tell me there's more.'

'This meeting will explain all.'

Scullion walked quickly; Perlman, darkly pondering Tay's interest in Colin's murder, lagged a few paces. They stopped outside the door to a conference room. Scullion entered, Perlman followed. The room, overlooking Pitt Street, was furnished with a long table and a set of chairs; Perlman noted water jugs and plastic glasses, notepads, dark blue Strathclyde Police ballpoints, a box of tissues.

DS Mary Gibson sat at the top of the table. She smiled in a restrained manner at him. She wore a peach-coloured scarf of some gauzy material and a pale tan blouse and matching skirt. Immaculate, he thought. Hair exact, lipstick just so. A certain kind of perfumed, permed perfection. When she walked, her feet probably didn't make contact with the ground.

To her right DI Paul Newby, from the Partick Office, sat slouched. He was distinguished in a crumpled way; his silver hair fell against his collar. He had the bearing of an academic who favours the shaggy laid-back look. He blinked at Perlman, as if he'd emerged from a long sleep and was uncertain of his whereabouts.

Sid Linklater, a bespectacled young forensics expert, sat across the table from Newby and drew Gothic crosses on a notepad; Sid's hobby, Perlman remembered, was to make charcoal rubbings of headstones – a cheery wee pastime for a pathologist. Sid had a thing about crosses.

A third man leaned against the wall with his arms folded. Flint-eyed, head shaven smooth as an egg, black three-piece suit: Perlman recognized him at once. Fraser Deacon, Special Branch, sometimes known as the Big Frase. One of the bright stars in the firmament of Special B. One of the smart boys with the well-buffed halo. He was Going All The Way. He was riding an express train to Glory.

He caught Perlman's eye with a hard look. Perlman thought: in that one look our shared history is encapsulated. Deacon sniffed the air and turned his face up towards the ceiling, as if he wanted to pretend that Perlman wasn't in the room.

Mary Gibson asked, 'Your alarm clock let you down, Detective-Sergeant Perlman?'

'I was unfortunately detained,' Perlman said. He noticed leaflets on the table, and he recognized them as the yellow sheets distributed by White Rage. 'My apologies.'

'Just don't make a habit of it,' Mary Gibson said.

Perlman didn't respond. He'd been chided quietly. Mary Gibson scolded with grace and objectivity. He sat down at the opposite end of the table from her, drawing a chair up alongside Scullion.

Mary Gibson said, 'For your benefit, Sergeant, I'll repeat what you've just missed – Ajit Singh died half an hour ago. He never regained consciousness.'

Perlman had been halfway expecting Singh's death – you came to fear the worst in this job – but the confirmation still upset him. Another sorry corpse, this one a potential witness to a killing. Now he was a victim, the other half of a double slaying inside the Sunshine Day School.

But there was more to this meeting than the news of the death of Ajit Singh. Otherwise, why was Newby here? And why Sid Linklater? And why above all was the Big Frase present?

Mary Gibson looked down at her wedding ring in a some-what wistful way, then she glanced at Deacon. 'I'm sure most of you already know Detective-Inspector Deacon from Special Branch.'

Deacon cleared his throat, pressing a fist to his lips. He

had big mauve hands that suggested a circulation problem. He gestured towards the pile of yellow papers on the table. 'You've all seen these things already, I expect. They've been stuck under wipers on cars. Pinned to telephone poles, super-market bulletin boards. In the past two or three days they've been spotted around the city. We've had similar groups in the past. They make a few threats. Sometimes they assault a few people. Do a bit of damage. Maybe a car overturned and burned. You know the kind of thing. Usually these fringe idiots run out of energy before they get into anything really serious.'

Big Frase paused. It was a good theatrical pause, Perlman thought, a kind of rehearsed suspension. The room was very still; all faces were focused on the man. Deacon enjoyed this, you could see. Captive audience in the palm of his hand. Centre of his own ever-expanding universe. He dominated space like an actor.

'Last night a Nigerian called Ochoba was stabbed to death in the West End. You're all aware of this. The crime was seemingly without motive. Ochoba led a normal life, no criminal sheet, no immigration hokery-pokery. Visa status shipshape. He was just a man trying to get a university degree. So why was he stabbed? Casual street violence? Something out of his past? Or just because he was black?'

Deacon walked to the window, where he turned his back on the room. The stage detective preparing his denouement, Perlman thought. When he spoke again, Deacon didn't turn around. Instead he addressed the window, or perhaps Pitt Street below, maybe even the city beyond, delivering a speech that was being transmitted, by telepathic means, to all citizens of Glasgow: *there is an evil among us.*

'A young woman's body was found this morning on Knights-wood Golf Course. She'd been murdered. Like Mr Ochoba, also a student. And, like Ochoba, also black. She was from Zambia. Her name was Helen Mboto. I'll ask Sid Linklater to fill you in on the physical details. Sid?'

137

Linklater resembled an eager schoolboy, the one who's always reluctant to leave the chemistry lab. Let me stay, sir, let me mix chemicals together and play with the Bunsen burners, oh please sir. My ambition is to be a mad scientist. 'Emmm. The victim had been beaten to death with really unusual brutality . . . My primary examination leads me, ah, to believe she was battered to death by a hammer or some similar object. Forced, I'd go with a common everyday hammer. Her cheekbones were broken. Jawbone. Skull. The ferocity of the blows to her jaw had driven her teeth through her tongue. She'd been battered thirty-five to forty times in the ribcage. Her fingers had been broken, her left thighbone shattered . . .' He shook his head, took off his glasses. Without the specs, his face looked truly youthful; bookish and innocent, the swot. 'My guess is that the blow to the skull was the killing one. Savage business altogether. You don't usually see . . .' He didn't finish his sentence.

Perlman listened to the wind on the pane. It was finally dying now, drained of energy. He thought of a hammer rising and falling, forty times, fifty, more. He thought of a black girl lying on Knightswood Golf Course, and a black man stabbed in Ashton Lane. His mind drifted to Indra Gupta, and Ajit Singh gunned down as he stepped out of his classroom. And then he wondered about Tilak Gupta: jumped or pushed?

The shades of the dead; black and brown, night and sand.

Was this the reason for the meeting? Connections between the killings? Perlman knew where Deacon was going, and it was related to the yellow papers on the table.

Frase Deacon said, 'Sid has omitted one detail. He hasn't mentioned the scars.'

'I left it to you, Inspector,' Linklater said.

'Why? Finish your story.'

'There's, ah, not much more . . . Somebody had carved two letters of the alphabet on Helen Mboto's right breast. Not a very good job, I have to say. Legible, though. W and R.'

'White Rage,' Deacon said, and turned quickly to Paul Newby, who sat upright for the first time. 'Tell us about Mr Ochoba, Paul.'

Newby ran a hand through his hair. A few flecks of dandruff fluttered to the shoulder of his jacket. 'Here's what my people have pieced together since last night. Ochoba was on his way to an assignation with Helen Mboto. According to his flatmate, one Fernando Gostabana, Ochoba was beginning to entertain 'serious' feelings for Helen. Ochoba never made the date, of course. But Helen Mboto was seen leaving a café called the Tinderbox at approximately ten p.m. in the company of a young white woman described variously as 'attractive', 'sexy', or if you like the more colloquial description, a 'smashing wee bit of crumpet' . . . Two dead black people, and one firm connection between them – namely, a relationship. Admittedly, we don't have any evidence that Ochoba was murdered by this White Rage outfit, but I think we can surmise, with a degree of certainty, that the killer or killers of Helen Mboto were connected with his death.'

'How?' Perlman asked.

Newby puffed his cheeks, then expelled a little blast of air. 'If we know the killer of Helen Mboto was a member of White Rage, does it make any sense to ascribe the murder of Ochoba – Helen's *boyfriend* – to another party? If White Rage killed Helen Mboto, it seems perfectly sound to assume that the murder of Ochoba was committed by the same party. Is it not one hell of a bloody coincidence otherwise – two separate and unconnected killers whose victims were friends?'

Perlman felt his stubborn streak work in the same involuntary way some people crack their knuckles. 'They left their calling card on Helen Mboto. But not on Ochoba.'

Deacon intervened. It was his show, after all, and he was from Special Branch, and he needed to stamp his authority on this meeting. He acted like a man who knew there was an empty seat just waiting for him in the corridors of true power. 'Obviously they didn't have time to leave their mark on Ochoba, Perlman. They had plenty of time for Miss Mboto,

139

though. All the time in the bloody world.' He paused, gestured at the yellow sheets. 'The inescapable fact is we've had four murders of non-Caucasians in Glasgow in the last twenty-four hours. So we have to be alert to the possibility that White Rage *could* be involved in all of them.'

Perlman was silent. Death and complexity. Murder had its own inverted logic. He saw the hammer rise and fall and fall and rise and he heard metal rap on bone and bone breaking. He imagined wind and rain blowing against the black girl's body on the golf course. He was suddenly shot through with sadness: once upon a time you took murder in your long stride, Lou. But time buffs the protective veneer. Death was a younger man's business. He thought about Murdoch, whom he'd dispatched to Bargeddie. Indra Gupta, and Dev, and Barry Gupta, these faces suddenly formed a crowd in his head.

Mary Gibson asked, 'This girl in the café who left with Helen Mboto – do we know anything about her?'

'We have a computer-generated rendering,' Deacon said, 'based on descriptions made by the cappuccino brigade who were in the Matchbox last night.'

'The Tinderbox, actually,' Linklater said.

'Whatever,' Deacon said, clearly annoyed that anyone had the temerity to correct him. 'Let's see the picture, Paul.'

Newby opened a briefcase that had been jammed between his feet, and removed a sheet of paper. He set it down on the table, placing it on top of the yellow leaflets. Perlman's view was upside down. Faces were always bizarre from this perspective, like creatures in the kind of dreams you had when half-digested vindaloo was rocketing through your system. He walked round the table to get a better look. Computerized sketches usually lacked vitality, reminiscent of faces in the morgue. He found himself gazing at a young woman, eyes large and dark, lips full, mouth downslanted in what might have been a slight petulance.

He imagined that in real life she'd be pretty.

140

But what else could you tell from this image that was based on the varied recollections of different people who'd seen her from assorted angles in a Glasgow coffee shop? Intelligent, murderous, innocent, sweet – what could you deduce?

Sometimes, with a photograph, you could imagine the subject's inner self, you could divine his or her state of mind up to a point. But this lifeless rendering granted you no such access. The girl could be one of thousands in the city, walking along a street, riding the Underground, climbing into a taxi.

Mary Gibson said, 'And this is all we have?'

Deacon said, 'All we have on the girl, yes.'

'Nobody saw where she and Helen Mboto went when they left the café?'

'Nobody's come forward so far,' Deacon said. 'We may not know anything about this young woman . . . but we do know something about White Rage.'

'I'm listening,' Mary Gibson said.

Deacon walked round the table. He paused directly behind Sandy Scullion. 'Special Branch has been aware of White Rage for the past few weeks. Certain information has been gathered . . . I'm not at liberty to say how. It's scant and it's not totally reliable, but we're working on it twenty-four hours out of every twenty-four.'

Perlman thought about how Special Branch operated in the crevices of the city, in those twilit places where terrorists and/or subversive groups gathered with malicious intent. Mad bomb-makers, disaffected citizens with burning grudges against a System that had foisted injustice on them. Anyone who was a menace to public order came under SB's scrutiny, and SB were furtive bastards.

Deacon said, 'The members of WR are probably hard-core neo-Nazis, fall-outs from organizations that have already gone out of existence. Membership is probably constructed on the cell principle. Nobody knows anyone outside his own cell, which may consist of only two, three or four people. Messages between cells are always conveyed anonymously. *Noms de guerre* are always used. These people keep moving. They don't linger.'

'And do we know the real identities of any of these people?' Mary Gibson asked.

Deacon looked deflated. He shook his head, then recovered his buoyancy. 'Not yet. But I think we're getting close.'

'How close is close?' Perlman asked.

'I can't tell you specifically. I can't say we'll catch them tomorrow or next week or next month. It doesn't work that way.'

'How does it work then?' Perlman asked.

'I can't reveal the inner mechanism of an ongoing operation, Perlman.'

'Why's that?'

'Why's that? Because I can't endanger the lives of people engaged in secretive work.'

'What do you think Helen Mboto would say if she heard that? Or Ochoba? What would they say if they knew their lives just might have been spared if SB had shared some of its information with us regular-type policemen, us low-ranking schmucks?' Perlman caught Scullion's eye and read the look as clearly as a banner headline: *Don't push it, Lou*. Pish off, Sandy, I'm playing my own game, he thought. 'If White Rage is out there in a murderous frame of mind, how are we supposed to stop them from killing again if you hotshots at Special Branch don't provide us with what you've dug up?'

Mary Gibson interrupted. 'I take your point, Detective-Sergeant, even if I find your approach disrespectful. But you know as well as I do that certain types of operation are fragile and have to be kept under very tight wraps.'

Perlman clasped his hands together and cracked his knuckles. *Stop. Fall silent*. He knew he should, but instead he raised another question. 'Why weren't we informed that SB knew about White Rage weeks ago?'

'*Lou*,' Mary Gibson said.

Perlman thought: quit before they toss you out of the room – but he was rolling along, enjoying Deacon's expression of disapproval. 'Now you're telling us that the murders of Indra Gupta and Ajit Singh might have been the work of this group. Right? So what I'm saying is it would be bloody helpful to have a gander at some of SB's info. Instead, we only hear what Inspector Deacon wants us to hear. I don't call that useful. Also, how is SB making inroads into this group exactly? Undercover cops, paid informants? I feel like I'm working blind. Somebody pass me a white stick.'

Mary Gibson sighed and said, 'Sergeant, I'm quite sure there's no deliberate obstruction here. Drop the matter now. Please.'

Perlman pushed his chair back from the table. 'Certainly,' he said. He heard his stomach rumble, acid churning. 'It's dropped.'

There was a silence in the room. Perlman thought of the stresses that boiled under the roof of Force HQ, the games, the one-upmanship, the sniping and the begrudgery; people built their own kingdoms and protected them any way they could, with threats, malicious rumour, brute power. It's time to get the fuck out, he thought. Take the high road to Somewhere Else. A clean place. By yon bonnie banks, yon bonnie braes. I kid myself. I stay until they carry me out. It's in my system.

Deacon addressed Mary Gibson. 'When I have more knowledge, you'll be notified. It's not in Special Branch's interest to sit on anything that might be useful to police operations – despite what our outspoken Sergeant here might think.'

Mary Gibson stood up and looked at Sandy Scullion. 'Make sure the picture goes into circulation right away, Sandy.' Then she faced Deacon. 'I'll expect daily updates, Frase. I don't want to wait until we're awash in blood.'

'Nobody does,' Deacon said.

People began to file from the room. Mary Gibson asked Lou to stay behind a moment. He'd been waiting for that. The bad pupil.

The rotten apple. He lingered until he was alone with her. She told him to sit, which he did. He watched lead-coloured clouds fly across the sky above Pitt Street.

'You're like a bear,' she said.

'I've got two dead people on my mind, and that flyboy from Special Branch flapping like a Cold War operative. Now I've got to start thinking about the notion, which may or may not be remote, that my two victims were killed by this scum, this White Rage.' He wondered about the possessiveness he experienced towards the kindergarten dead. *My two victims*. Was that what he felt – the dead belonged to him? He had some kind of right of ownership? 'Shoot me for expecting some cooperation,' he added.

'I'd love to shoot you for your bad manners, frankly,' she said. 'I know there's bad blood between you and Deacon.'

'Some people just rub each other the wrong way.'

'It's more than that, Lou. And you know it. You had a falling-out.'

'It was more than a mere falling-out, Superintendent.'

'You worked a case with him involving drugs.'

'Right. Before he became the blue-eyed of Special Branch. We knew a shipment of heroin was coming into the city. We knew where, we knew when, and we knew the principals involved. Piece of cake. But Frase gets it into his head that if he somehow infiltrates the smugglers, we can grab all the local boys and then go back down the trail to the point of origin, and nab the guys at source as well. Which, in this instance, happens to be Morocco, where Frase has absolutely no jurisdiction. Does that bother him? The world's his playground. He can strut where he likes. He infiltrates the Glasgow locals – but when he flies out to Morocco to bag the biggies, he's rumbled. They're expecting him. He's been sniffed out. It's all downhill then. The shipment never leaves Morocco, the big boys scatter and play elsewhere, and the Glasgow muppets are left with nothing. Frase comes back about to explode. He's got this look like a tomato that's been boiling in a greenhouse. Somebody's given him away. There was a leak. It wasn't his fault, of course. Oh no, heaven forbid. It was *mine*. I gabbed in the wrong place. I whispered and somebody overheard and a warning went out to abort the whole smuggling exercise. Frase blamed me. He *still* blames me. He had egg on his face, but I was the one responsible for splattering him with it. I'm an amateur, a clodhopper. Frase, who leads a charmed life, becomes a high-flyer in SB. As for me – well, here I am.'

Mary Gibson asked, 'You ever hear of kiss and make up?'

Perlman dismissed the idea with a slight shudder. 'What's so special about Special Branch anyway? How did they get that name? Did they apply for it? Did they say to the Chief, hey, we're special, so can we be called Special Branch?'

'You have no excuse for being confrontational, Lou. Nor sarcastic.'

'Take into account I also have Tay on my back like a carbuncle. He says he's looking for more action on my brother's case.'

'Still no excuse,' Mary Gibson said.

'And then there's George Latta, all sweetness and light.'

'Latta's piddling into the ocean, Lou. That's what he does for a living. He shouldn't alarm you.'

Perlman slumped, stretched his legs, gazed at Mary Gibson. She had a look of professional sympathy, such as you might see on the face of a trained counsellor; and yet there was more – a sincere softness in the eyes.

'When did you last have a holiday?' she asked.

'I forget.' When indeed? He couldn't recall.

'Take some time off soon. Get out of Glasgow. Or maybe you believe nothing exists beyond the city limits. Are you one of those people, Lou? Leave Glasgow and you fall off the edge of the planet?'

Perlman smiled. 'I was in Largs a few years ago.'

'Largs? Did you get a nosebleed? I'm thinking more of Malaga or Malta.'

'I'll have plenty of time for that when I quit the Force. Can I leave now?'

She nodded. Perlman moved quickly to the door.

'I know it's far too late in the day to tell you not to get devoured by the job.'

'That advice might have been useful thirty years ago.'

She smiled faintly. 'Shackled to the cause of law and order.'

Perlman reached for the door handle. 'I can think of worse causes.'

'That's what I told my husband even as he was packing his suitcases,' she said.

Perlman hesitated. 'You're separated?'

'Last week.'

'I'm sorry, Mary.'

'I wouldn't mind so much except it's such a damn cliché. Husband neglected because of wife's career. Decides to move on. Maybe there's another woman. I don't know. I doubt it.'

Perlman wasn't sure what to say, what comfort to give, nor did he understand why she'd chosen him as the recipient of her bad news. I must have a kind face, he thought. Mary Gibson's husband worked for the Inland Revenue; his name was Maxwell. Or maybe Martin. Perlman had seen him only once, at a Christmas party three or four years ago, and couldn't bring an image of the man to mind.

'He might come back,' he said.

'He might.' She made an uncertain gesture. 'Go do your job, Lou. Just remember to take a few steps back every now and then. You get a better view of the landscape that way.'

'I'll keep it in mind.' Perlman left the room.

Scullion was waiting a few yards down the corridor.

'Whatever she said to you, you deserved it,' he said.

'She chastised me,' Perlman said.

'Bloody right. What did I tell you less than twenty minutes ago? Try to play the game.'

'I tried. I failed.'

'You didn't try very hard, Lou.'

'I'll give it more effort, I promise,' Perlman said. 'Have you re-scheduled that fish pie?'

'I thought you hated the stuff.'

'Fish pie. Humble pie. I'll swallow whatever it takes for a quiet life.'

21

Bobby Descartes' head felt like the inside of a battered galvanized rubbish bin crammed with fishbones, furry pizza chunks, buzzy bluebottles, and an assortment of wee crawling things. His breath was as foul as sulphur. His throat ached and his teeth, his fucking *teeth*, actually *hurt*. How could that be? This was the Big Kangaroo of all hangovers. This was a hangover so huge it spawned screaming baby hangovers of its own. His brain was bleeding and leaking. Physical movement was barely possible, and his thoughts, such as they were, arrived like slabs of black ice on a frozen sluggish river.

He staggered out of the tenement and into the street. Thank fuck Sandrine was still asleep. He wasn't in any mood to face her. Seven hooded dopers smoked crack on the corner. They surveyed him with no interest and then went back to their ritual pipe-passing. He saw seven crows on a telephone line and he wondered about numerical correspondences, and superstitions.

He'd vomited last night on his mother. Why did he remember that particular humiliation? *Your starter for ten, Descartes.*

He saw Annie, the Tezzie addict, on the other side of the street.

She crossed towards him. Skin and bone, all she was. Her eyes were half-shut.

'Hey Bob, Bobbyman,' she said. She wore a short suede skirt and calf-length boots and her greasy fair hair hung down her back. She was barely a teenager and already she was strung out on Temazepam and hoored to score.

'Annie, hello doll,' he said. A vertebra moved in his spine. Click click click. It wouldn't stop. He straightened his back. The click went on, except the rhythm was changed. Maybe the noise was inside his head. I'll never drink again.

'You're bruised,' Annie said. 'There's a big blue mark on the side of your face.'

'Fell on my arse down a flight of stairs.' He'd been in Maryhill at one point late last night. He had a flash of himself rolling around on a pavement outside a pub, and people shouting at him angrily. What had he done to deserve a kicking? Told a few home truths, that was all. Stated the facts. People didn't want to hear.

Annie rubbed herself against him. Her lips were dry, cracked. 'I had a rough night.'

'One day we'll sit down and compare notes,' he said.

'Could you take me to a posh restaurant sometime? Could you do that? As a favour like.'

'You like Chinese?'

'Love Chinese, love it.'

'Right then. We'll go to the Canton Express, Sauchiehall Street. Great place.'

'Tonight?'

'Naw. Some night when I'm free.' Chinese food. Jesus Christ, rice and ribs and sweet-and-sour pork. His stomach rushed to the back of his throat. The afternoon sky was spinning. It hurt to speak. His throat was sandpaper.

'I got a fortune cookie once,' Annie said.

Bobby Descartes patted her shoulder. 'See you soon, pet.' He moved away. Fourteen, one of the walking dead. The streets round here were filled with the damned. Me included. He felt the tenements caving in on him. A collapsed universe. He stopped at the corner of the street and threw up some guff at the foot of a lamp-post. Hot belly broth. He walked unsteadily until he came to a stretch of waste ground.

She was already waiting for him. She wore a black leather jacket and blue jeans tucked inside brown boots. She had her hair drawn back and held by an elastic band. No make-up. She's beautiful and she scares me, he thought. *Fuck, I scare myself.* He was dizzy as he approached her. His gut rumbled.

'You look like shite,' she said.

'I feel like shite.'

'Get in the car.' She pointed to an old Mini parked a few yards away.

The upholstery on the passenger side was shot. Springs and tufts of padding, cracked vinyl. The dashboard had been stripped. No radio. Wires hung loose. The floor was rusty and thin.

He drew a hand across his face. He was going to puke again. He fought it. He tipped his head back in the seat. Don't close your eyes whatever you do. If you close 'em you get dizzy and you chuck your guts. He concentrated.

She said, 'This is simple. You make a delivery.'

'That's it?'

'You think you can do it?'

'I can do anything,' he said. 'Didn't I show you that last night?'

She drove, looked tense, didn't speak.

'I'm not sorry about last night,' he said. 'I was given a job. I did it.'

Still she said nothing.

'Like at the kindergarten,' he said.

She looked directly ahead. Fuck this silent act, he thought. Women did the silence thing when it suited them. What was her problem anyway? He'd done the work last night. He'd done it the way she wanted. He had a memory of the black bitch screaming. He saw the hard metal head of the hammer and heard her jaw crack under the force of the blow. He couldn't stop himself. Couldn't stop. Actually got used to it. Liked it. After the first few blows it was just a piece of fucking meat you were pounding to tenderize. That was it. A slab of cow, a black carcass. Blood everywhere. Blood on walls. Floor. Blood and more blood, rivers flowing out of the black cunt's veins.

'This is just a delivery,' she said. 'Nothing more.'

'Right, right, I got it.' He gazed out of the window. Garscube Cross, St George's Road. A couple of turbaned guys walked along like they owned the place.

Then he saw the spires of the university. Wind blew through a screen of trees and created an impression that the towers were swaying side to side. I don't like this feeling, he thought.

He hung his head from the window.

Fresh air, gimme buckets of it.

She said, 'Not much longer. Five minutes.'

He glanced at her. Fine straight nose except at the end, where it developed a tiny little bulb he longed to kiss. No way. She was untouchable. Even if he risked a kiss, his breath was stupendously *scunnering*, like he had a long-dead weasel in his mouth.

The roaring engine echoed inside his head. A Mini, what year, 1962, '63? He found himself staring at shopfronts. Dead animals hanging in a butcher's window, an inverted rabbit not yet skinned, fish on slabs of slushy ice, so much to eat, so much to choke down.

She parked the car, pulled on the handbrake. 'Here we are.'

'What now?'

She reached under the seat, produced a small padded white envelope. 'You go to that shop,' and she pointed. 'You ask for the owner. You give him the packet. He's expecting it. You come back to the car, I drive you home.'

'Easy as that, eh?'

'Easy as that, Beezer.'

She handed him the envelope. It weighed a few ounces at the most.

'You're up for this?' she asked.

'This is a stroll on the beach.'

He got out of the car and walked to the shop. She watched him. He seemed to drag himself through the dull light of the afternoon. Last night he'd beaten a woman to death: look at him now, hungover, a shambles.

He stopped outside the shop, knocked twice. He entered, and the glass door slapped shut behind him. She drove away instantly.

She thought: Thanks for the memories.

22

Perlman was glad to escape Force HQ. He regretted, if only in a half-hearted fashion, how he'd opened fire in front of Deacon and the others; presumably his behaviour would provide more howitzers for the stone-hearted Tay to hoist. *Perlman lost it at a meeting today. Out of control, Super. Do something about him . . .*

Too much, Perlman thought. Too much weight in the baggage I carry. Heart beginning to soften with time, you can't hide from your own humanity. Once upon a time you exorcized the dead with ease. Now they stalk you like demons. They congregate in the corners of your brain, shrouded and horned.

At 3.10 he entered Bewley's Hotel in Bath Street, where Dennis Murdoch was waiting in the bar. The young constable was dressed in a beige raincoat and dark brown suit and black shoes. Perlman thought: He looks like a policeman. No matter what he wears, he gives out the same aura. It was like a sonic warning: I am a copper emitting noise. It was his height, Perlman thought, and the size of his shoes, and the evangelical look in his eye. Either a big-footed Bible salesman or a policeman – and who was selling Bibles door-to-door in these heathen times?

Perlman ordered coffee, dropped a lump of sugar in, stirred it. 'Tell me about scenic Bargeddie, Dennis.'

'It doesn't have a lot to offer, Sergeant.'

'You josh. No tourist attractions? No beauty spots?'

'It's the back of beyond. There are places out there I've never even *heard* of – Birkenshaw. Langmuir. Crosshill. You wouldn't go to Bargeddie unless you had a specific destination in mind.'

'People tell me Drumpellier Country Park is pleasant.'

'I didn't see any park,' Murdoch said.

'But you saw Bargeddie Haulage.'

'I did. The depot is situated just off Gartcosh Road. One huge metal building and a wire perimeter fence. The site is probably about a couple of acres big. Trucks coming, trucks going. I counted about twenty. What you'd expect to see at any haulage operation, Sergeant.'

'How close did you get?'

'I drove right up to the front gate,' Murdoch said. 'A guy came out, asked me what I wanted. Said I was looking for directions to Edinburgh. He told me I was trespassing on private property and piss off. Helpful bugger.'

'Maybe he was just trying to spare you the genteel horrors of Edinburgh.'

Murdoch sipped his tea. He held the cup clamped in his big hand. 'I didn't hang around. The place has a sort of tense feel to it. And when they say no trespassing you get the sense that there might be a shotgun concealed nearby.'

'Anything else?'

Murdoch produced a little green notebook. 'Only what's in the computer. Public knowledge. Bargeddie Haulage is owned by Zahar Industries, a subsidiary of Ramesh Holdings. The directors of Ramesh are Bharat, Madhur, Indra, Dev and Tilak Gupta. A family firm, clearly. Registered offices Crown Street, Glasgow.'

'Who's Madhur?'

'Bharat's wife,' Murdoch said, consulting his notes.

It occurred to Perlman he'd never seen Mrs Gupta. 'So Bharat

154

stuck family members on the board of his holding company. Nice way of keeping total control. Wife, daughter, son . . . and nephew. I wonder why he went outside the immediate so-called nuclear family to bring the nephew in.'

'Tilak Gupta's official position was Company Secretary.'

Perlman considered another coffee, decided against it. The caffeine jag made him cranky. And he'd been cranky enough today without the help of stimulants. 'Any irregularities?'

'It's a clean company. They own thirty vehicles. They had one offence two years ago, when one of their vehicles had invalid insurance. An oversight in their accounts department, seemingly. That's it.'

'Any idea what they carry?'

'They have a couple of refrigerated vehicles, so foodstuffs would be one.'

Perlman imagined truckloads of frozen peas roaring down motorways. 'What else?'

'I saw some small cardboard packing crates inside the compound stencilled with Indian lettering,' Murdoch said. 'I *assume* it was Indian. Maybe they import spices. Or tea.'

Perlman heard a pert little waitress sing *'the tide is high, I'm moving on'* as she sashayed past the table, balancing a tray. He watched her go. He thought about Miriam. Why hadn't he accepted the offer of the sofa last night? The Puritan Jew.

'It would be useful to get something more specific on the cargo.'

'I'll dig around,' Murdoch said.

'With the utmost care, son.' Perlman looked out at Bath Street. A very light rain fell. Black taxis, buses, a city on the move. Faces in bus windows watching the street, or reading newspapers, or just dreaming whatever kind of dreams the city provoked. They hadn't heard of White Rage yet. It was an oil well waiting to be drilled by the media – and then, *gush*, Glasgow would be awash in geysers of newsprint and fear. He heard headlines roar like runaway trains in his brain. He saw the computer impression of the young woman's face splattered across the tabloids and broadsheets alike. *Do You Know This Girl? Is She A Cold-Blooded Race Hatred Killer?* And all the tumult he'd lived through in the aftermath of Colin's death would come back again as the fife and drum bands of the press assembled and played their bloodcurdling tunes.

Terry Bogan appeared in the doorway. He wore a tweed overcoat and a deerstalker bent slightly out of shape. He looked like a penniless squire reduced to living in a ruined tower, which he shared with some stray cattle. He spotted Perlman, raised a hand, then marched across the floor. There were tiny drops of rain in his whiskers.

'Thought I'd find you here. They tell me this is one of your regular haunts.'

'It's convenient and the coffee's passable,' Perlman said. He introduced Murdoch. 'Dennis here has been on the Force for – what? Three years?'

'Two,' Murdoch said.

Bogan took off his hat and shook rain from it. 'Two years? Enjoying it so far?'

'Absolutely,' Murdoch said.

'Ah, youth, youth,' Bogan said. He stuck his hat back on his head. 'Remember those carefree days, Lou? Remember when it was a joy just to come into work, and you jumped out of bed a little bit quicker?'

'Dennis is enthusiastic, Terry. Don't discourage him.'

Bogan said, 'Far be it from me. Can we talk about Tilak Gupta? A barman at the Corinthian remembers seeing him the night he died.'

'Ah. Alone?'

'He was draped all over some pretty young thing. Glued to her, the barman said. They might have been epoxied together. They danced most of the night. He was practically slipping her a length on the dance floor. The barman's not sure the exact time they left.'

'Had he seen her before?'

'No, but he gave me a description. About five-two, weighed

156

maybe seven stone, slender, black hair to the shoulder. Wore designer blue jeans and a blouse – white, he thinks. Might be beige.'

'I wonder if she looks anything like this,' Perlman said. Worth a shot. Why not? When you were fumbling in the dark you reached for the light switch. If you found it – *illumination*. If you didn't, you kept groping. Besides, there were connections here, albeit thin ones: if the girl was involved in White Rage, then she couldn't be overlooked in the matter of Tilak Gupta's death. She had to be located and interviewed. He took a copy of the portrait from his pocket and handed it to Bogan.

Bogan said, 'Beat you to it, Lou. I got a copy of that earlier. I showed it to my man at the Corinthian.'

'And?'

'He says mibbe aye, mibbe no. He tells me the face hasn't got the mouth right, plus the brow's too narrow. The girl looked happy when she was with Gupta. The face here makes her seem like somebody having a bad period.'

A *farbishener*, Perlman thought. He took the picture back, looked at it. The eyes stared straight through him, as if fixed on a point far beyond his own field of vision. Perhaps she'd been the last person to see Tilak Gupta alive. Perhaps she'd been the one who'd led Helen Mboto out of the Tinderbox. Mibbe aye, mibbe no. A policeman's life; the only gospel truth was that uncertainties abounded.

'We need to find this young tottie, don't we? We need to sit her down –' He was interrupted by the sound of a mobile phone ringing. He reached without thinking into his pocket, but his own phone was dead. He shook it vigorously, as if he might infuse the moribund battery with life.

'You're supposed to keep these things charged,' Bogan said. 'Did nobody tell you that? Did you not read the wee book of instructions?'

'Pish off,' Perlman said, annoyed with himself.

The ringing phone had been Murdoch's; the young constable

was speaking into it. He handed it to Perlman and said, 'It's for you, Sergeant.'

Sandy Scullion's voice was stressed, like that of a man trying to kick a drug habit. 'Get over to Partick,' he said.

'Specifically where?'

'The fish and chip shop. The one your pal owned.'

23

When he was angry Leo Kilroy developed several new chins. He looked like an overfed parakeet ruffled to the point of insanity. His plump face was blood-pressure scarlet. He wore a long black double-breasted jacket with velvet lapels, tailored for him in Genoa. His boots, Blum observed, were Texan-style, hand-carved and decorated with turquoise ornaments.

'Let me say this once and for all,' Kilroy said. 'I don't recognize the voice. I've never heard it before. For all I fucking know, it might have come out of the ether, or through the wooden head of a ventriloquist's dummy. Am I getting through to you, Nat?'

'I'm listening,' Blum said.

Kilroy sat in a pink cane chair in his conservatory and gazed across the garden where the waterfall slid over stones. He was fuming, hugely irritated by the tape Blum had played for him. His heart was going a little too fast. Fucking tape, fucking Perlman, fucking anonymous voice on an answering machine.

'I am up to here, Blumsky. Up to *here*. I feel pressures you would not *begin* to believe. All I ask is sweet sweet peace. Now I'm being hounded and harassed, and I don't have to be a fucking *mindreader* to guess who's behind it.'

'Perlman says there's no trickery, Leo. He received the message on his home phone. He's as puzzled by the ID of the caller as you are.'

'Aye, right, oh I bet he is. Listen, Blum, he's playing a bloody game. And you're falling for it because you Jews, you stick together. You're like members of a club. But keep in mind I didn't come up the Clyde on a water lily, old china. Fat Leo conceals a shark. Remember? A sleakit bastard shark.'

Blum's face reddened. 'I remember, Leo. As for your comment on Jews sticking together, you're off target. Perlman doesn't get special treatment just because we share a heritage that doesn't mean a whole lot to me, frankly.' He tightened his grip on the cassette. The Fat Man was a trial, an ordeal. He longed to ask Kilroy if he remembered his exact whereabouts on the night of December 15 last year, but he choked the question back. Beware Kilroy's wrath. Beware the anti-Semite. Did Porky Pig really believe there was some international Jewish freemasonry, a conspiracy? Or was he just anti-Semitic in the way of most goyim, a reflex thing, like a sneeze caused by a mild allergy?

Kilroy said, 'Don't get so touchy.'

'I wasn't being touchy, Leo.'

'You people are always touchy.' Agitated, Kilroy tapped his knees with his fingertips in the manner of a compulsive sitting at a typewriter. 'All I ask is you use your noodle, Blum. What would I be doing driving down Dalness Street that late at night? I don't even know where Dalness Street is.'

'It's in Egypt, where Perlman makes his residence, Leo.'

'And I'm supposed to know that?' Kilroy asked.

Blum turned his back on the waterfall. Tacky. The whole house was a flamboyant exercise in very bad taste. He surveyed the objects gathered on Kilroy's travels – African spears, leopardskins, sombreros, rhino horns, Stetsons, muskets, Navajo blankets – and thought how mismatched it all was. The collection suggested the work of an indiscriminate jackdaw. The world was Kilroy's to plunder.

'What worries me is the fact the caller makes a reference to unspecified evidence, Leo.'

'Am I talking to myself or are you going deaf? How the fuck can there be any evidence when I wasn't even in the bloody car? Open your ears, sonny. Listen to the client. The client is always right. The lawyer is only a glorified dog-walker. He creeps along behind the client carrying a wee brush and pan and he sweeps up the jobbies the client drops. Don't forget that, Blumsky.'

I went to law school for this, Blum thought. This abuse. The pooper picker-upper. Sod that.

'Give me the tape,' Kilroy said.

Blum handed it over. Kilroy ripped the plastic case open and yanked the tape out and cracked the cassette in his fingers, then he tugged the tape loose, section by looped section, until a long brown coil lay on the floor.

'And don't even tell me Perlman has a copy,' Kilroy said. 'I just wanted the simple satisfaction of tearing the shite out of this one.' He ground the plastic with the heel of his boot. 'Fucking tape, fucking fairytale *shite*. It's not even clever, as ploys go. Who does Perlman think he's fooling, eh?'

Sweat oozed from his face as freely as juice squeezed from a blood orange pulverized in a vice. He experienced a light-headed sensation that passed in a matter of seconds. Anger, sudden exertion: how unfit he was, corrupted by his own lifestyle. He spread his legs and felt a nagging pain clutch the centre of his chest. His bloody ulcer. Stress. Absolute undiluted stress.

'You all right?' Blum asked.

'Don't I look all right?'

'You look in pain.'

'Imagine I kicked the bucket sitting right here in my conservatory. Let's say the old ticker exploded and I expired. Would you miss me, Blumsky? Or would you miss your bloated retainer more?'

'That's an insult, Leo,' Blum said.

Kilroy smiled and rose slowly. 'I pay you enough. That gives

161

me a right to insult you. I fucking *own* you. You're a chattel. What are you, Blum?'

'I'm a lawyer.'

'You're a *what*?'

'A lawyer, Leo –'

'I'm not hearing you, Blum. Say it. Say chattel.'

'All right. I'm a chattel.'

'Oh, sonny, you disappoint me. Why don't you tell me to go fuck myself?'

Blum said nothing. His stack was about to blow. Consider the consequences of telling Kilroy to eat shite. He was calculating how the lack of the Fat Man's retainer would affect his lifestyle. He'd have to make changes. Then he realized that if Kilroy took his business elsewhere, so would all the other scum the Fat Man had brought him as clients, and then what? Where would he put up his brass plate next? He wouldn't have the plummy offices in Waterloo Street. He wouldn't be able to keep up payments on the penthouse. He'd have to downsize somewhat.

Downsize? Who was he kidding? He'd be lucky if he had enough work to afford a semi in Pennilee and share an office with an ambulance-chaser in a rundown Victorian ruin in a less than salubrious part of town south of the river. He'd be taking on charity cases and wearing off-the-peg suits – hell's bells.

Frankie Chasm appeared in the doorway that led from the conservatory to the house. He moved, grim and silent, bearing a tray of drinks. Two glasses, one that held G&T for Kilroy, the other sparkling water for Blum. Blum picked up his drink, caught Chasm's eye a moment, then looked away. There was a provocative aggression in Chasm's stare, like that of a man seeking any old pretext for punching your face in. He always made Blum very uneasy. What did he do for Kilroy anyway? What role did he play? Blum wasn't falling for this butler pantomime.

Kilroy picked up his drink, sipped, then looked strangely poignant and calm, as if the brief scene with Blum eased him. 'Once upon a time, I was the proprietor of this bloody city. I owned it. Nothing touched me. I had absolute *immunity*. Cops? They didn't give me any trouble. They were my friends, some of them my best pals. As for villains, they knew better than to give me any grief. And now . . . ffff. The roof falls in. The world changes.'

'Change isn't always bad.'

'Oh aye it is, Blum. It can be downright shite. Know what's the worst thing? There's bugger-all you can really do to stand in its way.'

'I suppose,' Blum said, watching Chasm leave the room.

Kilroy turned his glass round and round in his hand as he stared out at his garden. 'But a man can try, Blumsky. If he has the balls.' He winked, one blubbery lid rising and falling, then he hummed 'I Was Born Under a Wandering Star' before he was interrupted by the reappearance of Chasm.

Chasm held a white envelope. 'This just came, Leo.'

'What is it?'

'Special Delivery. I don't know what it is.'

'Who delivered it?'

'The van was from TransClyde Express Services.'

'Open it carefully,' Kilroy said.

Chasm slowly slit the envelope with a penknife. Inside, he found a single sheet of blue-lined paper wrapped round a photograph. He handed these items to Kilroy.

Kilroy read the note. He looked at the photograph.

He said, 'Fucksake.'

'What is it?' Chasm asked.

Kilroy's ulcer kicked like a mule's hoof. He was thinking: Perlman, you fucker, you kike fucker.

'The bastard has gone a wee bit too far this time,' the Fat Man said.

24

The windows and doors of Cremoni's had been blown out, the interior reduced to broken fragments of furniture and crockery, the ceiling brought down in piles of rubble: a bomb might have fallen from the sky. Perse McKinnon's office in the rear had been ground zero, desk flattened beyond recognition, computer equipment squashed, filing cabinets picked up and hurled in disarray around the room.

Perlman smelled the chemical stench of scalded plastic. He moved carefully around the edge of the office, skirting the engrossed figures of the forensics people, hearing glass and unidentifiable items crunch under his feet. He saw Tizer Dunlop take photographs of the wreckage.

The scene distressed him. All McKinnon's labours, his years of obsession, had come down to this: records ruined, a life terminated. Blood, flecked with powdery plaster, stained the walls.

When he couldn't breathe the air any longer, Perlman walked outside and cleared his throat and spat on the pavement. The street was thick with patrol cars, assorted cops, bystanders – more than two hundred of them, two fifty – gawking from the other side of the crime-scene tape.

He thought how still the day had become. No wind blew. The soft rain had stopped. The city seemed motionless all around him, suspended, as if waiting for a transfusion of life. He stared the length of the street, then turned his face to the sign above the restaurant. Only the C of Cremoni's remained, a blue letter on lemon glass that had somehow escaped the blast.

And he remembered: Perseus McKinnon had been black.

He'd never thought about McKinnon's colour before. He'd been indifferent to the man's pigmentation. McKinnon was a friend, a confidant.

But now he was also black.

Scullion moved along the pavement towards him. Glass crackled underfoot. Scullion knew the role McKinnon had played in Perlman's world. Archivist, collector of facts. He'd been Perlman's connection exclusively. Nobody else in the Force ever asked favours of McKinnon.

Scullion said, 'I'm sorry, Lou.'

'It was a risk he always ran,' Perlman said. 'It never seemed to bother him. He kept all that information, some of it obviously dangerous for him to have . . .' He waved a hand, indicating the wrecked restaurant, and the adjoining tenements, some of whose windows had been shattered in the blast.

'They're trying to ID the other body,' Scullion said.

'Amazing there's enough of anyone left to examine, Sandy.'

Scullion watched Perlman light a cigarette. The hand that held the match trembled a little. He thought Perlman looked haggard.

Perlman said, 'It could've been worse. It might have happened when the restaurant was crammed . . . Anybody got any idea how the explosion happened?'

'Not yet.'

Perlman said, 'Christ, I badly want to believe it was a faulty gas main, something like that. I don't want to think it was anything except an accident. Trouble is, my heart's singing another tune.'

Scullion touched the sleeve of Perlman's coat. 'Can we feed

you tonight, Lou? I'll call Maddy, make sure she's got enough in the house for a guest.'

'I don't have an appetite, Sandy.'

'You need to eat some time.'

'Later maybe.'

It was the response Scullion expected. Perlman never did the right thing when it came to his own needs. When it was time to eat, he didn't. When it was time to sleep, he lay awake. When it rained, he forgot his raincoat and didn't seem to notice he was being soaked. How the hell did he survive? He didn't look out for himself, he lived in that bloody damp house in Egypt –

Scullion stopped this rattle of carping thoughts. It wasn't his business to look after Perlman. And yet he spent a lot of time doing it anyway. Shielding, protecting him. He went too far at times in his behaviour towards Perlman, and he knew it, and he realized some rules got bent along the way. But what was he supposed to do? Leave Lou hanging out to dry? Sometimes Maddy chided him for being over-supportive: *I'm very fond of Lou, but he's a grown man, he can take care of himself, Sandy.* And so he could, up to a point: after that he often vanished into a fog of absent-mindedness or elsewhereness. How did he explain to Maddy that Perlman was more than a colleague? *He's like an older brother I never had.* But that was trite and untrue. He had no fraternal feelings for Perlman. It was something else. How to say it? *Maddy, for all his flaws, he's probably the best friend I have in the world, but he's his own worst enemy sometimes, which is why he needs me . . . And I need him.*

Perlman wandered along the pavement, hands deep in his pockets. There was a hint on the air of burnt cooking oil. He noticed Terry Bogan in conversation with Detective-Inspector Newby some yards away. Their heads were inclined together, like two men sharing a deep secret. Yards behind them – lo and bloody behold – Chief Superintendent Tay stood with his hands in the pockets of his overcoat and a mobile phone attached to his ear. Perlman couldn't remember when he'd last seen Tay at a crime scene. Years, it had to be. He had the bearing of a

166

colonial viceroy surveying a natural disaster, a flood, say, or an earthquake. His face was regally impassive. Mary Gibson stood at the Chief Super's side. She looked unhappy. She'd given up smoking recently for the umpteenth time, but now she had the desperate expression of somebody pining for a nicotine infusion.

Perlman listened to the crackle of messages on car radios, mobile phones ringing; he saw the usual gathering of newshounds arrive in their flashy media vans. He walked to where Scullion stood talking to a teenage boy with hair dyed green and white. This kid had studs attached to his earlobes and lips. A resident Martian, Perlman thought, somebody beamed down to report the stuff of Glaswegian life for the edification of viewers on a distant planet.

Hello, fellow Mars Beings, I bring you today's news from Weegietown.

Scullion said, 'Lou. This is Tommy Flynn.'

Perlman looked at the teenager. 'Do those things hurt?'

The boy said, 'You get used to them.'

'Do you attract lightning?'

'Aye right. And I set off metal detectors in airports as well.'

Perlman glanced at the green-and-white-striped hair. A head like a badger gone wrong. Or a brush in a car wash. Celtic colours. This one was a big fan. 'Who's your all-time favourite player?'

'Larsson,' the kid said. 'He's the best.'

'What about Bobby Murdoch?'

'Who?'

Perlman let the kid's response go unanswered. Football legends of the 1960s were fossils for today's young fans, who were interested only in the current heroes and their haircuts. Bobby Murdoch, half-forgotten forty years after his prime, was a Celtic Park ghost with a Brylcreemed head.

Sandy Scullion said, 'Tommy saw somebody go inside the chip shop, Lou. Just before the blast.'

'Tell me about it, Tommy.'

167

'I already told this man here,' and Flynn indicated Scullion with a quick nod of his head. Barely perceptible. Cool, Perlman thought. *Gallus*, in the patois.

He said, 'Tell me as well, son.'

The boy sighed. 'I live over there. That tenement. Top floor. Good view of the chipper. I was looking out of the window. It was about quarter past three. Can't be sure. Don't have a watch. A guy comes into the street from the direction of Dumbarton Road. He knocks on the chipper door. I know the place's shut, because it closes between three and half-five. The black guy who owns it opens the door. The other guy says something, then steps inside. Door closes. Thirty seconds later, mibbe more, there's this noise like a bomb going off and the chipper explodes. Wham. Glass flying. The doors blown off. All this thick black smoke pouring into the street.'

'Did you get a look at the man who knocked?'

'His face? Naw. He had a hood. You know, one of them hooded jackets?'

'You remember the colour?'

'Green. Definitely. He was wearing tracksuit trousers. Purple and green. Blue and green. One or the other.'

Like the kindergarten killer, Perlman thought. He imagined a Glasgow of hooded assassins. He imagined them sitting in spartan tenement rooms in front of formica tables scattered with digestive biscuit crumbs and pizza crusts, shadowy faces, men who spoke only in monosyllables and who oiled handguns to while the time away between acts of murder. He thought of tracksuit trousers of green and purple and blue and red. Colours spilled and ran in his imagination. He felt strangely dizzy. The sky shifted sideways in his line of vision. The tenements tilted. He placed a hand to his forehead. What was happening inside him? Was this the harbinger of some serious malady or just the giddiness of a blood-sugar dip induced by hunger?

'Can I skedaddle now, Mr Polisman?' the kid asked.

Scullion said, 'Aye. I've got your address if I need you.'

Perlman felt a flap, a flying sensation, in his heart. It passed quickly. I need a check-up. Blood pressure. Liver tests. Cardiac exam. The lot.

'Bobby Murdoch, son,' he said. 'Ask your dad about him.'

'What Dad?' the kid said. He slipped away, moving swiftly between police cars and media vans and the legion of reporters.

'Tracksuit trousers, hooded top,' Scullion said. 'We're thinking the same thing?'

'No doubt about it.'

'We could be way off the mark. You see clothes like that all over the place.'

Perlman caught Tay's eye briefly; a chill Presbyterian eye, like that of a Freemason's symbol, all-seeing, disapproving. Tay made him feel guilty of some nameless sin.

'Here's what puzzles me, Sandy. Say this fucker shoots Indra at the kindergarten, then he flees. So self-preservation is high on his agenda. Then the very next day he comes here and what – blows up a restaurant and self-destructs? Why?'

'An accident,' Scullion suggested.

'What kind?'

'We don't know.'

'And did he come here in the first place to murder McKinnon?'

'Let's assume so.'

'Okay. I'll buy a ticket for this hall of mirrors. He comes to kill Perse. Does he bring his gun? Or does he intend to employ some other means of destruction? An explosive device, say? He plans to hide it in the chipper without McKinnon seeing? Except the timer goes kaput before he can make an exit.'

'It's a possibility.'

Perlman lit a cigarette. Picture Miriam, he thought. Imagine your head between her breasts. Soothed, oh definitely soothed. Who needs nicotine? He longed to phone her. She was an island of calm in this ocean of wreckage. Be my *gueleebte*, Miriam.

'An observant man like McKinnon wouldn't notice somebody carrying an explosive, Sandy?'

'A small device, easily concealed, hidden in a pocket perhaps.'

'Perse had antennae coming out of his skull. He had built-in sensors. He had some really lowlife types coming to see him. He could smell out a liar. The same with anyone menacing. He'd sniff them out. I'm sure of it. So in this one instance his system was down?'

'Maybe he knew the visitor.'

Perlman took off his glasses and rubbed his eyes. He longed to take a walk along the riverfront, which was located minutes away on the other side of the expressway. He needed an environment that didn't reek of molten plastic. Even the Clyde had to be perfume by comparison.

He saw a group of reporters edge towards Mary Gibson. She turned them aside with a gesture that meant 'later'. But they persisted in the manner of their trade. They panted for material. Poor Mary. Abandoned by her spouse, now hounded by the zealous dogs of print and graphics.

Scullion said, 'We'll have some information on the dead man when forensics are through with him. Which may not be very long . . .' He was quiet for a second. 'I haven't had time to tell you this, but the news of Helen Mboto's death has already been broadcast. Radio Clyde was in like a bloody whippet.'

'How much did they get?'

'I think the phrase was "viciously slain",' Scullion said.

'No blow-by-blow mathematics?'

Scullion shook his head. 'Nor any mention of the initials cut into her breast. But it'll come. It always does.'

'We work in a fucking colander,' Perlman said.

Scullion looked at him with renewed concern. 'Lou, I wish you'd go and sit down somewhere, have a sandwich, take the weight off your feet.'

'Who made you my nanny?'

'Seriously. I've seen healthier-looking characters in the terminal ward.'

Perlman said, 'You're a fucking nag, Scullion.'

'Please yourself. I've tried.'

'And I'm thankful.'

Perlman looked out at the crowd beyond the yellow tape. These people had come from their flats and their shops and offices, they'd abandoned whatever it was they'd been doing to look at this tragedy. He wanted to tell them to fuck off back to their lives, if they could still find the way.

He scanned the gathering, thinking that the explosion might have happened when he'd been on the premises earlier. The leaflet stuck under the closed door might have been an explosive. And then – welcome to the big cheerio, Lou. Nighty-night. A plot of land near where Colin lay, in damp Barlanark. And maybe Miriam would come to place a pebble on your grave. And the Aunts would gather, weeping copiously, oh poor Lou.

He thought about Perse McKinnon, and the figure who'd come knocking at his door. One day the guy has a gun. He shoots to kill. The next day he doesn't. Did he leave his gun at home? Why?

I live a life of tough questions, he thought, and precious few answers. He continued to watch the crowd, which was growing steadily. His attention was drawn to a small dark-haired woman who stood on the outer edge of the gathering; he guessed her age in the late twenties. He found himself scanning her without thinking, a cop's habit. Then she moved and turned in the direction of Dumbarton Road.

Wait, he thought.

Wait just one minute.

He felt a faint feathery touch of recognition. He followed her, pushing his way through the thicket of the crowd. He saw her cross Dumbarton Road. She was walking swiftly east in long strides. Her hair bounced against her shoulders.

The computer sketch, he thought. You could find matches for it anywhere you looked, if you wanted them badly enough. He crossed through traffic, hands held aloft as if to suggest he had some divine means of parting the sea of vehicles, a Moses of Partick. Horns blared, drivers shouted at him. *You trying to commit suicide, ya daft shite? Take an overdose of sleepers, bawheid.* He reached the opposite pavement and moved about thirty or forty yards behind the woman. She glanced at something in a greengrocer's window as she moved.

I need to see her face close up, he thought. I need to *evaluate*. He removed the copy of the computer-drawn sketch from his coat pocket and glanced at it. What the fuck could you tell from this shite drawing? A Renoir it wasn't. How was he supposed to play this? Ask her if she minded him comparing her to an image he happened to have in his hand? She'd think at first she'd been accosted by some sad street loony, a sorry schizo kept afloat on an armada of NHS downers.

Suddenly the woman stopped and swung round to face him. 'Something on your mind?' she asked.

'Maybe.'

'You should be ashamed,' she said. 'I'm young enough to be your daughter.'

Haughty, he thought. Commanding green eyes. And good to behold, sweet on the vision. 'You misunderstand,' he said.

She pushed her hair over her ears. 'I think I understand you too well. You're a creep. A DOM.'

'Take a shufty at this.' He held the paper towards her.

She backed away. 'Is this some religious hand-out? Don't tell me you're one of God's infantrymen?'

'Me and God don't have an amicable relationship, dear. Just look.' He flashed the picture in front of her face.

She gazed at it, smiled. 'Who's this hag supposed to be?'

Perlman shrugged. 'No idea.'

'She's a real Cro-Magnon babe. Look at that forehead. Are you doing some baffling kind of market survey or something?'

Perlman took out his ID and showed it to her. 'Just so you know. I'm not a dirty old man, and I'm not conducting a survey.'

'Detective-Sergeant, eh? I'm suitably impressed. You finished with me? Mind if I go now?'

'Can I see some ID?'

'Are you accusing me of something?'

'When did I say that?'

172

'I get it. *You* think I look like this *beast*, right? You're a real master of the sly insult, Sergeant.'

'I'd still like to see some ID.'

She took a wallet from the inside pocket of her jacket. 'I hear we live in a free country. I have a few reservations about that fable. Have a shufty, sturmbahnführer.' She shoved a credit card and a driving licence at him.

'I look like the Gestapo to you?' he said.

'Let's debate civil liberties,' she said.

He examined the licence. Celia Liddell, born 5 January 1978. Address 4 King Edward Road, Glasgow. He knew King Edward Road. It was in Jordanhill, a comfortable suburb a couple of miles west of Partick. He checked the photograph on the licence against her face, glancing with half an eye at the computer impression – then realized with a flush of embarrassment how fucking ridiculously *mistaken* he was, how bushwhacked by the explosion at Cremoni's and the death of McKinnon, how lopsided his connection with the world had become: there was no similarity between this idiot caricature and the photograph, no resemblance *whatsoever* between the computer's ham-fisted rendition of an imaginary creature and the woman who was presently grabbing back her belongings from his hand.

Blood fired to his face. Was he blushing noticeably?

'You'll be all right if I leave now, I take it?' she asked.

'I had to check,' he said quietly.

'You don't need me to phone somebody to collect you?'

Funny girl. She was attractive. She had a self-assured quality, a proud intelligence about her. 'I had to check,' he said again.

'Now you get to say it's a messy job, but some poor bastard has to do it. Right?' She moved away. He watched her step inside a car parked about twenty yards from where he stood.

Celia Liddell, I'm sorry. Wrong woman. Totally wrong. He skipped through traffic back to the other side of the street. He felt out of synch, displaced. He felt – what was the word his mother had used – *dershloguen:* despondent. He was in no hurry to return to the crime scene. He needed time out, a break.

He stepped inside a grotty little pub of the old Glasgow kind, where everything was covered with a patina of dust, and the room hadn't been ventilated in so many years that the amalgamated odours of booze and smoke had created their own biosphere. A couple of leathery punters studied the racing pages of newspapers.

He looked at the menu, ordered a fizzy lemonade and a roast-beef sandwich with chutney. The girl behind the counter, twentyish and wearing gaudy earrings in the shape of parrots, vanished into the kitchen area, then popped back a minute later with his order.

He carried the sandwich and lemonade to a table. He took off the top slice, gazed at the marbled texture of the beef and the thick smear of chutney. His appetite was dying in slow stages. It wasn't food he needed, it was freedom from a world of suspicion and violence, his world.

Escape From Perlman's Planet.

He thought of his encounter with the young woman, and he had a sense of the whole investigation slipping away. It had an amorphous feel he didn't like. If you gathered all the murders under the rubric of White Rage, if you worked on the hypothesis that the dead were victims of race hatred, then maybe you'd be able to impose a design. Just maybe.

Who made the decisions? Who fingered the targets? Were they randomly selected? Was it as arbitrary as sticking the tip of a pin into a phone directory and choosing a victim on that basis?

He shut his eyes and thought: I was desperate to nail her, desperate to nail *somebody*. This is the measure of the place I've come to. So you were wrong. You made mistakes before, you'll make them again. Infallibility is the domain of the self-deluded.

Check. Check and double-check.

He rose, asked the barwoman if he could use the telephone. She told him it was fine. He punched in the number for Pitt Street and asked to be connected to PC Dennis Murdoch. He was informed that Murdoch was out of the building; he left a message for the young cop to run a question through the computer.

The barwoman asked, 'Did you hear about that explosion at Cremoni's?'

Perlman said he'd heard.

'Shocking. I mean, it's only just down the road. Somebody said it was an underground gas pipe just blew. You don't know when your nummer's gonny be called, do you?'

'You can't even guess,' he said.

One of the punters, who wore thick-lensed glasses, didn't look up from his *Daily Record*. 'Christ almighty, Glasgow's become a total pisspot.'

Perlman allowed his thoughts to float back to Miriam. She stood for serenity, the possibility of sanity, God knows what other good things.

'You mind if I use your phone again?' he asked.

'No, as long as it's not Tokyo you're calling,' the barwoman said.

'I don't know a soul in Tokyo, love. It's Rio I'm phoning.'

'Oh I'd love to visit Rio during the carnival,' she said. She did a slight samba sway. 'I can just see it. I'm yours, Miguel. Arriba arriba. Take me away from this humdrum life.'

Perlman smiled at her as he pressed in Miriam's number.

'I'm still waiting for that invitation to the Willow, Lou.' Miriam's voice gave him the notion that a fulfilling emotional life was still possible, and that the world might be a clean shining place after all.

'I wish I could make it today,' he said. 'I can't.'

'I read the papers, Lou. I listen to the radio. I know what you're up against. We'll do it some other afternoon.'

Be bold. Seize the day, Lou. An hour for yourself. Ninety minutes. It was so damn little to ask. 'I was thinking . . . how about tonight? A drink, maybe something to eat.'

'You're sure you've got the time, Sergeant?'

'I'll make the bloody time. I need to. I'm running on empty. How about La Fiorentina? Eight. Eight thirty.'

175

'Suits me. It's years since I've been there.'

He said goodbye and hung up. He took a single bite out of his sandwich before stepping out into the street and walking back in the direction of Cremoni's.

25

She abandoned the rotted Mini in a street near Kelvingrove Park, then walked to Kelvin Way where she hailed a taxi and asked to be driven to Dennistoun in the east end. The cab slogged her through the stop-start afternoon traffic of the city centre and past the giant dark edifice of the Royal Infirmary, then along Alexandra Parade, where the old red-brick cigarette factories lay vacant. She got out of the taxi at the entrance to Alexandra Park. She always followed the same route when she came here.

She entered the park, walked towards the large Victorian royal-blue fountain where water poured from the mouths of cast-iron lion heads. She glanced as she usually did at the four classical life-size statues of women who had the appearance of serene guardians; they were said to represent art, commerce, literature and science. She thought they always looked knowing, as if they'd penetrated some deep secret from the years of their vigil at the fountain. Something precious, something to do with patience.

Tell me all about patience and how to restrict my daft impulses.

You had to look, didn't you? You had to go back and check on Beezer's handiwork. You couldn't leave it alone.

She moved along the edge of the pond where swans sailed on the murky surface, and then past the children's playground. She was aware of elderly people on benches. Some gazed at her, the old men especially. She left the park and circled back to Alexandra Parade, where she walked in the direction of Kennyhill Square. A bowling green occupied the centre of the square, which was bordered by respectable red tenements, some of which had pretensions; columned entranceways, dense vine growing from sandstone, plants in hanging baskets. She heard the infinite drone of the motorway in the distance.

The day was calm, the wind dead, the air scented with cut grass.

Okay, she'd gone to look at the scene of the explosion, she'd joined the crowd outside Cremoni's. Probably stupid. No, *definitely* stupid. Slack, unprofessional. But why worry? She felt immune from the law. She lived inside a locked box, and nobody knew the combination. What legacy had she left the cops anyway? They might find her old car, the interior covered with her fingerprints – but since she had no criminal record, prints were useless currency.

She felt removed from the encounter with the man who carried a card that identified him as *Louis Perlman, Detective-Sergeant, Strathclyde Police*. Perlman had seen her close up, and he'd be able to give an accurate description, but when he tried to gain access to a copy of her driving licence from the central computer in Swansea, what was he going to find?

Just the same, she'd take the precaution now of dyeing her hair, changing the way she looked – maybe glasses, more make-up, whatever it took – then she'd find new rooms and move between them in her customary haphazard way. As for the computer drawing he'd shown her, a bad joke. It depicted a frightened zombie, a simian freak. The Missing Linkette. She wondered about the eyewitnesses who'd contributed their impressions to that poxy image. She'd been observed last night at the Tinderbox in the company of Helen Mboto – of course.

Which meant that the body had been discovered.

Good. It was time.

She stopped outside number fourteen. There were half a dozen nameplates. She rang the bell marked J K Oyster in two short bursts. She heard the buzzer, the man's voice from the intercom.

'Come up.'

The security door opened, she stepped into the building. The door shut behind her silently. She climbed the stairs to the second floor. Pale lifeless light fell inside the tenement from a pane set in the roof.

She stopped outside a panelled door with a brass knocker in the shape of a Celtic cross. She raised it, then let it fall twice against the wood. She heard noises from inside the flat, a footfall followed by the sound of a safety chain being slid back.

He opened the door, made a gesture with his head. She moved past him into the hallway. The flat was spacious, filled with the kind of dark furniture that suggested permanence, mahogany dining table and chairs, oil paintings depicting Scottish scenes, castles in mist, long-haired cattle in water. It wasn't her taste, but it was good stuff, expensive. She remembered the sticks of furniture her mother had gleaned from scrapyards and junkshops for the two-room flat in Govan. Every bloody thing broke so soon, she thought. Every bloody thing was so pathetic and smelled of other people's histories.

The man said, 'Sit.'

She didn't do so immediately. She liked a little show of independence. Nobody tells me. She looked out of the window; below, half a dozen senior citizens played bowls. A hump-backed old man in a blazer crouched over his bowl, then sent it skimming across the grass in the direction of the jack.

'God, it's exciting around here,' she said.

'I'm sure you get enough excitement in other places,' the man said. He had a strong Glasgow accent. 'Sit down.'

She sat in front of the unlit fireplace. The big velvet armchair engulfed her. The man leaned against the mantelpiece. He wore grey trousers and a grey open-necked shirt. It was all she'd ever seen him wear. She wondered if she should mention the encounter with Perlman, then decided against it. *You shouldn't have gone back*, she thought. You didn't take an accident of fate into account, a chance meeting with a policeman. She thought of Perlman's face. He had the look of a guy who'd innocently give sweeties to wee children, or help blind men cross busy streets, but she had the feeling that he'd be as quick to displeasure as he was to compassion. She could imagine him fishing, enduring long rainy hours on a riverbank, waiting for his float to be snatched under the surface. A man of some persistence.

The encounter was history. You can't alter it.

The man stuck his hands in his pockets and jingled keys. She knew him only as Jack Oyster. He wore smoked-glass shades. His black slip-on shoes had little tassels. He gave an impression of physical strength; he was someone who took pride in his condition. He was in his late forties, maybe fifty. Part of the attraction she felt lay in his impenetrability – he was a fellow-traveller of sorts, but he was also an enigma. She wanted to get inside him, to know him.

His money for one thing: where did that come from? He was generous with it but what was its source? And this flat – she felt that it wasn't where he lived, but simply a place he kept for meetings and assignations.

He sat facing her, legs crossed. 'You've been busy.'

'We keep on top of our work,' she said.

'This girl on the golf course . . .'

'Yes.'

Oyster adjusted his glasses. She wondered if Oyster was really his name. Most likely not. She'd never heard of anyone called by that name. She remembered a piece of childhood verbal nonsense: *what noise annoys an oyster*? She watched him and wondered if he knew she'd go to bed with him if he asked her. She wasn't sure how he'd react if she made the first move.

He gave off no spark of interest. She always knew when a man desired her. She studied the tiny scar that ran from the shadow of his earlobe to his jawbone. A couple of inches long, and discoloured. An old injury.

'And the explosion today,' he said.

'A job done.' She got out of the chair. She walked back to the window. The bowling green was empty now. The players had gone inside the pavilion for afternoon tea.

He said, 'You set off some pretty fireworks.'

'Is that a compliment? It must be your first.'

'If it's wee puffs of praise you're after, you've come to the wrong man.'

'I don't need praise.'

He said, 'If you did, I don't think we'd be doing business together. I help with a little finance. Sometimes our interests coincide.'

'We're *simpatico*,' she said.

'At times.' He was quiet for a while. 'One day you'll come here and I'll be gone. The place will be empty. I never existed.'

'I assumed as much. There's a touch of the mirage about you anyway. You're like something seen from a distance.'

'I come, I go. The longer I keep doing the same thing, the more chance of exposure. So I close shop and come back again a year or two later doing business under another name.'

'And this is going to happen soon?'

'I can't give you a time. There's still work to be done.'

'But you expect our organization to hibernate?'

'That's up to you. I'm telling you this just so you know that our relationship is finite.'

She said, 'And if I see you in the street, I look the other way.'

'You won't see me in the street,' he said.

'It's a small world.'

'Not as small as some people think.' He unlocked the drawer of a writing bureau. He took out a white envelope and handed it to her. 'The regular contribution.'

'The organization thanks you,' she said.

181

He ran a finger under his glasses and scratched the top of his nose. He had the lined face of a traveller accustomed to long trips by rail across dry landscapes.

He said, 'I always had an urge to ask you what drew you into this "cause" of yours in the first place. Now I'm not so sure I want to know.'

'I believe some people don't belong in this country,' she said.

'Well well. You surprise me.'

She ignored his sarcasm. 'They don't have rights. But they come anyway, and they keep coming. They come in like this endless fucking tide. They come illegally, they make demands. And the system can't cope and the people who have genuine rights, the citizens, are the first to suffer. Meantime, the dregs are saying give us food, give us proper houses and money for cars and free health. It's all gimme gimme gimme. And the country goes to hell.'

'Simple as that, eh?'

She saw a small patronizing smile on his mouth. She said, 'I'm giving you the basic version.'

'Racism Lite,' he said.

'Is it racism to protect yourself? If somebody pitches a tent in my backyard without permission, don't I have the right to kick him out?'

'You sound like a landlord,' he said.

'Only I don't bother with eviction orders.' She knew he was scrutinizing her, although she couldn't see his eyes.

'What if this trespasser is white as bone?'

'Then it depends.'

'On what?'

'Ethnic background. Immigrant status.'

Oyster paused. 'A Jew, say.'

She closed her eyes. She had an image of a transport train, Jews peering through slatted wood on their way to a death camp. 'I don't altogether believe they *rule* the world, but they have power out of all proportion to their numbers. Zyklon B wouldn't be my first choice.'

182

'Hitler had the right idea, but the wrong techniques?'

'He might have benefited from more sophisticated technology.'

'You're a cold wee bitch.'

'More compliments,' she said. 'My heart's racing.'

'Your heart's iron.'

'I like to think it's an alloy.'

'Of what?'

'Steel and patriotism.'

'Patriotism? I think your version of that idea is the sanctuary of some sorry people who don't know how to make it in the everyday world.'

'Let me guess. You look at me and see just one more sad lonely bastard who spends too much time on Internet chat-rooms talking to kindred spirits about how to rid our country of its unwanted scum. But you associate with people like us anyway, because you need us now and then. You're not exactly in the running for a peace prize – so what does that make you?'

'I'm a businessman,' he said.

'A bloody judgemental one.'

'I don't hold the necessary moral high ground to make judgements,' he said.

'Killing blacks and Asians is okay if it suits you, and wrong if it doesn't.'

'I don't give a fuck either way. I'm not lumbered by a racist agenda. Blacks, Indians, Jews. I'm a pragmatist.'

'That covers everything,' she said.

'It's a handy word. It means I can associate with anyone I like, provided there's some mutual advantage. Now, if we're finished . . . I'll walk you out.'

'I'm not finished,' she said.

'I am.'

'I want to tell you more about how I got to where I am.'

'Assuming I want to know your history, of course.'

'Fuck you, Oyster. You're dying to know.'

'Some other time.' He went with her to the front door. He

touched her elbow briefly. She felt a slight thrill. Also some anger. She didn't want to leave. The conversation dangled unfinished.

He said, 'Phone me tonight. The usual number. Usual time . . .'

'By the way.' She took a handkerchief-wrapped gun from the inside pocket of her leather jacket, and handed it to him. He unfolded the linen and examined the weapon.

'One little gun duly returned,' she said.

'Hold onto it,' he said. 'You never know.'

She stepped onto the landing. She heard the door shut behind her, and the chain slot back in place. She stuffed the gun back inside her pocket, then she headed slowly downstairs and out into Kennyhill Square.

After the still silence of the tenement the traffic roaring along Alexandra Parade was a cacophony; it was as if she'd passed from one city into another, the first quiet and cloistered and safe, the second raucous and exposed and volatile.

26

Perlman drove back to Pitt Street, parked his car. He needed focus. He needed a break of some kind, a passing of the clouds in his head and a moment of illumination. His thoughts had congealed, a form of cerebral constipation. How long before he met Miriam? He was impatient, wishing the hours away.

He entered the building. A woman approached him as soon as he stepped into the foyer, laying a hand on his arm. He'd never seen her before but he knew at once that she had to be Madhur Gupta; she was small and delicate and tragic, eyelids swollen, mouth sad. She was in her mid-forties and might have been pretty, but grief had robbed her.

'Is there a place where we can talk?' she asked.

'Upstairs –'

'No, not here, not in this building. Too many policemen, they remind me . . . I prefer to walk. The open air.'

Perlman followed her into the street. She wore a long dark blue coat and matching trousers. She had a blue scarf drawn round her head. She moved on high-heeled shoes with an air of uncertainty, as if she might keel over any moment.

'I'm Indra's mother,' she said.

'I assumed that.'

They walked slowly down Pitt Street. The recent rain had left the pavements slick. Without thinking, Perlman offered his arm to the woman; he didn't want her to slip and fall. Her grip was tight.

'I don't have much time, Sergeant. I have many things to attend to at home. Things I wish with all my heart I could avoid. You understand that.'

'Of course. Do you want to get a cup of tea somewhere?'

'I prefer to keep walking. I can't stand being still.'

They turned left into Waterloo Street. Madhur Gupta said, 'This morning I heard Indra's alarm clock go off. I'd taken some sleeping pills but they didn't help. I lay all night long with my eyes open and I kept thinking that what had happened was not real. Then I heard her little clock and I had to go inside her room and turn it off and I drew her curtains back to let light in, to wake her – the bed was empty, of course. Silly of me to think I might find her there. Isn't that silly, Sergeant?'

Perlman said, 'I don't think so. It's natural.'

'Natural? Tell me what is natural? For a mother to survive a child – is this natural?' She stopped, turned to look up into Perlman's eyes for an answer. Some faces hide nothing, he thought. Some people have no masks to protect themselves. Madhur Gupta, in her grief, looked as if she'd been scooped out inside, and sorrow was the only sensation she'd feel for as long as she lived. He had an urge to put his arms round this little woman and hug her. Oy. This loss of detachment was a sign of the downhill path he was on. He needed diplomatic immunity from feeling.

He said, 'No, that's not remotely natural.'

'A man kills my daughter, Sergeant. Shoots her. I feel her pain.'

Madhur Gupta gazed down Waterloo Street, which ended at Hope Street. *Hope*. Finding irony in the street name was too easy, Perlman thought. What in God's name was he supposed to tell this woman? How was he to help ease her pain? *We're doing all we can*, he might say. That chestnut had been in the fire too long. *We'll bring this criminal to justice*, another candidate. But Madhur Gupta didn't look like a woman who wanted justice. Revenge was what she sought. Blood. She wanted a gun and she wanted to blow the killer away.

'Your investigation,' she said. 'How does it go?'

'You want me to say we're close to the killer?'

'I don't want lies, Sergeant.'

'You won't get them from me, Mrs Gupta. We're not close. We have a couple of avenues of exploration, but I'm not going to tell you we've got anything substantial. Not yet.' Christ, how he hated pap: *avenues of exploration*. 'There's a lot of work ahead, and it requires a lot of questions. Takes time.'

'And luck too, I imagine.'

'I wouldn't spit in the eye of a lucky break,' he said.

They moved along the block in silence. At the junction of Wellington Street, Madhur Gupta stopped. She released Perlman's arm. 'Poor Indra. She didn't do anything to deserve what happened to her.'

She's going to tell me something, Perlman thought. He had the feeling that Madhur Gupta, who'd lived quietly in the background of her husband's life, a dedicated wife and mother, had decided to step, however briefly, out of the shadows.

'She had the misfortune to be Bharat's child, Sergeant. Do you think Bharat's nephew Tilak *fell* from the balcony of his flat?'

'I'm not sure.'

'Such terrible luck in one family? You think this is chance?'

'I'm not a big fan of chance, Mrs Gupta. What are you telling me?'

'This is difficult for me. To be open . . . Our lives have been less than ordinary in the last couple of years, Sergeant.'

'How so?'

'Are we talking in confidence?'

'Complete.'

187

She paused, stuck a finger under the watchband of her small silver watch, then twisted the links nervously. 'My husband has various businesses – I pay little attention, it isn't my place. I manage our household. I tell the cleaners what to do. This is my role. I understand some of Bharat's enterprises are – let me say, not always run by the book of rules? Do you understand me?'

'Dodgy,' he said.

'Yes. In the last two years or so, there have been events that have made me uneasy, and others that frightened me. But Bharat always said they were the work of business enemies.'

'What kind of events, Mrs Gupta?'

'Anonymous letters of a threatening kind. I received a few. I know Indra got at least one. She told me. Bharat always said they were empty, they meant nothing, we should destroy them and forget them.'

'Which you did.'

'Destroyed, yes. Forgot, no.'

'What kind of threats?'

'Some were vague,' she said. 'Others were death.'

She glanced at her watch, checked the time. Perlman guessed she'd slipped out of her home unseen, and she'd have questions to answer when she returned. Only desperation could have driven her out of a house of mourning.

'Your husband did nothing about these letters?' he asked.

'You have to understand this – Bharat is a good husband. He has always, *always*, looked after the family. He has never consorted with other women. He loves his children. He's protective of the family, the home. When he said the letters were worthless jokes in bad taste, I was ready to believe him. Perhaps I hid from the truth.'

'Apart from the letters, anything else?'

'Anonymous phone calls. Always the same rough voice, the same message. *You're going to die. You can't escape.* Somebody once slashed the tyres of Dev's car. Somebody also broke into Tilak's flat and wrote obscenities on the wall. Racial nonsense.

Then there was the stranger Indra said was following her. Bharat continued to be very reassuring. But I began to pick up little stories. A dry-cleaning establishment he owns had been set on fire deliberately. A supermarket in which he has a sizeable investment was vandalized. I asked him why did he not go to the police. It was a private matter, he said. It was something he'd settle himself. He's a very proud man, Sergeant.'

Pride's fine, Perlman thought, but it didn't explain why Gupta refused to report these events to the police. Something else. Maybe he just distrusted the authorities. Maybe he didn't want cops involved in his business affairs.

Madhur Gupta said, 'He had a company install security devices in our house. Alarms, sensor lights. He always has some of his employees watching the house. They sit in a van parked in the driveway. When he drives each morning to his office, he always travels with two men whose purpose he has never explained to me. I'm certain they're bodyguards. Meanwhile, the van always stays behind, parked outside the house.'

A siege condition, Perlman thought. 'If he's so keen on security, why didn't he send somebody to make sure Indra reached school safely?'

'Indra trusted her father's attitude to the threats. Why wouldn't she? She adored him.'

Perlman thought about this. Fearless Indra. She didn't need protection. She felt safe. Complacency kills. He thought of her staring into the killer's gun, and all her assumptions of security draining out of her. He gazed at Madhur Gupta; her face, framed in the dark scarf, seemed almost white. 'You think your husband's enemies are behind her killing?'

'I think it is a possibility you must consider, Sergeant. Think of Tilak too. He wasn't the kind of boy who'd take his own life. Believe me. Wild, certainly. Self-destructive, never.'

They reached the corner of Hope Street now. Central Station lay across the way. An early evening traffic jam sullied

189

the air. Fumeous Glasgow. A newspaper vendor called out *Evening Times, Getcher Evening Times here,* in an accent so impenetrable it might have been Estonian. Perlman pondered Barry Gupta's business dealings. What was the extent of them? Maybe Perse McKinnon could have told him more: the silenced oracle.

'I must go now, Sergeant.'

'I appreciate you talking to me,' he said.

'I knew my husband wouldn't tell you anything of this. I had to do it. It may just be the rambling of a woman whose world is in disarray. I leave it to you, Sergeant. I ask only that you do not tell Bharat that I came to you.'

'I won't.' He shook her tiny hand. She turned and slipped through the traffic and walked towards the taxi rank outside Central. He saw her climb into a black cab, then he walked back up Waterloo Street, thinking about death threats, anonymous letters, phone calls. What was in Bharat Gupta's life that he didn't want the police to explore?

He reached Force HQ. He hesitated outside, smoked a cigarette. He wondered how many times over the years he'd stepped inside HQ. Thousands, he supposed. *My days are numbered.* He flicked his half-done cigarette away, turned, entered. There was a buzz about the place, phones ringing, people coming and going up and down the stairway, voices. Destruction and murder activated cops, filled them with purpose; a strange force had galvanized them.

Dennis Murdoch appeared. He was still out of uniform. He had a couple of sheets of paper in his hand. 'I was just looking for you, Sergeant. That stuff you wanted.'

'Remind me.'

'The licence –'

'Oh aye. Right.' Perlman experienced a little mind-drift. Concentrate, concentrate. 'So?'

'Seemingly there's no such person as this Celia Liddell,' Murdoch said. 'The Motor Department in Swansea has never issued a licence for anyone of that name at 4 King Edward

Road. Not surprising, I suppose, since there's no number four in King Edward Road.'

Perlman felt a little stab of excitement, a jump-start. He heard himself say, 'The licence was a fine fake, a beautifully skilled piece of work,' but he wasn't really listening to his own words. He was thinking about the woman who'd called herself Celia Liddell: that *ligner* fucking fooled me. He thought: *It's important to remember what she looked like.* Don't let the mental snapshot fade. Her features, her clothes, everything. A woman you mistakenly thought resembled a face in a bad sketch turns out to have her own secret identity, *plus* she's in the vicinity of Cremoni's at the wrong time . . .

He grabbed the sketch from his coat pocket and stared at it, and yes, okay, it *was* downright awful, but maybe, just maybe, there was some very thin resemblance after all to the woman who'd called herself Celia Liddell, something you'd overlooked at the time of talking to her, because in your heart you never dreamed you'd gaze at a crowd in the street and *just happen to see* a person wanted for questioning in a murder inquiry. She wasn't in hiding, she'd brazenly come out into the daylight, she was close to the explosion –

Murdoch said, 'One other thing, Sergeant.'

Perlman coughed, felt light-headed. 'Bad news or good?'

'You judge. A truck belonging to Bargeddie Haulage went out of control on the M73 about three miles from Gartcosh this afternoon. The driver was wheeched to hospital. DOA.'

'Any more details?'

'Only that the whole thing burst into flames. I'll get more info as it comes in, Sergeant.'

'Do that.'

Perlman moved towards the stairs. He climbed them two at a time. Celia Liddell. You fooled me so easily and I don't like that: Perlman, *shlemiel*. Who and where are you, Celia?

He saw Scullion appear at the end of the corridor.

'Still no ID of the second victim,' Sandy said. 'You've got a funny look on your face, Lou. What is it?'

'I think I got sprayed by the musk of that very rare creature, the femme fatale.'

'I daresay that's a damn sight better than the smell in my nostrils. Burnt chemicals and smoke.'

'I wouldn't bet on it,' Perlman said.

27

Kilroy roared into his mobile: 'You unload the shipment *after* you pay the asking price, or you don't unload it at all. I'll send the whole fucking thing right back where it came from. My last word.' Angrily he switched off the phone and stomped heavy-footed around his Daimler, which was parked in a street alongside the Necropolis, at the back of St Mungo's Cathedral.

Frankie Chasm got out from behind the wheel. 'What's the problem?'

'You make deals with some people then they think they can change the financial details at the last minute. Sometimes I wonder. Am I doomed to spend the rest of my days doing biz with clueless wankers?' He sighed, and slumped against the body of the Daimler and slapped the mobile up and down in the palm of his hand.

Chasm recognized this as the Fat Man's Serious Huff Mode. Pieces of his world were going out of shape. Life was not always the orderly thing he wanted it to be.

'What do you think? Will these characters pay?'

'Frankie, do I seem like a reader of crystal balls to you? I *shudder* when I contemplate the lack of honour in business circles. I remember when a deal was a deal. A handshake was like, like . . . an Eleventh Commandment. Thou doth not goeth back on a handshake. But nowadays . . .'

Chasm looked at the skyline, against which stood hugely elaborate tombstones, great vaults and mausoleums built by Victorian sentimentalists and death-freaks. Hundreds of crosses cast shadows; you could call this place Crosses R Us.

Seven thirty and the sun sliding from the sky. He glanced back at Kilroy. It wasn't the shakiness of a business deal that troubled the Fat Man, although that certainly irked him. No. It was the note and the photograph that had been delivered by TransClyde Express.

Especially the photograph.

Frankie Chasm watched Leo's face, which in the last few seconds seemed to have deflated, like a big red football with a puncture. 'Look. The fucking note's a joke, Leo. Come on.'

'You see me laughing?'

'Plus that photo's a fake. If that's a genuine photo I'm a fucking yodeller in an Alpine band.'

Kilroy stared across the Necropolis. He wanted to be buried up here when his time came. He imagined himself wrapped in a burgundy velvet shroud, svelte in death. The shark at rest in Glasgow's damp black earth. The rich and the pious would come to his funeral. His eulogy would be read by one or other of the famous actors he knew. *A big man, yes, but with a heart to match. At the setting of the sun we will remember him.* It would be a memorable pageant attended by thousands.

I am not yet ready to shuffle off, he thought.

He slid a hand into the pocket of his powder-blue cashmere coat and took out the photograph and the note. He read the green ballpoint words: *If you don't want Perlman to see this, it will cost you a fortune, fatso. I'll be in touch.*

He gazed at the photograph. It depicted his beloved old Bentley passing under a streetlamp at night. The light falling from the lamp illuminated the presence, if not the features, of the driver, although a naked eye could tell that the man behind the wheel was a figure of some proportion. A printed date was visible on the front of the picture, lower right corner: *December 15*, followed by the year.

And there was a street sign in the background, clearly visible: Dalness Street.

Fucking *Egypt*.

Kilroy had a curdling feeling, pit of gut. 'They have computers, Frankie,' he said. 'Blum says they can work miracles, they bring out the face right down to the colour of the eyes.'

'How many times, Leo? *The pic is fucking rigged*. It's all trickery. They can enhance it all they like, it doesn't fucking *matter*.'

'Trickery, oh sure, I *know* it, you *know* it. But Perlman could use it to put my arse in a sling, Frankie.'

'Think, Leo. Don't wilt. He's pressuring you. A fake photograph and a ha-ha tape and a joke note, and you're coming apart. Get a grip, big man.'

'Ignore it all, you say?'

'Exactly. Perlman's thinking he'll keep up the pressure and you'll crack like a fresh Ryvita. Maintain. Endure.'

Kilroy seemed not to have heard. He blinked at the fading sun. 'I bet Perlman can make his colleagues *believe* the picture is real. I bet he can persuade the Procurator-Fiscal he's got a case.'

'Blum wouldn't let it go that far. He'd have the photo analysed to death by experts.' Chasm thought: Jesus *Christ*, the Fat Man was imploding like an amateur's soufflé.

'Blum? I think they can just brush that shyster aside any time they like. I've had my suspicions for a wee while now that he's really a lightweight. Scratch his Boss suit, and you get a wee boy whose rib-bones are showing. He's breakable, Frankie. Anyway, Perlman could manipulate the whole fucking system against me. Cops and judges stick together.'

Chasm experienced deep frustration. 'But you're *innocent*, Leo. You're being hounded by a demented fruitbat whose obsession with trimming your sails is away out of control.'

'Since when did a man's innocence matter in our legal system?'

195

Chasm shrugged. 'Sometimes justice is tough to get.'

Leo Kilroy thought about all the things he disliked in Perlman. 1. He's a Jew. 2. He's a cop. 3. He has a naff haircut. 4. He wears stupid glasses. 5. He's obsessed with his dead brother. 6. He never quits, never goes away, never, like a bloody tick under your skin.

Chasm said, 'Sometimes you need to seek out other avenues. Take an unexpected turning here, another one there.'

Justice is tough. Kilroy let the phrase roll round his mind.

Chasm whistled the first notes of 'Mairzy doats and dozy doats'. 'Incidentally. There was a serious accident on the M73 this afternoon.'

'Oh?'

'One dead driver, unfortunately. Blood everywhere. One truck out of commission.'

A breeze came up and blew over the crosses and the vaults. The dank smell of the dead, Kilroy thought. He imagined rotted coffins and hanks of desiccated hair and bones stripped clean of flesh as if having been immersed in acid. He belched, leaving a gassy explosion of garlic on the air.

He picked a stray thread from his sleeve. The echo in his head was louder. 'Tough justice, eh?'

'I'm not saying it's the only way, Leo.'

Kilroy examined the thread in his fingers. How did a green thread become attached to a pale blue coat? He let it slip from his fingers to the ground. 'I dislike intricate details, Frank. I like some things to happen far outside my field of vision.'

'I know.'

'Way way *way* beyond my auditory range.'

'That's a given.'

'Fine.'

'The less a man knows, Leo.'

Kilroy stood motionless a moment. He felt a strange little tingle go through him, an icy hand on the back of his neck. 'This place gives me the creeps when it starts to get dark, Frankie. I imagine the graves bursting open. Let's get out of here.'

Frankie Chasm ushered the Fat Man into the back of the Daimler. Kilroy's weight crushed fine leather.

'Remind me to call my chemist in the morning, Frankie.'

'Right.'

'Certain sharp edges need blunting. Very sharp ones.'

28

It was sunset when Perlman parked his car in Paisley Road West, just south of the river. Ahead, he saw the entrance to La Fiorentina and he thought: *I need this, how I need this time, this space*. Was it so much to ask? He raised his face, eyes drawn upward to the stone angel on top of the building that housed the restaurant. Perched four storeys above street level, the angel was lit gold by the dying sun. An easy dramatic effect, he felt, a piece of theatre, but what the hell – he liked the sight of the creature and had sometimes even imagined it rising from the rooftop and gliding over Glasgow, bringing hope and joy in a whisper of wings. No more badness. An end to malice. Greed banished.

And this is where I wake up, dream over.

The human condition, that minestrone of desire and charity, hate and love, was beyond the attentions of any merciful angel. That soft flap of wings you heard was nothing more than the product of your own yearning for a kinder world.

He stepped inside the restaurant, wondering if Miriam had already arrived. Max, Perlman's favourite waiter, a small Italianate Glaswegian with a little moustache, helped him out of his coat.

'How come we don't see you here so often any more? Huh? You found a better place to eat, Sergeant?'

'Impossible,' Perlman said.

Max hung the coat. 'I thought, hey, maybe the Sergeant has started to patronize some of those fancy new Italian places in Sauchiehall Street or Merchant City.'

'Fancy, I don't like. You know me.'

Max smiled. He had a gold tooth. 'People come, people go. Fickle.'

'I always come back,' Perlman said, and wondered when he'd last patronized this place. Two years? Surely not. He couldn't keep track of time. 'I'm expecting somebody.'

'She's here already. A real beauty, if I may say so. In the corner. This way.'

A real beauty: Perlman felt he'd been complimented on his taste. He followed the waiter across the room, past the fringed lampshades that muted the light, and the tangled green-black plastic foliage. He experienced a slight tension, and almost collided with one of the Roman statues lingering in the shadows.

He saw Miriam watching him from a corner table. She'd glossed her hair back flat against her scalp. It had the effect of making her forehead higher and her eyes wider, so that she resembled a woman in a painting by – what was that Dutch artist's name? Holbein?

'I'm late,' he said. He sat facing her.

'Ten minutes. Pardonable. I half-expected you to cancel.'

'This is my private time. I'm out of commission. I'm at liberty. For a while anyway.'

She wore a thin blue necklace and a matching bracelet. He couldn't name the stone, which sparkled slightly in the dim light.

'Drink?' he asked.

'I'd like some white wine.'

He summoned Max, who brought menus and took the drinks order. Perlman asked for ice-cold lager. He needed something to take the *drouth* of nervousness out of his throat. He studied the menu quickly. He wasn't in a fussy frame of mind. When Max brought the drinks, Miriam asked for lemon sole and Perlman spaghetti with meat sauce.

'Cheers.' He clinked his glass against hers.

'I'm not going to ask you about your day.'

'A mercy, believe me.'

'What the hell is *happening* to the world?' she said.

It was, he knew, a rhetorical question. She leaned a little across the table. She sipped her wine. Her white blouse was silk with small pearl buttons.

'Maybe people hate too much,' he said. 'Or maybe God died and left us this planet as his legacy, and we haven't got a clue how to care for it.'

She toyed with her napkin, unfolding, refolding. 'While you were talking, I was remembering when we first met. Colin introduced us.'

'I remember. He told me he wanted to meet me at Ferrari's. I was expecting him on his own. And there you were, hanging on his arm.'

'I did a lot of hanging in those days,' she said. 'I used to feel like a fashion accessory he wore.'

'I remember his exact words. This is the girl I'm marrying.'

'He hadn't even *asked* me when he made that announcement. Give him points for self-confidence.'

'He was always sure of himself,' Perlman said.

'He was a lot of things.'

Perlman closed his eyes briefly. 'You were wearing a black velvet miniskirt and white boots. Your hair was down to your shoulders. You had big bangles on your wrists and hooped earrings.' *And I lusted after you like a beast freed from a cage after years of imposed abstinence,* he thought.

'I remember those boots,' she said. 'Squeezed like hell. The way we looked back then. All that hair and those flash colours and microskirts. You've got a good memory.'

'For some things. Others just vanish completely.' He sipped his lager, and realized he was about to mention the message he'd received on his answering machine about the night of Colin's murder; no, don't steer the conversation in that direction, keep away from crime and murder and mutilation. It's just you and her on this oasis of wine and cold beer. And then he had another urge, this time to mention his encounter with Celia Liddell, and how easily he'd been fooled. Or maybe he could talk about his meeting with Madhur Gupta, or the tortuous half an hour spent describing Celia Liddell's features to the computer wizard who seemed affronted that anyone would question his efforts, and how, after some argument, a revised copy had gone into circulation, and Terry Bogan was taking it back to the Corinthian in the chance of shaking a barman's memory, the links between things, the little details, the broad ones, the *stramash*, the *ravel* of it all –

Why the fuck couldn't he drop work completely? Was it the only definition he had of himself? Was this all he amounted to?

She said, 'Let me see . . . you were wearing one of those really wide ties . . . Come to think of it, your taste in ties hasn't changed all that much in thirty years, Lou.'

'Ties. Who cares about ties?' But he was suddenly conscious of the gold-tinted kipper-shaped job hanging from his throat, and he fingered it with annoyance.

She reached out and caught his hand. 'I was *kidding*,' she said. 'You're right. Who gives a damn about ties? You're no fop. If you were, you wouldn't be you.' She held his hand a moment longer, then she drew her arm back and raised her wine glass and smiled at him.

That *touch*, he thought. He had an intense buzz of pleasure that rushed from head to groin. The stirring, the fabulous fire in the bloodstream. *There are no criminals in Glasgow, every evildoer is behind bars, tranquillity and sanity prevail over the entire city*, he thought. Even his lager tasted richer all at once, as if embellished with an exotic spice. *A love drug*, he thought.

Max arrived with the food. 'Made with passion,' he said. 'The chef sends you his good wishes.'

'Tell him the same,' Perlman said. 'Could we have refills?'

Max sprinkled flecks of Parmesan cheese on Lou's pasta, then he went to fetch fresh drinks. Perlman watched Miriam cut her lemon sole, which lay in butter. She carved with a delicate touch. He wound some spaghetti round his fork with as much care as he could gather, and raised it to his mouth. Spaghetti with red sauce was a potential disaster. He wished he'd ordered something less *menacing*, less likely to drip and stain, a chop, say, or a piece of steak.

Miriam said, 'I like it here.'

'It's a constant,' he said. 'Unusual in these days when every-thing changes. Things come and go overnight. Today's hot spot is tomorrow's empty shop. It's the speed of life.'

'Are you going to give me a life-was-slower-and-better-when-you-were-a-kid-speech?'

'It was slower anyway,' he said. 'I don't know about better.'

She smiled at him. 'Don't take this the wrong way. But sometimes you just look so serious, Lou, I feel like laughing.'

'At me?'

'No, not like that. Not *at* you.'

'Like how then?'

'I don't know. I get down-hearted and sort of disjointed sometimes, and you brighten things up, and you don't know you're doing it.'

'So this is a good thing, this ability to make you laugh?'

'Of course it is.'

'I'm not, God forbid, some court jester?'

'Not remotely.'

Perlman started on his second beer. I brighten her world, he thought. I make a contribution to her life. It's something. A step forward definitely. He hesitated, then took the risk – and why not, why not after the passage of so many restrained years? – moving one hand boldly across the table and allowing the palm to fall on her wrist, and she didn't react, didn't pull away, she just gazed at him with an expression he wasn't sure he could analyse. It wasn't cold and at the same time it wasn't inviting; there was a quality of assessment in her eyes, as if she were trying to work something out, perform complex mental arithmetic or spell an impossibly tricky word.

'Lou, listen, I need to tell you . . . I know how it is, how you feel,' she said.

His scalp burned. She knew, after all. She *knew*. And he'd never been entirely sure if she did. And now she'd told him. 'Oh, it's, well, I suppose it's, it's, ah . . .'

'Obvious? Is that the word you're stumbling for?'

He cleared his throat quietly. His earlobes were hot. 'Close to that. Yes.'

'I know you tried to hide it, Lou. I know how long. I'm not blind.'

He had a weird little pulse in his throat. He rambled. 'A man can get, uh, expert over the years at concealing things that are important to him. He isn't sure if he can say them out loud, or if he's going to make some bad blunder and come off like a total arse. At the same time he doesn't want to be dishonest, he hates concealment, em, he'd like to get it out in the open –'

'You're babbling, Lou.'

'Right, I am. So excuse me. I didn't mean to.'

She set her fork down on her plate. 'Also you're hurting my wrist.'

'I'm sorry.' He lifted his hand from her.

'Gentle, Lou. Go gentle. Can we take a walk?'

'Anything you want,' he said, and he was out of his seat at once, rushing to ease her chair back from the table and help her rise. He was a gormless boy offered a waltz with his sweetheart at a school dance. And yet even as he assisted her he wasn't sure what had just passed between them, whether she'd really told him she'd readily dance with him, or if she was simply saying that she was aware of the music.

He dropped a bunch of money on the table. He helped her into her coat. He slipped Max a few pounds as he headed to the front door; the waiter understood the impulses of romance, and nodded discreetly. And then Perlman and Miriam were outside, where the night air was cold and the lamplights were hazy. Hesitantly, he held her hand and they walked a few yards from the restaurant in silence.

'I don't know where any of this goes,' she said eventually. 'I don't have a bloody clue.'

'I could say the same.'

'I've been living day to day. I don't have any plans. I never saw any space in my life for any kind of . . . involvement, anything like that. I don't know.'

Involvement: the word was encouraging. He saw her shiver. 'You're cold.'

'Just a little.'

This wasn't the greatest neighbourhood in the city; it was alleged to be 'up & coming', but that could mean anything in Estate Agent Speak. He saw the lights of the Old Toll Bar across the street, and led her in that direction.

'Let's have a drink,' he said.

The bar, which had once belonged to a famous but doomed footballer, had been refurbished recently. It bore no resemblance to Perlman's memory of the place. It was all polished dark wood, artfully carved, and old wooden casks, and early twentieth-century mirrors. A poster from a long-demolished cinema in Hillhead announced a film called *Annie Laurie*, starring Lillian Gish; May 1928. Miriam sat down at a table under the poster and asked for a small Scotch.

Perlman fetched two glasses of Johnnie Walker and carried them to the table. He felt – uncomfortable? Apprehensive? Something had changed between himself and Miriam. A frozen pool had suddenly cracked, but there was no way of knowing how deep the water might be underneath.

'You've been so very patient,' she said.

'Years of police work helped.'

'Years of silence too, Lou.'

'My brother's wife,' he said. 'What was I supposed to do? What am I supposed to do now?'

Miriam drank half her Scotch. 'I don't know, Lou. I don't know what happens next.'

He wanted to ask her if she could define her feelings; then decided it was a step too far too soon. Take it slow. Besides, did he want an answer just yet? She might tell him how 'fond' she was of him, and how this 'thing' between them could never go anywhere. She might bandy around words like 'regret' and 'sadness' and he didn't want to hear her prepare an escape route from the possibility of a relationship. *I'm flattered, but . . .*

He lived in hope. Hope was frail. You couldn't trust hope to carry your weight. Sometimes it was all you had. Perlman: suitor, lover.

He leaned towards her and kissed her on the mouth. Pure be-damned impulse. He'd imagined kissing her so many times before, but hadn't really dreamed how sweet the connection would be. She tasted of Scotch and lipstick. Her lips were warm and a little dry. He saw her shut her eyes and observed the pale veins in her eyelids. He imagined her breasts under his hands. He imagined running a fingertip round the rim of her navel, and down, and down. He closed his own eyes. The pub ceased to exist. It became a spaceship floating across the city. It was a starry ride and his heart provided the fuel. And it didn't matter if his specs got in the way, or that this was a very public place for such intimate contact.

'Aw, my my. This is a lovely sight, lovely.'

Perlman knew the voice, and realized at some level of awareness he'd been expecting to hear it, but not precisely now. He drew his face back from Miriam and stared at the behatted Latta, and the anger he felt was like a snake hissing in his head.

'Very touching,' Latta said.

'Piss off,' Perlman said.

'That's not nice, Lou.' Latta propped his hands on the table and inclined his body towards Perlman. His hat was soft brown felt, pulled forward a little way. He had hairy hands, Perlman noticed. A fucking werewolf.

'You call spying nice?' Miriam said.

205

'Duty, my dear lady. I go where duty takes me. Nice doesn't come into it. Nice is when you're all snuggled up in a woman's arms. Right, Lou?' Latta smiled.

Perlman stood up. Miriam tugged at his sleeve. 'Let it go, Lou. It's not worth the bother.'

'Smart lady you've got there,' Latta said. 'Very smart.'

Perlman fumed. He felt violated. He groped for an insult, couldn't find anything suitably cutting. He knew that news of this kissing scene would go through HQ like a gale. So what? Did it matter? He could take it.

'Is this how you catch killers? Snogging your sister-in-law in a pub?'

'This is time off, time out, call it what you like.'

'Charming. Perlman and his squeeze. While the city smells like a butcher's shop.'

Miriam stood up. 'I'd like to go, Lou.'

'Stay just a moment, my dear,' Latta said. He took a folded sheet of paper from an inside pocket of his grey overcoat and waved it in front of her face. 'Care to explain to me how you managed to transfer eight hundred and ninety-three thousand pounds into a savings account at the Manx Bank on the Isle of Man from the Allied Irish Bank in Dublin the day before yesterday?'

'What's to explain?' Miriam asked.

'The origins of this tidy wee sum, for one thing.'

'I don't have to answer your question.'

Perlman asked, 'How did you acquire that information, Latta?'

Latta said, 'I can't disclose sources, Lou. You know better.'

'You got it under the counter, is that what you're saying?'

Latta sighed. 'I'm asking the lady a question she apparently doesn't want to answer. I can go another route. I have a legal arsenal at my disposal.'

'You bringing charges?' Perlman asked.

Latta shrugged. 'One always looks for cooperation before taking that step, of course. Why the hell are you so interested anyway? Playing the gallant in front of your lady – or do *you* have something to hide about the source of this deposit?'

'I can't take this creep a minute longer,' Perlman said to Miriam, and he escorted her towards the door.

'Hang about, Lou,' Latta said. 'This creep comes with a message for you.'

Perlman turned. His neck muscles were rigid with tension.

Latta grinned at him. 'I hear people are looking for you. People are seeking you everywhere. You're the Clydeside Pimpernel. Seems your phone's on the blink. Seems a certain corpse disfigured in an explosion has been identified. If I were you, perish the thought, I'd hasten to the nearest public phone and contact Sandy Scullion.'

Perlman went outside, his arm linked with Miriam's.

'The night's over,' Miriam said.

'I'm sorry.'

'Maybe we broke off at just the right moment.'

Perlman didn't want to explore the meaning of this one. For him, Latta's intrusion had come at the wrong moment altogether. He gestured towards the pub. 'That wanker –'

'He's not worth it, Lou.'

Perlman felt the nippy air of the real world. He preferred the world of magic. 'I'll put you in a taxi. Phone you later.'

'That's fine,' she said.

'I don't know what time.'

'It's okay.'

He gazed along Paisley Road West, thinking how Latta's appearance had drained the night of some of its wonder. Then he pondered Miriam's transfer of such a large sum of money, and he realized that Latta had done more than devalue the evening, he'd poisoned it.

He hailed a taxi, watched it cruise to a halt. Miriam kissed him quickly on the cheek, then stepped inside. He closed the door for her. She raised a farewell hand in the window. Her face was set in what looked like resignation or regret.

He didn't have time to decide. He walked back in the direction of La Fiorentina to ask for the use of their phone, all the while aware of Latta, shadowy under the brim of his hat, observing him from the doorway of the Old Toll Bar.

29

He drove north to Possil, pustulent Possil, his ears still echoing from the sound of Scullion's voice on the line. All right, so Sandy had a genuine grievance: his number two, his right-hand man, had gone AWOL at a bad time. And incommunicado. *You know how many fucking times I've tried to call you, Lou? This keeps happening.* Contrition didn't dent Scullion's anger.

White Rage had made it to the evening news on TV, Scullion had said. You could practically *hear* the city shut and bolt its doors against the horror. People are scared, and we owe it to them to say the city will be made secure. We want to tell them it's safe to go out and walk their dogs.

And where are you, Perlman? Out with your brother-in-law's widow. *Out on a fucking date!*

He imagined Latta clyping on him in unctuous tones. *Found your wandering DS, Sandy. Out on the town, no less. My, you should keep your man in check, Sandy . . .*

So Possil. Head aching, chest aching from the cigarettes he'd smoked all the way from the Old Toll Bar to the western side of the city, Perlman drove his faltering Mondeo. When he reached his destination it was like driving into a sudden pall; this blighted place, this *carbuncle* of a suburb. It dismayed him.

He found the address Sandy had given him. He parked his car, turned on the interior light, scanned the car for a sign of his mobile. It wasn't in the car and it wasn't in a pocket of his clothing. It wasn't anywhere. The mobie goes missing. He'd lost it, dropped it, whatever. It had been a fucking *ludicrous* attachment anyway, something with which he felt no kinship.

He locked the car, conscious of various phantoms gathering in the blacked-out places where no streetlamps shed light. There were few functional lamps anyway, and those that remained were curiously prominent, like sorry afterthoughts. Who the hell was in charge of changing bulbs anyway? Some corporation flunkey too afraid to enter this place?

He thought: £893,000. That was a considerable stash. That was hefty money. No, not now, Lou. Leave it among everything else piled up behind you, all the unanswered questions that spread out from the murder of an Indian girl.

He caught a smell of dope on the air. Whatever could be inhaled or snorted, you'd find it here. He saw Scullion's Citroën, and a Strathclyde Police patrol car parked behind it. Two uniformed constables stood guard outside the patrol vehicle and looked more wary than vigilant. Perlman recognized one as PC Anstruther from HQ, a kid with a fuzz of fair hair on his cheeks. The other was a young WPC, whom Perlman had seen at the Sunshine Day School. Meg, he remembered. Meg Gayle. Good oval face, a sad kind of intelligence in her eyes.

Something cracked against the pavement. Perlman, startled, watched a rock hit concrete and bounce a few feet away from him. Bombardments. The air was rich with menace. The night vibrated. You half-expected to hear war drums. Glasgow Mau-Mau.

Anstruther flinched. 'Jesus Christ,' he said.

'Rough territory, my children,' Perlman remarked. 'You might want to sit inside your car. For your own protection.'

Anstruther peered into the dark, as if trying to assess the

extent of his and WPC Gayle's personal safety. Perlman entered the tenement. The security door hung off its hinges. The close smelled of urine so intense the stench was a weight in the air.

He climbed the stairs to the second floor. The door of a flat was open. He stepped inside a living room. Scullion was sitting on a sofa with a woman whose age was impossible to guess. Her flesh was like cracked parchment, and her wispy uncombed hair was crowned by an aura of cigarette smoke. Her fingernails were scarlet and bitten down. She had a maroon shawl drawn around her shoulders.

Perlman caught Scullion's eye. Sandy got up and crossed the floor. 'I don't have the time to keep on being pissed off with you, Lou. Nor the energy.'

'I thought your spleen was well and truly vented anyway.'

Scullion made a querulous crescent of one eyebrow. 'Let's take it as written that my anger's now on a very low flame. Just don't aggravate it.'

'Got it.'

'I'll bring you up to speed.' He lowered his voice, leaned his head towards Lou. 'Positive ID of one Robert Descartes. He'd been booked about fifteen years ago for a DUI offence. It wasn't a big deal. Thirty days or a hefty fine. He paid up. No further trouble with the law. At least on record. He lived right here with his mother, Sandrine. He survived on unemployment benefits. The mother's French. Says she is anyway.'

'Have you had a good look around the place?'

'I'm working in that direction. Slowly. I want her to okay it. Saves time if she agrees to a brief inspection. Right now she's in shock. Seems she expected Robert – or Robair, or just plain Bobby – to get into deep trouble eventually. He was a doomed boy, she says. Born under a bad star.'

Perlman scanned the room. New TV, fake lilies in a porcelain vase, assorted tabloids and TV magazines on the stained carpet. A tarot deck lay open on a small coffee table alongside a big green glass ashtray overpacked with butts. The Four of Wands overlapped the Five of Swords and the Fool. Did this have any meaning? He studied Sandrine Descartes' face. The pale blue eyes looked as if they expected to see tragedy at every turn.

'Is she talkative, Sandy?'

'Comes and goes. Weepy. Chatty. Weepy again.'

Perlman approached the sofa. Sandrine Descartes lit a fresh cigarette from the end of an old one.

'I'm Detective-Sergeant Lou Perlman, Mrs Descartes.'

Sandrine Descartes stared at him. 'And? Are you here to tell me why my son was killed?'

'I'm here to see if I can find that out,' he said.

'Your colleague, he said the same thing.'

He sat beside Sandrine. He had the impression of a person sunk in shallow water and far too weary to rise. Life had scuttled her.

'What do you think Bobby was doing at Cremoni's?' he asked.

She shrugged. 'How can I answer this? Bobby was a mystery.' She said the last word in such a way that she might equally have said 'disappointment'. 'Until tonight I had never heard of this Cremoni's.'

'He never mentioned Perseus McKinnon to you?' Perlman asked.

'He never mentioned *anyone* to me. If he had friends, I never met them.'

Scullion stood close to the sofa, his shadow falling across the woman's face. 'What did he do, Sandrine? How did he pass the time if he didn't work?'

'He played on his computer,' she said, and shrugged. 'How do I know what he did? We shared very little. I never understood him. Sometimes, you know, I felt I was close to reaching him. Not often. He was like soap, slippery.'

Scullion said, 'He spent a lot of time on this computer?'

She nodded fiercely. 'Yes, yes. This is what he did. Sat at the keyboard. Tap tap tap. Like *un pic*. A woodypecker. Is that how you say it?'

'Close enough,' Perlman said.

Sandrine found a clump of tissues under her shawl, and blew her nose hard. 'And now he's dead. And I say it's a waste. A life goes out, pah, *snuff*. What was he here for? Why was he born? Just to die in this damp fucking city. This place. *This fucking place this fucking city*,' and she screamed at the room, the cords in her neck stretching and tightening. She sobbed, and held her shawl against her face.

Perlman said, 'Can I get you something? Do you have wine? Brandy?'

'Nothing,' she said.

'You sure?'

'I want nothing.'

Perlman asked, 'Can we see Bobby's room?'

She indicated a door to her right. 'Why not.'

Perlman opened it, entered a dark stale space. He found a light switch. The room was small and panelled. Assorted items were pinned to the walls.

A bumper sticker: *My Country, Love It Or Leave It.*

A ragged slip of paper torn from a pamphlet dated 20 April 1998: Concerned Citizens for a White Britain, 7.30 p.m., Govan Cross.

A creased snapshot of a boy, possibly Bobby Descartes, in a Cub uniform. Undated.

Scullion entered the room. 'What have we got here?'

'Bits and pieces.' Perlman indicated the stuff on the walls, then moved to a table that held a computer. Although he had an urge to turn it on he knew he'd better leave that task to Scullion. He'd only press a wrong button.

He found a stack of envelopes to the side of the keyboard and he flicked through them. They were all addressed to R Descartes. He opened a few, enough to get an idea of the kind of post Bobby received.

None of the material suggested Bobby was a man of toler-ance. There were leaflets from various 'patriotic' societies that extolled the merits of the Monarchy and something called 'the British Way of Life', even as they excoriated Britain's attitude to immigration and the lack of truly strict laws that would keep 'the unwanted' out of this concrete Jerusalem. Read this stuff and you could imagine crazed people scribbling their ravings in bedsits or cold attics, the demented and the deranged in whose dislocated minds Britain had become no more than a gathering place for the scum fugitives of the planet. You could hear their clamour, their slogans, their hatred. Send all those niggers back the way they came. Stuff 'em in the holds of bug-ridden ships and float their arses out of God's Country.

Perlman stilled his anger. Racism was one of the planet's conditions; all your outrage didn't make a flake of difference. You could rant until your face was heliotrope and in the end you'd only sound hysterical, the flipside of the message the racists were screaming.

Scullion sifted the material, shaking his head. 'Let's say the delightful Bobby Descartes wants to kill McKinnon – so are we really looking at a kamikaze act? Does he go inside Cremoni's on the understanding he's not coming back out again alive?'

Perlman didn't know. 'Why McKinnon anyway?'

'Surely obvious? The man's colour.'

'A few people, not all of them racists, might have been interested in the removal of Perseus. His records . . . some of that stuff he collected was more than enough to make certain villains very nervous, Sandy. In any case, do you look around this sorry room and get the impression that our boy Bobby had a kamikaze streak? I see some pitiful hate mail from dubious organizations and hysterical individuals, aye, but do you know the overwhelming impression I get here?'

'You tell me.'

'Bitterness. Despair. The place reeks.'

'All I smell is damp,' Scullion said.

'Pay closer attention to your senses, Sandy. This computer, for example.' Perlman laid a hand on top of the dead screen. 'I don't know shite about these things –'

'Seconded,' Scullion said.

'But I know enough to tell you this is one of those home-made jobs. Look at it. All the pieces are different brands. The screen's one thing, the keyboard's another, the disk-drive is stuck inside some scratched metal box, and this doodah –'

'The external modem, I believe.'

'Whatever it's called. It's battered and dented, and the cable looks fucking lethal. Touch it, I bet you fry like bacon. Here's what I see. Some downright fucking sorry loser sitting here in this gloomy room attaching all this *shmatte* together, bits he picked up probably for a few quid in junk shops and second-hand joints. Look at it, Sandy. It's pathetic and rundown, and those wood panels look like they'd fall off if anybody as much as raised their voice in here . . .' Perlman paused. This was the underbelly of a dead man's life. The unmade bed and the objectionable leaflets and the used grey Y-fronts on the floor and the discarded socks that lay in balls and the low-grade home-made computer system.

'You think, what? Bobby was set up to be blown to pieces?' Scullion said. 'He knew nothing about an explosive.'

'It's one possibility. Or maybe he just happened to go into Cremoni's when a device, intended for McKinnon, went off. Wrong place, bad timing.'

'That kid Tommy Flynn said Bobby knocked on the door and McKinnon let him in, right? So why was he going inside Cremoni's at a time when the restaurant was closed? Did he know McKinnon? Was he a friend? Was he delivering some-thing?'

Perlman folded his arms and leaned against the wall and the panel at his back shifted slightly under his weight. The day coming to an end was beginning to vaporize. He felt fatigue move just behind his eyes. How long until he hit his bed? Even then, head on pillow, would he sleep, or would his mind, like a greyhound, chase the evasive electric hare hour after hour? He gazed at Bobby's mail again: a racist, but nothing here to connect him *obviously* with White Rage.

'Why don't you switch the computer on?' he said.

'I was about to.' Scullion pressed a key and there was a flurry of whirring and clicking. The screen burst into colour, exploding orbs, zigzagging lines, then the words *Property of Bobby D.*

'Now what?' Perlman asked.

Scullion stared at the screen. He tapped the keyboard and a list appeared, white letters on a blue background. 'Word processing. Calculator. Internet connection. Email. Pretty basic.'

'Can we check his mail?'

Scullion opened the file that contained Bobby Descartes' email program. Nothing. Outbox, inbox, trash – all empty.

Perlman asked, 'Does this mean he never used email?'

'It's more likely he deleted it.'

'So we don't know who he communicated with?'

'Presumably that's what he intended. Keep everything secret.'

'Where does email go when you delete it?'

Scullion said, 'I think it just gets zapped. Gone and goodbye. I did hear once that some smart characters had ways of retrieving pulverized mail.'

'We can locate such a *vunderlech*?'

'I'm sure we can.'

'So we schlep the machine out of here.'

'You think you can carry it?' Scullion said.

'My age, I still get the donkey work.' Perlman stared at the tangle of wires. He didn't fancy touching any of them. Begin by unplugging, for safety's sake. He dropped to hands and knees and crawled under the table and carefully yanked plugs from the wall. He stood up, lifted the assorted pieces of the machine. Scullion helped, picked up the hefty monitor, clutched it to his chest. Perlman balanced keyboard, modem and disk-drive in a stack.

They hauled the stuff inside the living room.

Sandrine Descartes stared at them. 'Take it. Take anything you like. You don't need my permission. Bobby's dead. I don't want this stuff. Wait. I have something else for you.' She got up from the sofa and went inside the kitchen and when she returned she was holding a wooden-handled hammer in her hand. Tears slid from her eyes and ran in random lines

216

down her face and the corners of her mouth were flecked with saliva.

'Bobby brought this home with him.'

Scullion stared at her over the top of the monitor. 'Why do you want us to –'

Then he stopped, struck by an understanding of what she was holding. He glanced at Perlman, whose attention was focused on the metal head of the implement, which Sandrine Descartes brought very close to his face. He saw how the head was stained brown-red and covered with tiny dried specks of organic matter he couldn't identify. He placed the computer components on the floor and reached for the hammer, which Sandrine Descartes stuck into his open hand.

The shaft was a little gummy.

He knew at once how this hammer had been used. The recent history of this tool vibrated inside him. He wanted to drop the thing and scrub his hands clean in scalding water. But he held on to the hammer tightly, like a man frozen to a surface of ice.

30

She asked, 'You don't like the hair, Pegg? At least I don't look anything like this,' and she pushed the early edition of the *Daily Record* across the formica table top.

Pegg glanced at the computer sketch of the dark-haired girl on the front page. *Do You Know This Woman?* 'How did they get this to look so bloody accurate anyway?'

'I don't think it resembles me at all,' she said. It was different from the picture Perlman had shown her originally; that old fart, naturally, had had her features revised by somebody who knew his way around a photo-fit programme. 'The nose is too long. The eyes are too far apart.'

'By a fraction of an inch maybe.' Pegg frowned and turned his face to one side. He plucked at the rubber band of his eyepatch, as if it were too tight. A Chinese waiter hustled past carrying a tray stacked with sizzling pork.

'You're not telling me everything, are you?' Pegg asked.

She folded the newspaper over, hiding the sketch of herself and the banner headline *Racist Killings Shock Glasgow*. What was she supposed to tell Pegg? That she'd run into Perlman by sheer chance? That she'd jeopardized herself by going back to the vicinity of the explosion? No. Pegg was already simmering. He'd never accepted her entirely into the cell that was the province of himself and Swank. Maybe he was sexist. Maybe possessive of his little kingdom.

'Tell me why I'm getting the feeling you're not being straight?' he asked.

'You're a suspicious bastard.'

'I need to be.'

'Come on, Pegg. People saw me in the Tinderbox. Which incidentally was where you wanted me to be, because Helen Mboto was going to be there, and you wanted a double chocolate scoop, didn't you? Okay. People described me to the cops. What difference does it make now? This black-haired little number in the newspaper has ceased to exist, Pegg. In her place, you see a neat blonde cutie in tight blue jeans and scarlet lipstick and a low-cut blouse – and these sparklers.' She spread her hand, flashed her big cheap rings.

Pegg pushed aside a half-eaten eggroll. His one eye blinked rapidly a few times. 'Somebody will recognize the face in the newspaper. Somebody will come forward and say I remember her. You're arrogant if you don't believe that. Arrogance doesn't have any place in our movement.'

'Arrogant, my arse. I'm good at what I do, that's all. And who's going to catch me anyway? I'm on the move, Pegg. I'm quicksilver.'

'The blonde hair and those idiot jewels – you think you can hide behind all that?'

'I know I can, cutie.'

'You're . . .' Pegg didn't complete the sentence. He poked at the eggroll. 'Why do I eat this crap? I hate Chinese. You're the one who wanted to meet here.'

'It's open all hours and it's out of the way.'

'MSG makes me sweat,' he said. 'You look like a two-quid tart.'

She lit a cigarette and winked at him.

Pegg made a face. 'I don't appreciate this.'

She thought: Humourless little git. Did he stay home and jerk off? She decided he was a virgin. She was tempted to rub him under the table, a tiny provocation, but that was a move too far. You didn't joke with Pegg. She looked past him at the post-midnight diners. Some used chopsticks drunkenly, and sniggered when rice dropped.

'I got the *job* done,' she said.

'We could have done without the theatrics.'

'Look, I do what I'm supposed to. The point is, it gets accomplished. What time is it?'

'One a.m.'

'I have to make a phone call.'

'To who? Your Mr Big?' Pegg sneered; he did it well.

'He donates, Pegg. Hard *cash*.'

'I don't like the arrangement.'

'Because it's mine. Because you didn't initiate it.' She rose, adjusted the silver strap of her shoulder bag. She went down the hallway that led to the toilets, passing the open doorway of the kitchen. Thick smoke rose from hot woks. Chefs yammered in Chinese. She kept moving until she reached the telephone. She shoved a coin in the slot, punched in a number.

Oyster answered, second ring. 'I like your punctuality.'

'You can count on me.'

'You're compelled. You're driven.'

'Driven?' she asked. 'I like to think I'm the one doing the driving.'

31

2.08 a.m: Perlman badly wanted to wrap the day and go home,
but here he was in Scullion's office where a technical support
operative called Alec Desert had Bobby Descartes' computer up
and running. Desert was a miserable thin-necked little man who
hated his job, his wife, his kids and his three-bedroom semi in
Dumbreck. Roused from sleep and summoned to Pitt Street, he
was more crabbity than usual; he had the brow-scrunched look
of man who'd accidentally thrown away a winning lottery ticket
and couldn't find it. He wore a cheap blue suit over his striped
pyjamas, but he'd forgotten to put on outdoor shoes. Battered
tartan slippers covered his feet.

He studied the screen. 'I wish some of you Force guys would
get really computer-literate. It's not rocketry, you know. It's not
even Rubik's fucking cube. It's dead simple.'

Scullion said, 'It's a knack, Alec. Some have it, some don't.'

'Any schoolboy could do this half-asleep.'

Perlman said, 'So you wanted to be something else when you
grew up, eh? Welcome to the lodge.'

'I wanted to play football. I had a trial for St Mirren. I
wanted to turn pro. Instead I go around with my head stuck

inside computers.' He smothered a yawn and rapped at the keyboard, fingers long and bony. 'Okay. Lemme explain to youse thickos. You delete something on a computer, it doesn't mean it's disappeared for ever. It gets relegated to another sector of the hard disk, and it might stay there for a long time. You can't find the deleted message by typing in the file name because the computer won't recognize it. Following me this far? Now the email system here is standard. What I have to do is access the datafiles and see if I can open them without having to drag this piece of home-made shite to a lab. What we'll see, with any luck, is a bunch of deleted messages. Okay? So you want to know what he sent and what he received?'

'Just don't get technical,' Perlman said.

'Am I being technical so far? I'm talking like one of the fucking Flowerpot Men. I'll give you technical if –'

The phone rang. Scullion picked it up, then passed it to Perlman. Terry Bogan was on the line. 'Score. The barman at the Corinthian says yes, definitely, no two ways. This is the girl.'

'One hundred per cent?'

'Absolutely. I hope it helps, Lou. Jesus I'm knackered.'

'Thanks.' Perlman put the phone down.

'Something to share?' Scullion asked.

'Bogan got a yes from the Corinthian.'

'Now you're sorry you didn't cuff your femme fatale, right?'

Perlman didn't answer. Sandy's question was more mild criticism than inquiry: *How did you let her elude you, Lou? Pops up right in front of your eyes, and you let her walk.* You don't usually get second shots at coincidental meetings, Perlman thought. One jolt from the blue, then gone and goodbye. You could wait a lifetime for the next occurrence.

Perlman watched the screen change. His attention drifted to a memory of the hammer, and the feel of wood against his skin, and the revulsion he'd experienced when Sandrine Descartes had placed it in his hand. The hammer had already gone to Sid Linklater for examination. Now he thought of the golf course, and Helen Mboto, and Linklater's assessment that the dead woman had been struck – what? Thirty times? More? Perlman hated having to recall the stats of death, how many hammer blows, gunshots, knife wounds. If Bobby Descartes' hammer had been the killing instrument, it tied him, beyond doubt, with White Rage. And the girl who'd called herself Celia – identified now as the wee *stoater* who'd been gyrating with Tilak Gupta the night of his death – had she lured Helen Mboto out of the Tinderbox? Maybe Helen had been conned to death by kindness. And maybe on a dark street close to the Tinderbox Bobby Descartes had been waiting with a hammer in his pocket.

Desert said, 'Okay. You see what's coming up on the screen? These are deleted emails. Some complete, some truncated. There's a bunch of code splashed around – all these digits and slashes and weird symbols – but ignore that. I'll start scrolling slowly and you can tell me when you want me to stop.'

Perlman refocused, gazed at the monitor. Scullion huddled close, all attention.

'Stop there,' Scullion said.

Sahara looked at the screen. 'This is a message sent by somebody called Beezer to somebody by the name of Paprika. It says: *See you when I'm next in Edmburra.*'

Beezer and Paprika, Perlman thought. A name from an old comic and a Hungarian goulash condiment. Email offered a gateway to a world of unlikely conjunctions. 'Who the hell is Beezer?' he asked.

Desert scanned the screen. 'All the outgoing emails are from Beezer, so I assume he's the owner of this shambolic mutant of a computer.'

Perlman thought, Bobby Descartes: AKA Beezer. Why choose that as your nom d'email?

Scullion asked, 'If we wanted to know the identity of this Paprika, how could we find out?'

'It's difficult. Paprika has a Hotmail account. You sign up with Hotmail, you don't have to give an address or a phone number.

You don't even need to give your real name. Hotmail doesn't care who you are. It's one of those email servers popular with backpackers who send and receive from Internet cafés all over the world. Paprika could be anyone, anywhere.'

'And this one?' Scullion prodded the monitor with a fingertip.

'The message from clydevalley dot net? Is that the one you're looking at?'

'Right. From this . . . Magistr32. It just says Go.'

Sahara shrugged. 'Clydevalley is another free-serve op. Customers don't pay a fee to send or receive emails. Also popular with students, travellers, holidaymakers. There are so many of these outfits. Talk about proliferation.'

'So Magistr32 is basically untrackable.'

'You might get lucky and find the point of origin, then you'd probably discover it's an Internet café somewhere, with a hundred clients a day.' Sahara scrolled a little further. 'Beezer obviously answered Magistr32's message. Look.'

Perlman read aloud the words on the screen. 'Beezer will do his duty.'

'I wonder what his duty was,' Scullion said.

'Whatever, this Magistr32 is the one giving out the orders,' Perlman said. The screen was crucifying his eyes; he felt sharp pressure behind his eyeballs.

'There's a date and a time,' Scullion said. 'Hey, I just realized – he sent this email two hours before the shooting at the kindergarten.'

Two hours before. Perlman's headache was worsening. He thought of a rainswept school playground, and a hooded figure moving through the prematurely dark afternoon with a gun in his hand. And then his mind went to Magistr32's command, and Bobby Descartes' response, and the curious way Bobby referred to himself in the third person: *Beezer will do his duty*.

Alec Desert said, 'If youse two don't need me any longer, I'm for the off. I need some kip.'

'I think we can release you, Alec,' Scullion said.

Desert said, 'Remember. If you want to read more, just keep pressing that arrow key, the one that points down. Got it? Or is that too difficult for your wee brains? I'll leave written instructions if you like.'

Perlman said, 'Piss off home.'

'Matter of interest, do I get overtime for this?'

'Take it up with the management.' Perlman picked up a paper dart from Scullion's desk and aimed it at Desert, who ducked halfway out the door before the missile struck a wall and dropped gracelessly to the floor.

'Oh aye, one last thing,' Desert said. 'The name Magistr32?'

'What about it?'

'It's the name of a common but nasty stealth computer virus. Nice wee in-joke for nerds. It's as if Lucretia Borgia had email and used the name Toxica or something.'

'Funny,' Perlman said.

'Thought you should know.' Desert left.

Perlman picked up the dart, smoothed it back into its original flat form, then sat on the edge of Scullion's desk and stared at the light-strip in the ceiling.

Magistr32 and Beezer. Beezer and Magistr32.

He thought of the young woman in Dumbarton Road, the attractive Celia, but this time, strangely, he couldn't bring her face to mind as he'd been able to do with such clarity before; it blanked in his head, turning into an expanse of undetailed flesh, something rising up from the fog of an uneasy dream.

Scullion looked at the computer. 'What do you think, Lou?'

'I'm probably thinking what you're thinking, Sandy.'

'The Go message. The Beezer response. The timing.'

'The timing. You can't ignore that.'

'Magistr32 and Celia – one and the same?'

Perlman nodded. 'Maybe. But it doesn't bring us any closer to nailing her.'

'Her picture will be in every morning paper, Lou.'

'And we'll get lucky and somebody will see it and the case will break open like a jimmied safe. Right?'

'It happens. We'll get a uniform to run through the rest of Bobby's messages tomorrow.'

'Am I free to leave?'

'It's late,' Scullion said. 'Enjoy your liberty.'

Perlman edged off the rim of the desk and creaked to a standing position. I don't want to go home, he thought. Back to Egypt, back to that cold house. But it was too late to phone Miriam, and he didn't relish the idea of spending a night in a nearby hotel. I'm a man of limited options.

'Get some sleep,' Scullion said.

'Remind me how.'

'Say your prayers and close your eyes. If you're still having trouble, count all the good-looking women you failed to bring in for questioning when you should have.'

'Hit me below the belt, Sandy. *Bilik vi vorsht.*'

'What the hell does that mean?'

Perlman headed for the door.

'I hate it when you talk Yiddish,' Scullion said.

'Oy vey.'

32

Perlman didn't drive straight home, although he was weary and his brain was malfunctioning. He parked in the street outside Miriam's building and lit a cigarette to steady his wobbly hand. He looked up, saw no light escape from her loft. *Maybe she's sitting in the dark, waiting for you to ring, Lou.* Aye, and in this perfect wee world bumblebees play tunes on paper-combs.

I underestimate myself. She's up there, sleepless, waiting for me. Of course she is. He crushed the cigarette out. Go home, he thought. He looked the length of the dark street. No Latta in evidence. He lit another smoke. Tomorrow I quit. He rolled down the window. The 3 a.m. air was chill and a little hazy and the city quiet as the inside of a crypt.

The kiss, he thought. That's why I'm here. Seduced by a kiss. Wanting more. An addict in need of his fix. He shut his eyes and pondered Miriam's mouth and remembered the taste.

My brother's wife. £893,000.

You keep stumbling into things that take the breeze from your sails. He got out of the car and walked to the thick front door of the building. He poked the button for the buzzer; Miriam, take me in.

'Lou?' Her voice was clear over the speaker.

'I wake you?'

'No, no. Come up.'

She buzzed, the door opened, he entered the building and moved towards the stairs, unaware of a little skip to his step. He climbed. She was waiting for him outside her loft. She wore a dark green velvet robe, knee-length, belted. She was barefoot. Her hair, no longer gelled and flat, had been brushed out, given fuller life. He half-expected – if not a fierce hug, a fiery passion – a brief embrace at the least, but instead she simply smiled and turned and went back inside. He followed, hands dangling idly at his sides, palms cold.

One lamp was lit inside the loft, a tiny gasp of light in an expanse of shadow.

'I just finished at HQ. I was going home.' He wondered why this meeting was suddenly awkward, why there was a sense of frozen space between them. Where was the Miriam who'd held his hand and kissed him and understood his longings? He stared through an open doorway at her bedroom, seeing an edge of bed, sheets disturbed where she must have risen minutes before to answer the bell, a pillow dented where her head had lain.

'Solved everything?' she asked.

The question was ambiguous; did she want to know if he'd cracked the code of the human heart, or if he'd swept the streets of Glasgow free of criminals?

'Solve one thing, another puzzle comes along,' he said. 'Crime never sleeps.'

'Like you.'

'Crime and emotion,' he said. 'They're resurgent things.'

'Do I want to talk about emotion? I don't know, Lou.'

'In the pub tonight –'

'I kissed you. You kissed me.'

'It was more.'

'Lou, it's far too soon.'

'So I wait for a better time, if such a thing ever happens? Is that what you're telling me? I go about my daily business and

228

hope you get everything sorted out in your mind and one night you call with your decision?'

'No –'

'By which time, *neshumeleh*, I could be drawing a pension.'

'Lou –'

'I'm aching inside,' he said. 'I yearn. It's like having a fucking ulcer, Miriam, only there's no medication.'

'I'm not acting like this to *hurt* you, Lou. I'm not playing games. I swear, I know what you feel. I know what you go through. But I need time. Please understand I'm not being some fifty-year-old cocktease, Lou.'

He looked at lamplight reflected in the black skylight overhead. It resembled a small alien moon. How patient could he be? How patient could any man be? He'd soldiered for years in the trenches of endurance. He'd been sitting in the anteroom of Miriam's love for as long as he'd known her. You wait for a sign. You think the kiss is such a thing. You hope.

A Catholic might have called his life a purgatory.

He reached for her and drew her towards him. She let him kiss her. She didn't fight him off; there was no hardening of her body against him. He was captivated by the exciting privacy of the kiss, a man journeying into emotional hyperspace where time is fragmented and you're joyful, joyful. He touched her naked breast, moved by the warm softness of it even as he was amazed by his own lack of clumsiness; she let him caress her like this for a time, then she stepped away from him.

He hadn't come here to impose himself on her body. He'd wait, sure he'd wait, but maybe it would be a different kind of waiting than before: he'd glimpsed a tiny flutter of optimism, and that was enough to sustain him for the time being. He was aware he'd developed an erection, which was already in a state of collapse: a minor matter. You go from the promise of cosmic bliss to detumescence in a flash – was any journey ever shorter?

She shoved her fingers through her hair. 'Bear with me, Lou.'

'I'm bearing,' he said.

She looked at him. She had a frank gaze, direct and true. 'I'm thankful that you are.'

He walked towards the door, where he stopped. 'Tell me. Has Latta been bothering you again?'

'I try not to think about Latta,' she said.

'He'll keep on about that bank transfer. You know he will. He's a *nudnik*. He digs in with claws.'

'Why are we talking about Latta? You're as curious about that money as he is, aren't you?'

Of course he was curious. 'It's none of my business, Miriam.'

'You know what I sometimes feel, Lou? I'm destined to be haunted the rest of my life by your brother's ghost. I transferred some money, and suddenly people imagine Colin's sinister handiwork in the transaction. I spend money living in Florence for three months, and people want to know if I'm using a private slush fund Colin left me. Money he embezzled, money that rightly belongs to his victims, money the tax people are interested in, and the cops.'

'I don't wonder about the money,' he said.

'Of course you wonder, Lou. You can't help yourself. Go. Solve some crime. Make Glasgow healthy again. Call me.'

He stepped out of the loft. He didn't want to leave her. He heard her close the door behind him. He went downstairs and out into the street. Nothing moved. Glasgow was possessed by the curiously unreal stillness of the sleeping city. Traffic lights changed, but no traffic materialized. He got inside his car and headed east towards the Trongate, past darkened buildings and shuttered shops. He felt the spectre of Miriam's mouth: *Give me a kiss to build a dream on.*

Deeper into the east; London Road, Bridgeton, Belvidere Hospital, until recently a geriatric care facility, now closed. He reached the cemetery at Dalbeth, where he dozed a second, then pulled himself out of it just in time to avoid a man running directly in front of the car, a figure wrapped in headscarf and clothes so dark he would have been barely visible in the best of light. Perlman stamped on the brake and the Mondeo went into a short skid and the man vanished in the direction of Braidfauld Street.

Perlman heard the siren of a police vehicle, and saw a flash of lights about a hundred yards ahead of him. From the dark of the cemetery more black-garbed figures appeared, twenty or so scarpering and scattering across London Road, some rushing into Braidfauld Street, others making for Downfield Street. The air was cut with the occasional cry or shout in a language Perlman didn't know. The police vehicle was a black van that came to a halt alongside the Mondeo, and four uniforms jumped out, their boots clattering on stone as they raced after the fugitives.

A man in a blue raincoat emerged from the front of the van. Curious, Perlman got out of his car and walked towards him.

'Problem?' Perlman showed his ID.

The man said, 'Lou Perlman, eh? Sergeant Joe Adamski, E-Division.'

'What's going on?'

Adamski was a heavy man whose florid neck overflowed his shirt collar. 'Round-up time,' he said. 'This lot was dropped off by a lorry back there,' and he jabbed a thumb in the general area of the cemetery. 'But we had the information. So we were waiting. They usually give us a good work-out. Not for long. They don't have the stamina. Starving, most of them.'

'Illegals,' Perlman said.

'Yep. I think this lot is from the Middle East. Some will apply for asylum. Most get their backgrounds investigated and then offksy. There's always another load arriving. They come in the holds of ships, under piles of cargo, sometimes they're buried beneath rotting fruit, frozen beef . . . a fucking desperate state of affairs. It costs them a fortune to get here, and they don't know where they're going to end up. I hate this part of my job, chasing these people.'

Perlman, drunk on lack of sleep, had the feeling of being in a city he didn't know. Glasgow was suddenly a place he'd entered

231

unwittingly, where men chased other men in a pantomime played out in front of tiny audiences.

'They think it's all milk and honey here,' Adamski said. 'They have this notion they can come two thousand miles and the government just spews out cash for them.'

Perlman looked a little longer into the dark, hearing angry or impatient voices now and then break the silence. He had to get home. 'Happy hunting, Adamski.'

'We always get them,' Adamski said.

Perlman drove up Braidfauld Street. He saw nobody, no movement. He parked outside his house. Depleted, depressed by the idea of homeless refugees fleeing in the night, and the basic inequities of the world, he barely made it to the front door. He stroked the mezuzah as he always did.

He undressed while he climbed the stairs, kicking off shoes, dropping overcoat and trousers. By the time he reached his bedroom he was down to shirt and underwear and socks. He lay on the bed. A Celtic Football Club pennant hung aslant on the wall. *European Cup Winners, 1967.* There was a small framed photograph of that legendary team tacked just under the pennant. Heroic Glasgow men, toiling in the Lisbon sun to defeat a bunch of tough Italians. A couple of old football programmes were pinned around the pennant. Real Madrid v Eintracht Frankfurt, Hampden Park, 1963. England v Scotland, Wembley, 1967, a rare, famous Scottish victory.

The thought struck Perlman, as it had done before, that this was a boy's room, with its sport souvenirs and discarded clothes piled here and there; it wasn't a grown man's bedroom. It wasn't a seduction chamber, a babe-box.

He fell asleep quickly, and dreamed he was pursuing a band of fugitives down Hope Street at the height of rush hour.

33

At dawn she walked towards the Clyde, where she listened to the cry of gulls and the occasional noise of a delivery van carrying morning rolls and newspapers to shops. There were no buses in the streets, no taxis. A dirty yellow light slit the dark sky. The night withdrew at the pace of a garden slug. Streetlamps were still lit in the city.

She passed a bundle of newspapers stacked and twined outside a shuttered newsagents, and helped herself to one, yanking it out under the string. Hysteria on the front page: *Racist Killings*. A group called White Rage was being 'hunted'. Police spokesmen said rhubarb rhubarb. Only a matter of time. We'll bring them to justice. A Roman Catholic bishop called for calm and courage and prayer. Muslim leaders urged people to be watchful. An inner-city politician took advantage of the situation, as politicians will, and railed at the inadequacy of policing, and how stronger punishments for race crimes were needed.

She saw her own face stare at her from the page.

If you have seen this woman, please call 888-8787.

Pegg had said it was a good likeness.

She couldn't see it. People never really know what they look like to others. Check a mirror, and you see what you're inclined to see. She walked to the river's edge and ripped the newspaper in a dozen pieces and let them go from her hand towards the water, where they floated in gradually discolouring strips.

Then she began to run. She moved into an easy jog when she reached Anderston Quay, picking up speed along the Broomielaw. She turned round as soon as she reached Central Station Bridge, and jogged back the way she'd come. Good for the heart. Good for the lungs. She needed to be fit. She needed clarity of mind and strength of purpose. Her skin felt warm now under the grey cotton tracksuit. Her breath created little clouds in the air.

She stopped at the end of Lancefield Quay. She could hear sparse traffic on the Clydeside Expressway. A drone, then silence, then another drone. She took a couple of deep breaths and ran again, heading back towards Central Station Bridge. She saw a man come towards her, late thirties, expensive black tracksuit, top-of-the-line running shoes. He smiled at her. A couple of pavement pounders exchanging affectionate understanding, like members of a club recognizing each other's badges. We must be mad to do this. She predicted he'd say something like that.

What he said was, 'Are we crazy?'

'Probably,' she said.

'I haven't seen you around here before.' He'd changed direction, slipped into step alongside her.

A duo of joggers. He fancied his chances. 'I don't come here often,' she said.

He was breathing hard. 'The fight against flab knows no bounds.'

'I don't have any flab,' she said.

'I can see that. So you exercise for what? Fun?'

'I'm fighting middle age before it arrives.'

'Precautionary measures. Smart.'

She spurted a few feet ahead of him, then he caught up with her.

'Is this a race?' he asked.

'I'm only doing what I do.'

'You're in great shape.'

She stopped. She walked a couple of paces, turning into McAlpine Street. He followed her.

'You jog up here?' He gestured towards the network of little streets – Crimea Street, Balaclava, Washington – that ran south of a main thoroughfare, Argyle Street.

'It's quieter this time of day.'

'It's not exactly crowded anywhere this early, is it?' He had black hair, a few lanks of which toppled over his brow.

'I like the quiet,' she said.

'I'm a noise person myself. Too much quiet, I'm going out of my mind.' He fluttered his index finger rapidly against his lower lip to suggest gibberish and lunacy.

She was supposed to laugh at this, so she did. 'We're all different.'

'Thank God for that.'

She stared at the ground. She knew he'd ask her out. She sensed him gather the nerve. Men were vividly transparent most of the time. Only Oyster was different, difficult to read. Maybe that was why she found him so appealing. The sense of inner privacy he projected: you'll never know me.

'You ever been to Café Arta?'

'Are you inviting me?'

'Why not? We runners should stick together.'

She put her hand in the pocket of her trousers. 'You want an immediate answer?'

'If you've got one.'

'I'm the girl with all the answers.'

She took out her gun and shot him. She shot him in the right eye. He went down, stunned and blinded, and tilted his face up as if to say *There must be some mistake.* She shot him again, this time in the neck. He fell on his side and his blood gathered on the pavement around his head. It looked darker than blood in the bad light, more like spilled wine. She didn't wait. She ran north to Argyle Street and jogged under streetlamps even as the sky lightened inexorably. She kept going north up Wellington Street, then she made a right turn along St Vincent Lane, just a runner, just a pretty blonde jogger pursuing good health.

Any pedestrian passing on his or her way to a sedentary job might look and think: More people should do what she does. *I* should do what she does. Get the blood going, stave off a coronary, tone the muscles. Yes indeed.

A healthy young woman. Sound of body, sound of mind.

34

It seemed to Perlman he'd hardly slept more than a few minutes
before his alarm clock raged. His dreams vaporized. He woke
empty-headed, dry-mouthed. He rolled out of bed and stumbled
to the shower and stood paralysed under the blast of water.
When it began to run cold he stepped out, towelling himself as
he returned to his bedroom to look for something to wear.

He found a clean white shirt folded badly in a drawer of his
dressing table. He decided yesterday's socks had another day
left in them. Clean boxers, blue and white striped: he felt sporty
in these, vaguely pugilistic. Come out of your corner fighting,
champ.

He knotted his tie, not yesterday's embarrassing kipper of an
attachment, but a slimmer tie one of the Aunts had pressed
on him a couple of Chanukahs ago. Blue, silver flashes. *Here,
Louie, do yourself a favour, brighten yourself up, what bird whistles
at drab plumage?* He checked inside his wardrobe. He had a
charcoal-grey suit hanging there. It had a faint pinstripe that
was almost invisible. The suit was ten years old and the trousers
were tight at his waist. He'd get by.

He put on his shoes and went downstairs where he stuck an

old vinyl disc on the turntable and listened to Fats Waller sing 'Ain't Misbehavin'', and then he continued into the kitchen. Coffee, tea – decisions. He plugged in the electric kettle. He made instant coffee. He drank it standing at the kitchen table. He glanced at the clock on the windowsill. Eight oh seven. He had a very bad feeling about the day ahead. More death. More violence. A panicky city.

He walked to the stairs, picked up his coat where he'd dropped it about five hours ago, and then left the house. He stepped inside his Ford. Ready ready ready. Hit the road, Jack. As he drove off, he slid a CD of Nigel Clark's *Grand Hotel Europa* into the deck, and realized he'd forgotten to turn the damn turntable off. He drove towards the city centre through draggy traffic, wondering where he'd lost his mobile. You could go crazy pondering the loose ends and missing objects of a life – the record player running, the AWOL mobile phone, the light he realized he'd left on in his bedroom.

He made it to Force HQ by eight forty. He parked his car on a double yellow and entered the building. He was filled with a quiet dread that lay in his stomach like an undigested slice of Dundee fruitcake. He saw Scullion coming quickly down the stairs, and Mary Gibson hurrying behind him. They looked grave.

Scullion said, 'Just in time.'

'For what?'

Sandy didn't answer. A rough day loomed: you could read it in his frown. Mary Gibson's face was knotted with tension. Perlman followed Scullion and Mary Gibson out into the street. The morning was cold, the sun a furious red. Scullion zapped the central-locking device of his car, opening the doors. Mary Gibson took the passenger seat, Perlman slid in behind her.

'Will somebody tell me?' Perlman asked.

Mary Gibson didn't turn to look at him. 'Nat Blum,' she said.

'Blum? What about him?'

'Dead. Shot twice. Cold blood.'

238

'Blum's dead? *Blum?*'

Sandy Scullion said, 'His body was found at six a.m. approximately, just off the Broomielaw. He was carrying no personal items, no wallet, nothing. It took more than an hour and a half to ID him.'

'Blum,' Perlman said. 'I can't believe Blum's . . .' He hadn't cared for Nat, he'd considered him greedy and slick, but he'd never have wished him dead.

Scullion turned his car into Bothwell Street, and then Waterloo. Perlman remembered how he'd come this way yesterday with Madhur Gupta, and how long ago that seemed. It was as if Indra Gupta's murder had been driftwood sucked away by a ruthless tide. If he didn't reel it in soon there was a risk of it vanishing completely.

And now Blum.

Okay, Nat kept bad company: maybe somebody in that circle of thugs he represented had decided he knew too much, and a man with an insider's knowledge of illicit acts is always vulnerable, always a possible liability.

Scullion parked the car outside Blum's office building, where Perlman's urge to blame a gangster element for the lawyer's murder dissipated as soon as he saw the graffiti spraypainted over the windows and entranceway. Shocked, he got out of the car. He opened Mary Gibson's door for her. Scullion was already on the pavement, staring at the riot of paint.

'Fuck me,' Perlman said. He studied the collection of red swastikas and tried to define what was going through his head, what this blood-coloured symbol caused him to feel – sadness? Anger? Or just a reaction to his own powerlessness to make a change in the world, and promote a little understanding, a little tolerance? Fuck it, he wasn't a social worker, a shrink, it wasn't his place to alter the attitudes of men and women –

Scullion said, 'Pretty sight, eh?'

Perlman made no response. He was conscious now of uniformed cops cluttering the scene, keeping at bay the growing number of spectators. He recognized Dennis Murdoch among them.

Perlman wondered when he'd last seen a swastika in Glasgow. He'd spotted one now and then in the arches under old railway bridges, usually surrounded by the spraypainted names of gangs and crude religious slogans. He'd noticed the symbol in a peripheral way only, viewing it as the work of ill-informed boys, the same yobs who splashed the acronyms IRA and UVF here and there throughout the city. But this serious assault on a building in the business heart of Glasgow was a different piece of work, offensive, nakedly public.

He counted more than twenty individual swastikas. Then he noticed the initials *WR* in white paint dotted here and there between the red; white streaks had slithered to touch the red, and the red had run here and there as well, creating a pink pattern, as if the stone itself were leaking a pale blood.

WR.

Nat Blum had been white; no matter, his Jewishness had put him in the same category as Ochoba, and Helen Mboto, and Perse McKinnon. There was no such thing as a white Jew, not if you were a member of White Rage.

Perlman entered the building. He followed Mary Gibson and Scullion into the lift and they rode in silence upwards. Inside Blum's suite, there were more swastikas, dozens splattered across blond wood and chrome. In Blum's private office, filing cabinets lay toppled, plants overturned, pots shattered, the lawyer's sound system smashed.

A couple of fingerprint guys worked in their careful way, stooped, almost monkish in their devotion. Tizer Dunlop appeared, photographing the wreckage. Fraser Deacon entered Blum's office, looking gaunt in a black suit and black polo-neck sweater. His shaved head gleamed like bone under the recessed spotlights. Did the Big Frase bring news from Special Branch? Perlman wondered. Was there somewhere a nugget of precious information?

Deacon said good morning in a curt way, then indicated that

he wanted to talk in a small conference room that adjoined Blum's office. This was a place where Nat met his clients, where legal strategy was discussed and options assessed. Perlman sat down beside Mary Gibson. She had her hands folded demurely in her lap. No wedding ring, marriage still out of commission. Scullion remained standing, his back to the window that overlooked Waterloo Street. Deacon stared at Perlman, as if surprised to see Lou here. Perlman thought, Maybe he expected me to walk away from this case, citing 'personal differences'. But I'm sticking to it, Frase. Trust me.

Deacon said, 'First, we're inclined to believe the weapon that killed Nat Blum was the one used in the shooting of Indra Gupta. Thirty-two calibre in both cases. We won't know for sure until further tests are done. But we're working on the assumption that it was the same weapon.'

The same gun, okay, Perlman thought, but how did it get from Bobby Descartes into the hands of whoever shot Blum? Did it come from Magistr32? Was she the provider, the quartermaster?

'Second, the hammer that was in Bobby Descartes' possession,' Deacon said. 'Linklater phoned me an hour ago to confirm that the tissue samples and the blood matched Helen Mboto.'

Since when did Sid Linklater report to Deacon? Special Branch, of course, those bastards took control, they had secret tracks they could pursue, quietly sinister avenues along which they could move. Deacon made no acknowledgement of how the hammer had been acquired. He talked as if the implement had just materialized, a miracle akin to the face of Christ appearing on the surface of a potato scone.

Nice to get credit, Perlman thought. 'Are you taking questions, Inspector?'

Deacon narrowed one eye, as if he were looking down a microscope at a dubious specimen. 'Depends on the question, Sergeant.'

'Bear with me. I thought the investigation of these various murders came under the aegis of Superintendent Gibson and

241

DI Scullion, with a team member such as my humble self somewhere down the pecking order. Are you saying Special Branch has stepped in, and this is now a joint op? Or are you saying you've taken control altogether?'

'No, we haven't taken control –'

'Fine. So my next question is whether you have fresh information re White Rage that you're prepared to share with Superintendent Gibson and the team.'

'All in good time,' Deacon said.

'When is a good time, Inspector? I mean, how many people have to shuffle off the mortal coil before you deem it a good time?'

'That's an impertinence, Perlman.'

'Look. I'm sick and fucking tired of being up to my knees in blood, Inspector. If you can help us in any way?'

Deacon said, 'I'm not being uncooperative just to obstruct, Perlman. There are some things I can't divulge.'

'Because they're – *sensitive*?'

'Exactly.'

'And how do you define sensitive, Inspector?'

Deacon made his right hand into a slack fist, and glanced at Mary Gibson. Did something pass between them at that moment? Perlman wondered. A look of complicity, a tell? Was Mary Gibson in league with the Devil here?

'You don't qualify on a need-to-know basis,' Deacon said.

'Um, a need-to-*what* basis? Excuse me, when exactly did we become the Glasgow sub-branch of MI6? Did I miss an in-house bulletin or something?'

'*Lou*,' Mary Gibson said.

'I'm sorry, Superintendent, but people are being killed and pardon me, I feel a responsibility. I don't sleep well. I'm not eating. My nerves are shot. I just don't think we're getting any fucking help from Inspector Deacon's clique.'

There was a silence in the room. Scullion, who'd grown pale over the last few days, studied his watch. Fraser Deacon sighed. Mary Gibson looked down at her own shadowy image in the polished surface of the table. Perlman got up and gazed into Waterloo Street, where a growing crowd gathered, and a line of uniforms prevented them from getting too close to the building. He blew on the glass and watched it steam up; the morning sun, red as a drunkard's nose, rose slowly over the rooftops.

He turned to face the room. 'Question. Is there some governmental involvement here? Are we getting too close to an area where ordinary foot soldiers shouldn't be straying?'

'Governmental?' Deacon asked.

'Don't play games with me, Inspector. You haven't intervened in this investigation simply because you want to make us flat-footed plodders look like inferior dullards, have you? There's something else at the nub of this. Something you don't want us to know. Maybe something the Scottish Office doesn't want us to know. Or Whitehall. I'm guessing, I'm stabbing in the dark.'

'Has Perlman become the department eccentric or the resident conspiracy theorist, Superintendent?' Deacon asked.

'He has his odd moments,' Mary Gibson said quietly. 'But he's a good policeman, generally.'

'I'll have to take your word for that,' Deacon said. 'Just the same, I'm wondering if perhaps the Sergeant is a little burnt out by his workload. It's a heavy one.'

Only an idiot could have missed the point: Perlman was being undermined. Doubts about his energy were being cast. 'I can handle it,' he said.

'Glad to hear you say so,' Deacon said. 'But still, you know . . .'

'No, I don't know. You tell me.'

'This is nothing personal, Perlman, but we all reach a certain stage of life when the reflexes aren't what they used to be. The muscles lose their elasticity. The brain slips up when it comes to concentration . . . The human condition, Sergeant. We're all going in the same direction.'

'Thank fuck I'm not a horse,' Perlman said. 'Or I'd be off to the abattoir at the crack of dawn. I'll go cheerfully when my time comes, not before. And especially not now, when it seems that

White Rage has declared open season on Jews.' He was furious with Deacon, and trying to tamp the feeling down. 'Doesn't it seem that way to you?'

'It's hard to predict,' Deacon said. 'But you're right, it seems that way.'

'So I should watch my back?'

'You should always watch your back.' Deacon smiled in a frosty way and lowered the register of his voice so that he sounded soothing, like a smooth late-night deejay playing bluesy old standards for insomniacs and lovers. 'Listen to me, Lou. And don't get petulant. If you feel you want to take some holiday time, I'm sure Superintendent Gibson would be sympathetic. We'd all understand.'

How deplorably heavy-handed Deacon could be, Perlman thought. It was the *worst* suggestion he could make. Deacon didn't have a clue who he was dealing with. Sideline Perlman? Give him time out and maybe he'll bugger off? A beach somewhere, a bottle of vino, chickadees walking past in G-strings and leaving the tang of suntan lotion on sultry air. No fucking *way*, Perlman thought. Not in a thousand years. *Leave the job now?* Leave Glasgow because it might be more convenient for Frase Deacon, who doesn't want me aboard his mystery train?

Why did everybody suggest he take a fucking holiday anyway? Fat Leo had advised a sea cruise. Mary Gibson had suggested Malaga or Malta. Now here was Deacon making a contribution to Lou's vacation plans. I'm in everybody's way, he thought. My realm of influence, that tiny fiefdom, is being reduced by the minute. My movements are being curtailed. Never mind what the grown-ups in Special Branch are doing, you're not part of the team. *The human condition, Sergeant.*

He wondered if Tay was behind this, or if Tay and Deacon were in collusion; what if Mary Gibson was a player in this sorry game too? Add Latta, and pretty soon you've got all kinds of officers aligned against you. And, God help you for wondering, was Scullion blameless?

He looked at Scullion, who half-smiled, as if to say: It's okay,

I understand, Lou. Come home with me, it's fish-pie night again, we'll relax, sup a few brews.

I can't do fish pie tonight; sorry, Sandy, Perlman thought. I still have the killer of a young Indian girl to find, and it doesn't matter that I hate the taste of bureaucratic fodder, and the shit-stink of interference from High Places, and the condescending suggestions of Baldyheid from Special Branch.

He thought of Nat Blum, Kilroy's front, his decoy, the glove puppet that fitted neatly on Leo's fat hand. Poor ambitious hotshot Nat. Now a dead man. Why? Why out of all five thousand Jews in the city had Blum been chosen? Why not a prominent rabbi, or a community leader? Why not *me*, a policeman?

'I'll ponder Inspector Deacon's suggestion about a vacation,' Perlman said, and addressed the remark to Scullion, who knew that dismissive tone very well. 'Meanwhile, I've got some paper-work to catch up on. Reports, Sandy. Right? Detailed reports? Up to the minute, nothing overlooked, right?'

'Right,' Scullion said.

'*In my hour of darkness*,' Perlman sang, as he left the room and walked towards the corridor. He kept moving, although he thought he heard Mary Gibson call his name. Keep moving, keep singing. '*O Lord grant me vision, O Lord grant me speed.*' Was that meant to have a drug connotation, or did Gram Parsons believe God could give you wings so you could fly fast? He walked to the lifts, pressed the call button.

Fucking Deacon. Patronising me, suggesting I can't cut it.

He stepped into the lift. He had a pain at the back of his eyes. New glasses is what I need. Take a vacation. Aye. Up yours. He exited the lift at street level. The entrance was crowded with coppers. He pushed his way through, trying with each little thrust of his elbows to keep calm, restore sanity, straighten his gyroscope.

He made it to the street. An inquisitive crowd blocked the pavement. He squeezed through. When he was free of the spectators, he walked to the nearest corner and lit a cigarette.

He sucked the smoke deep and long. He realized that this was the corner where he'd stopped yesterday with Madhur Gupta. Waterloo and Wellington Street, Hope Street ahead. A grieving mother.

He didn't see Dennis Murdoch approach. In uniform, he looked very young, a pink boy. He had good trustworthy eyes.

'The pits,' Perlman said.

Murdoch nodded. 'It's hard to know what to make of it all. The why of . . .'

'Don't worry, Dennis. I've been round the block a few times and the whole circus still wrecks my head.'

'I'd been looking for you, Sergeant, but then all this happened,' and Murdoch gestured at the crowd, the swastikas, the situation in general, 'and I didn't have a chance to catch up.'

'You don't have to make excuses,' Perlman said. 'What did you find out about the accident?'

'It's a wee bit strange. The driver was identified as one Willie Glone. The cab exploded. He died of massive burns. According to the person I phoned at Bargeddie Haulage, they didn't have a driver by that name.'

'Meaning what? They're lying, or the truck was stolen?'

'They hadn't reported it stolen, Sergeant.'

'Either it was stolen, or the late Willie Glone had permission to drive it. One thing or the other. If it's the latter, then it's downright weird his name isn't known to Bargeddie Haulage. What's the name of the person you spoke to?'

'I didn't get a name, Sergeant. Some guy in the office.'

'What cargo was the truck carrying? Any idea?'

'None,' Murdoch said. 'I spoke to the officer who'd been at the scene, and he said the vehicle was empty.'

'Cause of accident?'

'Not yet established. All I heard was "out of control".'

Sort of like the way I'm going, Perlman thought. He laid a hand on Murdoch's sleeve. 'Let's take a drive, Dennis.'

Murdoch gestured in the direction of the crowd. 'I'm supposed to –'

246

'Just follow my orders, son,' Perlman said. 'We'll walk back to Pitt Street and pick up my car.'

Murdoch looked uncomfortable countermanding an order to protect the graffiti-stained building. A conscientious cop, Perlman thought, an honest man.

Good.

35

'I think she's fine, she's great,' the man called Swank said.

'Because you lust after her, don't you,' Pegg said.

Swank said, 'Lust, me? No, mate. I happen to think she's terrific at her game.'

'She loves drama,' Pegg said. 'She should have been an actress.'

'Look, I think she's pulling her weight. She's a good girl. It's not like she's some skinheid with blue tattoos on her skull. Or some common yobbo screaming monkey slogans at a football match.'

Swank lit a briar pipe and sucked on it. His cheeks imploded. He had a cadaverous face, deeply engraved by premature ageing. His long thin hair, a straggle of black and grey, hung down over the shoulders of his brown velvet jacket.

Pegg waved away an aromatic fog of tobacco smoke and looked round Swank's flat in the basement of a tenement in Garnethill. Paint peeled from the walls like skin. The ceiling had been water-damaged at some time, and had developed an eczematous look. The sweet smoke killed the smell of rising damp. An enormous bank of computer equipment, stacked

248

against the back wall, gleamed incongruously; there had to be four or five grand's worth of equipment here. Swank enjoyed the computer culture.

'Don't like my digs, do you, Pegg?'

'It reeks in here. Socks. Damp. Tobacco. Sweat.'

'Nobody's keeping you. You're not shackled to the bed.'

Pegg asked, 'Have you ever fucked her?'

'Don't make me laugh.' He swallowed smoke and coughed. 'Fucked her? Have you looked at her closely, Pegg?'

'Can't help it, seeing how her face is in newspapers everywhere today.'

Swank said, 'She's gorgeous, mate. She's a wanker's dream. What could I offer her?'

'You know about her family background?'

'I don't think that's relevant.'

'Her mother liked to fuck blacks,' Pegg said. 'She brought them home.'

'So.' Swank relit his pipe.

'You know she committed suicide?'

'I heard it was something to do with diabetes.'

'You could say. She OD'd on insulin. Coma. Death. Our girl found her mother lying naked on the kitchen floor. Needle right beside her.'

'How do you know all this crap?'

'I make it my business to ask around. It only takes one weak link, Swank.'

'Wowch.' Swank burned his finger on the flame of a match.

Pegg said, 'She told me her mother died of diabetic complications. She's in a dream world, Swank. She makes things up. She's just reinvented herself. Plus she's too *secretive* at times.'

'Precaution,' Swank said.

'Oh yeah? What about that idiot she brought in. That Beezer.'

'She cleaned up her own mess.'

Pegg said, 'And this Oyster. What's his game?'

'He supports the movement.'

'He gives money, right,' Pegg said. 'I'm fucked if I know

what he really *supports*. How did she find him? Why doesn't she introduce us to him?'

Swank had the pipe properly stoked and primed now. His face was eclipsed by smoke. 'We need contributions, Pegg. Maybe the guy prefers anonymity.'

'Cash is the only thing that concerns you so you can buy more bells and whistles for that computer of yours.'

'We need the fucking computer. Who's going to pay our expenses if this Oyster folds his tent?'

Pegg stared at his companion for a while. 'You think the sun never sets on her, don't you?'

'You might be right there.' Swank seemed regretful. 'I wish I was twenty-five again, instead of this raddled old misanthrope you see before you. I'd be in with a shot. Wham. Watch my afterburn, baby.'

Pegg said, 'All I'm saying is we should be re-evaluating her on a constant basis.'

'We all need re-evaluation, Pegg.'

'I couldn't agree more. Complacency is death.'

Pegg stared at the remains of Swank's breakfast on the table. Cornflakes, tinned strawberries, a banana skin. 'She's blonde now.'

'Are you trying to excite me, Swank?'

'It's not hard.'

'Naw, but it could be.' Swank laughed as he grabbed at his own crotch.

Pegg plucked a squashy strawberry from the open tin and popped it in his mouth. 'We just need to be careful. Okay?'

'I don't disagree with that, brother.'

36

Bargeddie Haulage was hidden behind a stand of trees on Gartcosh Road in the far east of Glasgow. Perlman parked outside the wire fence of the compound and walked with Murdoch to the padlocked gate. About fifteen big trucks – each identified by the logo BH, two letters circled by flame – stood idle inside the yard. There was no sign of life. A long metal building dominated the area. A garage probably, Perlman thought. Somewhere out of sight a dog barked with unrestricted fury.

A man emerged from a prefabricated office and walked to the gate and looked through the wire at Perlman and Murdoch. He was small and sinewy, and had the collapsed cheeks of someone with no back teeth. He wore a baggy brown uniform with the BH logo on his breast pocket.

'Aye?'

Perlman showed his ID.

The man said, 'Yews here about the accident, eh?'

'Got it first time,' Perlman said.

The man unlocked the gate. Perlman and Murdoch stepped into the yard. Perlman scanned the compound quickly. Cardboard boxes, wooden pallets, used tyres.

'I didn't get your name,' Perlman said.

'Jimmy McCutcheon. Cutch is what I use.'

Perlman looked beyond Cutch at the prefabricated office, a simple construction erected on breeze blocks. 'What do you know about the driver of the stolen vehicle?'

'He didn't work here, Sergeant.'

'So he came in and stole the truck right out from under your noses?'

'People come and go here. During a hectic spell, you've got a dozen trucks in and out. A guy could come in and he might not be noticed driving a lorry away.'

Perlman wasn't buying. He had the feeling that security was a little more tight than Cutch wanted him to believe. He turned to see Murdoch strolling between parked trucks, glancing inside the big metal building. Good, Perlman thought. The boy was sneaky: showed promise.

'You any idea what caused the accident, Cutch?'

Cutch took a tube of lip balm from his pocket and applied it to his cracked lips. 'It's a write-off, zall I know. Mibbe a steering fault. A blow-out. Lotsa things can go wrong. These machines.'

Perlman noticed two cars parked behind the prefab office. A Jaguar and a VW Golf. He gestured towards them.

'I suppose the Jag is yours, Cutch?'

'You've got a bloody good sense of humour. Mine's the VW.'

'So who owns the Jag?'

Cutch didn't reply. Perlman moved towards the prefab, and Cutch scurried after him.

'This area's private, Sergeant.'

'Stop me,' Perlman said.

Cutch caught his arm. Perlman gave a hard stare and shrugged Cutch's hand aside.

'You'll get me in trouble,' Cutch said.

The door of the prefab office opened. Perlman looked at the man who stepped into the frame. He hadn't expected Bharat Gupta to be here. He'd assumed that Gupta would have stayed

252

away from his place of business in the aftermath of his daughter's death.

'Sergeant Perlman,' Gupta said. He came down the short flight of wooden steps and strolled towards Perlman.

Cutch said, 'I tried –'

'It's okay, Cutch. Everything is fine. I know Sergeant Perlman. Don't worry. Run along.'

Cutch shrugged and walked off in the direction of the metal building, presumably to eyeball the roving Murdoch. Bharat Gupta held out his hand for Perlman to shake. 'You must excuse Cutch, Sergeant. He's over-protective. He knows when I want to be bothered, and when I don't.'

'Your personal bodyguard,' Perlman said.

'I fear he isn't physically imposing enough.' Gupta wore a black jacket and a white shirt open at the neck. His hair looked buoyant, as if blow-dried only moments before. There were small dark circles under his eyes, and the whites were cracked with pink lines: the eyes of an insomniac. 'When it comes to protection, I prefer to rely on Kumble,' and he turned to look at the chained mastiff, huge and brown and bellicose, snarling in the doorway of the prefab.

'Spooky,' Perlman said.

'Very effective. He roams the area at night. Quiet, Kumble! Quiet now!' Gupta made a chopping gesture with his hand. The dog grumbled, then settled down.

'I heard about the accident,' Perlman said. 'I understand the dead driver wasn't an employee.'

'Indeed. We'll investigate how he managed to steal one of our vehicles, of course. The missing truck was unnoticed for some time, it seems . . . Perhaps some of our security procedures need to be reassessed.'

'Frankly, I wasn't expecting to find you here today.'

'A truck was stolen and a man died. There were other policemen asking questions before you came along. And as you can see my yard's at a standstill today, because I've closed the business for this period of mourning . . . so who else is going to cope

253

with the accident and its insurance consequences? Cutch? He has serious limitations. And Dev isn't really mature enough to deal with the practicalities of running this enterprise.' He put his hands in his pockets and looked directly at Perlman through his clouded eyes. 'If I'm not being imprudent, let me ask . . . are you making strides in the murder investigation?'

'A little headway,' Perlman said.

'But you can't say how much, of course. The discretion of the police is sometimes admirable, but more often frustrating.'

'I don't like to raise false hopes. I've seen them collapse too many times.'

'I am reading about this group White Rage in all the newspapers. Suddenly they're everywhere. It crosses my mind to wonder . . . did they kill Indra? And then I sometimes think, does it matter who pulled the trigger?' Gupta paused, ran the back of his hand across his lips. 'Even if you find the killer, it will not assuage our grief. Not by one tear.'

Perlman was quiet. Murdoch had surfaced about a hundred yards away, and was talking to Cutch. Cutch was listening to whatever Murdoch had to say; he shook his head every now and then.

Gupta said, 'Perhaps you are being just a little furtive, Sergeant. Perhaps the conversation you had with my wife made you curious about my businesses, and brought you all the way out here.'

'She told you we met?'

'She didn't have to.'

Perlman thought, Okay, a man might have a number of reasons for having his wife watched – he was jealous, he suspected some extra-curricular slap and tickle. But he didn't think these applied to Gupta's marital espionage. He assumed Bharat had bodyguards tracking Madhur for her own safety.

'She no doubt spoke to you about the phone calls, the anonymous notes,' Gupta said.

'Yes, she did.'

'And about sabotage at a dry-cleaning concern? Or vandals in one of my supermarkets? You don't have to worry about breaking a confidence, Sergeant. She has anxieties, and it's quite natural she'd voice them to a policeman.'

'All the more so since you haven't reported any of these matters yourself,' Perlman said.

'I can take care of my own family,' Gupta said.

'Really? So what happened with Indra – an unfortunate failure of your policy?'

'I wish you had kept that comment to yourself, Sergeant.'

Perlman instantly regretted his remark, the unintentional cruelty. 'I'm sorry. I should be more diplomatic at times. But the fact is, your daughter received threatening mail, and you didn't take steps to contact the police. You failed to report criminal offences. You preferred to construct a private fortress, complete with soldiers and watchdogs, around your business and your family. But you fucked up.'

'I don't think you should be involved in affairs that don't concern you.'

'Barry, the law gets broken, I'm involved.'

'Some matters are immensely personal, Sergeant.'

'I don't give a flying fuck how personal you might think they are. If the law's been broken, it's black and white.'

'How tidy your view of the world is,' Gupta said.

'Only where crime's concerned.'

'An orderly universe,' Gupta said. 'You're fortunate to have such a clear vision.'

'I didn't say it was always clear.'

'You have moments of doubt? Surely not.'

'More like moments of terror, Barry. What's happening to our world. Why are people so homicidal. The usual everyday matters.' He felt the mid-morning sun emit a little miserly heat, but enough to take the chill from the day. 'You have enemies, Barry? People who don't like you? People who'd steal your property and threaten your family?'

'I can't think of anyone in particular.'

'Come on. They crash your trucks and vandalize your super-market and light fires in your dry-cleaning store. You've stepped on toes, and some people don't like that. Question: Who are they?'

'Even if such enemies existed, do you think I would *name* them?'

'So you've got a bizarre notion of honour? The villains' guild, eh? Misguided, Barry.'

'I'm no villain, Sergeant. But I have my own code.'

Perlman said, 'It's a dangerous one.'

'In your Old Testament it says an eye for an eye.'

'I cancelled my subscription to the Old Testament years ago.' Perlman laid a hand on Gupta's arm. 'Talk to me. I can help you.'

'I don't think I need your help, Sergeant. Kind of you to offer, of course. But what do these tiresome business matters have to do with the death of my daughter anyway? What does her murder have to do with some anonymous people who may have developed a dislike of me? You are wasting valuable time looking in the wrong places, Sergeant.'

Perlman tipped his head back as if to draw a deeper warmth out of the sun. He suddenly remembered a matter he'd pondered some time before: the fact that White Rage was getting money from somewhere. People were backing hatred with hard cash. The race junkies had access to a computer, weapons, explosives.

Okay. Imagine these backers had some role to play in infusing money into White Rage. Did they also have *some* say in picking and choosing the targets? If so, what could possibly have induced them to sanction, for example, the murders of Oçhoba and Helen Mboto? Two African students, innocents, what the fuck had *they* done that they had to die?

They hadn't done anything. They didn't *have* to do anything. They were black. Look no deeper. White Rage didn't need any help with its agenda. They called their own shots.

He lit a cigarette and blew smoke away from Barry Gupta's

face. 'Private vendettas are often very bloody, Barry. I could help you, but I'd want you to be more open with me.'

'We all want something we can't have,' Gupta said.

'Point taken.' Make the dead come back to life. Raise them up, Lord. 'So, back to where we started. What caused the accident to your truck? Do you know?'

Gupta said, 'The wreckage is being examined. Of course, you assume sabotage.'

'Recent events in your history suggest it's a possibility,' Perlman said. He saw Murdoch come towards him. Cutch stood in the background, leaning against the cab of a truck. There was an element of wariness in the small man's pose.

'We'll talk again, Barry,' Perlman said.

'I anticipate it.'

They shook hands and Perlman walked with Murdoch in the direction of the gate. The unlocked padlock clanked against wire as Murdoch thrust the gate open; the mastiff, tuned to such sounds, barked angrily a couple of times. Perlman got behind the wheel of the Mondeo and Murdoch folded his long frame into the passenger seat.

Perlman changed the angle of the rearview mirror just slightly. 'What were you talking to Cutch about?'

'He wasn't very happy with me snooping round,' Murdoch said. He put his hand in his coat pocket. He removed a couple of objects. One was a child's sandal, the other a rolled-up magazine. 'I picked these up when Cutch wasn't looking.'

'What have you got there? A kid's shoe?'

'Found it in a rubbish bin inside the metal shed.'

'A sandal. What's so special about a sandal?'

'The imprint on the sole caught my attention.'

Perlman adjusted his glasses, glanced at it. The maker's name, scuffed and illegible, was carved into the sole. At least he assumed it was the manufacturer's.

'The writing's Arabic,' Murdoch said.

'I see that. And what's the magazine?'

'It's a comic book.' The young constable unfolded it, straightened it on his lap. The garish front cover depicted a space creature with demonic features in pursuit of two young characters, clearly earthlings, in space helmets. Murdoch flicked the pages. Inside was a Spiderman adventure, lurid in colour.

The speech balloons contained Arabic letters.

'There was more stuff lying around,' Murdoch said. 'I didn't have time to grab it all. Sweetie wrappers, cellophane bags, a few toys, items of clothing.'

Perlman braked when the car was out of sight of Bargeddie Haulage. He pulled to the side of the road and skimmed the magazine. 'I assume Bargeddie Haulage sends its drivers overseas, Dennis. Places like Bahrain. Qatar.'

'And they come back with kiddie sandals and Arab comics, Sergeant?'

Perlman stared through the windscreen at a stand of birch trees. Sandals and comic books. 'Which wouldn't generate much in the way of income for Barry, would it?'

Murdoch said, 'I have one other thing.' He reached into his pocket again. He pulled out a sheet of paper charred around the edges. 'This was inside the comic,' he said. 'Here.'

Perlman took the paper carefully from the young cop. It was clearly some kind of official form, perhaps a document of identification; in the lower right-hand corner of the page was a small photograph depicting a boy of thirteen or fourteen. A rubber stamp had imposed an inky blue circle over the photograph. The words on the page, like the words in the comic book and on the sole of the sandal, were Arabic.

'Well?' Murdoch asked.

Perlman had the feeling he was on the edge of some luminous perception that would clarify all the mysterious connections that bamboozled and teased him. But then, like an elusive muse, the sense of expectation vanished.

'Find out if we know anything about this Willie Glone when we get back to Pitt Street,' Perlman said.

'Will do, Sergeant.'

'You drive. And lend me your mobie, will you?'

37

On the way to Pitt Street, Perlman tried to reach Joe Adamski a couple of times on Murdoch's phone, but the Sergeant was out somewhere. Murdoch drove while Perlman looked at the city going past in a gloss of sunlight. Even Duke Street, a thoroughfare he usually found claustrophobic, was enlivened, shop windows glowing, buses reflecting squares of light.

Newsagents advertised the day's papers outside their shopfronts: *City of Death*, according to the *Daily Mail*. *Hate Killings Shock City*, the *Daily Record*. *Glasgow's Bloody Broken Heart* – the *Sun*, making a valiant tabloid attempt to be maudlin and sensational simultaneously. Here and there, instead of newspaper headlines, he saw copies of the picture of the girl who'd called herself Celia.

The mobile rang in Perlman's hand.

It was Sandy Scullion. 'Where are you?'

'Duke Street approaching High Street,' Perlman said.

'You walked out.'

'Don't tell me somebody noticed?'

'You don't like Deacon, fine. But you're doing yourself no favours by exposing your feelings.'

'I'll wear a mask next time.'

'Sometimes you're so diabolically hard to talk to, Lou. All I'm trying to say is I don't want you to get the axe just because you can't stand the sight of Deacon.'

The axe, Perlman thought. Guillotine for a gendarme. 'Fucking Deacon's up to something. I wouldn't be surprised if Mary Gibson knows what it is.'

'She's on *our* side, Lou.'

'People are sometimes on both sides. And sometimes they just sit on the fence and watch what happens before they declare themselves.'

'Whatever.' Scullion sounded weary, a man whose friendship was forever being tested. 'The gun checked out, by the way. Same weapon both times. What we thought.'

Perlman listened as Sandy went on about the explosive used in Cremoni's – a North Korean variant of the old Czech Cold War favourite, C-4 – but he was thinking of the gun. He imagined Indra Gupta looking into the barrel of it in much the same way as Nat Blum must have done, a microsecond of realization, a moment out of time, the inevitability of that last lethal sound, then a world of silence.

'How long before you come in?' Scullion asked.

'Ten minutes.'

Perlman switched off. He tapped the end of the mobile phone against his lower teeth in an absent-minded way, then decided to try Joe Adamski again. Still no reply.

Murdoch drove into the busy heart of the city. George Square was crowded. Lunchtime diners took advantage of a rare sun and sat on walls and benches. They ate sandwiches and sipped coffee from cardboard containers and studied newspapers, looking for some kind of explanation of what was happening to their city. Nothing's easy, Perlman thought. You can't just reach up and pull a solution from the sky. Poverty, an impoverished health service, low-grade housing, drugs – you couldn't add up these social problems and hope the total would provide a satisfactory answer. There was no mathematical formula, nothing you could crunch through machines.

Murdoch drove up St Vincent Street and found a parking space half a block from Force HQ. Perlman got out, and as soon as his feet hit the pavement he felt a muscular ache in his lower back and remembered the Dalmatian that had bushwhacked him – when? How long ago had that been? He couldn't recall. Another man's history. Days bled into other days.

Inside Force HQ he walked directly to the stairs.

'Don't forget Glone,' he said to Murdoch.

'ASAP.'

Perlman left the young cop and continued upward until he came to Scullion's office. Sandy was sitting behind his desk, shirtsleeved.

'We're getting a lot of calls about the computer sketch,' he said.

'Anything positive?'

'Funny how one image can be open to so many interpretations,' Scullion said. He picked up a bunch of phone messages from his desk and waved them at Perlman. 'She's Jean such and such from Carmyle, she's Mary so and so from Stepps, she's Martha this from Possilpark, she's Denise X from Castlemilk. Oh, this one's a beauty, you'll love it – she's Yan Yomomata, a Japanese terrorist.'

'She couldn't look oriental if you met her in a bloody geisha house in Tokyo,' Perlman said.

'This is definitely a round-eyed girl we're chasing.' Scullion tossed the papers down. 'It's a slog now.'

Perlman picked at a loose button on the cuff of his coat. 'Am I still up shit creek? Do I still have pariah status?'

'Not from where I sit,' Scullion said. 'Except you haven't done anything about Tay's request concerning Colin, have you?'

'No, not yet, I've been diverted, you know that.'

'He phoned me again ten minutes ago. Not in a good mood, Lou. He wants those files. He wants you to get all your reports updated, start building again.'

'Why?'

'Only a psychic could read Tay's mind,' Scullion said. 'All I can tell you is you're going to have to spend some time on this business, Lou.'

'I feel a tide rising around me, Sandy.'

'Find a way to stem it.'

'I'm Canute. Turn back the fucking sea. Is that the way? Regal fiat?' He laid his hands flat on Scullion's desk. 'You got an aspirin or five?'

Scullion took a box from the drawer of his desk. 'Nurofen. Help yourself.'

Perlman shook three pills into his palm and swallowed them dry, even as he twisted to reach behind himself and massage the pain at the base of his spine. 'Jesus. This just kicked in a quarter of an hour ago.'

'Try sitting down.'

'Better if I stand.' Perlman had a bitter taste at the back of his throat from the Nurofen. He walked slowly around the room. He shoved his hands in his coat pockets and leaned against the wall. He had the odd feeling that Scullion was withholding something, although he wasn't sure what.

What the fuck is wrong with me? Everywhere I turn I sense conspiracy, legerdemain under the surfaces of everyday life, furtive acts of behaviour. The holiday idea everyone had bruited about seemed suddenly ripe with wonderful promise. Malaga, yeah. Malta. The boat to Dunoon, the train to Troon. There were all kinds of places he could fuck off to, and shake the smell of Glasgow out of his system.

'So I'm to collate my reports and update all the bumph I've collected?'

'Fast as you can, Lou. That's what the man wants.'

'Did he say I should abdicate the Indra investigation?'

'Not specifically. He indicated that you were too engrossed in other matters for his liking. I surmise he meant White Rage, what else? But he didn't issue a *verboten* dictate. I had a feeling he wanted to, but then how would it look to take an experienced officer off a case as big as White Rage? Somehow you're going to have to make the time to do several things at once.'

'I'll get it done, Sandy. I promise.'

'I'll be watching you.'

Perlman sat in puzzled silence, his mind picking away at the why of Tay's urgency. He supposed a meeting with Tay was always a possibility, but would any of his questions receive straight answers?

'What news on the Indra front?' Scullion asked.

'I'll talk to you about Indra after I make this phone call.' He'd absconded with Murdoch's mobile. He punched in the number he'd been trying for the past hour. This time Joe Adamski answered.

Perlman said, 'I'm going to send you a document by email, Joe. Have a look at it. Then phone me right back at Pitt Street. Give me a few minutes.'

Perlman switched the mobile off.

'Joe who?' Scullion asked.

'Adamski. E-Division.'

Scullion rapped his fountain pen on the desk. 'Did I hear you say email? Do you *know* how to scan a document into a computer, Lou?'

'Ah. Problem there. I was hoping you'd show me.'

'Where's the document?'

Perlman took the charred paper out of his inner jacket pocket. 'Here.'

Scullion glanced at it. 'Any idea what it means? What language is it?'

'I'm hoping Adamski knows.'

Scullion walked to the computer terminal in the corner of his room. He stuck the document into the scanner as Perlman watched with a bewildered, suspicious eye. The modem kicked in, making a series of squeaks and beeps. Scullion tapped the keyboard with fast fingers. The whole chore was completed quickly. He removed the paper and passed it back to Perlman.

'Very impressive,' Perlman said.

'I can perform certain basic tasks, but I'm limited. Now tell me about that document, Lou.'

'Murdoch came across it at Bargeddie Haulage.'

'And you think it has some significance?'

Lou bit on the fingernail of his fourth finger, right hand. 'In a roundabout way.'

Scullion sighed. 'Remember when cases were smooth sailing? Remember when you had a crime here, and a criminal there, and all you had to do was join the two? Or am I dreaming it was really like that?'

Perlman smiled. 'We had easy ones, also tough ones. Like this one now, which is all over the fucking place. One thing leads to another, and the pattern goes round and round. Roll up, step on the merry-go-round, it birls you in a circle but it takes you right back to where you started.' Perlman shut his eyes for a second. *Imagine a candle in the dark of your head.* He'd read that in a feelgood book in a dentist's waiting room. He could never get the candle to light.

The telephone rang. Scullion reached for it.

Murdoch appeared in the open doorway, bulky in his dark uniform. 'Am I interrupting, Sergeant?'

Perlman looked at the young man. When was I ever this eager to please? he wondered. 'What's up, Dennis?'

'I thought you'd want to see this,' and he handed Perlman a sheet of paper. 'From the National Crime computer.'

Perlman looked at it, but before he could absorb the information Scullion called him to the phone. 'Adamski. For you.'

Perlman took the handset. 'Joe,' he said. 'You checked that paper I sent?'

'Yeh. In fact we picked up this kid a couple of nights ago, Lou.'

'Where?'

'He was wandering around Shettleston. Not a great place for a young boy to be, especially when he doesn't speak English and he's freezing his arse off, and he's penniless and starving.'

'Where's he from?'

'Damascus. Name's Achmad Aballah.'

'Where is he now?'

'We shipped him to London. He'll probably stay in a camp for a while.'

'How did he get to Glasgow?'

'By truck from Calais. He believed he was going to Dublin. The destination's always a mystery for these people. They never really know where they're going. The drivers don't tell them. They drop them anywhere they feel like. It's not as if Achmad can claim compensation under the Fair Trades Act. Where did you get this ID?'

'Let me get back to you on that, Joe. Thanks.'

Perlman experienced a quiet stirring of life, as if he'd risen refreshed from a deep sleep. Achmad Aballah. Bargeddie Haulage. The connection quickened him.

And then something else touched him too, a shadow thrown by fire on the pocked face of a subterranean wall, a ghost locked in the busy arteries of memory. Leave it alone. It'll come. Just don't labour it.

Something to do with Kilroy –

He looked at the paper Murdoch had handed him. 'Nice,' he said. 'Very nice. A wee bit surprising, mibbe. But it's the kind of surprise I can deal with.'

'Explain,' Scullion said. 'I'm all ears.'

'Willie Glone,' Perlman said. 'Mean anything to you?'

'Not a dicky.'

Perlman said, 'Six years in Peterhead for GBH in Dundee.'

'Out of my district,' Scullion said.

'Not entirely, Sandy.'

The pain in Perlman's spine was easing already. Fast-acting Nurofen. He felt clear-headed. He looked from the window into Pitt Street and saw a familiar elderly man walking a highly strung Dalmatian.

He thought: Don't let it slip the leash again. He felt a moment of tension as the big dog lurched forward, pulled by God knows what canine impulse, but the elderly man held tight, even though he was dragged several yards down the pavement by the beast, and almost lost his balance. But he remained standing, and the dog was brought back to still, if resentful, obedience.

A small triumph of the human will, Perlman thought. Such little victories always lifted his spirit. He watched man and dog go out of sight and wondered what it was that had risen from dormancy at the back of his brain to make him think of Leo Kilroy.

It had to do with the sea, he was sure of that. With the sea and ships. But what? So much of the past, he thought, was debris hidden behind muslin. And what good was a policeman with a flaw in his memory circuits?

38

She liked the feel of mid-morning sun in her blonde hair. She jogged through Tollcross Park at a steady rhythm, passing the glass structure of the Winter Palace where sunlight the colour of beaten copper was thrown back from the panes. She saw her own reflection slide past in a smooth sequence of moving pictures, as if she were trapped in celluloid like an actress in a film. Black glasses, grey tracksuit with the red stripe in the trousers, Walkman plugged into her ears, the easy stride of her taut body; the compleat jogger.

She stopped, caught her breath. She bent, placed her hands on her knees. She saw her long shadow on the grass. She wanted to lie down, stretch out, but it wasn't a sunbathing day. She watched a couple of mothers push prams past her along the path. They glanced at her, and she thought: They don't recognize me. These women look at my figure, they see a fitness they left behind when they gave birth, and now they're dough-faced and flabby, they have stretch marks and I don't. *They walk the baby, go to the shops, buy mince, get the man's tea going later, make sure it's on the table at the right time, then after a night of dreary telly they might be asked for a quick fumbling fuck from work-knackered hubby . . .*

How did some women live that way, leaving unexplored the possibilities of life?

She started to run again. She thought of Blum jogging along the Broomielaw in the first light of morning, making his move on her, sure and smooth as a fine Scotch, thinking, Hah, my ship's come in, a pick-up, an easy score.

She reached Wellshot Road, ran past the children's zoo where she heard a pony neigh, then kept running along the edge of the park. Pound pound, elbows pistoning, hands clenched, calf muscles tensed, sun glowing on her shades. The Walkman played a tape of nature sounds, running water, birds whistling in trees, wind roaring through a canyon. *The Best of Nature, Vol 1.*

She crossed Wellshot Road. She went right on Ardgay Street. The houses around her were 1930-ish two-storey blocks, plain, each constructed in imitation of its neighbour. Lives of uniformity, she thought. An elderly man in a flat cap, a tweedy bunnet, stepped from one of the buildings and stared at her as if he couldn't understand her purpose in this place. *Saw a fucking jogger, so I did, swear to God.* But he smiled at her in a wolfish way, a reflex reaction to a pretty female going past. He might think she was a stray from the Leisure Complex in the park, just a good-looking girl running free and easy. She knew he was still watching her even as she'd passed him.

She took another right. She was panting a little now. She kept moving, beating the pavements, listening to the slap of her trainers. The tape in the Walkman stopped. She heard dead noise, static.

She ran a little harder, slowing once, and then only for a moment, outside a house that was unlike any of the others around, a narrow black stone front with a blue door and curtains drawn shut at every window. A quiet black house. She slipped the tape out of the Walkman, flipped it over, listened to the other side as she started to run hard again. Her head was filled with the liquid roar of a waterfall.

39

'I always find it strange to think the Romans were here once,' Kilroy said. 'They must have *hated* the climate.'

Frankie Chasm said, 'They brought their own vino. It was some consolation.'

'But not much.' Kilroy studied the scant remains of the Roman Baths that had been dug out of this small corner of Bearsden. It was more an outline of stones than a massive reconstruction. The little noticeboards helped identify what you were looking at: over here was the *frigidarium*; and there the *caldarium*. To an unenquiring eye, the whole thing might have suggested a pile of old rocks rather than an ancient and sophisticated bathing system.

Traffic moved west along Drymen Road, east to Milngavie. Slightly glazed by ten milligrams of Valium, the Fat Man listened to the hum of vehicles even as he detected another sound that floated above the commonplace noise of the piston engine. A lark, high and invisible, but a lark decidedly. He hadn't heard a lark in years. He thought pollution had done them all in.

He sat down on a wall. He carried a gold-knobbed walnut

stick, with which he prodded the earth between paving stones. Chasm sat beside him, crossing his legs.

'You hear that, Frankie?'

Chasm heard nothing. His affinity for the world of nature was nonexistent. His natural habitat was one of bars, restaurants, casinos. But he was agreeable and said yes, he heard it, definitely, whatever it was.

'Rare. Used to be dirt common. Not now.' Kilroy launched into a spiel about birds. Birdwatching had been a boyhood hobby of his. He spoke of how, at the age of seven or eight, he'd considered a career in ornithology. Chasm didn't listen. The Fat Man was sensitive to Diazepam and sometimes babbled on the drug. Chasm could eat Valiums like fucking Smarties, but Leo had zip tolerance.

'Let's walk back to the car, Frankie.'

'Any time you're ready.'

Kilroy rose from the wall. He hummed 'Getting To Know You' all the way back to the Daimler. Frankie opened the door, ushered Kilroy into the back seat, then settled behind the wheel.

'Straight home, Leo?'

'And no radio, if you please.'

Chasm headed down Drymen Road and turned right on Ledcameroch where sunlight burned pleasantly on thick trees. The soft fleshy underside of Glasgow, Chasm thought. The sweetest of suburbs. He zapped a remote for the gates to open, and drove the Daimler through.

His attention was drawn to the rearview mirror. Behind him, a car he didn't recognize squeezed between the gates just as they were closing. Instantly, he reached under his seat and found the automatic he always stashed there, a Llama 45 with a thirteen-shot magazine. He gave the Daimler a little more fuel and swung it in a tight circle in front of the house. Tyres screeched. The air smelled of scorched rubber.

'What the fuck?' Kilroy said, yanked from his Diazepam lull.

'The floor, Leo. Get down.'

Kilroy slid from his seat. 'Do we know them?'

'I'm not taking any chances,' Chasm said.

The car was foreign. He couldn't say what make. He watched it approach the Daimler and then, twenty or thirty yards away, it stopped.

'Who is it?' Kilroy asked. He was in a heap on the floor.

'I don't fucking *know*, Leo. Be still. Do nothing until I tell you.'

'Right, right,' Kilroy said.

Chasm held the gun in his lap, waited, watched the metallic silver car. He enjoyed the tension. He fed on the adrenalin of the situation.

He saw the two front doors of the silver car open.

The driver was a man Chasm didn't recognize. The passenger, on the other hand, was familiar.

'It's Perlman and a sidekick,' he said. He slid the Llama under his seat.

'I'm lying here like a bagman in a shop doorway on account of *Perlman*?' Kilroy struggled up into his seat and watched the cops through the back window. 'The other guy is Scullion. Detective-Inspector.'

Chasm got out of the car. Perlman and Scullion walked towards him. Perlman peered into the back of the Daimler and said, 'Leo. Did I surprise you? Should I have phoned for an appointment?'

Kilroy smoothed his coat as he shoved his door open. Grunting, he stepped out. 'You shouldn't come up behind people like that.'

'Call me a sneaky bastard,' Perlman said.

Scullion said, 'Pity about your lawyer, Leo.'

'A great tragedy,' Kilroy said. 'A kid filled with such promise.'

'Lawyers are ten a penny.'

Kilroy said, 'You've got a big heart, Inspector.'

'You find the culprit yet, Perlman?' Chasm asked.

'Not yet, but we will.'

'Racist trash killed the boy,' Kilroy said. 'You should be turning Glasgow upside down to find these cunts.'

Perlman turned, looked directly at Chasm, who hadn't aged greatly since the last time he'd seen him. Maybe he'd developed a little more flesh in the jowl region, a slight fattening, but not much. The body was trim and hard. 'How long has it been, Frankie?'

'Years,' Chasm said. 'See you wear the same specs.'

'They suit me.'

'Nothing else matters. If you're happy.'

Perlman said, 'See you got yourself a nice wee job looking after Leo. Into the bargain a terrific car.'

'You're not here to talk about bloody *cars* again, are you?' Kilroy asked. 'When you get going on that subject you're like a runaway train.' He wondered if he should play nice and invite the coppers indoors, then decided against it. He couldn't remember where he'd put the photograph. He panicked, wee birds flew round his heart like sparrows descending on a stale loaf. His ulcer scorched him. His tubes might have been stuffed with hot cinders. What if he'd left the photie lying on a table and he asked this pair of jokers to come indoors and they *saw* it? Would Perlman pretend to be shocked by it? Would he seize it in the fashion of a man seeing something for the first time and gasp? *What's this, Leo?* No, you couldn't tell what the yid would do. He was cunning, he'd play you like a cat a dying mouse.

Scullion said, 'Lou likes antique cars. He likes old Bentleys especially, Leo.'

'Oh, Lord, let it go,' Kilroy said. *Old Bentleys.* Why was Scullion bringing this up now? Had he participated in the creation of the photo? He must have. Perlman & Scullion, it was like they shared a fucking *pod.*

'Lou gets a thing in his head, there's no shifting it.'

'It just *lodges* there,' Perlman said.

'This is the same old harassment, Lou.'

Perlman lit a cigarette. 'Funny to see you without poor Nat draped round you.'

272

'He was smart. Dedicated. Loyal –'

'And greedy as shite,' Perlman said.

'That isn't fair, Lou. That's a libel.'

'Right, I shouldn't speak ill of the dead. It's bad luck they say.' Perlman laid a hand on a wing mirror of the Daimler. 'So life's been good to you, Frankie.'

Chasm said, 'I'm a changed man, Perlman.'

'Walking softly with the angels these days, eh?'

'I wouldn't go that far.' Chasm smiled. He had an effortless smile, casual, calculated to put people at ease. Oddly, this same expression sometimes had the opposite effect: sinister, mirthless, cold.

'You miss jail?' Scullion asked.

'Aye. Constantly. I lie awake at night pining my heart out for the snoring and the stink of pish and the sound of boys being shagged by brutes and the screws clattering people with sticks. I miss all that, Inspector.'

'I'll narrow my question. Miss anyone in particular?'

'Come again?' Chasm cupped a hand behind his ear, a gesture of mock deafness.

'Old cellmates,' Scullion said.

Perlman asked, 'Need a clue? Willie Glone.'

'Willie. I remember Willie all right. Nice guy.'

Perlman said, 'Lovely guy, Chasm. He scalped a man behind a bar, as I remember. Took a knife and cut off the top of some poor tosser's head. He also lacerated a young woman's skull with a beer bottle.'

'These things happen,' Chasm said.

'In your world,' Scullion said.

Kilroy flapped a hand. 'What are you here for anyway, Lou? My factotum is a busy man.'

'I just want to talk to your, uh, factotum about Glone,' Perlman replied.

'Is this important?' Kilroy asked. Glone, he thought. Was that all? Just Glone? 'Poor Nat Blum's lying stone-cold in the morgue and his building's been daubed with these bloody swastikas, and

273

you come here asking about an obscure ex-con, when you really should be hunting down this White Anger or Rage or whatever it's called. What kind of music hall are you running down there in Pitt Street anyway?'

Chasm said, 'It's okay, Leo. I don't mind.'

Scullion asked, 'You heard Glone died?'

'Did he? I'm gobsmacked.'

'Smashed a truck he was in the act of stealing.'

Chasm said, 'Glone couldn't drive a golf cart, never mind a lorry.'

'Why steal something you can't even drive?'

Chasm said, 'Maybe he was on the bevvy at the time. He was fond of a tipple. Too fond.'

'The stolen truck was the property of a company called Bargeddie Haulage. You ever heard of them?'

Chasm said, 'Do I look like an anorak that memorizes the names of haulage companies?'

'When did you last talk to Glone?' Perlman asked.

'Must be months.'

Kilroy interrupted. 'What are you hoping to catch here, Lou? A cold?'

'Always the same commodity, Leo. Information.'

'You're just fucking *fishing*,' Kilroy said and tried to keep the stress out of his voice. 'People are dropping like flies, and all you do is come out here asking questions that have SFA to do with the general situation in Glasgow. You're talking dolly mixtures compared to what's going on out there.'

'Indra Gupta, Leo. Dead kindergarten teacher?'

'What about her?'

'Her father, Barry Gupta, owns Bargeddie Haulage.'

'So?'

'Bad things are happening to Barry. Deaths in the family. Business sabotage. Theft. You name it. He's got some enemies.'

'And you think Chasm might be helpful just because he shared a cell with this whatshisface . . .'

'Glone.'

274

'Glone, right. I think it's downright *scandalous*, frankly, that you can throw a man's past into his face –'

Chasm said, 'Leo, it's okay, I don't have anything to hide.'

Perlman dropped his cigarette, flattened it underfoot.

Kilroy said, 'Be my guest, Lou. Drop your cigarettes on my good gravel. You know what that stuff *costs* by the ton?'

'Looks just like old dirt to me,' Perlman said.

'It's pulverized rock from an Ayrshire quarry,' Kilroy said. 'It's the twenty-five-year-old single malt of gravel.'

'I wish I'd known,' Perlman said.

Chasm stooped, picked up the cigarette butt.

'Is that what a factotum does, Frankie?' Perlman asked.

'I'm a jack of all trades.'

Chasm gazed at Perlman in a challenging way. Perlman didn't flinch from the contact. He enjoyed a little eyeball competition.

Kilroy said, 'Open the gates for these guys, Frankie.'

'We being thrown out?' Perlman asked.

'Not so much as a cuppa,' Scullion remarked.

'I heard stories about the service here, Sandy.'

Kilroy said, 'Lock the gates behind them, Frankie.'

Perlman walked in the direction of Sandy Scullion's Citroën. He paused with his hand on the door handle. He gazed beyond Kilroy and Chasm at the splendid front of the large house, white stucco, Spanish effect, Kilroy's hacienda, a touch of the Ibizas. But it wasn't the impressive house that caused Perlman to stand so very still, it was a shift in memory, a word on the tip of his tongue – he had it, he didn't have it, he'd lost it. It was as irritating as a tiny *krishel* of food stuck between your teeth. Cursing himself, he yanked the passenger door open.

'Don't be a stranger,' Kilroy said.

Perlman stared at the Fat Man. 'Boats,' he said. 'Something to do with boats.'

'Boats? Eh? You lost your compass, Lou?'

'Cargo boats. That's it.' Perlman pointed a finger at Kilroy. 'You own some cargo boats.'

'I didn't know that was a crime. Is it new on the statute book?'

275

'Boats *and* trucks,' Perlman said. He clicked thumb and middle finger together: *Eureka*. 'The name of the company. What's the name of the company? Dammit. *Dammit.*'

Kilroy said, 'Memory breaking apart? Let me help you. Bute Transport.'

'That's it,' Perlman said.

'The boats are long gone, Perlman. Uneconomical. As for the trucks, the company runs only five or six these days.'

'And they go where?'

'Anywhere,' Kilroy remarked.

'You don't keep in touch with your own business?'

'Lou, you are *embarrassingly* out of date. I'm not involved in Bute any more. The boats went to auction in '98. I wasn't happy in that line of business anyway. I like hands-on, and who wants hands-on when it comes to some smelly old cargo boats and rough seagoing sorts with holes in their jumpers and jock-rash? Not my style, Lou. I sold the trucks and the company name five months ago.'

'Who's the new owner?'

'I am,' Chasm said.

I didn't expect that, Perlman thought. 'Really? Was it a credit sale, Frankie?'

'Ex-cons don't usually have loads of the spare lying around, Perlman.'

'You got finance?'

'Nah, I bought it with Monopoly money. What do you think?'

'And somebody holds the paper?'

'Somebody always holds the paper, Perlman.'

'This might be light years off target. Is Kilroy the note-holder?'

Chasm said, 'He was generous when I needed it.'

'Cosy. What do you think, Sandy?'

'I think Frankie Chasm landed on his feet,' Scullion said.

'Embraced by saints,' Perlman said, and slid into the passenger seat.

Scullion slammed the door and turned the car towards the

gates. They opened automatically, then closed as soon as the Citroën had cleared them.

Chasm brought Kilroy a G&T in the conservatory. He tossed it back, one gulp. He stared moodily at the waterfall.

Chasm sipped a Diet Irn-Bru.

Kilroy said, 'Our Jew friend remembers everything. Eventually.'

'So it seems.'

Kilroy smacked the palm of his hand on the arm of his chair. 'Why hasn't there been a follow-up to that bloody photo? Even if it's Perlman playing a stupid fuck blackmail game, you'd think there might be another note by now. Except he comes here to ask about Glone. Fucking Glone.'

'He wants you simmering.'

'Where did I put that photograph anyway?'

'In your desk,' Chasm said. He laid a hand on the Fat Man's shoulder. 'You want another G&T? Another pill? Tell me, I'll fetch it.'

'Bring me both.'

'Living dangerously?'

'Why not?'

Chasm stopped on his way out of the conservatory. 'You weren't happy with Blum, Leo. A waste of money, you said.'

Kilroy watched tumbling water fall against rocks and vanish inside crevices, alive in the way lava is alive. He felt sluggish and uncertain of himself. And fat, fat beyond the boundaries of obesity, a gross figure in whom the shark must surely have been devoured. For so many years he'd been confident and self-assured – how had he fallen from that high place so *quickly*? What wrong turning had he made along the way? Could he take a couple of steps back and bring about repairs and restorations, so that everything might be resurrected as it had been? The Fat Man in all his roaring ostentation and glory, a dazzling rage of colour on any drab Glasgow day, a zappy eyecatcher on the streets, powder-blue mohair coat, scarlet alpaca scarf, a crazy quilt waistcoat, red and white two-tone shoes he'd picked up at the Italian Centre, a walking wobbling marvel of a man.

With some effort, he stood.

Remember this: a few days ago you were a ruthless machine. Be one again. The sleek creature in blue waters. He called out for Chasm, who came back with a second G&T and a small blue pill.

Kilroy cleared his throat. 'See it through, Frankie.'

'It's in motion, Leo. It's running under its own steam now. I couldn't raise a finger.'

40

Perlman shaded his eyes against an afternoon sun that had turned unexpectedly brilliant. In the start-stop traffic in Maryhill Road, where a crew of men in hard hats dug a trench for some inscrutable purpose, and the air was jarred by the sound of pneumatic drills, Scullion was becoming impatient.

'What the hell are they digging for?' Scullion asked.

Perlman said, 'Who knows? It's a quick-change world we live in, Sandy. Think about it. A man like Frankie Chasm comes out of Peterhead jail and straight into ownership of a fleet of trucks.'

'Thanks to a line of credit extended by the Fat Man.'

'What are friends for?' Perlman looked at the beery red face of a weary worker leaning on a shovel. 'They lend money. They find jobs for each another. Consider Glone, another Peterhead alumnus. He gets out of jail and friendly Frankie Chasm contacts him and says, I've got a wee job for you, Willie. There's a few quid in it.'

'And sends him out to Bargeddie to steal a truck . . .'

'Aye. People are trying to derail Barry Gupta's empire. Family members die. Strange "accidents" happen in his places of business. Somebody nicks a truck from his yard and demolishes it.

279

I don't think it was meant to turn out badly for Willie Glone, but somehow he made a ballocks of it and got barbecued in the wreckage.'

'And you think Chasm is undermining competition.'

'Waging war may be the better term.'

'There's no direct evidence.'

'Okay. But I don't like the fact that Chasm and Glone are fellow graduates of the Peterhead Academy for Bad People, and Glone's the one who steals a fucking truck from Gupta. That link makes my baw-hairs *tingle*. You imagine Glone woke up and said to himself, *I must steal one of Gupta's trucks today*?'

'Assume Chasm asked him. Where does the death of Indra fit into Chasm's demolition of Gupta's kingdom? We've attributed that killing to White Rage. Are we saying, what – let me get this straight – that Chasm is connected with White Rage?'

Perlman took off his glasses and peered through them just as the light changed and the car moved. He breathed on them, wiped them on the cuff of his shirt, put them back on. 'All I'm suggesting is a possibility worth exploring, Sandy. You see anything better in the distance?'

'We should talk some more to Barry.'

'Feh. He's in denial. He's all: *What enemies?* He's from the school of bruised machismo, thinks he can handle everything his own way. Barry's not the right approach.'

'You've got another?'

'Young Dev.'

'He's sullen. Trapped in big Daddy's shadow.'

'Sullen? Not after I talk to him about matters of cargo.'

'Fine. Do that. I'm also thinking it wouldn't do any harm to send a few uniforms out to Bargeddie for a look-round.'

'Try Joe Adamski,' Perlman suggested, and he remembered the dark shapes fleeing the posse of policemen across London Road; asylum seekers, economic refugees – what did it matter how you labelled them? They were scared people a long way from anything familiar: they were coming to a cold place where they knew nobody, and nobody wanted to know them. The disenchanted. The disenfranchised. The shoeless. 'I think Joe would like to be in on this. You got E-Division's number?'

'It's programmed into the mobie.' Scullion took out his phone, and drove one-handed while he punched in a couple of numbers.

The city centre loomed beyond St George's Cross and the high ridge of Garnethill where, months ago, before Colin had died, Perlman had stood with Miriam outside the synagogue and surveyed the wintry lights of the western reach of the city and understood how much he loved her. He remembered how desirable she'd looked in the hazy darkness and his heart had stammered.

One day she'll be mine.

Scullion, who'd been speaking to Adamski, switched off his mobile. 'Okay, done.'

'I don't want to go barging into the Gupta household like a couple of plodders,' Perlman said. 'I'll call Dev. Get him to meet us elsewhere.' He took Murdoch's phone from his pocket and asked the directory operator to connect him.

Dev Gupta answered, his voice sombre.

Perlman said, 'This is your favourite policeman. I need a few minutes of your time.'

'When?'

'Twenty minutes, say?'

'I can't get away from here.'

'Try, Dev. It's about the stolen vehicle.'

'Bad timing.'

'I know, and I'm sorry.'

A pause. 'Okay. Where do we meet?'

'You choose, Dev.'

'Crossmyloof Station?'

'Fine,' Perlman said.

He switched off.

Scullion parked the Citroën in the car park at Crossmyloof Station. Thirty minutes had passed since Perlman's phone call, and there was no sign of Dev Gupta. Perlman rose stiff-limbed out of the car, walked up and down to get blood circulating in his legs. There was that spasm in his back again, damn it. A train rattled past heading from Glasgow towards the suburbs of Priesthill, Nitshill, Barrhead.

A blue MG approached. It halted beside the Citroën. Dev Gupta stepped out. He was dressed entirely in black. Perlman knew nothing about fashion, but he understood enough to realize that the young man's suit was implausibly expensive. Well tailored, perfect.

Scullion got out of the Citroën. He said, 'Nice suit.'

Perlman said, 'I was thinking just the same, Sandy.'

Dev Gupta said, 'I agreed to meet you, so let's get to the point.'

Perlman glanced at the MG. 'I bet you pull birds out of the trees.'

'Now and then.'

'Enjoy while you can. Nooky lasts only so long. One day you just can't get it up so easily.'

'I didn't come here to discuss your sexual inadequacies,' Gupta said. 'The accident, remember?'

Perlman said, 'Ah, right, the stolen truck. You heard any more about it, Dev? How it happened, anything like that?'

'I thought the whole point was that you were going to tell me.'

'I brought you here under false pretences, son.'

'Then I'll turn around and I'll pish off.'

Perlman caught Gupta by the sleeve. 'You go when I let you go, my wee man. I'm going to ask you something, and you'll answer me truthfully.'

'And if I don't?'

'Oh sonny.' Perlman frowned. 'Don't make me work.'

Dev Gupta said, 'You're a hard man, Sergeant. I'm dripping sweat. Look.'

Perlman ignored the bluster. 'Here's my question. Who the fuck is trying to wipe out your dad's business?'

'Come again?'

'Just name the enemy, son. And we can all go home.'

'There's no enemy,' Gupta said.

Perlman tugged harder on the sleeve. The material was soft and weightless. With a suit like that, a man would feel he was wearing air. What was it – cashmere? Alpaca? He wondered how he'd look in such a suit: would he make Miriam's head spin?

'Just *name* the fucker, son.'

'There's nobody to name. Jesus Christ, let go, you'll tear the sleeve.'

'I'm clumsy at times,' Perlman said.

Gupta, profoundly irritated, his threads threatened, shook his head. 'Piss off.'

The sleeve came loose from the shoulder, in a series of quick little pops of stitching. 'Ah Jesus,' Perlman said. 'Sorry.'

'Fucking hell,' Gupta said. 'This cost me a fortune.'

'It must have been *shmatte*. I hardly touched it.'

'I'll vouch for that,' Scullion said.

'Pair of tossers,' Gupta said, and opened the door of the MG. Perlman kicked it shut and Gupta took a step back to avoid being struck.

Perlman said, 'All I want is an answer, Dev.'

'Nothing to say, Perlman. Where do I send the repair bill for my jacket?'

'We'll get to that. Let's talk about something else first.'

'I'm going home,' Gupta said.

'Just hang on.' Perlman stuck his foot against the door panel. 'Let's talk about cargo, Dev. Let's just talk about what it is that Bargeddie Haulage hauls.'

Dev Gupta had a way of looking arrogant with a mere motion of eyelids. 'We move whatever we get paid to move.'

'Does that include people?'

'People?'

'Illegals.'

'What the hell are you talking about, Perlman?'

'It's big business, I suppose. Poor bastards pay their life-savings for a long ride to a strange land, heads stuffed with notions of freedom and buying a car and strolling the aisles of well-stocked supermarkets and oh look at all the break-fast cereals and biscuits, *scrummy*, and then they get dumped by the side of the road, or in a ditch, or the middle of a field in the centre of nowhere, and who gives a shite about them.'

'Our company doesn't do anything like –'

'Oh but it does, it does, son. You bring them in. You drop them off. Thanks for your *shekels* and cheerio. Find your own way in the dark.' Perlman rubbed the top of Gupta's head like an ominous uncle, a nasty little gesture.

Gupta ducked away. 'You're out of your turnip, Perlman.'

Sandy Scullion looked at his watch. 'Even as we speak, Dev, policemen are searching the premises of Bargeddie Haulage on the basis of information received.'

'Fuck this, I'll talk to my lawyer before I say another –'

'Lawyers, lawyers, all I ever hear is lawyers.' Perlman leaned close to Gupta, faces almost touching. 'All right, don't tell me anything. Let *me* see if I can tell *you*. It's Frankie Chasm, right? It's Bute Transport.'

Dev Gupta was silent. Perlman smelled mint on the kid's breath.

'Don't waste my time, Dev. Cooperate with me. And when you've satisfied my curiosity, you can go back to acting all smart and cool and drive home in your chickmobile. You can go back to being a *macher*.'

'A what?' Gupta asked.

'Think of it like a lightning rod for babes,' Perlman said.

Gupta looked at Scullion, then gazed across the car park. He was quiet for a long time. He chewed on his lower lip, looking years younger, and for all the world like a kid caught shoplifting. He scanned the area, as if the possibility of making a run for a place of illusory safety had crossed his mind.

'There's nowhere to hide,' Perlman said.

Gupta said, 'Right. All right. Fuck you. It's Chasm. It's Bute. There. You happy with that?'

'See how easy that was,' Perlman said. 'There's one thing I don't get. There are plenty other trucking companies all over the city. Why did Chasm pick on yours?'

'You stupid?'

'No more so than the next punter, I hope.'

'Because he's in the same fucking *game*, diddy.'

'The people game,' Perlman said, letting the insult slide off him.

'Right, right. You got it. He moves flesh from here to there. He wants a monopoly. We're not talking about loose change. This is big business.'

'And merciless,' Perlman said.

'Money's money, no matter how you make it.'

'All those poor suffering bastards you transport, they'd agree with you, eh?'

'I look like I give a fuck, Perlman? Why don't you just nail Chasm, okay? Castrate him. Hang him up somewhere and leave him until his fucking skin rots off.' He shrugged, kicked stones, walked in small restless circles. 'If my father . . . if he'd had enough brains and guts to report everything to the cops at the time when we received those threatening letters, if he'd picked up the phone and called you, if he hadn't acted in such a pig-headed way, then maybe all the other crap would never have happened, and Indra . . .'

Perlman watched a train go in the direction of Glasgow Central. 'Go home, Dev.'

The young man opened the door of his MG and sat behind the wheel and inclined his face against it in an attitude of defeat or sorrow, or both. Neither Perlman nor Scullion could see his expression.

Scullion said, 'Pitt Street.'

41

At Force HQ, Perlman found a memo from Tay on his desk. Terse, as Tay's messages usually were, it read: *Request update on Colin Perlman data ASAP.* Tay was relentless about this. Yielding to an impatience he wished he didn't feel, Perlman took ten quick minutes to study Colin's file. He was squeezing this chore in between what were matters of greater urgency, a realization that caused him a stab of guilt. I should've done more for Colin, he thought. Pushed harder. But other developments occurred, diversions arose, and the business of policing this city brought new situations daily. How could you concentrate on just one? Crime was sometimes tidal, sometimes a typhoon. You couldn't get out of its way.

Perlman still couldn't understand Tay's interest in Colin. Months, he'd never enquired. Never a word. He was apparently catching up for lost time. But why now?

He leafed through the file. It contained the pathologist's report, a description of the bullet that had killed Colin, and Perlman's own account of what he'd seen and heard in Dalness Street that night: the big car, the Bentley of legend and myth, the gunman's shot. There were a couple of photographs of the victim. Hurry, hurry past them, they still cause pain. There was a list of Colin's clothing. His possessions. These were scraps, assembled quickly.

The file also contained a report of the discovery of the burnt-out Bentley in a wooded area near the Ayrshire town of Dalmellington, and a statement, made to a constable in U-Division, by the ten-year-old kid who'd come across the wreck of the car. *I was taking a shortcut through the woods . . .*

The good discoveries only happened when people were taking shortcuts, Perlman thought. And only then if they were going through the woods.

He'd appended printed notes of his interviews with Kilroy and Blum, and an opinion from the Procurator-Fiscal's office that there was no evidence of Kilroy's involvement in Colin's death, and therefore no case to bring. He rapped out a short account of the anonymous caller on his computer keyboard, then printed the sheet, the only electronic task he knew how to perform. He slid the sheet from the printer and put it in the file. The next step would be to include a transcription of the message he'd received on his answering machine. He looked in the middle drawer of his desk, saw the cassette resting on a salad of rubber bands, paperclips, and varied scraps of paper.

Later, he thought. When there was time. Tay would have to wait. He closed the drawer, locked it, then rolled his chair back from his desk. The castors squeaked on the floor. He took off his glasses, rubbed his eyes. Without the specs, he always had a slightly startled look.

He went in search of Scullion. Sandy was studying some papers on his desk when Perlman came into his office. 'You done that stuff for Tay?'

'Most of it.'

'He'll come looking for you, Lou.'

'I'll make sure I'm out of the building.' Perlman followed Scullion down the stairs. 'Where is this place we're going?'

'Near Hillington.'

Outside, they walked to Scullion's car. The city was darkening.

287

Perlman felt hunger; his stomach whined like a bow drawn badly across a fiddle string. When would the day end? He strapped himself into the passenger seat and imagined food: good thick chips with little bits of skin still attached, HP sauce, a thickly battered lump of cod and a wee drizzle of hot grease.

Later. Like Colin's file. Life was all postponements.

Scullion was racing through the Clyde Tunnel now. Here and there the walls were damp where the river had seeped through. Perlman never liked being in the Tunnel. He imagined a deluge one day, total disaster, water crashing mercilessly through plaster. He was glad when the car emerged from the cylinder and the Southern General Hospital came in sight.

They travelled along Shieldhall Road and then skirted the edge of Hillington Industrial Estate. 'It's somewhere around here,' Scullion said. He took a left turn and drove into the estate.

Perlman asked, 'Street name?'

'Gladys Road.'

Yellow streetlights were coming on. The area, caught between the last of the day's natural light and the glow of the artificial, had a look of unreality. It was as if the whole place lay under a haze the colour of daffodils. Low concrete buildings housed small companies, light engineering, electronics, all shut and shuttered at the end of the day's business. These small enterprises were dwarfed by huge warehouses that contained thousands of barrels of whisky.

He spotted the sign for Gladys Road at the same time as Scullion.

'Here we are,' Scullion said, and parked alongside a fence built out of tall steel poles that rose to a height of about eight feet and then tapered into ugly swordpoints. A sign welded to the front gate read: *Bute Transport*.

Perlman got out. He had a limited view of the yard between the slatted poles. Some kind of galvanized metal structure, about the size of a small garage, sat dark and unlit in the middle of the compound.

Scullion said, 'See anything?'

'Not a thing. Place looks abandoned.'

'I don't see any kind of transportation.' Scullion grabbed the gate and shook it, a fruitless effort. 'No trucks. No cars.'

'I get the funny feeling Bute Transport has moved on,' Perlman said.

'You think Bute did a flit?'

'It's possible. Things were getting a wee bit too hot for Chasm.'

Scullion kicked the gate, grunted. The steel poles didn't yield. 'Okay, we find him and ask where and how he operates his business these days. Especially the how.'

'You got a number for him?'

Scullion said, 'No, but I assume Kilroy does.'

'Kilroy's bound to be ex-directory.'

'I can run him down through Pitt Street. We've got to have his details on file.' Scullion produced his mobile and tapped numbers into it.

He stared into the gathering dark while Scullion talked on the mobile. He walked the length of the fence, peering between the poles at the empty compound. He heard something. He wasn't sure what or where exactly it came from. It might have been the sound of a stone falling from a high place, a cat disturbing loose masonry on a wall; or it might have been a footfall nearby, somebody's stealthy walk arrested in mid-movement. He listened hard.

Some yards away, Scullion was pissed off with the person at the other end of his phone, and raising his voice. 'Don't tell me we don't have it. I know for a bloody fact we do.'

I'm jumpy, Perlman thought. He tried to listen to the silences that lay under the surface of Sandy Scullion's voice, as if they might suddenly yield another sound. He had a moment when the night seemed totally disjointed, and his surroundings were as much out of alignment as his spinal column, which throbbed again. Why this sense of danger, if that's what it was? Maybe it was something else, a consciousness of being observed by an invisible onlooker, say. My own stalker. Somebody to watch over me.

Scullion said, 'It's like pulling teeth to get information out of people.'

'Did you see anybody just then, Sandy?'

'No. Why?'

'I thought somebody was hanging around nearby.'

'I don't see a soul,' Scullion said, looking this way and that.

Perlman shrugged; the feeling of uneasiness didn't lift.

Scullion said, 'Anyway, I got Kilroy's number. *Finally.*' He held the handset to his ear, tapped the keys, waited. He looked jaundiced in the lemon light. 'No answer.'

'So do we run out to Bearsden?'

Scullion said, 'I'm dead, Lou. We'll track down Chasm in the morning, first thing. I think it's time I remember I have a home life I neglect too much.'

'Fine, I'll go back and transcribe the cassette,' Perlman said. 'One chore less, then I can sleep without dreaming of Tay.'

They walked back to the car. Perlman had a last look round. He saw nothing. He settled in the passenger seat and wondered if the sound he'd heard was merely a little blip in the radar of his imagination.

Scullion dropped him off at Pitt Street. Perlman walked inside the building, climbed the stairs, passed a few WPCs drinking coffee. One of them was Meg Gayle, the others he recognized but didn't know by name. He smiled at Meg, and she returned the expression in a coy way.

'Would you happen to have an aspirin, Meg?' he asked.

'I can find one for you, Sergeant.'

'I'd appreciate it. I'll be at my desk. Thanks.'

He moved down the corridor. He sat in front of the computer console. He unlocked the drawer where he'd stashed the cassette.

Meg Gayle appeared with a small cardboard cup of water, and two aspirins in the palm of her hand. 'Here,' she said.

'Thanks, dear.' Perlman swallowed the tablets, washed them down with water.

'You look a wee bit weary, Sergeant,' Meg Gayle said.

'I don't think I'm alone,' Perlman remarked.

'I know what you mean.'

Perlman noticed the young woman's long thin neck, the sweet small mouth, the darkly serious eyes. He wondered what had compelled Meg Gayle into a police career, but he didn't ask.

'Anything else you need, Sergeant?'

'I'm fine,' he said, and his attention was drawn to a small rectangular envelope propped against his keyboard. It was addressed to him. He opened it – it hadn't been gummed very well – and removed the contents. A photograph slid into his hand face down. He turned it over and felt a rush of recognition.

'Did you put this envelope here, Meg?'

On her way out, Meg Gayle paused in the doorway. 'No, I didn't.'

'Any idea who might have been in here?'

'Sorry, Sergeant. Is there a problem?'

'No, no, it's fine.'

'Right, goodnight,' she said.

He didn't answer. He looked at the photograph for a long time.

A classic Bentley, a driver, a streetlamp, a street sign, a date and time. It was night-time in the photograph, and the driver's face was obscured by shadow. *I was there when this was taken,* he thought. And so was Colin. He got to his feet and stuck the photo in his coat pocket and rushed downstairs to reception.

'Jackie, has anybody strange gone upstairs tonight?'

'People going up there are usually strange, Sergeant,' Wren said.

'Seriously.'

'I haven't seen anyone unfamiliar, if that's what you mean.'

'Fine, thanks.' Perlman walked outside. Go home, he thought.

Leave the transcription of the cassette for tomorrow. Tay can wait.

He'll have to.

He walked to his car and sat behind the wheel and smoked a cigarette. He removed the photograph from his pocket and examined it under the interior light. Who took this? Who sent it to me? Was this the evidence the anonymous caller had promised?

He peered hard at the shot. How could you tell if the picture was real or fake? And if it *was* real, who was the photographer? Who could possibly have been in the street at that particular time on that particular date armed with a camera? He pushed back his seat and stretched his legs. Three miles to Egypt. Three miles to ponder the photograph. After that, he'd call Miriam.

42

He let himself into the dark house and touched the mezuzah, then turned on lights as he moved down the corridor and into the kitchen. He opened the refrigerator and seized a brown-spotted chill-skinned banana he found in the salad tray. He unpeeled it quickly and crammed it into his mouth. He scanned the refrigerator again: slim pickings. He found a triangle of plastic cheese and picked the packaging off clumsily. As you got older, packaging irritated you increasingly. At sixty-five he'd probably have to set half an hour aside to crack open his cigarettes. At seventy, senile and trembling, he'd be totally bamboozled by a bag of potato crisps.

He walked inside the living room, his attention taken by a slight whispering sound. The turntable. The stylus had gone back to the off position automatically, but the disc was still turning round and round. A flawed device; it must have been spinning for hours. He chose another album to put on, placed the needle carefully on the slick surface of the record and listened to the first bars of Billie Holiday singing 'What is this Thing Called Love'? He moved some newspapers and magazines from the sofa, tossed them on the floor, then sat down and undid his tie.

The music calmed him. At times there was a sweet ease about it, at other times an eerie doomed optimism. *I saw you there one wonderful day . . .*

He opened the envelope and studied the photograph. You couldn't see the driver's face. But he didn't have any doubt that it was Kilroy. The man behind the wheel, although half-lost in an obscurity of shadow, was undeniably big and bulky. Blow this up and you'll get the Fat Man, he thought. If it isn't a fake. Why send a fake anyway?

Who'd falsify evidence? The picture needed to be examined by experts. And if it was real –

The Proc-Fisc couldn't disregard this item. He couldn't just cast this one aside.

He leaned towards the telephone, dialled Miriam's number. *I saw you there one wonderful day, you took my heart and threw it away . . .* 'Hello, Lou,' she said.

'How did you know it was me?'

'Would you believe psychic?'

'I keep an open mind.'

'The truth is banal. I have caller ID.'

'Damn, that's one mystery less,' he said.

'I'm sure there are plenty of other mysteries.'

'You're telling me? I'm falling over them all the time.' He tried to picture her, what she was wearing, whether she was standing or sitting or lying down. He had the mind of the inquisitive lover, possessive and yearning for detail; the fact that he wasn't a lover he deemed a mere technicality. They'd kissed. He'd touched her breast. He'd crossed barriers he'd never dreamed of crossing. In time, he'd span others.

He was about to mention the photograph, but why turn the conversation towards Colin? This is my dime, my time, he thought. I'm hungry and selfish in matters of the heart. Colin had her to himself for years.

'Is that Billie Holiday?' Miriam asked.

'Yes.'

'I like her.'

The things you learn about the people you love, he thought.
'When are you free?' he asked.

'Are you asking me out again?'

'I think I am.'

'You're becoming very bold, Lou.'

He gazed round the room. Lamplight made crevices in the shadows. 'How about tomorrow,' he said. 'I'll rearrange my cluttered world for you.'

'Lou, you never know what you'll be doing one hour to the next. If you're free, call me.'

He didn't want the conversation to end in uncertainty. He needed to know that tomorrow held romantic possibilities. 'When I saw you, you know, in your dressing gown –'

She laughed. 'When you copped a feel, you mean?'

'Take me seriously.'

'I do.'

'Right, when that happened, I felt like a kid doing somersaults. Am I sounding daft and soppy?'

'Totally. I don't mind.'

She opens the door a crack further. She says she doesn't mind. This is the kind of thing you pounce on. 'So many things I've been meaning to tell you –'

'Then tell me to my face.'

'I will.'

'Save them. Call me tomorrow,' she said.

'Count on that.'

'Goodnight, Lou.' She hung up before he could think of a way to detain her. He rose from the sofa and bopped round the room in happy dancing mode.

He stopped suddenly.

Somebody was in the room with him. Standing directly behind him. He didn't have to turn and check. He knew. The chill on the back of his neck, the sudden surge of heartbeat. He knew.

'You're obviously in love, Perlman. What a surprise.'

She was blonde and she'd cut and curled her hair, and she wore a grey tracksuit and running shoes, but he knew that face.

He felt foolish. She must have been watching him, and listening to his conversation with Miriam. Tracksuit, running shoes, kitted out for jogging.

Blum had been a jogger too.

He saw the little gun in her hand.

'Love at your time of life,' she said. 'There's still hope for the rest of us.'

'Some things take you by surprise,' he said.

'I'm going to shoot you,' she said.

'I guessed when I saw the gun.'

'I don't want to especially.'

'But it's the programme. It's White Rage. You're doing Jews now.'

'Flavour of the day,' she said.

'Like Blum.'

'Creepy type. Thought he was God's gift.'

'But you were under orders.'

'The movement needs victims, Perlman.'

'And killers.'

'I believe in my work,' she said. She had a mouth you could imagine doing outrageous things. Her green eyes shone with fervour.

'What's your real name anyway?'

'Names don't matter, Sergeant.'

'You're subsumed by the movement. You give up your identity.'

'I'm a wee cog in the big machine,' she said. 'You like the hair?'

'It suits,' he said.

'Cut and curl,' she said. 'This house was a piece of cake. I thought a cop would be more security conscious. Back door, crappy latch, I'm inside in a flash. What's she like, this love of yours?'

'Let me count the ways,' he said.

'You've got it bad.'

'My soul's affected,' he said.

'Deep stuff, Sergeant. You should have arrested me in the street, you know.'

'Hindsight's easy, lassie. I couldn't make the match.'

'And I couldn't believe you walked away.'

'Mistakes, I've made a few.'

Billie Holiday was singing 'Do Nothin 'Til You Hear From Me'. Perlman heard the words, but his mind was working elsewhere: a way out, an exit route, how? The gun sorely limited his options. His heart banged like a fist against a concrete wall.

'Never mind, Sergeant. We all make them.'

'That's such a wee gun,' he said.

'It does a big job.'

'Bobby used that one on Indra,' Perlman said.

'How right you are.'

'And you're the virus. Magistr32.'

'You dig a bit, don't you?'

'I like standing in holes.'

'Good, because you're in a deep one now. And you can't get out.'

Perlman eyed the gun. He had a floating sensation, as if, filled suddenly with helium, he was rising to the ceiling. An out-of-body experience already, and you're not dead. He wondered about all the trusted responses, the suicidal rush, head down like a battering ram, the fast backward retreat, the *Me Jewish? You must be mistaken* strategy: none of these ever worked. He thought, this is going to hurt, no matter what I do. She has a bullet and my picture's on it.

'Did Helen Mboto scream a lot?'

'Playing for time isn't going to win you a reprieve, Sergeant.'

'A hammer, repeated blows, she –'

'She wasn't conscious much.'

'Tilak Gupta, now, he really fell, right?'

'He needed only slight encouragement.'

'You get around –'

'Speaking of getting places. This has been very nice, and I'd love to stay and chat.'

297

'Wait,' and he raised his hands in front of his face.

She brought the gun up. Billie Holiday sang, *True I've been seen with someone new.* He stepped back half a yard. He'd miss fish suppers. He'd miss music. He'd miss Miriam. He had a hundred reasons for not dying. He wanted to tell this woman what they were, and how unfair it was to die when you'd finally *almost* declared your love.

He took another step back. The hallway was behind him, the door open to the corridor, the front door beyond that, the street. He wondered if he could edge out of the room in steps so small she'd never notice. Not even Houdini had a chance.

She fired a shot.

He'd never known such *intensity* of pain could exist. It put all the aches of his life in perspective. The bad back, the toothache, the sinus pain behind the eyes, the front of the skull, these were nothing, motes in the great cosmic drift of things. He brought his right hand across his chest to his left shoulder, which is where he thought he'd been shot. His fingers were instantly wet with blood. He couldn't stand up. Legs gone. He went down on his knees, rolled onto his back, groaned, *Christ such pain.* He slid towards the hallway like a man with his hands tied behind his back. She'd fire again, he knew that. She was looming down on him. His eyesight was tinted now, everything deep red at the edges, like paper burning.

He heard the gun again.

The shot missed him by the width of a thread. He heard the bullet kick into the floorboards beside his head, splintering wood. His thoughts swirled. The gunfire was audible in his skull. His body was sliding down towards the combustion chamber of a crematorium. Already he felt the raging heat. He slithered backwards through the fog and fire and smoke of his pain, even as she tracked him, gun held aloft.

'Fuck it,' she said.

He reached up with his right arm, grabbed the edge of a shelf, brought it down in a clatter of books and old souvenirs he'd collected over the years with no real purpose in mind, war

298

medals of WWI, a couple of old brass telescopes, some primitive flint tools gathered at an archaeological dig in Stornoway by Colin in the days of his youthful innocence, big glass jars of old pennies, florins, half-crowns, pre-decimal coins he'd collected just because he liked that metal-smelling dirty weighty old currency. The jars shattered, the coins rolled everywhere, the flint pieces broke, the medals clanked on floorboards. He was covered by his own silly keepsakes. He found the strength to keep pushing himself backwards, spine to floor, hips working, feet kicking for purchase against the floor.

Somebody was banging on the front door now. Thumping. Or was it a tattoo in some fevered corner of his own brain? And now a voice. Several voices, male, rough, upraised.

He saw her stare at the door. She was surprised, and then indecisive, caught between the sudden sounds from outside and the sight of Perlman lying before her. She fired another shot, this time levelling her gun at the door. The bullet split wood high, almost at the lintel level. He twisted his face and looked backwards and saw the front door open – not in any normal way, no geometric opening of space, the door was battered off its hinges and fell inwards and figures entered the hallway. He wanted to warn these intruders, *Get back, she'll shoot again*, but his mouth was too dry for speech. His tongue was numb, a flat stone between his teeth. Head tilted, he recognized a couple of faces, neighbours roused by shots, neighbours tired of the cyclical crime and violence in the city – vigilantes of a sort, he'd always supposed. There were three or four of them. They were men he talked to on the street from time to time. He knew some of their names. McQuillen. Spiers. Dunn. They asked him questions about becoming police volunteers, part-time cops on the beat, what did it take, how did they qualify? Sometimes he thought, *I look like a recruiting poster?* They wanted to meet violence with an approved, city-regulated violence of their own. Batons to the head of wrongdoers. A boot, a knee to the groin, to the skull. They wanted to be a posse. He'd always mildly disapproved of them for this urge to take the law into their own hands, but not now, they were heroes, saviours, fighters at the borderline where civilization met brutality. They'd come to his rescue. Praise them. Bless 'em all.

'You awright, Sergeant Perlman?'

'Fucking not awright, can you no see he's bleeding like a pig?'

'Call an ambulance somebody.'

'Where'd that bitch go?'

He was no longer conscious of his shoulder. He was going down into a steep dark place. He struggled to stay above it. With a great effort, he raised his face up. The woman was gone.

Somebody he didn't know helped him stand. He glanced at the man, thick dark eyebrows, a doleful face that might have made John Knox look like a stand-up comic. He wasn't one of the local vigilantes, some of whom were thundering through the house into the small yard at the back in pursuit of the woman; only one of the locals – Dunn, snub-nosed, chubby, effervescent – had stayed behind to help Perlman. Dunn's shirt was soaked with Perlman's blood.

The man with the dejected face said, 'No sense in waiting for an ambulance. You could bleed to death. I've got a car outside. Can you make it?'

'I've got a choice?' Perlman said.

Assisted by Dunn on one side, the stranger on the other, Perlman hobbled down the hallway and outside into the street. He was dopey suddenly, due to blood loss and shock, and the realization of how close he'd come to shuffling off on a permanent basis.

Easy easy, Dunn kept saying. Go easy.

Like there's another way I could go, Perlman thought.

Somebody draped his coat round him. A thoughtful touch.

He was led, very carefully, to a car parked in front of his Mondeo, and then lowered into the passenger seat.

'I'll bleed in your car,' he said.

'Plastic seat covers,' the stranger said.

Perlman still held one hand to his wound. He thought: I've

never been shot before. He felt the car move. Dunn remained behind outside the house.

The man said, 'The Royal's the nearest hospital.'

Perlman couldn't think. The Royal's the nearest, whatever. The man drove hard into Shettleston Road, turned west, raced towards Biggar Street. Perlman shut his eyes. He had no sense of direction. He was trying to imagine that candle in the deeps of his brain, but he couldn't get it to light; all he could see was the woman's face, the gun in her hand, the lethal determination in her eyes.

'Hang on. Not much further.'

'I don't know you, do I?' Perlman said.

'No.'

It was too much effort to engage in talk. Perlman let his head sag back. He tried to envisage the route: Duke Street, High Street, Glasgow Cathedral, Castle Street, the Royal Infirmary, the ancient core of the city. The car stopped. Perlman heard the driver get out and come round to open the passenger door.

'Grab me for support, Perlman.'

Perlman reached for his Samaritan. He was always moved by unexpected kindness.

'A few yards, okay?'

'I can make it,' Perlman said.

They entered Emergency. The man led Perlman to a desk where a nurse was bent over a file. She looked up. She was West Indian. 'Oh my my my, what happened?'

'He's been shot.'

She glanced at Perlman's wound and she picked up a phone. 'Dr Gordon, can you get out here quickly?'

'I'll leave you now, Perlman,' the man said.

'Wait. I didn't get your name.'

'Take this.' He pressed a wadded piece of paper into Perlman's hand. 'They'll clean the wound and give you painkillers. You'll be okay.'

The nurse led Perlman to a wheelchair. He watched his benefactor walk towards the exit door. He wanted to call the fellow back and thank him for his generosity, but he didn't have the energy. The wad of paper he clutched in his hand was damp with blood. He managed to stick it in a pocket of his trousers.

And then he was exhausted.

The man paused at the exit door as if he meant to look back, but changed his mind and went out. Perlman gazed at the image of his benefactor passing through the black space of the doorway and out into the night. And then the thought struck him for the first time that something must be wrong with the fellow's eye.

He wore a patch the colour of skin.

43

She was running through narrow dark streets of small houses. The men had been in pursuit of her for a while, but now she no longer heard their shouts or their hoarse panting. She passed windows with drawn curtains and bright TVs glowing behind the drapes. This is the life, ladies, your own little house and telly, you settle into the deadness and dread of it all and you die, smothered. She couldn't live like that . . . Forty, abandoned one night by the hubbie, used up, hung out like a limp old wash-rag on a line to dry and wither, the way her mother had been treated. Husband upped and gone. O Canada. No future. Just men she fucked and drinkies she drank.

It was a kind of a life, she supposed. One you lived in the silt of things.

Fuck that.

She kept running. She wondered if the men had telephoned the cops and whether there were patrols searching for a female in jogging gear in the east end of Glasgow. Okay, right, she was noticeable. She stood out. When she passed under lamps her blonde hair shone. She had to get away from here. She needed a street where taxis ran.

Then there was the question of where to go.

She could return to one of the several rooms she rented throughout the city, and change her clothes, dye her hair again, do what she had to do. She clenched her hands in anger. Bastard Perlman had slipped away from her, blessed by luck. Weren't the Jews said to be the Chosen People? God's favourites.

She stopped running now. She was whacked, out of breath. She'd dropped the gun somewhere along the way. And the Walkman. The loss of these possessions panicked her a little. Especially the gun. It could be used in evidence.

What did it matter about the gun? Perlman knew where it had been fired and who it had killed. Maybe he'd die too. Loss of blood. His age. Didn't look to be in great shape. Maybe he couldn't be saved. But he had the face of a survivor. Oh, she was furious with herself for failing to get one in his heart, and the way she'd shot without pause, her aim shite, and how she'd lost control when the door was kicked in, firing wild, stupid stupid stupid –

She knew better. She knew how she should have done it. With cool, with detachment. She'd allowed herself to become flustered.

She walked across a patch of wasteland. She saw lights in the distance. The green neon of a petrol station, pale white street-lamps floating in midair. She moved towards them cautiously. First priority: a place with a telephone. When she reached the forecourt of the petrol station she saw a woman through the plate glass of the shop feeding a roll of paper into a cash register, and a man filling his car at one of the pumps. There was a public phone situated close to the door of the shop.

She took some coins from her pocket. She dialled a number. It rang and rang and no answer. She hung up. Okay. Think. Phone for a taxi. Logical. There was no directory attached to the phone. If there ever had been, it was long gone. The absence of the phone book unnerved her – little things like this jangled her suddenly, things she'd have sailed past before.

Maybe a taxi would come.

She punched in another number and Swank answered.

She said, 'There's been a fuck-up.'

'How bad a fuck-up, love?'

'I don't know how bad. Is Pegg there?'

'You only ever talk to Pegg,' he said. Swank could be petty. He wanted to own her.

'Is he there with you?'

'He left a while ago. Why don't you tell me what's wrong?'

'Just tell Pegg I called.'

She hung up, walked to the edge of the street. She wasn't sure of her surroundings. Somewhere east of Perlman's house, maybe north-east. Springboig? Carntyne? She stared the length of the street, noting the scarcity of traffic.

The man who'd been filling his car walked over to her. He was fortyish, short, drinker's nose red as the flesh of a blood orange. 'You lost, hen? Are you wanting a lift?'

'Piss off.'

He said, 'This is what kindness gets you. Try to help and what happens?'

'A kick in the teeth, buster. The world's like that.'

'Your world mibbe. No mine.' He stalked back to his car and slammed the door. She watched him drive past very close to her. He flashed her a vigorous V, then he was gone. What did he think she was – a hoor in jogging gear? She watched his car vanish and then, thankfully, a taxi appeared in view, vacancy sign lit. She hailed it, got in the back.

'Where to?' the driver asked.

'Govan,' she said.

'Govan it is.'

He looked at her in his rearview mirror and winked.

44

Perlman woke sweating. He wondered where he was. When the pain kicked in he remembered: he'd been shot and survived.

Shot. You never think it's going to happen to you. You come across firearm victims in your work, you never *dream* you might become one of them. Maybe he should pray, offer up a word of thanks. *Dear God.* He stared at the pale blue curtain stretched round his hospital bed. A lamp burned beyond, and an oval of light was trapped in the texture of the curtain, like a spirit emerging from a nether world.

Death waits for me. G Reaper, Esquire, extends a willing hand.

He was hooked up to a drip. He raised his face to look at the bottle that contained the intravenous liquid, whatever it was. He followed the line into his arm and saw an Elastoplast covering the spot where the puncture had been made to accommodate the needle. *I want out of here,* he thought.

Scullion appeared like a magician's assistant conjured from a concealed cabinet. A parting of curtain and there he was. He drew a chair up to the bed and smiled at Perlman. 'Couldn't get out of the way in time, eh?'

'Not nippy enough on the old feet,' Perlman said. His voice was hoarse, his mouth stuffed with dry balls of saliva.

'Must be a funny feeling being on somebody's hit list.'

'You see me laughing?'

'We're still looking for her, Lou. Your concerned neighbours, a really concerned gung-ho crew, gave us a description.'

'Which she'll have changed by now.'

'Naturally,' Scullion said.

Perlman moved. A flash of pain in his shoulder caused him to suck air. 'We don't even know her name. Celia Liddell. Magistr32 –'

'Or Yan Yomomata.'

'She's Glaswegian,' Perlman said. He struggled for speech. 'It's the only thing I don't doubt. Her accent.' He drifted a moment, remembering the guy with the eyepatch. But that seemed faraway to him now. He thought of the bullet that had gone into his flesh; something he shared with Indra Gupta and Nat Blum, an intimacy he hadn't wished for. He was bonded with the dead. They'd all been victims of the same gun.

'Pass me that water, Sandy.'

Scullion filled a glass from a pitcher on the bedside table. Perlman, who noticed a telephone on the table, sipped through a double-jointed straw. 'Have the reports of her so-called sightings been checked out?'

'The ones that weren't silly hoaxes, sure. Nothing so far. How are you feeling?'

'I need painkillers.'

'You want me to call a nurse?'

'Mind? What time is it?'

'Six a.m.'

'I must have slept for hours.'

'They shot you up with morphine.'

'Very nice it is too. I recommend it.'

Scullion vanished beyond the curtain. Perlman tried to raise the damaged arm. It was bandaged and stiff; he winced at how it hurt. He closed his eyes. Sleep floated close, wraithlike.

Scullion came back. 'Here, one painkiller.'

Perlman looked at the capsule in his hand. 'What is it?'

'I didn't ask.' Scullion sat again. 'Take it.'

Perlman swallowed it with some water, which tasted stale. He laid his head back on the pillow.

Scullion said, 'You'll be bedridden for days.'

'Who says?'

'I was talking to your doctor.'

'I don't plan to lie here, Sandy.'

'Superlou thinks he's going to just *bound* out of bed? Your arm's useless, for Christ's sake, and you're on painkillers.'

'So I walk tilted to one side and my thoughts get fuzzy. Is that such a big deal?'

'Forget the bloody heroics.'

'Sandy, she came *that* close to making me permanently inactive. I want her.' Perlman felt drowsy. Heroics, my arse, he thought. Somebody tries to kill you, you're supposed to stay in a hospital bed and suck narcotics? He'd find a way to get out of here. But it's not a fucking movie, Lou . . . it's not where the hero, like Lazarus, picks himself up and comes back to life, eager for conflict and confrontation.

He drifted away again. He remembered the cowboys of his matinee mornings, Roy Rogers, Hopalong Cassidy. They wouldn't lie in a hospital bed. Despite all the gunplay in which they were involved, they never even got *shot*. And then there were the G-Men, the Feds who came and went in shadowy black and white serials, brushing wounds aside as casually as men flicking flies off their skin.

Scullion said, 'It's frustrating and I sympathize. But the muscles in your upper arm and shoulder sustained damage. Some bone is splintered there. The doctor removed the slug, but that doesn't mean you can hop out of bed, Lou. Let's be realistic. Your system's in shock. You don't move. How come you never want to do what's best for you anyway? What is it inside you that makes you think you're invincible? Twenty years younger, maybe you could've been released from this place within twenty-four hours. Even then, you wouldn't go straight back to work, you'd convalesce.'

Perlman was tired listening. His brain darkened. Going down the gutters of no return. He must have slept, because when he opened his eyes again Scullion was gone. A little hop-skip in time. He had the strange feeling that Miriam had been sitting by his bed. A dream? He remembered opening his eyes and she was watching him with a look of concern but then she'd faded into shadow. He wondered if Scullion had told her about the shooting.

A nurse came in and took his pulse, his blood pressure. She was a big woman with a perm that had imploded in a thicket of flattened curls.

'What time is it?' Perlman asked.

'Midday.'

'Are my glasses anywhere?' he asked.

'Right here.' She picked up his glasses from the surface of the bedside table and passed them to him.

He put them on one-handed. How clear the world looked again. A couple of discs of simple glass bring you back from the murk. 'How's my blood?'

'Acceptable,' she said. 'Considering.'

'Here, any chance of a smoke?'

'Aye, right, about as much chance as me and Richard Gere making a wean thegether.'

'You and Dick would make great parents, pet.'

'None of your flannel,' she said. 'I'll be back with some grub.'

Perlman watched the wide-hipped nurse disappear beyond the curtain. He wondered where they'd put his clothes. What had he been wearing anyway? A blood-soaked shirt? Trousers, probably also bloodstained. What were a few stains, if you weren't particular? Had he been wearing his coat? He scanned the space. No closet. The big drawer of his bedside table was the best candidate. The trick was to lean from the bed and slide the thing open.

If you can't manage that, Lou, you're going nowhere.

But it was dumb and stupid to *think* about movement. Here's the chance to kick back, cool your beans, get pampered, fed, never have to raise a finger to help yourself, get bathed in bed, you want anything you just press a wee bell and somebody eventually comes, easy living, no problems.

I'm in a movie, he thought.

I'm the man who has to rise up from his sickbed and, no matter what the cost, go in search of justice.

I'm the Federal Agent who groans as he gets up. He's still clinging to his badge of office, his responsibilities, his sense of duty. *He has to get up.* Bed just isn't an option.

I'm the *parshoin*, the superhero.

He twisted, groaned, *oh God have mercy*, stretched for the handle. Then rested. He was breathing hard. Shattered muscle, chipped bone, God knows what else the bullet had done. *I'm kidding myself about getting out of here.* His face was damp and cold. His body sweated. He felt mildly fevered. Scullion was right when he'd asked: How come you never want to do what's best for you?

Because it's in the fibre. The marrow. You're an *eigueshpart* bastard. What other kind of man could have silently loved a woman for so many years? Only a stubborn one. Only a single-minded old bastard who wouldn't listen to the cries of his own body but preferred instead to stare at the grainy silver screens of childhood, where men absorbed their pain without fuss.

He removed the drip, lowered his hand, grasped the handle, slid the drawer open. The pain pincered his upper arm and shoulder. Tears came to his eyes. He needed pethidine, morphine, whatever took away this sense that somebody was boring a hole through flesh and nerve and bone with an electric drill.

He saw his clothes piled in the drawer. The shirt was bloodied. The trousers looked okay, give or take some red stains. His coat had been folded. His shoes were on the floor, half under the table. He lowered the uninjured arm, plucked the trousers from the drawer, drew them up to the bed.

Christ, all this was *tiring*. He remembered now. Hadn't his benefactor given him a wadded-up piece of paper last night? Or had he conjured that up from his opiated sleep? He stuck his hand in the pocket of his trousers and fumbled among a keychain, coins, a book of matches, some indescribable lint – *oose* was the word for it – and retrieved the paper, which he spread on the bedsheet.

A name and an address.

He didn't know the name, and the location of the address was only slightly familiar to him. Okay, it meant something, otherwise the Samaritan wouldn't have given it to him. Was it the one-eyed man's address? Or something else? Perlman's head felt like a basketball being tossed through a series of hoops and hitting the rim each time.

Who the hell was the benefactor anyway? And why had he been outside Perlman's house at the *exact* time of the shooting? He didn't believe it was pure chance. He had the feeling that the Samaritan had been lingering nearby for a purpose.

But what?

He *craved* answers. He let his head slide back towards the pillow. Another big question: how to get into his clothes and out of here with a minimum of suffering? He lay very still and considered the problem. He needed help. An assistant.

He knew of only one candidate who'd obey without creating problems. He reached in an awkward manner for the telephone, imagining his hand to be pale grey suddenly, and the slats of venetian blinds laying darker strips of shadows across his skin. Any moment now the credits would roll and he'd be out of this monochromatic world of pain and whooshed back into the drably sensible reality with which he was familiar.

45

She left her room in Langlands Road shortly after 2 p.m. She hadn't slept all night – mind meandering, thoughts tumbling, memories of Perlman flitting through her head – but she felt alert. She'd cut her hair even shorter than before and rinsed the blonde out of it, and now her style was that of a very young schoolboy, side-parted. She wore a pair of granny glasses, baggy old jeans with holes in the knees, tan trainers, a brown wool jacket and a dark paisley scarf. The charity-shop eclectic look, a kind of downmarket fusion, the style – or lack of it – that might be adopted by an impoverished student finishing her thesis on some arcane aspect of Elizabethan theatre.

She walked to Govan Underground station. She passed a veiled woman selling copies of the *Big Issue*, and a couple of beggars she'd seen a few times before, shivering young dopers in balaclavas, chalk-coloured hands held out for alms. The board of a newspaper stand read: *White Rage Killings: More Fears*

She went inside the station and down to the platform and heard the rumble of an incoming train approach from the black of the tunnel. She boarded, avoided the faces of her fellow passengers, rode to Buchanan Street, exited, walked to

Killermont Street. She'd given up her usual long stride; the clothes she wore somehow imposed a slight shuffling mode of walk, modest, less self-assured.

I fucked up, she thought. *I missed an open goal.*

She passed the bus station and moved along Hanover Street.

She'd look for a cab. She was forever looking for cabs. Sometimes she felt she lived her life in the back of black taxis. She coughed in the polluted air. The stench of diesel from the bus station was overpowering.

She saw a taxi, raised a hand, watched the cab come swooping in to the kerb. She climbed in the back and the driver swivelled his red razor-nicked neck and said, 'Let me take you away from all this, sweetheart.'

'Any time,' she said.

'My wife's an awfy jealous woman,' he said. 'She'd have a fit.' He laughed at his own banter. Running off with a woman half his age, leaving a scandal in his slipstream after a life of respectability and fidelity, fancy that.

She settled back in the seat and took off her glasses and rubbed her eyes. She had a single lash turned inward against the eyeball and it pricked her. She pushed it aside with a fingertip.

She'd say, *I screwed it up. I need another chance.*

She pulled her scarf around her head and looked from the window. The city was washed in yellow light, and indifferent.

46

'Easy there, son,' Perlman said. 'Hard as it might be, think of me as very delicate porcelain.'

Carefully, Murdoch helped Perlman to a sitting position. 'I'm trying, Sergeant.'

'Just say porcelain porcelain over and over to yourself and you'll start to believe it.' Perlman's legs dangled from the bed. Call me Dick Tracy, he thought. 'What clothes did you bring me?'

'The best I could find.' The young constable opened a plastic grocery bag and spilled the contents on the bed. 'A shirt, a pair of trousers, socks. I tossed in boxer shorts.'

Perlman thought of the neatly dressed Murdoch rummaging through his house. Had he stumbled on the dirty laundry pile? Had he seen the heap of burnt-down cigarettes in the bedside ashtray and the crumpled sheets and the hole singed by loose ash in the mattress and the pillowcases that didn't match? Perlman felt a tiny tweak of shame. But was it his fault that his former cleaning woman, Maggie McGibbon, had quit the job a few months ago because of her bad back? Pardon me, I haven't had time to look for a replacement.

'You'll need to help me, Murdoch.'

'I don't think this is too smart, Sergeant.'

'Did I ask for an opinion, Dennis?'

'No, actually –'

'Then do as you're told. The underwear first.' Perlman stood upright. His head felt like an egg that had been spooned empty. His bandaged arm, stiff and useless, reminded him of stories told by amputees about how they could still feel missing limbs. His arm was a phantom.

A little embarrassed, Murdoch assisted him into the blue boxers. 'No need to be coy,' Perlman said.

'I'm just not used to helping grown men into their underwear.'

'Avert your eyes, Dennis. Now the trousers.'

Perlman couldn't recall owning trousers like the ones Murdoch produced; heavy and black and tight at the waist. Where the hell had they come from? What forgotten quarry of discarded clothing? He did up the zip without the constable's help.

'The shirt,' Perlman said.

'This is going to be awkward.'

'Drape the shirt over that shoulder, Dennis. I can manage the right arm.'

Murdoch held the garment in such a way that Perlman could push his right arm into the appropriate sleeve, then the young policeman gathered the left side of the shirt and hung it over Perlman's left shoulder. Murdoch did up the buttons.

'Never thought you'd signed on as a nanny, did you, Dennis?'

'No, Sergeant.'

'You're good. You've got that special touch.'

'I've waited all my life to hear that,' Murdoch said.

Perlman managed a very fragile smile. This is a fucking stupid mistake, he thought. I'll kill myself if I walk out of this place. My black and white world will be ablaze with colour, and I'll be dead.

'You've got permission to leave?' Murdoch asked.

'What am I, a prisoner? I leave when I like.'

315

Murdoch looked concerned. 'Sergeant –'

Perlman said, 'Don't nag, Dennis. You're too young to *kvetch*.'

'They won't let you out of here.'

'So they'll strap me in a straitjacket against my will? Coat, please. Then socks and shoes.'

Murdoch hung the coat over Perlman's shoulders. He stooped, slipped the socks on Lou's blue-veined white feet, then the shoes. He tied the laces.

'You brought a car, Dennis?'

'My own.'

'Good. Lead me to it. Slowly, slowly. Just until I get the circulation pumping again.'

Murdoch held the curtain aside. Perlman stepped through it, like a forgotten actor crooked with age, about to make a comeback appearance. A dilapidated old man, attached to an elaborate arrangement of tubes, peered at Perlman from the next bed. He was clearly edging towards the last exit. *The indignity of hospitalized death*, Perlman thought, and kept moving. Murdoch was wary at his side, ready to catch if Perlman stumbled.

The nurse with the wrecked perm appeared in the doorway. She looked as if she had a bedraggled miniature poodle on her skull. Perlman held up a hand, palm outward. 'Say nothing. Don't chastise me. I'm leaving.'

'You think you'll make it out of here?'

'I'd rather be out there than in here, Nurse. Believe me.'

'And when you need painkillers, what? You'll just ring some little bell in your head, will you?'

'I've got killers to catch,' Perlman said.

'So I'm told –'

'And I'm not going to catch them lying here.'

'You'll drop in the street.'

'I'm a durable old sod.'

'Stupid old sod is more like it.' She took a small pill box from her uniform. She opened it, removed two capsules, dropped them into Perlman's hand. 'You were due for medication anyway. You're going to need it, Sergeant. If you run into

316

the doctor on the way out, I never saw you. Do we have an understanding?'

'You're a wee darling,' he said.

'You might not think so well of me later,' she said.

He slipped the pills into his coat pocket and kept walking, Murdoch alongside him. 'Sometimes you find charity when you least expect it, Dennis.'

'And trouble,' Murdoch remarked.

'Trouble I always expect.'

They passed the front desk together, then walked out of the building. The sky was unexpectedly white and high in Perlman's vision. He blinked, felt woozy. A quick sharp ache hacksawed his upper arm. He was tempted to take one of the capsules, but he'd resist until he felt he was about to faint.

Murdoch's car was a bulbous little green thing, a Ford Ka.

'What planet's that from? Am I expected to get in there?' Perlman asked.

'It's bigger than it looks.' Murdoch held the passenger door open and Perlman, bending none too comfortably, made his way into the car. He grunted. The secret of movement, he thought, was to be aware of your limitations. Head upright, left arm completely still, don't bend unless you have to.

Murdoch turned the ignition key. Perlman asked, 'Did you tell anybody you were coming to the hospital?'

'No, Sarge.'

'Am I detecting hesitation, Dennis?'

Murdoch drove out of the car park. 'Hesitation?'

'A pause, a tiny wee measure of time?'

'You asked me to be discreet.'

Perlman checked the wing mirror. 'And?'

'I was discreet.'

'So why is Sandy Scullion right behind us, Dennis?'

Murdoch blushed, a boy with his fingers caught in the sweetie tin. 'Okay. I told him. He asked me if you'd called. I suppose he guessed you wouldn't stay in hospital.'

Perlman sat back, fell silent, sensed encroaching blackness. He thought of his pain, and then all the pain in the world, the whole sharply vibrating pulse of pain that held the planet captive. Babies dying for want of food and medicine and water, people mutilated by shells and shrapnel in stupid wars: the world was a great big globe of misery spinning pointlessly. I'd like to stop it, save just one child, just one small sad undernourished child –

Aye, the hero again, always the hero.

'Sergeant? Hello?'

Perlman opened his eyes, confused a moment. 'I must have dozed.'

'You were muttering,' Murdoch said.

'I was dreaming of something. I can't remember. Something unpleasant . . .' He stuck his hand in his pocket and fingered the painkillers. Now? No, wait, postpone the moment.

'Let me take you back to the hospital, Sergeant.'

'No.'

'Then just tell me which way we're supposed to be going.'

'Take me here.' Perlman gave Murdoch the slip of paper he'd received from the Samaritan.

Murdoch looked at it. 'If that's what you want.'

'It's what I want.'

Murdoch turned his car around, changed direction; in the wing mirror Perlman saw Scullion's silver Citroën, a metallic glint reflected in the glass. Murdoch glanced in the rearview mirror, presumably checking that Scullion was still keeping track. Satisfied, the young constable relaxed into his seat, his hands loose on the wheel.

'How you feeling, Sarge?'

'I think I'm alive.' Perlman felt his eyelids weighted, but this time he fought sleep off. He concentrated on the street. Tenements, small shops, cafés. People stared in windows, women pushed prams, toddlers clutched parental hands. A café door became a flash of light as it swung open. He glimpsed a black-haired girl frothing milk under the spout of a cappuccino machine, then the door shut and she was gone. A drunk stared in an estate agent's window, a shoe on one foot, the other bare.

Laundry hanging from a clothesline came and went. Old men and stout women walked dogs in a park, and children dipped their hands in a fountain and splashed. Perlman thought he saw a Dalmatian, but wasn't sure.

'We're almost there,' Murdoch said.

He turned off the main drag and parked his Ka under the dense branches of a broad-leafed tree. Scullion slid his Citroën in behind the Ka. He got out, hurried to open the passenger door of Murdoch's vehicle, and stared at Perlman.

'Explain this, Lou. Why are we here? Why the hell are you out and about?'

'Last night a man was generous enough to take me to the Royal after the . . . let's call it the incident.'

'And?'

'He gave me this address.'

'Who was this man?'

'Never told me his name. All he gave me was this paper. Why does he want me to come here, Sandy?'

'To thank him. He wants a medal. Who the hell knows?'

'I don't get the feeling he was looking for rewards. I think he had something else in mind. I don't know what.'

'So we check out this address and then . . . ?'

'We'll see.'

'Lou, for Christ's sake, you're not up to this.'

Perlman got out of the car, trying to make it look easy, he didn't have a care in the world. He took a few steps away from the vehicle. He was steady, balanced perfectly in an imperfect world. 'See, Sandy?'

'Great, you can walk a couple of steps.'

'Be impressed, laddie. Share my joy.'

'I'm over the moon, Lou.'

Murdoch locked his car and pointed to a row of sandstone tenements that overshadowed a bowling green. 'We're looking for number fourteen.'

'Ready?' Scullion asked.

Perlman was about to say yes he was ready, yes he was sharp, when he paused and stepped back, leaning against Murdoch's little car. 'Wait.'

'You okay?' Scullion asked.

'That woman.' Perlman nodded his head in the direction of the street that ran alongside the railings of the bowling green.

Scullion asked, 'What about her?'

Perlman studied the figure. She was about a hundred yards away, her eyes fixed to the ground as she walked, *trudged*, with the foot-weary manner of a person whose life has been one of rejection; broken hearts, strangers' beds, jobs that never lasted more than a week or two. She had a scarf pulled up around her head and she wore small round glasses. Her jeans were three or four sizes too big. She stopped, as if she'd heard a sound that troubled her. She stood in a cowed way, a half-stoop that suggested she expected to ward off a blow from an unseen assailant.

'What is it, Lou?' Scullion asked.

Perlman peered hard through his lenses, one of which was smeared with a pale rose spiral of dry blood. *Good act. One of the city's downtrodden.* 'It's her.'

'You sure?'

'It's her,' Perlman said again. 'I'm sure.'

'Let's pick her up,' Scullion said.

'Wait. See where she's going first.'

The woman stopped outside a door and rang a bell. Immediately, the door opened and she entered the tenement.

'She went inside number fourteen,' Murdoch said.

Scullion was impatient. 'We could have stopped her, Lou.'

'Right. We could have. Now my bet is she's going to see the guy whose name is on the paper.'

'Oyster,' Murdoch said.

'So we get them both,' Perlman said.

'What makes you think we *want* them both?' Scullion asked. 'This Oyster might be an innocent bystander. He might even be the guy with the eyepatch, Lou.'

'I don't think anything Celia does is innocent. I don't think any of her acquaintances would be innocent either.'

Scullion stared at the sandstone building. He shook his head in the manner of a man who never knows where his partner's impulses will lead him. 'Okay. Let's go.'

They walked alongside the bowling green. When they arrived at a spot opposite number fourteen, they crossed the street then stopped outside the security door where Murdoch looked at the buzzers and the nameplates.

Perlman saw the name: *J K Oyster*.

Scullion asked, 'I assume we don't ring the buzzer and wait out here politely to be invited inside, right?'

'Agreed.'

Scullion hesitated. 'Okay. You make the decision, Lou. You're the one who wanted to come here. This is your connection.'

Perlman thought for a moment. He knew there was only one course of action, and that was to enter the building now. What was the alternative? Wait in the street for Celia to come out? No. What if there was a rear exit she could use instead, a door that led to back courts, an escape route that gave her access to the nearby park? If she left that way, she could vanish entirely.

They had to get through the security door.

Perlman examined the names of the other tenants. There were eight in all. Choose at random. He pressed a button marked Quinn. No answer. Next name down: Clayne. He pressed this button also.

A woman's high harsh voice came over the intercom. 'Who's there?'

'Police,' Perlman said.

'Oh aye? Polis, eh? Prove it.'

'We need access to the building, Mrs Clayne. If you can come to the front door, we can show you ID.'

'I've been conned before,' the woman said. 'All kinds of rascals in the streets these days. And far worse besides. They scunner me, so they do. I'm no opening the door to a stranger.'

Scullion pushed his face towards the speaker. 'I'm Detective-Inspector Scullion, Mrs Clayne. I understand why you're reluctant, and I don't blame you. You're welcome to check my ID.

Or, if you like, you can telephone Force HQ at Pitt Street, and they can verify I work there before I show you my card.'

'If I come down, can you slip your ID under the door?'

'Gladly,' Scullion said.

'I'll phone the polis office first and make sure they've actually got somebody called Inspector Scallion –'

'That's Scullion.'

'Aye. Right. Whatever. Stay where you are. Gimme a few minutes.'

Scullion thanked her, then looked at Perlman and sighed.

'We should've kicked the bastard door in,' Scullion said.

Oyster and Scallion, Perlman thought. Items on a menu.

He wondered about the eyepatched man again, but then any questions he had just slid out of his mind. It was enough, he thought, to stay upright and keep going. Which he was managing: just about.

She stood at the window with her arms folded and her back to the room and said, 'I can go after him again.'

'Maybe,' Oyster said.

'I don't like to fail, Jack.' She turned to look at Oyster. He had the distracted expression of a man calculating. She wished she could read his mind. He seemed distant, and disapproving, and she felt she'd let him down on a profound personal level, failed him as you might a friend. But that was daft, there was no friendship between them. They used each other. They were in a partnership whose limits hadn't been well defined, but she knew how the deal worked anyway: either you succeeded, or you went your own way.

'I'll get him,' she said. 'I've never failed twice.'

'Why did it happen?'

'I was flustered. People came to the door.'

'Amateurs get flustered,' he said.

'I felt pressure,' she said.

'Professionals work best under pressure.'

Fuck you, Oyster. You weren't there. You don't know.

'Maybe you need more direction,' he said.

'From you?'

'Is that so ludicrous?'

'I don't know.'

'You think I don't do violence?'

'I think you're capable of it.'

'Why?'

'Something in your eyes I can't read. Something you hide. I don't know.'

'It's best you don't know,' he said.

He scared her suddenly. The light in his eyes went out and she found herself looking into a substance that resembled an icescape with no end to it.

She said, 'Then don't tell me.'

'Then don't underestimate me,' he said.

She walked round the room. 'Another chance,' she said.

'I'm not stopping you.'

'I lost the gun.'

'You're a careless wee thing,' he said.

'I was running. It slipped out of my pocket.'

'Now you need a replacement.'

'It would help. If I'm to finish what I started.'

He stepped behind her. Unexpectedly, he put his arms round her body, closed his hands over her breasts, held her this way for a moment. She shut her eyes. She realized she'd been waiting for this; hoping. She felt his breath on the back of her neck. He lowered one hand to her outer thigh, then moved it slowly inward, and she parted her legs a little to give him access to her, if that was what he wanted. His lips touched her neck so lightly she could barely feel the pressure. There was an inevitability about this. She covered his hand with her own, and forced it into her groin. He undid the zip of her jeans. His touch was sure. He edged aside the material of her underwear, and slid his fingertips inside her gently. She reached behind, opened his zip, felt how hard and swollen he'd become.

323

'Jack,' she said. 'Do me, do me from behind.'

She took his cock in the palm of her hand. She bent a little, tugging her clothes away from her body, sliding her jeans down, waiting for him to enter her.

Her voice had become wispy. 'Jack, do me, do me now.'

'Turn around,' he said.

'Any way you want it.'

'Let me see your eyes.'

She turned, mouth open, legs apart, clothing at her feet, and looked at him. 'Fuck me, hurry, fuck me, please.'

'Baby baby,' he said.

She shut her eyes and waited. She spread her legs wide.

He slid open the drawer of the lamp table at his side and removed a silenced gun and held it to her lips. She opened her eyes and said, 'Oh Jack, do we need special effects?' and he used the heel of his hand beneath her chin to push her away before he shoved the gun hard against her teeth and pulled the trigger.

She was blown back and fell, limp and suddenly heavy, tangled in her clothes. He looked at her for a time, then arranged her jeans and underwear to cover her nudity.

Too bad, he thought.

Perlman saw Scullion's ID card vanish under the door, but the woman didn't open up, nor did she return the ID.

'How do I know this is the genuine article, eh?' she asked.

'Just open the door and check the picture against my face,' Scullion said.

'I'm not opening. You could be these racist killers for all I know.'

'What would a racist killer want with you, Mrs Clayne?' Perlman asked. He was having a strange shivery spell. Floating in space. He fingered one of the painkillers in his pocket. Maybe this was the time.

'How do you know I'm not a Paki or something?' the woman asked.

'You don't exactly sound like it,' Scullion said. 'Did you phone Force HQ?'

'They said there was a Scullion, aye, but how do I know that's you?'

Murdoch made a lunging gesture with his shoulder; he'd break the damn door down if he was given the signal. Scullion shook his head. 'Naw naw,' the woman said, her voice muffled by the thickness of wood.

Perlman asked, 'Mrs Clayne, you a Catholic?'

'Aye.'

'As one good Catholic to another, I'm asking you to open the door.'

'What church do you go to?'

'St Anthony's.'

'Where's that?'

Perlman thought as fast as his dulled brain would allow. 'Drumoyne. The priest's Father Dow. Officiated at my daughter's wedding.'

'How old's your daughter?'

'Twenty-three. Philomena, named after her late mother, God rest her soul. I have one wee grandson called Aloysius McCracken.'

Scullion raised his eyebrows. He made a fanning gesture with his hand as if to dispel the heat created by Perlman's fiction.

'That's nice, so it is,' Mrs Clayne said. 'And your wife's long dead, is she?'

'Twelve years, Mrs Clayne,' Perlman said. 'I swear on my grandson's life, this is really Inspector Scullion out here.'

There was a long, promising pause. Perlman waited. The handle turned, the door opened a little way. The woman who appeared in the slit was about four feet nine inches tall and had a face like a tiny cat. She had a line of prominent hair above her lip and her eyebrows came together in the middle. She held Scullion's ID in her hand and compared the picture with his face.

'Aye, well, I suppose it's not a bad likeness. So who do you want to see in this building anyway?'

'A man called Oyster,' Scullion said.

'I don't know him personally. I see a woman come and go into his flat from time to time. I don't like the look of her.' She stared at Perlman. 'You're the Catholic?'

'I am,' Perlman said.

'You don't look Catholic.'

'It takes all sorts, Mrs Clayne.' Perlman stepped past her into the hall. Scullion came behind, then Murdoch.

'You know what, you look Jewish,' Mrs Clayne said.

'I get that dark complexion from the Italian side of the family.' Perlman headed towards the stairs. He grabbed the banister rail and made it halfway up, then felt he was about to slip. Scullion caught his elbow.

'When did you convert, Lou?' he asked quietly.

'Five minutes ago.'

'Pray to this new-found God you don't fall down the stairs and break your bloody neck.'

'It got us inside, didn't it?'

From the bottom of the staircase, the little woman was watching them ascend. 'Second floor,' she said.

Murdoch led the way now, his shoes clattering on the stone steps. Perlman paused, caught his breath. Enough's enough. This is it. Your body's crying out. He slipped one of the capsules into his mouth.

Scullion said, 'I saw that. Don't think I missed it.'

Perlman didn't respond. The tiled interior of the building was yellow with a dark green border. Light came from a stained-glass window set in the roof, a feature that took daylight and imbued it with different colours before diffusing it. You could hallucinate in here.

A door closed above. The sound echoed. Murdoch stood very still. Scullion raised his face, gazed upward. Perlman listened to somebody descend. A figure appeared on the stairs above Murdoch. A man. He came down, stepped straight past Murdoch, then stopped.

Perlman gazed up.

326

Scullion said, 'Funny old world.'

'I was thinking the same,' Perlman said.

The man didn't speak. He shoved a hand quickly into the pocket of his double-breasted overcoat. Murdoch reached out, his arm strong and straight, and caught the man's wrist. Murdoch twisted hard, and the man, stifling a grunt, was forced down on his knees.

'What the fuck,' the man said.

'I think there's a weapon in that pocket,' Murdoch said.

'Wouldn't surprise me,' Scullion said.

Perlman climbed the steps to where Murdoch had the man forced against the wall. 'You got a gun, Frankie?'

'You got a search warrant?' Frankie Chasm asked.

'Don't think we'll need one,' Scullion remarked.

'Fuck you, Scullion.'

'Likewise, Frankie.'

'Why don't we go back up to your flat and talk things over,' Perlman said.

'You sure that's what you want?'

'I'm sure,' Perlman said.

47

Distressed, Perlman looked at the dead woman on the floor. What was left of her face reminded him of something red and unidentifiable slaughtered under a truck on a highway. She was recognizable, but only just. He stood over her, bent down in an awkward angled way, touched the back of her hand. The painkiller was dissolving in his stomach and he felt nauseous, and the sight of the woman didn't ease the gastric discomfort. He found an armchair and lowered himself slowly into it. *I creak therefore I exist.* Those Feds in the movies never swallowed drugs, never felt faint and uncoordinated. They were machines. They functioned no matter what. They all had square chins and heavy overcoats.

He stared across the room, squinting for focus. Framed by the window, Frankie Chasm created a dark silhouette. He affected an air of disinterest. Somebody was dead on his living-room floor, so what? Murdoch gazed at the corpse. Scullion, scowling, stood with his back to the mantelpiece. The gun that had been in Chasm's coat pocket lay on the table alongside the silencer attachment.

'Why did you kill her, Frankie?' Scullion asked.

'Prove it.'

'Aw, come on, Frankie. You know it's only a matter of matching the bullet wound with that gun of yours.'

'But can you prove I pulled the trigger?'

'It's elementary, Frankie. You had the gun in your possession. The girl's dead on your floor –'

'It's not my floor, Perlman. It's not my flat.'

'Don't make this hard on us. Either you rent this place under the name of Oyster, or Oyster is some stooge you use for cover. We'll find out. And you *know* we'll find out. You're going back to Peterhead, sonny.'

Chasm said, 'I'm not taking *your* word for that, Perlman. I need to hear it from a jury of my peers.'

'Count on it,' Scullion said.

Perlman shifted in his chair. 'Tell us your story anyway. You came in the flat, found her dead on the floor, you picked up the gun then you left? That about right? It's a fucking weird sequence, Frankie. Why did you pick up the gun and go? If *you* didn't shoot the girl, why did you feel the need to purloin the evidence?'

'With my record, Perlman? Your people wouldn't give me the time of day if I called and reported a murder. You'd have me in handcuffs and back in the nick like shite through a goose.'

'So you were going to dispose of the gun and and and?'

'I hadn't thought that far.'

'Let me guess. You toss the gun, come back here, remove any traces of ever having been here, spot of house-cleaning, bit of elbow grease to get rid of the nasty tell-all fingerprints, then toodle off back to the Fat Man in Bearsden?' Perlman rose into a cloudy place where he felt like spirit matter. Concentrate on what you are saying, Lou. *Hard*. He cleared his throat. He heard his voice make sounds like dry grass stalks rustling. 'The girl rots. The smell. A neighbour complains. You're three or four days gone by then.'

'Nasty,' Scullion said.

Perlman asked, 'How did you get inside the flat if you aren't Oyster?'

'I have a key.'

'Oyster sort of "gave" it to you, did he?'

'We have an arrangement.'

'In your dreams.' Scullion yawned theatrically. 'This is crap, Frankie. If Oyster's real, tell us where can we find him.'

Chasm said, 'He comes and goes.'

Perlman said, 'The girl's still warm. So let's think about the time scheme here. You enter the flat, you see her on the floor, you pick up the gun, you head for the stairs. This takes, what? A couple of minutes while you ponder your actions?'

'I don't remember,' Chasm said.

'But you don't see the killer. So, you just missed him, a matter of seconds? And we're outside in the street arguing with some old biddy, but the killer quote unquote doesn't pass us either. So he skipped out the back way, did he?'

'I'd like to phone a lawyer.'

Murdoch, who'd slipped out of the room unnoticed, came back. 'Nobody seems to live here. The bed looks like it's never been slept in. The pillows are still in their plastic wrapping. The towels in the toilet are brand new. Bar of soap untouched. No clothes in the wardrobe, nothing in the chest of drawers. No personal possessions.'

'This is all a bloody sham,' Perlman said. 'It's a stage setting you've got here, Frankie.'

'There's no such person as Oyster,' Scullion said. 'Don't insult us, Frankie. You used this place. You met the woman here.'

'But obviously not to screw her,' Perlman remarked. 'Sex is messy. It leaves signs. Little disturbances. Towels in a laundry basket, soiled sheets, maybe certain kinds of discarded items –'

'You working from memory?' Chasm asked.

'Oy, hit me on the nerve endings, Frankie.'

Chasm said, 'I need a lawyer.'

'Here's what I'll do,' Scullion said, ignoring Chasm. 'Contact Force HQ, get some tech staff in here and dust the place top to bottom, fingerprint the gun at the same time. Who knows,

Lou? Maybe Chasm's telling the truth. Stranger things have happened.'

'Not much stranger, Sandy.' Perlman felt the medication kick in sweet and low. The pain went out like a slow tide. He could still feel it, but barely; it lay just outside the firewall of pethidine, or whatever it was he'd ingested.

'Hello, anybody listening? I want to contact a fucking *lawyer*,' Chasm said again.

'In time, in time.' Scullion took his mobile phone out and tapped the keys.

'You're calling HQ now?' Chasm asked.

Scullion said, 'Why wait?'

'What about my rights, Perlman?' Chasm asked.

'Even if you talk to a lawyer, it's a preposterous story you've got to tell him, Frankie. You're dead meat.'

'The fuck you say.'

Perlman smiled but didn't feel his lips move. This numbness was a lovely condition. 'Was this all your idea, Frankie? Renting this place. Pretending to be somebody else. If you didn't shag the girl here, what did you do with her? Why did she come here? It wasn't for tea and biccies, was it, Frankie? So what did you get up to when she paid a visit?'

Chasm didn't answer. He looked at Perlman with an air of nonchalant defiance: I don't have to talk to you, polis.

'I hate asking questions twice, Frankie.'

Chasm turned away, gazed up at the ceiling, tapped a foot on the floor.

Scullion closed his mobile and put it back in his pocket. 'They're on the way. Twenty minutes.'

'See, Frankie? The tech boys are coming. Whose prints are they going to find scattered round this nice wee flat? Yours. The girl's. Who else? These guys will find evidence – so small you don't even know it *exists* – that you fired the gun.'

'And you can throw me a life jacket, can you?'

'I can't throw you anything,' Perlman said.

Chasm was quiet a moment. 'Fuck it. All right. We met here. We talked.'

Perlman said, 'You didn't want to be seen with her in public, Frankie, did you? You knew what she was doing and what she stood for.'

'For the record, I didn't agree with any of it.'

'Do I look like I care? You agree with racism, you don't, means nothing to me. What did you have in common with her, Frankie?'

'She needed help now and then.'

'Money?'

'Money. Well, yeah.'

'Since you're not a registered charity, Frankie, I have to ask what was in this for you?'

'I got nothing out of it.'

'Hear that, Sandy?'

'He's a philanthropist,' Scullion said.

'She wanted money.'

Perlman asked, 'In your great generosity, what else did you give her? How about guns?'

Chasm shook his head quickly. 'No. No guns.'

'Bullshit,' Perlman said. 'I'm betting you gave her a weapon, didn't you? She killed Indra Gupta with it. She shot Blum with it. She tried to kill *me* with it. You and her met here because she was hitting you up for White Rage donations and because she needed weaponry. Tell me I'm wrong, Frankie.'

Chasm didn't respond. He stuck his hands deep in the pockets of his grey trousers and looked remote.

Perlman said, 'You gave her a gun and you gave her money. But you didn't agree with what she was doing? I'm missing something.'

'Like what, Perlman?'

'The big why, Frankie. That's what I'm not getting.'

Chasm made a casual throwaway gesture with one hand. 'I did what I had to.'

'What does that mean?'

'You're the bright boy. You work it out.' Chasm jingled some coins in his pockets and whistled a couple of tuneless notes.

Perlman knew he had to keep going, keep pressing. His present clarity was brief, fragile; he couldn't predict how long he might endure. 'Tell us about Bute Transport, Frankie. How much do you charge per head?'

'Per head of what?'

'What does it cost a refugee to be smuggled into the alleged land of the free? A thousand? Five thousand? Ten?'

'You want to know about Bute, speak to the Fat Man. He lied his arse off to you. He never relinquished control of that company. I don't care what he told you, it was just an old paper shuffle. I don't want to be sucked into any fucked-up deals where Bute is concerned. Especially when it comes to smuggling people. Okay?'

'I like an interesting mess.' Perlman wanted to get up, but remained a little longer in the chair. When he rose, he needed to appear collected. He glanced at the body on the floor. 'She was bad news, Frankie.'

'Hard reading, right enough,' Chasm said.

'I'm going to book you on suspicion of murder,' Scullion said.

Chasm said, 'I thought you'd never get round to it.'

'We get round to everything in time.' Perlman heard a crackling in his head, like low-level white noise reaching him from faraway. His ears were small caves where sounds resonated. High-pitched whistling from the distant estuaries of the universe.

He looked at Chasm and said, 'I'll speak to the Fat Man.'

'Good luck.'

'We have old scores.' Perlman rose finally, and remembered a question he'd wanted to ask for a very long time: 'Where does Leo go for target practice?'

'What makes you think he goes anywhere?'

'Just answer the question.'

'He doesn't leave the house, Perlman.'

'No?'

'It's clever and convenient. He has a shooting range in a sub-basement he dug out. Soundproof, state of the art. Spends an hour down there three days a week. Funny thing, he's got a photo of your face glued to one of the targets.'

'I'll bet,' Perlman said. 'He's a good shot?'

'What do you think?'

48

Kilroy woke in the late afternoon. He pulled on his robe, a Japanese silk garment big enough to house a small bridge party. A huge embroidered eagle with wings spread decorated the back. He padded downstairs, calling out Chasm's name. No response. In the vast white gleaming kitchen he drank three glasses of fresh orange juice and ate four croissants with butter, clotted cream, and rhubarb jam.

Burping slightly with each step, he wandered into the conservatory. Empty. He looked out at the garden, remembering that Chasm was away on business. But he'd been due back hours ago. His tardiness worried Kilroy.

He walked outside. Uneasy, he gazed at the waterfall. He checked the flowerbeds with no great interest – he'd lost his passion for lilacs and tulips – then he went back into the house just as the telephone was ringing. It stopped before he could reach it.

Irksome and unnerving, he thought. An unknown caller.

He entered the kitchen, toasted two muffins, spread them with butter, gobbled them standing at the counter. He wiped his lips with a napkin and went inside his office and made a business call. He checked a detail concerning pricing changes demanded by an unlicensed supplier of black-market beef to his fastfood interest, *Eat'n'Run*, known to some cynical consumers as *Eat'n'Runs*. Usually he left this kind of menial task to his managers, so why was he bothering with it today?

Checklist:

to keep my mind off things –

to pretend life is ordinary –

He opened the middle drawer of his desk and pulled out *the* photograph. He couldn't help himself. He studied it for a while. The figure in the car. The lamplight. The street name. He fetched a magnifying glass and peered through it, enlarging the details but clarifying nothing.

He stuffed the picture back in the drawer and went back to the kitchen where he took a tub of Cherry Garcia out of the fridge and dug a spoon into it and ate ravenously.

The telephone rang. He didn't want to answer it. He had a bad feeling. He picked up the stainless-steel handset.

'Leo?'

He knew the voice. He hadn't been expecting it.

'This is Leo,' he said.

'I'm thinking a meeting might be useful.'

Sweat poured over the Fat Man's cheeks. 'Our meetings usually are, Lou.'

Perlman said, 'That depends on your perspective. To keep you up to date with events – we have Chasm, Leo.'

'What do you mean you *have* Chasm?'

'He's in custody.'

'For what?'

'Better we speak face to face.'

'I get to look at your ugly fizog, Lou?'

'Your treat.'

'You come alone. I don't want a posse.'

'All right.'

'And not here.'

'Name a place.'

Kilroy thought a moment. 'The Bluebird Café. In Yoker.'

'*Yoker?*'

'I was born and brought up there. Call me nostalgic. One hour, Lou. No friends tagging along.'

'No friends,' Perlman said.

Leo Kilroy put the receiver down and pressed his fingertips very softly to his upholstered eyelids. He saw zigzagging lines created by his retinas. They reached back into the black of his brain.

You should be dead, Perlman.

Chasm is in custody.

He got up and stumbled into the edge of his desk. Rubbing his thigh, he rushed wobbling towards the stairs. He'd wear his black suit, it was properly solemn. A black shirt, say. A canary tie for a slash of colour. Black shoes, of course. Unless he decided on his two-tone slip-ons, black with white tassels.

What do you wear when the world is going awry?

Whatever the fuck your little heart desires, he thought.

When he stripped off his robe and stood naked in front of the mirror he sang, '*Some enchanted evening, you may see a stranger . . .*'

49

'You can't bloody well go alone,' Scullion said.

'He won't meet me otherwise,' Perlman replied.

'It's folly. It's lunatic.'

Scullion played the scold well. He'd had years of practice. Perlman gazed at him over the rim of his coffee cup. 'I can work him on my own.'

'I wish you could see yourself through my eyes, Lou.'

'I'll give that a miss.' Perlman drained his coffee, set the cup down. He looked round the café in Bewley's Hotel. He had a sense of mild bewilderment; he couldn't remember travelling here from Dennistoun. His memory highlighted bits and pieces in a selective way. His radar was malfunctioning. Don't look back. Keep going forward while you can. You know your name, rank and serial number, you know your purpose. All you need to know.

'We should just haul him into Pitt Street,' Scullion said.

'Grounds?'

'Conspiracy to smuggle illegals,' Scullion said. 'Suspicion of aiding and abetting in murder.'

'Whose? Indra Gupta's? Blum's? The gun isn't linked to the

Fat Man.' Perlman wondered about another cup of coffee. The caffeine in his system conflicted with the painkiller. One part of him was close to shutdown, the other up and jittery. 'Somebody can drive me to Yoker.'

'Muggins can take you.'

'Knew you would.' Perlman rose. 'I want to pee – and I have a phone call I have to make before we go.'

'I'll be waiting.'

Perlman found the gents'. The painkiller's effect was sub-siding. He felt raw. The outer layer of his flesh might have been skinned and a sensitive subcutaneous expanse exposed. He zipped up, looked at himself in the mirror: pale, bleached, sunken-eyed.

Scullion's right. It's folly to go to Yoker.

He splashed cold water on his face and hair and let it drip down his neck. He stepped out of the toilet and walked to the public telephone where he dialled Miriam's number. She answered on the second ring.

He asked, 'How are you?'

'Lou, oh God, Lou. I heard. Scullion phoned me. How are you?'

'Tidying loose ends.'

'Don't tell me you're *out and about*?'

'Very briefly.'

'Lou, you should be –'

'I know where I should be.'

She was quiet a second. 'I need to talk to you about Latta. He's been badgering me again.'

Latta? His mind flapped at the name. 'I'll come over when I'm done and we'll talk,' he said. 'I can't give you an exact time.'

She said goodbye, almost whispered the word.

He hung up with a feeling of – what? Disappointment because he hadn't told her how he felt, how much love he carried? Or was it irritation because Latta was still so fucking determined to occupy her world?

He returned to the table where Scullion waited. 'You ready, Sandy?'

339

'Ready and unwilling.'

'My destination is the Bluebird Café. In deepest Yoker.'

'Nobody goes to Yoker,' Scullion said.

Perlman followed Scullion into Bath Street. Traffic was gridlocked. Perlman sucked the bad air in lieu of a cigarette. His pain was creeping back. He reached in his pocket and touched the single remaining painkiller. Reserve supply. The last saviour. He postponed the moment. His brain was like a butterfly on downers, flopping in a wing-weary way from one leaf to another.

'What do you expect to come out of this meeting?' Scullion asked.

'Some simple truths, if I'm lucky.'

They reached the place where Scullion had parked his car. He unlocked the doors. Perlman slipped into the passenger seat. Scullion drove west along Dumbarton Road, following a line parallel to the Clyde, passing Scotstoun, Garscadden, iron works and engine yards and cranes and old buildings whose functions were unadvertised and therefore mysterious. Gulls swooped in the air, diving at the Clyde in the endless quest for scraps.

Gulls and cops, Perlman thought, always looking for scraps.

'You want me just to drop you off in Yoker?' Scullion asked.

'At the door of the Bluebird Café.'

'Then what? You'll call a taxi to get back into the city?'

'I expect.'

'Where is this café precisely?'

'Yoker isn't a big place. We can find it.'

Yoker, in the extreme west of the city, was an unadorned sub-urb Perlman usually found depressing. It lacked what – vitality? Charm? Character? Roofs and buildings were cluttered with satellite dishes. Endless TV was beamed at Yoker, a constant stream of dross from space, TV-made movies and American sitcoms and an assortment of hand-me-down programmes from a klatsch of religious evangelists who operated out of the US

340

Bible belt. Perlman stared at the array of small dishes. In the dire insomniac moments before dawn you could murder time shopping with a credit card, buying hair-curling devices and tacky ornaments.

Scullion spotted a sign for the Bluebird Café in a side street. He turned right, parked just beyond the front door. Perlman stepped out. *Fuck the Queen* had been whitewashed on a nearby wall.

'Christ, you look shaky, Lou.'

'Shaky? Not me. I'm walking tall.'

'Yeh. Right.' Scullion scanned the café, a greasy window, a half-length curtain drawn across, the menu on a single sheet of paper taped to the glass. 'It's not getting a Michelin rating any time soon, is it?'

'It's where Kilroy wants to meet.' Perlman felt a slight sagging of self, as if he were about to dwindle into a shapeless pile of flesh and fluid and bone right here on the pavement. To die in Yoker. It didn't have a *ring* to it.

'I don't suppose you have your mobie, do you? Take mine. In case.' Scullion handed him the phone. 'Don't lose it. Call Pitt Street if you need anything. It's programmed. Just press 3. Got that?'

'Got it.'

Perlman turned towards the café. He could smell fried food wafting out. Scullion wheeled his car around and disappeared in the direction of Dumbarton Road.

Perlman entered the café. A little bell rang overhead. The room was smoky, formica tables creating a grid, tomato sauce available in big tomato-shaped plastic containers, HP sauce bottles on every table, little tower-shaped containers of malt vinegar. It was like stepping back into a Glasgow that had vanished in the late 1950s.

He saw Kilroy seated against the wall. Perlman slid into the chair facing him. Kilroy smiled, gestured around the café, where a couple of white-faced dopers picked at their food because they needed stodge until they could score again.

341

'I came here as a boy,' Kilroy said. 'I return now and again. For auld lang and auld acquaintance, et cetera.'

'It's attractive,' Perlman remarked.

'It's a shitebox, Lou. It's greasy spots on the menus and cheap formica and the food is swill, but I happen to like it here. Don't be snobbish.'

'Snobbish? You're talking to a man who thrives on swill.'

'You look like you died and an electric shock brought you back to life. You sick?'

'You didn't know I was shot by a deranged young woman who broke into my house. She sank a bullet into my shoulder. An inch or two the other way – end of the line.'

'Christ in crutches,' Kilroy said. 'What an awful thing to happen.' He flicked a crumb of bread from the lap of his black alpaca coat. He wore a black suit and black shoes and a black shirt. His tie was offensively orange-lemon, the colour of a canary on a carrot juice bender. 'Broke in and shot you? This city's going down the pan, Lou. Are you all right?'

'I'll live,' Perlman said.

Kilroy made a few consolatory sounds, sighs and huffs, and then slid the menu across the table. 'I recommend the mixed grill. But I suppose you're not in a food mood.'

'Right,' Perlman said.

'Shame. They do a special for me. Three lamb chops, a nice hunk of fillet steak, black pudding, kidneys, fried onions, fried tomatoes plus a decent mountain of chips.'

'Are you sure that's enough?'

'Some people it's heroin, me it's grub. Tell me about the woman who shot you.'

'She was a racist.'

'Oh, God, not one of those, what do you call it . . . ?'

'A White Rager.'

'The same ones who got Blum.' Kilroy's puffy eyes widened from tiny slits to bigger slits. 'I hate those racist bastards, Lou. Oh, I despise them. Killing blacks and Indians –'

'Jews are a natural progression for them.'

342

An old woman in a dirty apron approached the table. She was wearing an old-fashioned clunky hearing aid. 'Mr Kilroy. Been a wee while. Where you been keeping yerself, eh?'

Kilroy, presumably to counter the woman's deafness, raised his voice to where it assumed a mighty *honk*. 'My dear Mrs Bane! I'd like you to meet Lou Perlman! Lou's a policeman!'

'Izzat so? We don't get many polis in here. Nice to meet you.' She looked at Kilroy. 'What can I get for you, Leo?'

'What else, my dear? The mixed grill.'

'And your friend here?'

'Coffee,' Perlman said.

'The last of the big spenders, eh?' Mrs Bane said. She gave Perlman a friendly nudge, which sent a painful reverberation up his arm.

'He has a stomach upset,' Kilroy said.

'I thought he looked definitely under the weather, so I did. Looks dead queasy.'

'Better dead queasy than dead,' Kilroy said.

'Aye, right enough.' She touched the back of Perlman's hand in a maternal manner, then shuffled off, vanished behind a curtain where the kitchen was situated.

Kilroy said, 'I've been coming here for years. I used to live in Yoker. I was a pupil at St Brendan's Primary, just round the corner. It's a comfort to come back sometimes. There's a sweet security about the past you can't get in the present, if you know what I mean.'

Perlman tapped the surface of the table. His fingertips felt numb. 'The woman who shot me is dead, Leo.'

'Is that a fact? Well. Quick justice anyway.'

'I'm not sure you can call it that. She was murdered by your friend and, er, factotum Frankie Chasm.'

'*What?*'

'In a flat in Dennistoun.'

'You're pulling my chain, sly dog. Why would Chasm kill this woman?'

343

'Maybe he couldn't find any more use for her. Maybe he wanted to break his connections with White Rage.'

'Come again? His *connections* with White Rage? Have you been imbibing some serious narcotics? What fucking connections could he possibly have had with that fascist gang?'

'He gave them cash. He provided at least one weapon.'

'Oh nonsense, Lou. It's a mistake –'

'No mistake, Leo.'

Mrs Bane came back with a cup of coffee and a plate of white bread smeared with margarine. She set the bread down in front of Kilroy, who instantly stuffed away a couple of slices.

Perlman tasted his coffee. The liquid had a chemical whiff. 'This coffee's shite,' he said.

'That's the worst instant money can buy,' Kilroy remarked. He dabbed his lips with a paper napkin. 'I seriously doubt what you're saying about Frankie.'

'He's in custody, Leo. He's confessed to the fact he killed the girl, also to gifts of money and procuring a gun. And he looks like he has plenty more phlegm to hawk up.'

Mrs Bane returned, carrying a plate piled with assorted fried meats and a large mound of thick glistening chips. Kilroy squeezed tomato sauce on the whole thing; the plastic tomato made a farting sound. He scattered salt on the food then shovelled forkfuls to his mouth. The sight was amazing. Perlman felt an odd admiration for the Fat Man's magical ability to make his grub disappear. Nor was there any visible evidence that Kilroy chewed his food before swallowing. It was seemingly conveyed whole into the cavity of his throat and from there began its voyage, intact, to the processing factory that was his gut.

Perlman said, 'I have the distinct impression, Leo, he's going to sing a wee bit more.'

'What tune and in what key?'

'Some sorry little song in a flattened minor,' Perlman said.

'I don't like the look in your eye, Lou.'

'What look is that?'

344

'Bleary but watchful. Under all that pink there's something ticking away, keeping score.'

'I'm always keeping score.' Perlman moved the troublesome wounded arm slightly, trying to find comfort, liberation. 'The point is, Leo, what Frankie might have to say could be highly problematic for you.'

'How so?'

'Consider what he knows about you.'

'He's not going to hang anything on me, Lou.'

'Don't count on that.'

Kilroy pushed his food aside. Unfinished. An historic first, Perlman thought. Alert the press. Send photographers. *Kilroy Leaves Meal Uneaten.*

'You're murdering my appetite, Lou. Let's get out of here.'

Kilroy left a stack of notes on the table and moved towards the door, and Perlman followed, trying to keep his back stiff, determined not to slouch. Pain had re-shaped him: he had limited parameters of movement. He forced himself to think bright thoughts; like nailing Kilroy. Like bringing him to justice for the death of Colin as well as any other crimes he could lay on the Fat Man's doorstep. *I'm after you, fucker, and homing in. I'm a lard-seeking missile.*

'Why don't we walk down to the river,' Kilroy said.

'Why not.'

They crossed Dumbarton Road. Perlman grimaced. He couldn't postpone the other painkiller indefinitely. He palmed it, took it from his coat pocket. Do it now. He held back. He needed an unclogged mind.

They walked past a pub called the Wharf Inn and stopped by the edge of the water. The river was grey and slow and narrow at this point. From the Yoker side you could take a ferry across to Renfrew, a journey of a few hundred yards that lasted a little more than a couple of minutes. Gulls screamed all around them.

Kilroy looked up at the birds. 'I hate it when they dump shit on you.'

Never mind the gulls, Perlman thought. I've got shit to dump on you. 'Chasm admitted his association with White Rage, Leo.'

'Until he tells me that straight to my face,' and Kilroy shrugged, staring at the opposite bank.

'He also denied ownership of Bute Transport.'

'Denied it? That bastard. See? *See*? You *give* to people. You act *kindly*. You offer a charitable hand to an ex-con and what does he do? I have a big heart, Lou. I should learn to be careful of it. Bute? I gave it up. I gave it to Chasm. There are papers. Official papers.'

'So he's the one responsible for importing human cargo?'

'*What* kind of cargo?'

'Asylum seekers. General illegals.'

'And he says Bute brings them into the country?'

Perlman remembered Chasm's denial. What the hell. The end justified the means. 'That's what he says.'

'I don't know what the fuck he's on about.' Kilroy stamped his foot like a petulant boy. Buy me that lollipop. Buy me that fucking lollipop, Mummy. 'I regret my generosity. I swear to Christ.'

'My understanding is there's a problem with competition. Bargeddie Haulage.'

Kilroy watched the ferry come in. He ignored Perlman's comment. 'Let's take a ride on the ferry, Lou. When did you last go across the Clyde on a boat?'

Perlman had a memory of sailing the small Govan Ferry with Colin – when? The middle of the 1950s? He recalled the stink of smoke, the dank smell of the river and rotted wooden steps and water seeping through his shoes. The craft approaching now bore no resemblance to the old ferries, which had been small soot-blackened tugboats. This new ferry was bigger, and wider. It didn't even look like a boat, Perlman thought.

The vessel docked. Perlman followed Kilroy on board. There were no other passengers. The Fat Man paid the conductor.

'My treat,' he said.

'Thanks.' Perlman leaned against the side and looked upriver. If Kilroy was uneasy, he managed not to show it. If he was worried about further revelations or accusations, he concealed the feeling. He was singing under his breath: '*Clang clang clang went the trolley.*' He beat one of his meaty hands softly against his thigh.

'So what about Bargeddie Haulage, Leo?'

'What about it? I'm not sure of the relevance.'

Perlman thought how good Kilroy was at bland statements of denial. He lived, when he so chose, in a sealed world of his own making. 'If you're at all confused, Leo, allow me to make it clear. Bargeddie is in the people-smuggling business too. But Bute Transport, in the great and good spirit of capitalism, doesn't like competition.'

'Is that a fact?'

'A nasty fact, Leo. The Gupta family, owners of Bargeddie, represent a jaggy thistle up Bute's arse. Two rival companies, only one can be the *balebhos.*'

'Is that Yiddish?'

'It means the boss, the big boss.'

Perlman felt the engine of the ferry throb. Coming aboard had been a mistake; the motor thudded inside him. He longed for the quiet stillness, the certainty, of dry land. The ferry edged away from the bank.

'The Guptas have experienced more than their share of misfortunes recently,' he said. 'But you know that.'

'I saw on TV a daughter was shot. I think.'

'Killed by White Rage. Also a nephew died falling from the balcony of his flat. Probably pushed. And one of their trucks exploded – the one Glone stole. Glone was a big mistake, Leo.'

'Glone. I never met Glone.'

'If he hadn't crashed that truck, I might not have had a connection to Chasm.'

'Chasm maybe. Okay. You can't connect Glone to me, Lou.'

'You don't know what Chasm's going to tell us, do you?'

Kilroy had the expression of a man who wished he was in the kind of location from which he might send postcards saying *Having A Great Time.*

Weakened, Perlman sat down. He thought of Chasm, of the money he'd invested in White Rage. The question reared up at him: Where did Chasm, ex-con, get the cash? From the moneyman, of course. And who was he? The answer was as obvious as a firework going off on a wintry night. Perlman hesitated a second, listening to pennies rumbling down a chute.

'You gave the instructions, Lou. That's how it worked.'

'Speak so's I can understand you, Lou.'

'You told Chasm what targets you wanted to hit.'

'You're a cherry short of an empire biscuit, Detective,' Kilroy said. 'Targets? Instructions? Where do you get this guff?'

'It makes sense. White Rage pops up on the scene. In your warped brain you get the idea this organization might be useful to you. Why? Because your competitors are the right colour for White Ragers to target. Chasm the factotum becomes the go-between. You give him money, he pays White Rage to kill people associated with the competition. The intention is a warning to Gupta to get the fuck out. He leaves the scene and tally-ho, the market's all yours again. You've blown your rivals out of the water.'

Kilroy said, 'Get a grip, Lou.'

'I imagine you also disposed of Perse McKinnon, because his computer records probably contained material a little too close to the bone for you, Leo. Who knows what lurked in the depths of that electronic box of his? And he happened to be black. Natural candidate for White Rage.' Perlman finally placed the painkiller in his mouth and swallowed. 'It's neat enough, Leo. White Rage go about their business as normal. Two Africans with absolutely no connection to you or Gupta. Fine. As for Indra Gupta, and the unfortunate bystander Ajit Singh, White Rage will get the blame. Who else? And Blum, alas poor Blum. When he gets shot, White Rage go over the top defacing the building where he works. Swastikas, no less. But it wasn't Blum you wanted, although I suppose he'd served a purpose, except he knew a wee bit too much about you, always a danger facing anybody who enters your employ.'

'This is like listening to a man trying to play the fiddle with woolly mittens on.'

'Blum got the chop, but it was me you had in your sights, Leo. Right? It was *me* you wanted. You just fucking *hated* the idea of me trying to dig up stuff about Colin, making a nuisance of myself. Blum was a good start. He was Jewish. Set a precedent. Kill a Jew or two. Maybe after me you might have singled out a rabbi, I don't know, any Jew to keep the anti-Semitic thread going. Suddenly Jews are dying, Indians, Nigerians, Zambians, White Rage knows no bounds . . . see tomorrow's headlines. City locked in more terror. But White Rage are just fucking fall guys.'

The ferry banked on the Renfrew side of the river. Perlman gazed at the pub beyond the dock. The Ferry Inn: imaginative. He wanted a drink, but he didn't want to move just yet.

Kilroy shoved his hands into the pockets of his coat. 'It's turning cold. I can't stand this city in the cold. Not that I don't love Glasgow, because I do. I love it less and less, that's all. It's been dismantled, Lou. So much of it is lost.'

Perlman waited for the drug to release him from pain. His lips were numb now. He wondered where Kilroy was drifting.

'What do you miss about the old city, Lou? Remember the Oswald Street Zoo?'

'The animals smelled like they'd been dead for years.'

'It was a zoo stink. Terrific, exotic. Wild animals right in the city centre.'

'Every Saturday night, Leo, we get wild animals in the city centre. You might not be aware of this.'

'Aye, I suppose you do. I also miss high tea at Pettigrew's, and the little trio that played. My mother used to take me there. We'd get all dressed up. I'd eat cream buns.'

'I remember the place,' Perlman said.

'And the Victor Sylvester Dance Studio? I learned to tango at that place. Can you believe that?'

Not easily, Perlman thought.

The ferry moved again, turning back towards the Yoker shore.

Kilroy looked suddenly fierce. 'Your accusations aren't really about Chasm or Bute or Gupta or White Rage or anything like that, are they? It's all about that fucking *photograph*.'

'The photograph?'

'Dalness Street. Night. Bentley. Man driving. You *should* remember. You sent it.'

'I never sent you anything, Leo. I received a photograph like the one you describe, but I never sent a copy to you.'

'Somebody did. Including a note that hinted at blackmail.'

'It wasn't me. Take my word for it. So who sent it?'

'You tell me, Detective.'

'I can't tell what I don't know.'

'I'm not buying your Lucky Bag, mister,' Kilroy said. 'The tape. The photograph. You're out to get me. You're conspiring against me. This story about Chasm and White Rage, that fucking photograph, it's all some plot to drive me up the wall, drive me fucking mental.'

Kilroy sat beside Perlman. Kilroy was breathing hard. Perlman felt the painkiller cloud his brain; a pleasing sensation. Dreaming your life away. How nice. Not a worry. Not a care. The world turns and turns. The bills pile up. Nobody gets paid except the man who brings the opiates.

'I didn't kill your brother, Lou. That picture is a bloody fake.'

'Maybe.'

'Colin just won't go away, will he? You'll twist anything to get me for Colin.'

Almost anything, Perlman thought. He heard water lap against the hull. Funny: the more I drifted away from Colin's death, the closer I approached it. You start on another case, a diversion, and somehow it takes you back to your point of origin. Connections. A dead nursery school teacher, a dead embezzler, neither of whom knew the other – and Kilroy was the glue that held the connection together.

Life has patterns, after all. The tapestry has a design, the watch a maker. Fancy that.

The Fat Man sighed long and hard and with the frustration of someone misunderstood. 'Despite my rep, Lou, I don't think I'm a bad man. I'm good to the people I like. I give money to charities. It's just the world keeps changing, and people keep changing too, and things get confusing. And I have a hard time keeping up, Lou. Younger people come along, scumbags and neds who see what I've achieved with my life, they want a share. They don't want to *work* for it. No, they want to seize a nice juicy chunk of it. Gratis.'

Everything you've achieved, Perlman thought: all of it ill-gotten, illegal, accomplished ruthlessly. 'Am I supposed to feel sorry for you, Leo?'

'I don't need your sympathy.'

Perlman stared at a crane upriver and a squall of seagulls that burst out of shrubbery on the south bank, and spun in the sky. He remembered holding Colin's dead body. He thought of grief: the narcotic had fucked with his filter system and suddenly he had a feeling he was going to break down. Him and Kilroy, casualties of a changing Glasgow. A pair of guys growing old. Reminiscing.

No, what in *God's* name was he *thinking*? He had nothing in common with Kilroy.

The ferry docked back on the Yoker side. Both men disembarked and walked in silence a little way. They turned onto Dumbarton Road and Kilroy said, 'Here's how I see it, Lou. You're playing a guessing game.'

'Is that what I'm doing?'

'You don't have a shred. You've got nothing to link me with Colin. A fake picture. A phoney tape. Why was I so worried about all that? You got under my skin, Lou. That's why. I dropped the ball.'

351

'And when Chasm opens his big mouth to sing opera?'

'You don't have anything except his word, and he's a known felon and probably a fucking perjurer into the bargain. So you lose on the Colin front, and you lose on the White Rage front. Life's hard.'

'You're scared, Leo. First time in your life, you're terrified. Admit it. You've had it all your own way for such a long time, you don't remember what it's like to be on the defensive. Chasm's in custody and ready to blab about your secret life – including that nice shooting range in your basement – because he wants to sell you to us, and maybe he can get the library slot in Peterhead, or some other cushy number. You're reaching the end of your road, Leo.'

Leo Kilroy laughed. 'Shooting range? He's lying.'

'I don't think so.'

'I couldn't tell a gun from a power drill.'

Perlman stopped, caught his breath. He wondered how much further they were going to walk. He was hovering a few feet above his wound; he knew that when this last painkiller wore off he'd fall back on the sword again. So this was nice while it lasted. But it wasn't for ever.

'Chasm says you practise shooting three times a week. You're a sharpshooter.'

Kilroy stopped outside the gates of the Scotrail Depot. 'He's talking ballocks.'

'We'll hear what tunes he whistles soon enough.'

'You don't look so hot, Lou. Out of energy?' Kilroy asked.

'This wound's a bastard.'

'Get a taxi. Go home. That's my advice.'

'And forgo the chance of being involved in your arrest?'

'It's not going to happen,' Kilroy said. He looked through the bars at trains idle on the tracks, trains awaiting repairs, or cleaning, in preparation for going back into service. There were scores of passenger carriages painted burgundy and cream, some with broken windows, others with dented panels.

Perlman said, 'I don't think we have a whole lot more to discuss, Leo.'

'You sure? I wanted to reminisce a wee bit longer about old Glasgow. I thought you'd be interested in a wee stroll down memory lane, Lou.'

'Perhaps another time.' Perlman took Sandy Scullion's mobile from his pocket. What was the number to press? Sandy had told him. Two? Three? Bloody memory, a curtain in the wind.

'St Enoch's Station,' Kilroy said. 'You remember that?'

Perlman said, yes, he remembered it.

'You remember the old subway, the way it used to smell?'

'I remember,' Perlman said. I remember everything except the correct button to push on the damn phone.

'Oil, water, damp, a whole underground strangeness. Nobody can ever describe that smell, Lou.'

Three. That was the number. Perlman pressed the button and Kilroy suddenly knocked the mobile out of his hand and it went flying in the air before it clattered to the ground. As Perlman turned to pick it up, the Fat Man pushed through the depot gates and ran towards the platform; he was an astonishing sight, the cavernous coat flapping like a marquee, the stubby legs working the air as if it were molasses, the arms rising and falling vigorously. He vanished among the engines and the carriages.

Perlman went after him, calling his name.

'Leo! Come on! Where the hell do you think you're going?'

No answer.

Perlman stood on the platform and scanned the area. He saw nothing except his own reflection in the windows of the motionless carriages. He walked the length of the platform. Somebody as gross as Leo couldn't simply vanish. Perlman opened a carriage door, stepped inside, moved slowly down the aisle between the seats. He looked left and right, trying to keep the carriages on the next track in view, as well as the platform; where was Leo?

Lost in the Scotrail Depot, Yoker. Me and the Fat Man.

Perlman moved into the next carriage. He called Leo's name a few more times. And still no sign of the man, no sound.

'*Leo!*'

He gazed through a cracked window at the carriages parked alongside. And there – he saw Leo's face behind a grubby pane for just a second before it vanished. Perlman opened the nearest door, stepped out, found his way across a yard of track and clambered into the carriage where he'd seen the Fat Man. Hide and seek. But only if you were young and had the energy and weren't fighting against battalions of pain.

He moved down the aisles, shoving doors, calling Kilroy's name.

Leo knows he isn't going anywhere. So what was this desperate scramble to flee? Fear of a trial, a guilty verdict, imprisonment? Kilroy would die in a prison. No freedoms, no luxuries, no exotic wardrobe. And no power. That was the worst of it. *No power.*

'*Leo, for Christ's sake!*'

The oxygen had gone out of Perlman's lungs. He felt airless, had to sit down. His heart was roaring. He had a rapid pulse beating in his throat. He saw midges jig in front of his eyes. I can't do much more of this. He turned his head to the right and glimpsed Leo again, rushing across a length of track. Perlman rose slowly, opened a door, lowered himself onto the rails. A hundred feet away Kilroy raised a hand in greeting, a challenging smile on the big porcine features.

'Catch me, Lou.'

Kilroy laughed and turned and ran a few yards down the track, glancing back to see if Perlman was still in pursuit. And Perlman was, his muscles screaming with every step. Leo was pulling further away all the time. Kilroy stopped again in a space on the tracks between one length of carriages and another, and he spread his arms wide as if he saw himself as some kind of superhero, his coat hanging like a cape.

'Catch me, Lou. Come on.'

'Don't do this,' Perlman shouted. 'It's ridiculous.'

'There's always an exit route, Lou.'

Perlman understood he had nothing left to give. If Kilroy wanted to flee, let him. Others, younger and fitter, could catch him.

'*What are you waiting for, Sergeant? Come on. You scared?*'

Perlman squatted at the edge of the rail, trying to catch his breath. He heard the sound of wheels rolling along the track some distance up the line. He stared at Kilroy who was still taunting him.

'*Can't catch the fat man, eh? Lazy bastard.*'

Perlman heard the sound grow: an engine was on the move.

He climbed from the track to the platform. He waved a hand frantically, warning the Fat Man. Something's coming. Move out of there. He shouted this aloud, but his voice was weak, and Kilroy was roaring anyway, a great blustering vain outpouring of words, a bitter rant. *I ran this city. I could buy and sell any policeman I liked. Nobody held me back. Everybody was scared of me. Everybody wanted to be my friend. Headwaiters licked my arse. None of that ever happened to you, did it, Sergeant?*

Perlman heard a clank behind Kilroy. The clatter of metal on metal. The carriages at Kilroy's back slid forward, propelled by the engine shunting them from the rear.

'*Get the fuck out of there!*' Perlman shouted.

Kilroy twisted his head, saw too late the carriages come rushing towards him, and then realized he was trapped between those moving at him and the stationary collection in front. He tried to get to the platform, but his coat had apparently become tangled in the hitch of the last forward carriage, and he was imprisoned. Perlman shouted again, *Get the fuck out of there*, and Kilroy made a great effort to grasp the edge of the platform, short arms extended in hope, plump fingers grabbing air, but as the carriages grew closer the more he was dragged down by his ensnared coat, and then he was gone, screaming as the two strings of carriages slammed fiercely together and the engine at the back fell silent.

Perlman, who'd been moving along the platform, stopped when he saw Kilroy. The Fat Man was crushed, sandwiched between carriages, his mouth open, his fingers broken and twisted in all manner of unlikely angles, and his hands flattened back against his shattered face.

50

In a pub called the Dry Dock Perlman sipped cold water, relishing shards of crushed ice on his dry tongue. He looked at Scullion and said, 'I wanted him in a courtroom. I wanted to make a case the Proc-Fisc couldn't toss out. I don't get any kind of joy him dying like this.'

'I understand that.' Scullion finished his half-glass of cider. 'I think I should take you back to the hospital.'

'I know what you think.'

'You need medical attention, Lou.'

Perlman shivered, though the air in the bar was warm. He knew Scullion was correct, but he felt no inclination to incarcerate himself in a hospital ward to be looked after by the sisters of the NHS. He could arm himself with a bottle of strong prescription painkillers and go home, of course – but the loneliness of his house held no appeal. In any event, the case that had begun with the murder of Indra Gupta wasn't closed: White Rage might have lost an operator, but there were others in the city, and he had no idea how many, and he didn't want to quit looking for them.

Who are you kidding, Lou? You don't have the strength now.

Other cops will take over. Same with the people-smuggling racket. You're out of that equation also. Leave it alone gracefully. You're not well. You need recuperation. The movie's over. No Fed ever felt a pain like the one you feel now.

He looked inside his glass at melting ice. Imponderables remained – the Samaritan who'd given him Chasm's address. The photograph he'd been sent, the anonymous caller. Look for joy, he thought. Look for the bright prospect. Amen.

He stood up. Scullion lingered at his side, concerned and fussy. 'Okay, I'll drive you wherever you decide to go, Lou.'

They left the pub. The sky was still light, but staining dark at the edges. Soon the sun would go. Night falls on Glasgow. Perlman held his injured arm flat against his side. Sandy opened the door of his car, helped Perlman climb in.

The car passed the street in Partick where Cremoni's had been; now a dark gash, plastic sheeting in place of glass, haunted. I can't find the bright prospect, Perlman thought. There's been too much death and God knows there might be more. The city was still subdued, still besieged. He could feel it. Turn a corner and you might collide with a killer whose agenda was white superiority.

'I want to see Miriam,' he said. He told Scullion the address in Merchant City, and then wondered if he was in any condition to climb to her loft.

Scullion said, 'I have to pop into HQ and pick up a couple of files. You can wait in the car if you like.'

'I don't intend to go inside Pitt Street looking like this,' Perlman said. He saw Miriam's face pass across his mind; he was hanging on the edge of sleep. Glasgow was suddenly a dream-state filled with shifting structures. Everything that had happened belonged in the fiefdom of mirages. He was shaking now, tremble in his legs, tic under his eye. The wounded arm had died entirely. He thought of Kilroy crushed between railway carriages, and it was as if he were looking at a single frame of a motion picture, incomprehensible, ripped from context.

The Fat Man dies on a railway line in Yoker.

Scullion parked. 'Back in a jiffy,' he said.

Perlman watched him go out of sight. Darker now, streetlamps pale against the coming night. He imagined Miriam's loft. He fancied dancing with her under the skylight, stars overhead. He dozed, dreamed that Kilroy, raised from the dead, was knocking on the window of the car. A horrific Kilroy, bloodied and skinned –

Perlman opened his eyes. Somebody *was* rapping at the window on the driver's side. He adjusted his glasses and focused on the shape outside. It was Frase Deacon, in a black polo-neck sweater and black and white hound's-tooth jacket. Inspector Cool.

He opened the door and stuck his head in. 'I hear you took a hit, Lou.'

'I'll get over it.'

'I was sorry when I heard.'

'Thanks.'

'Don't believe me? You're still projecting frost, Perlman.'

'You know what I think about the way you handle things, Inspector.'

Deacon edged into Scullion's seat. He emitted a rich aftershave scent like squeezed lime. 'You're entitled to your opinion.'

'Right.'

'You can think what you like.'

'I've tried all my life to do that,' Perlman said. He looked at Deacon for a moment. That well-sculpted face, the narrow nose, the perfect square of the jaw. 'Right from the start, you wanted me off the White Rage thing. All I got were these waves of hostility from you. The big man from Special B, and I'm just a low-grade flatfoot with more than thirty years' experience, what the fuck do I know?'

'You were the hostile one. You still are.'

'I happened to ask some questions, and they annoyed you.'

'I couldn't answer them.'

'Wrong. You *wouldn't* answer them. Take a holiday, Lou. Don't

359

you want a break, Lou? In other words, Get to Fuck, Lou. I wasn't falling for that.'

'You seemed, let me say, *fraught.*'

'Fraught doesn't make it. Try *steaming*.' Perlman jabbed a finger in the air. 'You didn't want me along, Deacon. You were running the show like a comic-book hero, and all you needed was a bunch of yes-men –'

'I'm trying to convince myself that some of your attitude is down to your present unsettled condition, Lou. And I'm not doing very well at it.'

'My condition? Forget it. People were dying and you were playing silly spy games. It was all bullshit. And you didn't want me asking awkward questions. And . . .' Perlman lost the thought a second. Something else he needed to say: what the hell was it? He still pointed a finger at Deacon but he needed words to back up the gesture. Got it. Right. 'Out of the blue I got this message from upstairs. Tay wanted me to concentrate on my brother's case. Drop everything else. Bring it up to speed, he says. Get the files updated. I might be as fuzzy as an angora sweater at this moment, but I'm seeing it now. You tell Tay I'm a troublemaker, and he says something like *leave it to me, I'll sidetrack Perlman*. Was that it?'

'I've got a job to do and I do it any way I see fit.'

'And I upset you?'

'You have a knack for that. But I don't let anything upset me for long. I prefer to deal with things before they get completely out of control. I don't like Bolshies asking unanswerable questions.'

'Forgive me if I failed to see how delicate your line of work is.'

'It's sensitive enough. I didn't need a bull in my china shop.'

'Now I'm a bull.'

'With your head down ready to lunge. You never change.'

Perlman wished he didn't have this wound, that he had the energy to take on Deacon; he wished he could align his thoughts in a sequential way, then nothing would slip out of the cerebral net. But.

'I want White Rage, Lou. But only when I'm ready for them.'

'And that means what exactly?'

'Why pull in one or two jackasses if you can get them all?'

'You think you can wipe them out.'

'I've got some good men working all hours in precarious conditions.'

'And when will you accomplish this destruction?'

'There's no precise timetable.'

'The long-serving sergeant, I know, don't tell him anything –'

'I didn't say that.'

Perlman looked ahead through the windscreen. 'What the fuck *are* you saying?'

'I crush White Rage when I know I have all the members lined up and ready. Right now, we can pick them off here and there in ones and twos, but there are others, and if I don't nail them they'll only reassemble. And I don't want any strays left over when I'm done. I want it dead and buried *completely*. I don't do half-measures, Perlman.'

'Meantime you let them continue?'

'Up to a point. But we try to inhibit some of their excesses.'

'Thoughtful of you, Deaky. So what? More people might just die while you wait for the chance to round up the whole network?'

'We'll work to make sure nobody gets hurt.'

'That's impossible.'

'I wish I knew a better way to accomplish the demolition of White Rage. But I don't.'

'It's fucked,' Perlman said. 'Whisper collateral damage in my ear, why don't you?'

'Some people we manage to take care of. Others we don't want getting in the way, maybe getting hurt.'

'How do you mean?'

'You're an example.' Deacon opened the door and stepped out. 'Think about it, Perlman.'

'Wait –'

Deacon cleared his throat and said, 'Remember this, Perlman?

A wee flashback for you. Ready? *I saw Leo Kilroy drive his Bentley on the night of December 15 at approximately eleven. He was heading along Dalness Street, driving at about twenty-five mph . . .'* The Inspector's accent had changed, shifting from narrow Glaswegian to broad, r's rolling, t's dropped, g's discarded like so many bent nails.

Perlman felt a weight shift and drop inside, and his heartbeat quickened. 'I remember.'

'And you went for it.'

Perlman said, 'You're a fucking actor, Deacon.'

'I have a small talent for accents.'

'It didn't occur to me.'

'It intrigued you, Lou. It served its purpose.'

'To make me all gung-ho for Kilroy.'

'Well done.'

'And the photograph. Am I such a *shlemiel*?'

'We're blessed with some smart tech staff. The picture was a stroll in the park. Fell for that too, right? Christ, did we light fires under you and Kilroy, or did we light fires? Okay, I didn't want you on the case because I don't like you, and we have a history I can't quite get over. So I tried to redirect you towards your brother's murder, just when it seemed your interest might be . . . is waning the word?'

'It never waned, Deacon. Don't say that.'

'Don't get so testy. Let's say you welcomed a diversion. A new case. A fresh start. Your other investigation was going nowhere. But I wanted you back on it. I wanted you snapping at Kilroy's heels and staying the fuck out of my way. And I wanted Kilroy feeling uneasy about your attentions. I got that, didn't I? Of course, I didn't realize at the time that Kilroy had an involvement with White Rage. But that worked out all right in the end.'

'Did it?'

'I believe so.'

Perlman arranged and rearranged these revelations as if they were tiles in a surreal game of Scrabble. Phone calls left on answering machines, a bogus photo got up by some computer wiz. Get Perlman off the stage, he's a pain in the arse, he'll intrude and make a mess, let him fart about with his brother's murder, that way he can't break anything, the china shop remains intact.

Deacon said, 'You got your reward, Perlman. We gave you Chasm. We didn't have to. But we did. We're not looking for public acclaim. Some of us work in places where it would be fatal if we were identified.'

Deacon turned and walked away. He strolled to the end of the street where another figure emerged from shadow and, moving in step with the Big Frase, walked towards a parked car. This newcomer glanced in Perlman's direction.

Perlman saw the fawn eyepatch for only a second before the man stepped inside the car, then the vehicle moved off and vanished down an adjoining street.

Some people we look after, he thought.

And I'm one of the chosen. Am I supposed to be grateful? Am I supposed to go on bended knee in a gesture of gratitude that I was rescued at the last possible moment from death by gunshot, while Deacon and his friends play out their tricky games? Am I to be thankful that the one-eyed man gave me Chasm and the woman on a platter? Here, Perlman, a wee present for you, delicacies, to make you feel good about yourself. You caught a killer.

No way. That wasn't it. They gave me Chasm and Celia because they couldn't come out into the open and grab them for themselves; they couldn't go public. Too risky. Deacon and his pals liked the milieu of unlit back closes, alleyways, abandoned buildings. They were in love with the notion of operating undercover.

I'm supposed to feel grateful. And I don't. He pinched the top of his nose. Oh Christ he was sleepy and didn't want to be. He needed to think a little more about Deacon.

Because it wasn't adding up. It wasn't coming out right.

He couldn't think why.

Scullion appeared, opening the door. 'You okay?'

'You just missed Deacon.'

'The Big Frase? My heart beats harder. You talked to him?'

'No. He talked to me, Sandy. There's a difference.'

'Anything interesting?'

A blackness crossed Perlman's mind. 'Did you know he wanted to speak to me? Is that why you left me here?'

Scullion laughed quietly. 'What the hell are you talking about?'

Perlman settled back: what the hell *am* I talking about? 'Maybe I dreamed him. Maybe he wasn't here at all.'

'You never know how drugs are going to affect your head.' Scullion smiled, twisted the key in the ignition.

Perlman saw a faint white haze around the streetlamps.

Scullion drove as far as George Square where the City Chambers were illuminated. Light glowed on the Cenotaph. It wasn't far from here to Miriam's loft. A short walk, that's all. He considered getting out of the car and making his way to her. *Darling, I'm home.*

Deacon. A devious bastard. A liar. Maybe it came to the man naturally. Maybe it was part of his job description: scheme, fabricate, manipulate, deny. Perlman rubbed his face wearily. He was in a place where that line between right and wrong – normally as faint as old chalk – had faded completely into the earth.

Something's wrong, he thought again.

Go back. Go back to when this first began.

The death of Indra Gupta. Back there. Think.

Perlman fumbled through his memory. He remembered the Dalmatian leaping at him. The dead gull in his driveway. What was he forgetting? He remembered the encounter with Blum and Kilroy at Force HQ and the urge that had come over him to strangle the Fat Man. But there was more, and it was simple, and he was missing it. He thought of Deacon. *Did we light fires or did we light fires?*

He turned to Scullion. 'Remember when Indra Gupta was shot?'

'How could I forget it?'

Perlman's memory was a boat becalmed. 'Wasn't it the night *before* her death I got the first anonymous phone call about Kilroy?'

Scullion looked surprised. 'You know it was. Why?'

Perlman slid his seat back and stretched his legs. Sweet Christ, was there no order in the world? Deacon knew in advance that Indra Gupta was to be killed the following day, he had the information from somewhere, from one of his infiltrators, say, one of his undercover glory boys, maybe even the Samaritan. Why make the phone call the night before? Why a pre-emptive strike, unless he wanted to make sure that Perlman had no choice except to concentrate on his brother's murder and nothing else?

Colin, remember? He's your priority, Perlman.

Deacon could have stopped that killing. He was as guilty as Bobby Descartes, as Celia, or whatever her name was. He was as guilty as White Rage. He'd allowed a young woman to die. And for what?

To protect his operation.

Now prove all this, Lou.

You can't.

'Stop the car, Sandy.'

'You said you were going to Miriam's.'

'Yes.'

'I can drop you right there. It's only a couple of blocks.'

'I want to walk.'

'You never mellow, do you, Lou? You can't stand to think you're somehow indebted, can you? You're the hardest person in the world to do a favour for. Fine. Open the door and walk. I think you're crazy, but what can I do about it? Promise me just one thing, you'll see a doctor before the night is out.'

'Dib-dib.' Perlman gave a Boy Scout salute and got out of the car. Scullion waved, drove away, glanced back once, then he was gone.

Perlman crossed the street, arm pinned to his side, his steps shortened. He could feel that blood had seeped through bandages into his shirtsleeve. He walked with fierce concentration like a drunk determined to remain upright. It was a matter of dignity. He passed under streetlamps and thought of Deacon again, the territorial nature of the man, the need to draw up and protect his own boundaries of influence. And yet these borders were more fluid than fixed; they were anything Deacon wanted them to be. And Perlman had trespassed. Perlman hadn't obeyed the Keep Out signposts. Perlman had wandered into Deacon's Kingdom.

I'm lucky to be alive. Think about that. *It's not enough.* I'm coming back, I'll expose Deacon. Somehow I'll do that. I'll find a way.

He paused, leaned against a building, threw up some thin coffee-coloured liquid. A pain gripped his stomach and wouldn't let go. He moved forward holding one hand flat against the wall. He rang Miriam's buzzer. *Liebling.* He slumped, heard her voice, raised himself upward.

'Lou,' he said.

'I'm coming, I'm coming,' she answered.

51

He lay on a wide couch under the big skylight. The city glowed in the expanse of glass. Miriam held a warm damp rag to his forehead. He looked up at her and wondered at her tenderness. He saw her compassion as if it were an aura that hung around her in a misty outline, and he was amazed.

'I've got some painkillers somewhere,' she said.

He heard her voice, seemingly very far away; a whisper in another room. 'Prescription ones,' she said.

'I have to get out of this shirt.'

'Let me help.' She took off his overcoat with great care. 'The shirt's soaked, Lou. Be very still.' She peeled the garment from his body. He looked down at the bandages. Bright red, sodden.

'I can change the bandages,' she said.

'Where did you learn that?'

'There's no great art in applying a bandage.'

He watched her go out of the room. He felt a slight uneasiness while she was gone, a vague fear she'd never come back. He was relieved when he saw her return with a first-aid box. She unwound his bandage and removed the dressing and although it caused him mind-numbing pain he stifled the urge to cry out.

'It looks bad, Lou.'

'How bad?'

'I'm an amateur. I can only give you temporary help. You need a pro.' She opened the first-aid box, retrieved a strip of gauze dressing, then cut a length of bandage; she applied both dressing and bandage to the region of his upper arm and shoulder, and he was moved by her solicitous manner. In his hypnagogic state, he understood he'd never felt anything like the emotion he experienced now, a love as vast as a great blue sky in which he floated. How close was he to delirium?

'You need a hospital,' she said.

'I keep hearing that.'

'You're sleepy.'

'I deny it.'

'Don't lie to me.' She rummaged inside the box again and produced a bottle of capsules. 'I got these a few months ago for migraine. Take two.'

He opened his mouth. She dropped the capsules on his tongue. She brought a glass of water to his lips. He drank, swallowed the medication. He held her hand and pressed it against his mouth. She smiled at him.

'I'm taking a holiday,' he said.

'Do you have a choice?'

'I doubt it. My heart's telling me.'

'Where will you go?'

'Anywhere. Will you come with me?'

She took off his glasses, held them to the light, sighed. 'How do you see through these things?'

'Apparently I don't. I miss a lot. Far too much.'

She breathed on the lenses, misting them, then rubbed the surfaces with a scrap of leftover bandage. 'That's better. A little.' She placed the glasses back on his face. He thought it the most intimate gesture he'd ever experienced, even more than the kiss they'd shared in the Old Toll Bar, more than the few seconds when he'd caressed her breast. The simple act of replacing glasses, and yet it assumed an unearthly beauty. He felt humble and speechless. He lost himself in the deep brown dark of her eyes.

'I'm a schoolboy again, Miriam. My heart's like a harp that's been silent half a lifetime until you came along and plucked it.'

She pressed a finger to his lips. 'Lou,' she said.

'You'll come away with me?'

She closed the lid of the first-aid box. She stood up.

'You're not answering me, Miriam. Wait, I remember now. You mentioned Latta before. He's bothering you? I can deal with him. He's nothing.'

'Things have changed, Lou,' she said. 'I'm scared.'

He couldn't bear to see the look in her eyes; the brightness went, a sorrow replaced it. 'I'm here, you don't have to be scared, Miriam.'

'It doesn't have anything to do with you,' she said.

George Latta appeared in the doorway of the kitchen. 'The things you learn when you eavesdrop. Fucking stunning. So I'm nothing, eh? I like how you hold me in such high regard, Perlman.'

'What the fuck do you want, Latta?'

'Ask your girlfriend.'

'I'm asking you,' Perlman said.

'It's a matter of money.'

'It's always money with you.'

'Don't blame me. It's the world I move in, Perlman. I see them all, the greedy, the conniving, the cunning, the white-collar boys who think they're immune to the law – they pass in a great parade in front of me, and all their crimes come down to greed.'

'What has this got to do with Miriam?'

'Leave it, Lou,' Miriam said. 'Please.'

'Listen to the lady, Lou,' Latta said. 'Leave it.'

'Leave what?'

'I can clear it up myself,' Miriam said.

'Clear up what?' Perlman asked.

'It's a technical thing, it's got to do with currency regulations, Lou. There's been some confusion –'

'That's one way of putting it,' Latta remarked.

'That money I transferred –'

'That money she transferred,' Latta said to Perlman, 'came from an account that ought to have been listed with the assets of your late brother and impounded by the Inland Revenue as illegal earnings. His widow, seemingly, had other ideas. What she calls a technicality, I call larceny. I love that word, Perlman. Nice how it rolls off the tongue. *Lar-cen-y.*'

Perlman stood up. 'She has no right to the money, you're saying?'

'Exactly,' Latta said.

Perlman looked at Miriam. How frail she seemed, how much in need of his protection.

'She's trying to walk away scot-free with £893,000 that belongs to our paternal and all-watchful Government,' Latta said.

'It's my own damn money,' Miriam said.

'It didn't have your name on it, my dear.'

Perlman moved towards her. 'It's something we can clear up. It has to be. Right, Latta?'

'Not that easy,' Latta said. 'I think there's going to be some bad publicity, and a sordid little trial, and she's going off for a year or two. If she's lucky, she'll get into one of those prison camps. Good library books, TV. Maybe some tennis practice. Cups of tea in the afternoon. All very jolly, I suppose.'

Perlman took a step towards Latta, his fist clenched.

'Don't even think about it, Perlman. Don't even let the slightest *prospect* of violence go through your mind. First, you're in no shape. Second, I'm a senior officer. Third, I'd probably smack you back very hard.'

Perlman felt a peculiar helplessness, a man inhibited by his own body; like somebody lame, a polio victim, a motorist dragged from a crash with a broken leg. He looked at Miriam. She didn't meet his eyes. She looked as lost as a small girl on a crowded beach.

'Your brother put me through hell for years,' she said.

'I know he did, love. I know –'

'His women. His whores. He flaunted them, Lou.'

'I know that.'

'If he'd been a wife-beater, it would've been easier to take. But he was far more subtle and far more nasty. I saw the money as pay-off, compensation for the way he treated me. It isn't much to ask, is it?'

'I'll help,' he said. 'I'll do everything I can, Miriam.'

Latta said, 'See, my dear? When Perlman offers his help, it's like a new dawn sneaking into the sky. You've got nothing to fear. Rest easy. The hero stirs.'

'Fuck *you*,' Perlman said. He couldn't stop himself, couldn't resist. He sucked air hard and swung his good arm, backhanding Latta, smacking his knuckles into the man's teeth.

George Latta stumbled back against the wall and laughed. He bled from the lip. 'Good bloody shot, Perlman. Probably broke something in my mouth.'

'No great loss,' Perlman said. 'I'll do it again. Happily.'

'I'd think twice,' Latta said.

Miriam said, 'Don't make this hard on yourself, Lou.'

Latta said, 'I bet this lip swells up nicely. Wait until people at HQ ask me how I got it. I wonder what I'll tell them. Tay's bound to ask. Me and him, we're like that, Perlman. Thick? You wouldn't believe it.'

Perlman ignored George Latta and placed his hand against the side of Miriam's face. He didn't have words for what he wanted to say. His vocabulary was stunted. He'd spent too many years in a world where nobody talked of love and loving; everything was greed and violence, everything buried under the sludge of mean-spirited people, whether criminals or cops.

Latta said, 'She's leaving with me, Perlman. She's coming down to HQ to answer a few questions. I don't have to explain procedure to you. With any luck she'll be back in the morning. She'll have inky fingers once we've put her through the process. But you know that. Wait for her here. It's comfy. You don't mind Perlman waiting, do you?'

Miriam looked at Perlman, then away.

Latta said, 'I won't handcuff her.'

'Generous of you, George.'

'People don't understand me, Perlman. I get a bad press.'

'You deserve it.'

'Tell me. Is this lip swelling?'

'It's a thing of beauty, Latta.'

'Great. Evidence of your violence on my own kisser.' Latta turned to Miriam. 'Fetch your coat.'

Perlman sat on the couch. He watched Latta lead Miriam out of the loft. He wanted to go after them, drag Miriam back; he remained very still as the door closed. He concentrated on the cold light that slanted from the kitchen. A fly buzzed in the loft, brushing the skylight now and again.

He lay down on the couch and stared up at the glass. The pills Miriam had given him were dissolving in his bloodstream; he could feel the glaze, the cowl drawn over his senses. He listened to the slow drumming of his heart. Then he was floating, flying as if by sorcery through the solid skylight and out across the electrified city; below him lay the river, and the cranes, and the moving light-show that was traffic crossing bridges or hurrying along motorways. He flew beyond the city and out over the black divots of the surrounding countryside, where occasionally he passed above the scattered lights of a small community, or the mirrored glint of a loch under a half-moon. He saw the sea in the distance, and the island of Arran rising out of the water like a great creature birthing, and he wondered if what he felt was like dying, the spirit unleashing itself from the body; and if it was, it was nothing to be scared of, it was sweet and painless, warm and hospitable, a kind of homecoming.

A thud, a sudden clap from above, made him open his eyes.

He saw a gull strike the reinforced glass of the skylight. Wings bent back in a dying flurry, head bent to one side, the bird folded and slipped down the smooth glassy slope of the skylight's angle.

His throat was dry and he had no idea of how long he'd slept. The sky was suffused with pale sunlight. He sat up. Then he realized that Miriam lay alongside him on the couch, fully dressed, her slender body squeezed into a narrow space. He hadn't heard her come back. He reached down for her hand, which was limp, a sleeper's hand.

He traced the ridge of her knuckles with his fingertips. Her presence elated him. He thought about the gull he'd seen: another omen?

Let it be good. It better be good.

He listened to Miriam's steady breathing and wondered what she was dreaming, or if she dreamed at all.

So much to learn.